Charade
(Heven and Hell #2)

By *Cambria Hebert*

Interior design and typesetting by Amy Eye, The Eyes for Editing

Cover design by MAE I DESIGN

Edited by Amy Eye, The Eyes for Editing

ISBN: : 978-1-938857-05-8

Dedication

To my writing buddy, Cocoa. For all the days you curl up in my lap, keeping me company while I write, and scratch at my arm for belly rubs and treats. Your furry ears have heard more about my characters than anyone and it is you that I tell their secrets (and mine) because you are always so interested and willing to listen.

.

Acknowledgements

Who knew the second book in a series could be more nerve wracking than a debut novel? Well, besides every other author with more than one book out there...

While writing *Charade* came easy... the rewrites, the editing and everything in between (marketing, proofreading, scheduling) was a challenge. I really dug deep to get to know the parts of my characters they wanted to keep hidden. It wasn't always comfortable, but I truly believe that this book is better for it. I can't tell you how much I've learned over the past year about publishing, editing and writing. I could write a book! But I won't. Not about that anyway.

There are many people who have supported me, cheered me on, and were there to give me my meds... just kidding! Well, kidding about the last one, anyway. But I have had a lot of support. I would like to acknowledge and thank my husband, Shawn Hebert. Ten years (almost!) together and I still like you — okay, I love you. If it wasn't for you, I would never take my pills (not crazy pills, its Nexium. I have reflux! Really, it's true). I would always be out of toothpaste (I squeeze the tube from the center) and I would sit around in the dark like a creepy woman (light bulbs + me = disaster). Thank you for taking care of me, putting on your glasses and beta reading this book and for supporting me when I was feeling discouraged. If it wasn't for you I *would* need pills — and not the kind for reflux.

To Kaydence and Nathan, for telling me to put down my phone or to get away from the computer. To Kaydence, for always keeping me grounded and asking me why I would replace the background on my phone from that pretty girl (Heven) to a guy showing his chest hair (Sam). He he he he. To Nathan, for not really caring that I write and reminding me that ice cream is indeed the ideal food because you don't have to chew it before swallowing.

To Amy Eye, my editor and my friend. For faithfully fixing all the text abbreviations in my manuscript (Is that a sign of a texting problem?), for telling me that I can do better and then holding me to it, while ignoring all the notes in the manuscript where I call you a poo poo head. Thank you for taking time out of your life to help me achieve my dreams and for teaching me so much about writing and editing (but you should just give up on the commas).

To Regina Wamba, my cover designer, I don't think that anyone quite understands my excitement over this cover but you. You knock me over with your talent and with your designs. You gave my Sam an identity all his own and brought him alive on the page. You gave me weeks and months worth of inspiration to write the hardest character I have yet. And to Forres Rasmussen, thank you for lending your face to Sam. I know your name is Forres, but you will forever be Sam in my mind and therefore more of a celebrity to me than anyone on TV.

To my Beta readers, Cassie McCown, Jenn Pringle, Shawn Hebert, Candice Wade Terry and Adriane Tait-Boyd. Thank you for taking the time out of your busy lives to help read Charade and spot anything that Amy's and my tired eyes might have missed.

To my fans, do not underestimate the power of your tweets, Facebook posts and emails. On the days that I felt unmotivated, it was you who gave me motivation. On the days when I wondered what all the work was for, you reminded me. With every single email, word of encouragement, and "like," I am truly humbled by you all and I hope that *Charade* lives up to everything you are expecting because you deserve it.

And finally, I would like to acknowledge myself. Ya made it, girl! Now do it all again for *Tirade*. He he he he.

Chapter One

Heven

"Chop it off," I declared and motioned with my hand just how far I was willing to go. The stylist nodded and smiled. I squeezed my eyes shut and waited, the snipping of the scissors followed by the blasting heat of the hair dryer made my stomach cramp with nerves. Was I really doing this?

"You can look now," the stylist said over my shoulder.

I opened one eye then the other.

I gasped. "Holy crap."

"I know." The stylist shook her head. "If we all could be so lucky."

"It's..." I stared at my image in the giant mirror for several beats. It occurred to me just how big this moment was. I was staring in the mirror—a *huge* mirror—with bright lights blazing and I was doing it willingly. Just a few short weeks ago, this would have sent me into a full-blown panic attack. *Before*. "I think I like it."

"You look gorgeous," the stylist said, smiling. Then she went about putting away her tools. I knew she was telling the truth. Auras don't lie.

I stared up at the mirror once more. I was no longer the girl who felt the need to hide. I didn't need a baggy sweatshirt with a hood... I didn't need a heavy, long mane of hair.

My days of hiding were over. So I cut it off.

Still stunned, I reached up to finger the new style, which just skimmed my collarbone. It was a blunt cut with the ends slightly layered. The stylist also got creative and added a long, sweeping bang toward the right, leaving the left side of my face exposed; the side where my hideous, disfiguring scars use to be. Now, the skin was smooth and creamy. It was bright and clear. My eyes seemed wider and more exotic, my nose smaller, perkier. And the dramatic way my bangs fell made me appear aloof and confident. I wasn't any of these things. *Before*.

Staring into the mirror now, I realized that I didn't really recognize this girl. I had accepted who I was with the scars, but now they were gone. I tilted my head, considering this new feeling, this new look. I could be whomever I wanted. Maybe I'd give this new me a try.

Hev? You've been quiet awhile. Sam's voice purred through my mind.

A shot of nerves jolted me out of my pep talk. What if he didn't like it? What if he thought it was horrible? Oh, boy, what did I do?

I cut my hair off.

Come see me, beautiful.

Yeah?

I'm waiting…

I smiled. The stylist came up behind me and ruffled my hair, giving it a playful, windblown look. "I don't mean to hurry you, but my next client is waiting."

"Of course!" I jumped out of the chair. "I'm sorry." I paid her, gathered up my bag, and slid on a pair of dark sunglasses.

Outside on the sidewalk, I couldn't help but notice the way the breeze tickled my neck and flirted with the ends of my hair. Wanting to get to Sam, I walked while rummaging through my bottomless bag for my keys and ran smack dab into someone.

"I'm so sorry," I gasped as the person grabbed my arms to steady me.

"Heven?" Cole leaned down so he was level with me.

"Oh! Hey, Cole."

He whistled between his teeth.

"Is it bad, then?" I asked, taking in his blank, shocked look.

He reached up and pulled off my sunglasses. My new bangs fell over one eye and I laughed, pushing them up out of the way.

"You look… awesome."

"Yeah?"

He nodded, still staring. Colors of the rainbow burst around him. "It's so shiny," he murmured and caught a strand between his finger and thumb. Magenta bloomed around his head. It always caught me off guard because he was still the only person I have ever seen with that bright mixture of pink and purple permanently in their aura. Usually pinks and purples were temporary clouds of color that burst, then faded. But with Cole, the two colors mixed, creating a color all their own and it was there all the time—it never faded. It puzzled me because I wasn't sure what it meant, and I always knew what the colors meant.

"What are you doing here?" I blurted, suddenly uncomfortable.

He grinned, releasing my hair, but not stepping back. "I work here." He motioned at the grocery store right next to the salon.

"Oh. Right."

He chuckled.

"Well, I was just going." I nodded toward Gran's new car. It's a wonder that she trusted me to drive it at all after I totaled the last one. Not that the accident had been my fault. I thought back to the months of being watched— stalked—by China, a hellhound that Sam had been living with. She was an evil person who did everything she could to kill me. She actually succeeded when she ran my car off the road. The crash was so severe I died. But thankfully, China wasn't the only one watching me. Airis, an angel who had also been keeping an eye on me, brought me back to life. But my life had come at a price. Now, Sam and I were indebted to her in way of the Treasure Map and getting it to where it belonged.

"I'll walk you." He fell into step beside me, his palm resting on the small of my back.

I couldn't help but think about Sam's reaction if he saw Cole and me together. He wouldn't be happy. Time definitely had not mellowed Sam and Cole's major dislike for one another. If anything, it was worse.

When we reached the car, Cole snatched the keys from me and opened the door, leaning in to start the engine and turn on the AC. When he pulled back out, he shut the door and leaned against it, crossing his arms over his broad chest. "Let it cool down for a sec." His eyes skimmed from my toes to my head.

"Cole," I began, but he spoke over me, his voice quiet, serious. "We're friends right?"

"Of course we are." I was surprised he had to ask. "Besides Kimber, you're my best friend."

He nodded, his eyes going warm. "I wasn't sure anymore."

"You mean because of Sam?"

He nodded. "You could do better, Hev."

I sighed—this wasn't the first time we have had this conversation. "I love him, Cole."

He made a face. "I just want you to be happy. And safe."

I felt my face freeze. My safety was not really a good topic these days. Not with all the attacks that Sam has had to ward off. "I'm happy," I said softly.

It was his turn to sigh. "Yeah." He scrubbed a hand down his face. "You look happy. You look real good, Hev."

"So why do you hate Sam?"

He pushed away from the car his chest puffing out, just slightly. His aura burst in deep, bright colors. "I'm not sure you're safe with that guy."

"I'm safe with Sam. Trust me." I was alive because of Sam.

He regarded me seriously for a moment, then hooked his hand around the back of my head and drew me forward. His palm pressed my cheek against his chest and he wrapped his arms around me for a hard hug.

"What's the matter, Cole?" I mumbled against his chest.

I felt his deep breath and he squeezed me tighter before releasing me. "I don't know." He sighed heavily and the color of uncertainty burst around his head. "I just feel like something is going on; I don't understand it. I can't help but feel like I need to protect you."

I didn't say anything; I didn't know what to say. Concern marred his features and I could sense he truly was puzzled. The uncertainty nagged at him. I could see the toll that it was beginning to take. Maybe Sam and I weren't concealing everything that was happening as well as we thought. "Everything is okay with me. I promise." My stomach cramped at the lie.

He only wanted to protect me. He was sweet. But it was also a tiny bit frustrating because everyone wanted to protect me. No one thought I was capable of protecting myself. Except maybe Kimber. The thought of my best friend had me pulling away from her boyfriend.

"I have to go."

He nodded and opened the door for me. When I was buckled in and ready to go, he was still standing next to the car. I rolled the window down, he put his forearms on the door and leaned in. "Be careful."

"I'll be fine." Even as I said it, I checked the rearview mirror, making sure there was no one there. Cole's eyes followed mine, then snapped back to me. Did he somehow know that I was in danger? The magenta around his head suddenly deepened and spread outward. The color was stunning and mysterious, and strangely, it made me want to comfort him. I put a hand up onto his forearm and squeezed. "Really, I'm going to be fine."

He nodded and handed my sunglasses back to me. I forgot he even had them. "Thanks," I murmured, slipping them on.

"Are you working later?"

"No. Tomorrow afternoon."

"Free ice cream?" he asked, grinning.

I laughed. "Sure. Come by."

"See you later." He looked like he might say something else, but then he stepped back and motioned for me to drive.

He watched me until I was out of sight.

Where are you?

I smiled. *On my way to see you.*

Are you all right? Any problems?

No. I looked in the rearview once again, just to make sure. Looks like for today I was safe.

How long? I could feel his agitation, his worry. I hated it. I had been out in town all morning and his nerves were stretched thin. Sam didn't like the thought of me going around alone, but there wasn't anything he could do about it. He had to work and I needed to have a life.

Five minutes tops. My response seemed to take the edge off his nerves and I sighed. Having a Mindbond with Sam was amazing. We could talk whenever we wanted, no matter the distance between us. Even in a room full of people, we could have a private conversation. I thought back to just last week when we were at yet another one of Kimber's legendary lake parties and I needed to be rescued from a seriously lame conversation. I thought it was cool I didn't have to invent any kind of eye roll or code word so that he would know I needed saving. I just yelled "Help!" really loud in my head. Then I realized that was NOT the thing to yell when demons from Hell were attacking me at random. The minute I yelled the word, extreme adrenaline and anxiety rushed through my body. I would have stumbled had I not already been used to being overcome by Sam's emotions.

Sam and I are so closely linked with the Mindbond that when we are in the same space, our strong emotions "bleed" through to each other. He had come barreling through the people and practically knocked everyone in my group down. It had definitely gotten me out of a lame conversation, but it had also gotten us some weird looks. I grinned to myself. We have a code word now for rescuing each other from lame conversations.

I pulled onto the narrow dirt road that led to the boat rental shack where Sam was working this afternoon. My stomach fluttered a bit in anticipation of seeing him. Even though I had just seen him this morning and spent all night in his arms, I was still excited for that first moment that my eyes would meet his. There was no other feeling like it; there were no words to describe it. I smiled at the thought of inventing such a word.

I parked the car on a patch of grass shaded by a large tree and hurried to turn off the engine and shove the keys into my bag. I shut the door behind me and turned to face the little shack, my eyes already seeking Sam's smile. He was down by the water watching a couple in a boat paddling out of sight. He turned slowly, drawing out my anticipation and making my heart thump unevenly.

We were staring at each other from across the soft expanse of bright green grass. My heart stopped altogether and a delicious warmth curled my toes and spread up, restarting my heart when it reached my chest. I raced forward, desperately wanting to close the distance between us. He was faster of course, reaching me in seconds, picking me up and swinging me around before catching me in a huge bear hug. I laughed. He squeezed harder and I squealed. He chuckled, planted me on my feet, and looked down.

I was nervous that he might not like my new style, but then I realized that *I* did and my nerves fell away. I smiled confidently as he slid his fingers through my locks and tugged at the corner of the side-swept bang. "I didn't think you could get any prettier." His voice was deep and raspy and it raised tiny goose flesh along my skin. "But you did."

I grabbed his wrists and kissed him, standing up on tiptoe to press myself as close as humanly possible. *I missed you this morning.*

Me too, Hev. Me too.

Suddenly, he pulled back, breaking off our kiss. I pressed my lips together, trying to make it last just seconds longer. "You were with Cole?"

My eyes shot up to his at his accusatory tone. "Yes... no." I shook my head trying to banish the haze of fog his lips left in my head.

He crossed his arms over his chest and stared at me. I glanced just beyond his shoulder, my eyes landing on a fish jumping in the lake. "I wasn't *with* him. I just ran into him in the parking lot of the hair salon."

His whiskey-colored eyes narrowed and I felt his anger.

"How did you even know?" I mumbled. I didn't like when he got mad at me and I looked away again. The water was still rippling with the force of the fish's jump. Must have been a big one... yet, it hadn't really looked like a fish, in fact, it looked like...

"You smell like him," Sam said, his voice hard, drawing me out of my thoughts and tugging my eyes back to his face. "What was Cole doing at the hair salon?"

"Getting a perm and some highlights." I giggled. Sam didn't seem amused. I let out an exasperated breath. "He works at the grocery store next door!" I demanded. Who cared anyway? Sam let out a gruff sound and then muttered something about Cole always being around, but I wasn't listening. I was staring at the water again. Something wasn't right.

Something was slithering closer to the shore, and the way it moved along the surface of the water half-in, half-out was creepy and odd. I watched as its long tail propelled it faster. Its skin was bumpy and green like a crocodile's. Except we didn't have crocodiles in Maine. "Sam," I whispered, but Sam was still muttering and making noise about Cole.

I watched as the thing rose completely out of the water, standing on two legs, and I gasped. In one fluid motion, Sam turned, tucking me behind him. I thought I heard him sigh before his back went ramrod straight and his body began to quiver.

I peeked around him to look. It was a crocodile. At least half of it was. The other half was a man. From the waist down, the crocodile man was green and scaly with a long, curving tail and wide feet tipped with sharp claws. From the waist up, he had skin that was olive toned and shiny with slime. His fingers were gnarled and crooked, and he didn't stand straight, but hunched over like his short reptile legs couldn't support his weight. His face was more disturbing than his half-man, half-reptile body. His nose was overly long and hooked, and his eyes were a flat-black color that stared at me with a surprising amount of hatred, considering how vacant they looked. His skin was not smooth, but rough, suggesting scales where there were none. He had no eyebrows. In fact, he had no hair at all and his aura was white.

All these things had white auras.

The absolute worst color an aura could be.

"Go hide in the office," Sam told me, not taking his eyes off the advancing creature.

I stifled the urge to argue. He knew how I felt about hiding while he took on all the danger. I splayed my palm along his back, spreading my fingers wide, while I debated my options.

Please, Hev. Don't make me worry.

I exhaled and stepped out from behind him to run toward the rental shack. Now wasn't the time to argue. The creature let out a long, loud hiss, planted himself firmly on his short crocodile legs, and tossed his tail in my direction. To my horror, he had a tail like Gumby that stretched with the force of his throw and I stared, frozen, as the thing wrapped around my feet and began to tug me closer.

His scales were slimy like his skin.

With a roar, Sam, now a sleek black hellhound, pounced and used his razor-sharp claws to sever the thing's tail. The crocodile man screamed in anger or agony, I couldn't tell, and he fell forward to land on all fours. I watched in horror as it scurried across the ground toward me. I shivered because it moved like a spider. Sam wasn't having any of it and rushed forward, landing directly on top of him as the demon thrashed about. A long tongue darted out of his mouth and began to wind around Sam's neck. Panic built up in me as I struggled to escape the tail, which was still wrapped around me amazingly tight. I struggled for what seemed like hours, desperately wanting to be free to help Sam.

I heard a sharp tearing sound and looked up just in time to see the creature's head splash into the lake.

I stopped struggling.

It was over.

I couldn't stop the tears that slipped down my face, so I settled for swiping them away quickly, hoping Sam wouldn't have to see them.

He came to me, his skin slick with sweat and slime from the creature, his pair of running shorts hastily pulled on backwards. I managed to get one foot untangled from the crocodile tail and was fighting with the other. Sam reached down, gently removing my hands and then grabbed the tail and yanked. It gave way, curling around his arm. He made a disgusted sound and jogged to the lake, throwing it out into the center, following the creature's horrid face, where it sank out of sight.

"Are you all right?" he asked, returning to my side to run his hands over me, checking for injuries that weren't there.

"I'm fine."

He kept checking.

"Sam." I took hold of his hands and squeezed. "I'm not hurt."

His shoulders slumped as he pulled me close, pressing a kiss to the top of my head. "I never meant to allow it to touch you," he said. "It's tail…"

I shuddered. "Are you hurt?"

"No," he said and pulled me along with him into the shack where he pulled a T-shirt out of his backpack and shrugged it on. "Where's the scroll?" he asked in a clipped tone.

I grimaced and pulled it from my bag.

He groaned. "Heven, I told you to stop carrying it around everywhere with you."

"I can't just leave it at home," I protested. "Gran was home. What if something went there for it?"

"Just give it to me."

"I can't." I felt like it belonged to me.

He groaned again and swiped his hand through his already messy dark-blond hair. It stood out all over his head. "You know I'll protect it."

I knew he would protect the scroll. With his life. All the more reason that I couldn't give it to him. It would put an even bigger target on his back. Then there was the other reason I didn't want him to have it…

"Heven?" He did a great job disguising the vulnerability in his voice. I would have never known it was there without the Mindbond.

I closed the distance between us, forgetting the conversation and momentarily letting go of my fear for his safety; my only thought was to soothe and reassure him. "I trust you." I moved forward, cupping his face in my hands. "Of course, I do," I murmured, lifting my chin until I could reach his lips with mine.

He accepted my kisses and returned them with a fervor that boiled my blood. It was enough to erase away the past few horrible moments.

"Then why won't you let me have it?" His finger trailed down the length of my nose.

I guess my kissing wasn't as good as his because he deftly stayed on topic. I sighed and pulled away. "I don't want you in danger and..."

"And," he prompted.

"I'm attached to it, okay?" I flung the words at him, exasperated.

His lips lifted in a silent smile.

"I know it sounds crazy, but I can't stand the thought of not having it."

It was his turn to sigh. "At least stop wearing the key that opens it, huh?"

I looked down at the bracelet around my wrist and all the keys dangling from it. I guess that wasn't my smartest move. All a demon would have to do is knock me out, then take the scroll *and* the key to open it. Something told me Airis would not be happy. A giggle escaped me. "Not too smart, am I?"

"Of course you are," Sam said, hooking me around the waist and towing me toward him.

I wrinkled my nose. *I'll stop wearing the key around.*

Good plan. Now, if I could only think of a way to keep from being attacked by demons on a daily basis.

* * *

When the hour finally turned late enough for me to feign exhaustion and slip upstairs, I did so gladly. As I trudged up the stairs to my room, I realized that maybe I really wasn't faking how tired I felt. Being hunted and unexpectedly attacked by demons all the time was draining.

I shut the door soundlessly behind me and turned, hoping to see Sam lounging across my bed, but he wasn't there. *Sam?*

Yes, beautiful? Is everything all right?

I smiled; his voice in my head was a very good thing. *Yes. How are you?* I didn't ask (even though I sorely wanted to) where he was and why he wasn't here yet.

Good. I'm going to be a while yet. Logan and I... his words trailed off and I understood that he was in a tough place, between his brother and his girlfriend.

It's no big deal. Gran and I were thinking of playing some cards, I lied, only because I didn't want him to feel torn.

Awesome. Have fun, okay? he said, and I sagged down on the foot of the bed. *I'll be there later.*

See you then.

I glanced around the room, wondering what to do. I couldn't really go back downstairs after making a big show of how tired I was. Plus, I didn't really want to. I *was* tired but I knew it would be useless to try to sleep until Sam was here. I glanced down and caught sight of the bracelet hanging from my wrist. The key to the scroll was there, the biggest key on the bracelet. I thought back to the night Sam had given it to me. How thrilled I was to have something from him and how *right* it felt when he clasped it on my wrist. I couldn't imagine not wearing it. Yet, I promised Sam I would stop walking around with the scroll and the key. Gently, I took it off, smiling a little as I pictured Sam's large hands laboring over it to fix the broken clasp. I lifted the gift up to examine it closer, wondering how difficult it would be to take off the one key that opened the scroll. Turns out, it was easy to get it off, and before I knew it, the key was lying heavy in my palm. I looked around for somewhere to put it and settled on hiding it between my mattress and box spring. It was not lost on me that I probably got the idea from—shudder—China. It is where she chose to hide the scroll containing the Treasure Map (which we learned is basically a list of all the people that God had assigned to do good in the world, like cure cancer and end wars) after she stole it from wherever she stole it. Fortunately, Sam killed her before she could do anything with it, and then we found it. I glanced over at my bag where the bronze end of the scroll was jutting out. It gave me the willies to think what she might have done with it and all the people who would have been hurt... I shook my thoughts and gathered up what I needed for a long, hot bath. Perhaps the water would wash away some of today's drama.

The heat of the water coupled with the softness and sweet fragrance of the bubbles was exactly what I needed to unwind.

Unfortunately, my break was short-lived.

My cell phone began ringing and I leapt out of the water and wrapped myself in a towel, hurrying to answer. It was my mother.

"It's been a while since we talked. How are you, honey?" I paused at the tone of her voice. A tone I hadn't heard in a long time. It was how she talked to me *Before*. Since she declared me evil and I moved to Gran's, her voice was always tense and short.

"I'm great, Mom. How are you?"

"Doing great!" she said, and I actually believed it. "I was calling to ask you if you would like to join me for dinner this week."

"Uh, that'd be great, Mom. I'll need to check my work schedule." This call just seemed odd. She knew I was livid over the fact that she refused to sign the permission slip for me to go to Italy and the fact that she was trying to ship me off to some cult-church camp where they could 'be gone' with the evil in me.

"Wonderful. And I was hoping that you could bring Sam."

My body jolted from shock and I almost dropped the phone. I sat there trying to decide if I had heard her right.

Her light laughter on the other end made my head reel. "I know it seems a little strange with me inviting Sam, but I have come to the conclusion that maybe I could accept him as part of your life."

"Uh," I stammered. "Yeah. I mean, sure, Mom. We'd love to come for dinner. Can I get back to you though? I'll need to ask Sam which night he is free."

"Of course! I can't wait!"

"So… everything is going good then?" I couldn't help from asking. Where was this change of attitude coming from?

"Wonderful."

"Well, all right then," I said, ready to end the call. I was getting cold, wearing only a towel.

"There is one more thing, Heven."

This was it. What I was waiting for, the price I would pay for her 'accepting' Sam. "Yes?"

"Someone else will be joining us for dinner," she began. When I didn't say anything more, she finished her sentence. "I—I've met someone."

I almost dropped the phone again. "What?"

"We've been out several times now and I'd like you to meet him."

My mother was *dating*? Ewww.

"Heven?" Mom said, the first signs of stress entering her voice. I guess I had been too quiet.

"That's great, Mom." I cleared my throat and forced the words out. "I can't wait to meet him. I'm sure he's very special if he caught your eye." Gag.

"Well, isn't that sweet."

"Listen; I'll call you tomorrow and let you know when we will be able to come." It was all I could do not to hang up. I could hardly believe that my mother was *dating*. I never in a million years saw this one coming.

"Great! It will be so good to see you. I've missed you."

My heart softened a bit at hearing this because, really, I missed her too. "Me too."

"Bye, then."

"Wait! Mom?"

"Yes?"

"I'm really happy for you."

"Thank you." She sounded so happy.

I hit the END button on the phone and dropped it onto my bed. I stood there, numb, in the center of the room, until my toes felt ice cold. I looked down at myself, half dried, dressed in only a towel and a hysterical laugh bubbled out of my throat. It was just too much. My mother had a *boyfriend*.

I couldn't help but wonder what the man would be like and if perhaps, my mother's new-found happiness might sway her to sign the permission slip for me to go to Italy.

Chapter Two

Sam

The trees were dense this far into the woods, which I liked because it was better to conceal ourselves; we had more freedom to move without fear of being seen. It was dusk and since it had not been a clear day, the clouds in the sky made it darker than what it might have been. It was oddly gray outside and the trees looked black against the sky, making everything appear as though it was a scene from an old black-and-white postcard that has yellowed slightly from age.

I glanced over my shoulder at Logan, who was trailing a few paces behind me. He didn't want to be here. I had to make him get in the truck and come. He needed this. I just wish he understood that. "I think we're far enough in," I said, stopping and turning around.

"Tell me again why we're here," Logan said, glancing around at the trees.

"We're here because you need to get more comfortable with the hellhound inside you. You have to learn some more control and how to shift."

"I don't want to shift." His eyes continued to look at everything but me.

"Yeah, I know." I sighed. When Logan first arrived, I really thought that he had just been confused, that he was scared and freaked about everything that had happened to him. He had been all alone at fourteen with strange, unexplainable things happening to his body. But the longer he's with me, the more that I see Logan's issues went deeper than I realized.

"Why don't you want to shift?"

His wandering eyes snapped to me. "I told you. I don't want to be a hellhound. I don't want to be a freak."

"I get you don't want to be a hound. But you aren't a freak. You just have abilities that other people don't have. I really think if you learn about them, about yourself, you won't be so freaked out about who you are." Logan lifted an eyebrow when I said "freaked." I shoved at his shoulder, "I wasn't calling you a freak. Not yet anyway."

The side of his mouth tilted in a half smile. First smile I got out of him all night—I'd take what I could get.

"Let's try something," I said and the smile vanished from his face. "There's a deer in here, in the woods. I smelled it on the way in; I can hear it too, shuffling around every few minutes. Tell me where it is."

Logan began looking around.

"You won't be able to see it. It's too far away. You're going to have to use your senses."

He gave me a 'yeah right' look. "You have amplified scent and hearing, Logan. Come on and try."

At first, I thought he would argue, but he didn't. He closed his eyes and I could see the concentration on his face. Long, quiet moments passed as we both listened to the sounds in the night. Finally, he opened his eyes and looked at me. He cocked his head to the left and made a slight motioning with his hand. "Over there," he said hushed.

I smiled. "Very good."

Logan grinned.

"Let's shift now and use our senses in hound form to find it. This time, though, we will sneak up on it. You'll have to move quietly so it doesn't hear us coming." I pulled my shirt up over my head and tossed it on the ground. I reached for the button on my jeans, then stopped and looked at Logan who wasn't moving. "I'm not wasting a perfectly good pair of jeans and a T-shirt. Come on, Logan. It will be fine; you'll see."

He nodded and we both stripped down. My body began to shake; the hound in me seemed anxious to get out. Then I was shifting; I was so used to it, I barely noted the way my bones and muscles seemed to stretch and re-align. The way my back arched up and my spine popped into place. It didn't hurt like it had the first few times and it only took moments for the transformation to be complete.

I stretched out two midnight-colored paws in front of me and flexed my claws into the earth. It felt good to give in to the hound sometimes, especially when it was because I wanted to and not because I had to (like when a demon was trying to kill Heven). This is the feeling I thought if Logan could experience, he would understand—he would see that being this way isn't the end of his world.

I stood up and looked at Logan, who still hadn't shifted and had begun to sweat. It was trickling down his bare chest and beading on his upper lip. I couldn't talk in this form so I tilted my head to the side, hoping he would understand I wanted to know what was wrong.

He was looking at me with fear in his eyes. I was standing in front of him, accepting who I am and exactly what he fought to ignore. Not knowing what else to do, I sat down and waited for him to shift. To my relief, I didn't have to wait long. He dropped down onto hands and knees and began to shift.

It was horrifying.

His body seemed to break itself apart; his skin stretched paper-thin and his bones poked at it until I was sure they would puncture right through. The sounds that tore from his throat were gut-wrenching and not at all what I had been expecting. Sure, I knew that shifting might hurt him a little (especially since he fought it so much), but not even my first time had been like this.

He seemed to scream and groan all at once. Sometimes he sounded like a hurt little boy and others like a beast trying to claw its way out of Hell.

I was completely frozen.

I sat there in shock not knowing what to do, knowing there wasn't anything I could do, and as his body writhed, I felt my instincts sharpen, to identify... a threat. I shut down that feeling immediately. Logan was not a threat to me.

He was my brother.

He let out another shriek, one that raised the hair along my back and I was sickened and mesmerized all at once because the way his skin stretched and bunched just made me think over and over that there was something inside him that wanted out.

And then it stopped.

He looked just like I did in hellhound form—only smaller.

The sight actually made me feel better. While I was watching his body literally rip itself apart, I had begun to regret forcing him to come here. Maybe Logan shouldn't have to face the hound in him... but looking at him now, sitting there peacefully with all traces of pain gone from his face, I thought maybe things would be okay after all.

I made a sound in the back of my throat, wanting to know if he was okay.

His eyes flashed—not quite gold—like mine, but more of an orange shade, like the color of a flame. I blinked and looked back, but the color was gone. His eyes were once again human-looking, a soft hazel shade, full of vulnerability.

He made an answering sound and stood up. He was ready to go.

Shaking off my doubts, I stood and moved past him to begin tracking the deer. I really doubted that we would find it; he made so much noise shifting that he probably scared every animal in this wood within ten miles. But it didn't matter if we found the deer. All that mattered was spending time in our hound forms so Logan could become more comfortable.

We moved through the woods as quickly and quietly as possible. I was more experienced than Logan, so I moved with more grace, but he seemed to learn fast, which I thought was a good sign. After a while, I sort of gave up on the deer, decided to have some fun and stopped abruptly in my tracks. Logan, who had been following behind, ran right into me.

I turned around, flattened my ears to my head and narrowed my eyes, giving him time to see what was coming. He seemed to brace himself and then I launched at him, both of us rolling across the forest floor. Because the trees were so dense, we didn't make it very far before we smacked into one. Logan acted fast and pinned me to the floor, snapping at my jaw. I bucked him off and lunged, grabbing at his tail and pulling him backward, then flipping him onto his back and pinning him down.

He was breathing hard when I looked down into his eyes, my own eyes laughing. *Gotcha.*

He growled and snapped at me. I let him up and we went round and round across the floor, leaves and dirt flying as my brother and I enjoyed our guy time.

18

He moved well. He was quick and seemed to be able to anticipate my moves seconds before I made them. Because he was smaller than me, he could move more quickly and leapt out of my way when I pounced.

I was actually very impressed.

When I was first learning, I hardly had any control. Learning to move on four legs instead of two was harder than it looked. The sheer weight of my form was something I had to learn to carry; it wasn't that I hadn't been strong enough — I was — but learning how to move several hundred pounds was a challenge.

We were having a good time and it made me wonder why he had been so reluctant to shift. But the question was short-lived as the memory of his screams and the vision of his contortioned body drifted into my head. It distracted me and Logan took the opportunity to slam me into the base of a large tree.

Pain shot through my back and side and I growled, adrenaline surged through me and I swung my head around and locked my jaws around his neck. He fought me for a minute, but I held fast and then tipped him onto the ground to pin him. I had never set out to hurt him. All our sparring had been in good fun and learning how to move.

But that had hurt. He saw my distraction and took advantage. He was my brother but I had enough hound in me to let him know that I was the one in control here.

After I had him pinned, he went still and waited for me to take my teeth from his neck, which I did.

Instantly, he was up and staring at me with a challenge in his eye. I saw a flash of that flame color and then he lunged. I braced myself for a true fight this time, but to my surprise, he raced past me and took off through the trees.

I went after him, wishing I had my human voice to call out to him, to see what he was doing. But I didn't.

So I followed him.

Logan was quick, but I could keep up. My legs were longer, giving me an advantage. I stayed back, just feet behind him, curious to see where he was going — what he was doing.

Then I picked up another scent.

The deer.

I heard it before I saw it. It was lunging away from us through the forest, eyes wide, knowing it was being stalked, and it's only thought was to escape. It's like it knew what was about to happen.

With a burst of speed, Logan disappeared through the trees. I heard a squeal and a thump. I raced forward, hearing my own heart pounding in my ears. Logan came into sight and he was standing over top the deer who was flailing about, trying to escape, its eyes wide and nostrils flaring in panic. It saw me and its efforts increased.

Instead of backing away like I would have done, he tackled it.

For the kill.

The deer let out one last scream and then Logan ripped its throat out.

He did it with such enthusiasm, I looked away.

The sound of tearing flesh and the smell of fresh blood made me queasy. I didn't understand what happened. One minute we were having fun, being brothers, and the next, he was attacking me and killing wildlife.

In all my years as a hellhound, I had never killed any other animals. I certainly never ate them.

I looked back at Logan who was still enjoying his kill and a growl ripped from my throat. He looked up. I stared him down, without blinking.

He glanced back down at the deer and then he walked away from it, without looking back, to stand in front of me. Gone was the color of flames. His eyes were back to normal and they held not one bit of remorse.

His fur was matted with blood, dirt and leaves. I walked away without a sound and he followed. We walked in silence, the only sounds were that of the night and as we drew closer, the sound of the lake rippling against the shore.

There actually wasn't much of a shore here at all. This was not a part of the lake accessible to the public. It just happened to be where the lake ended and the earth began. Without hesitation, I leaped right into the dark, cold water.

I loved the water. Sometimes it called to me. I was meant to swim and although I weighed hundreds of pounds, the water made me feel weightless. I remember when I first started changing; the water was the only place I felt truly like myself.

Hopefully, Logan would feel that way now. Hopefully, it would wash away whatever was going on inside his head. I poked my head up out of the water to look for him. He was still on shore, watching me swim.

I paddled over and pulled up out of the water, not bothering to shake the heaviness of the water out of my fur. I tilted my head toward the water and Logan shook his head.

Was everything going to be a fight with him?

Without even giving it a second thought, I charged him, and like a battering ram, pushed him into the lake. He seemed to hit like a ton of bricks and sink. Down, down, down he went until I thought he might not come back to the surface. Just as I was about to jump in after him, there was a commotion in the water and his dark head appeared. He flailed about, panic-stricken—like he didn't know how to swim. But that couldn't be because all hellhounds knew how to swim; we were waterproof. He caught sight of me and made a sound that could only mean *help.*

I jumped into the water to pull him back to shore when he went under again and all his thrashing stopped. I dove down, searching the dark water for him.

I broke the surface the same time he did, only this time he was in his human form.

"What the hell, Sam?" he said, his voice a little shaky. "How about a warning next time?" He swam back to shore and pulled himself out onto the dirt ground. I did the same, morphing back, so we could talk.

"Sorry, I didn't mean to catch you off guard."

"I didn't want to go swimming!" he demanded.

"You were covered in blood," I said flatly.

That seemed to shut him up and we both sat there, dripping wet in the dark. I wanted to ask him what happened. I wanted to ask him why he killed that deer. I wanted to know what it had felt like…

I wasn't sure I really wanted to hear his answers.

"Can we go now?" Logan eventually asked. He sounded tired.

"Sure." We both made the long walk back to the truck, silent the whole way until I couldn't stand it any longer.

"Logan," I began, "does it always hurt like that, every time you shift?"

Logan was silent for a few long moments and then his voice, soft and low cut right through me. "Yeah. The couple times I have shifted, it—it hurts. But mostly I don't remember when I shift."

"You don't remember?" I stopped to stare at him through the dark.

He seemed self-conscious and something else as he looked away. He shook his head. "Sometimes I wake up in places that I hadn't been when I went to sleep." He looked back at me. He was scared. More scared than I had ever seen him.

"That happen a lot?" I asked, trying to keep my voice light, not letting on to how much this disturbed me.

"Not for a while. It's better since I found you."

I nodded. "That's real good."

Logan sighed. "Please don't make me do this again."

"Yeah, okay. We won't do this—not until we know that you can control it. Not until you feel like it's part of you."

His shoulders slumped like he'd been told his best friend in the world died. "You don't get it. It isn't part of me. It's a stranger."

There wasn't anything I could say. Before he could move past me in the direction of the truck, I grabbed him and gave him a hard hug. It was meant to be quick and firm, but he grabbed onto me and wouldn't let go. His face buried itself in my shoulder and he shook like he might cry.

"Hey. Hey, bud, it's okay. We're going to figure this out."

He pulled away and nodded, walking off to find the truck.

I watched him go. I hadn't been around many hellhounds in my life—it's true we are a very rare occurrence, but I couldn't shake the feeling that the hellhound in Logan wasn't like the other ones I had known. Something was wrong. His words floated through my head, taunting me.

It's a stranger.

Angry, I pushed the thought away. He wasn't a stranger. He was my family. My brother. And whatever it was we would get through together.

* * *

Logan was still quiet and withdrawn when we got back to the apartment. Thankfully, he wanted a shower the minute we walked through the door and it gave me a few minutes alone to not have to be the one to hold everything together. I glanced at the clock and sighed. It was late. By now I was usually at Heven's with her body pressed against mine as she slept. I had grown accustomed to that, to her. It was the best part of my day. She was probably in bed already, the covers pulled around her, her blond hair spread out across the pillow. Usually all that hair kind of annoyed me. When I would breathe, it would go up my nose, it would get in my eyes, and I was always afraid I would roll on it and pull it. What I would give for some of that 'annoyance' right now. Besides, it smelled good.

I flopped down on the couch and leaned my head back against the cushion. *Heven.*

Hey! How was your guy bonding?

It was good. I took Logan out into the woods – you know the ones that back up against Lake Sebago? We lost track of time.

I'm glad you guys had a good time. I loved the way her voice sounded sleepy, even in my head. It was slower than usual and a little deeper. I closed my eyes.

Yeah, honey, we did.

Sam? You sound off.

Everything's fine, but Logan shifted, finally –

That's great! Is he a little more accepting of himself now?

It's been a hard night for him… I really hoped she wouldn't press the issue. I didn't want to tell her what really happened. I know she tried to hide how uneasy she feels around Logan sometimes, but it was something that I could feel anyway. It didn't bother me that she tried to conceal her feelings about my brother because I knew she was doing it out of love. So not telling her about tonight was kind of the same – I was doing it out of love.

Maybe if you stayed with him tonight it would help.

You won't be upset?

Of course not, Sam. Logan is your little brother. He needs you.

I miss you.

I miss you too. This bed isn't the same without you hogging it up.

I grinned. *I don't hog the bed.*

Yes, you do. But I like it, so that's okay. How about I bring some breakfast over in the morning before work? I'll bring Logan's favorite, donuts.

He would like that. Knowing that she felt uneasy around my brother and was still willing to support him lifted a huge weight off my shoulders. It was so nice to know I wasn't alone. I spent too long feeling alone and this was so much better. *I would too.*

Get some sleep, Sam. I'll see you in the morning.

Thank you, Hev. For understanding. For loving me. For bringing me a donut.

Anything for you. Now go take a shower. You probably smell after being in the woods.

I laughed out loud as Logan was coming out of the bathroom.

"What are you laughing at?"

I sat up and turned. He looked a lot better. His skin was no longer pale and he didn't seem weighed down with pain.

"Nothing. Just thinking."

"Some thoughts," he muttered.

I jumped up off the couch and headed for my dresser to pull out some clean clothes. Heven was right. I did stink. "I'm taking a shower."

Logan was busy looking through the fridge, which was probably almost empty. A trip to the store was needed.

"You hungry?"

He grunted.

"Me too. There's mac n cheese in the cabinet. Make enough for me."

"You're staying?" The slightly insecure tone to his voice had my gut tightening.

I turned from the bathroom door. "Yup. I want to hang with you tonight."

"Cool," he said and walked to the cabinet to find the mac n cheese.

Before he turned away, I saw him smile.

Heven

The shop was finally empty. With a great sigh of relief, I grabbed a cleaning rag and went around the counter to wipe down the tables and straighten the chairs. This afternoon, I think everybody and their mother wanted ice cream. From the minute I walked in to begin my shift, it was nonstop scooping and ringing at the cash register. About fifty people wanted milkshakes. I hated milkshakes. An odd thing to hate for sure, but with a line out the door and me as the only one working, every time someone uttered the word 'shake,' I cringed. They were a real pain to make. I had to get a tumbler, scoop out the ice cream, add the flavorings and the cream, hook the glass into the machine and turn it on and wait... then I had to put it all into a cup, add the whipped cream and a lid. I glanced over at the shake machine and stuck out my tongue. Did I mention what a pain in the butt that thing was to clean? Ugh. The bell on the door rang and I sighed. It seemed my reprieve would not be for very long.

"Hey, girl," Kimber sang. I looked up, surprised to see her. Things between us lately have been kind of strained, which I knew was my fault. It's hard to pretend to be a BFF with someone whose aura gave away that maybe she isn't as great of a friend as you thought.

"Hey!" I said, tossing the rag on the last table and turning around. From behind Kimber, Cole grinned and waved. I smiled even as my stomach did a little dip. I didn't want to feel uncomfortable around Cole. But ever since the other day in the parking lot, I did.

"What the heck happened in here?" Kimber said, looking around at the damage the crowd had left.

"I think everyone in Sebago Lake stampeded the place this afternoon." I finished wiping up the last table and turned my attention to the floor. It was littered with napkins and sample spoons. I sighed. "What can I get you guys?"

"I'll take a scoop of Moose Tracks," Kimber said, coming to stand at the counter.

I looked over at Cole, but he wasn't paying me any attention. He was picking up the trash-littered floor. "You don't have to do that Cole."

He shoved a handful of trash in a nearby wastebasket and straightened, our eyes meeting for the first time that day. He was such a great guy. "It's no big." He smiled.

I smiled back, then went to work scooping out Kimber's ice cream and handing it over. Then I looked at Cole, lifting a brow. "Peanut Butter cup." He pointed to the flavor he wanted.

I scooped out a huge cupful and then added a drizzle of caramel to the top. It was the way he always got it. "Thanks, Hev," he said around a huge mouthful.

"So what are you guys up to today?" I asked, turning away to begin the dreaded cleaning of the milkshake machine.

"Shopping," Kimber answered. "My wardrobe for Italy is completely lacking."

The mention of the trip made my stomach go tight. I still wasn't even sure I was going to be able to go. I *had* to go. Returning the Treasure Map to its rightful place was the only way Sam or I would get any peace. I pushed away my thoughts and worked to make my voice as light as possible. "The trip isn't for a few weeks yet and already you're shopping?"

"A good wardrobe takes planning," Kimber said, exasperated.

"Did you get your mom to sign the permission slip yet?" Cole asked.

"Not yet," I hedged. "But I will this week." I had to. Mrs. Britt told me if I didn't get it signed by the end of the week, she couldn't hold my spot any longer. I felt the first tingling of panic curl through my belly and stifled the urge to groan. I thought I was past this panic stuff. *You are stronger than this!* I yelled at myself. Still, the thought of Sam flying off to Rome with the scroll and without me made my heart race. Sam could get hurt, the scroll could get taken, and then... people would die.

"Heven?" Cole spoke from behind me.

I spun around, the warm soapy water in the tumbler spilled over onto my sneakers. "Sorry, I was just thinking."

"You okay?" he asked, concern darkening his brilliant blue eyes, eyes that seemed to see too much these days.

"Sure," I lied, forcing a smile and looked around him at Kimber. "Heading into Portland to shop?"

"Of course, so we better get going." Her aura was huge and bright, the colors always bursting around her erratically. Sometimes it was hard to focus when she was around; it was so distracting.

"Sure. Thanks for coming by." I took a deep breath and realized that I had managed to calm myself down. *Way to go!* I was so much stronger than I used to be and it made me proud of myself.

To my relief, Cole moved off to stand at Kimber's side. His aura was a lot less intense than Kimber's, but it was still distracting. Why was his different than everyone else's? Before going out the door, he fished a five-dollar bill out of his pocket.

"It's free," I reminded him of our free ice cream deal.

"I know," he said, sticking the five into the half-empty tip jar.

I opened my mouth to respond, but my vision clouded with red. Kimber's aura was practically exploding with jealousy. *Not again.*

"That isn't necessary," I told Cole, hoping he would take the hint and take his money back.

"You give us free ice cream all the time. It's the least I can do," he said.

My shoulders slumped while Kimber glared between us. Didn't he see that Kimber was seething?

"Well, have fun you two," I said, choosing to ignore the situation and went back to the milkshake machine.

The doorbell rang behind them and I let out a sigh of relief. Thank goodness they were gone.

How much ice cream have you eaten today? Sam's voice floated through my head. *Did you save me some?*

Sorry, chocolate's all gone. I teased, smiling.

Guess I'll have to get my ice cream somewhere else, then. He made a dramatic sound and I laughed out loud. Good thing I was here alone or people might think I was crazy.

All right then. I guess I will have to find another way home from work. There was this guy in here earlier that left his number in the tip jar...

A growl vibrated my brain and I laughed again. Leave it to a hellhound to figure out how to growl in someone's head.

Down, boy. I'm only kidding.

Just for that when I get there I am ordering a large milkshake.

I call a truce! I was NOT making any more milkshakes today. Ugh.

Truce, then. I'll see you in a bit.

I glanced at the clock and willed the next two hours to pass quickly.

* * *

Ten minutes left until my shift ended and Sam still wasn't there. Usually by now, he was, but Logan called and asked him to pick him up so he could get some ice cream, too. So instead of being here, he was on his way to get Logan. After spending all night with him. We hardly even had a moment alone this morning when I brought breakfast over. I sighed, I didn't like feeling jealous and I realized that I was being stupid. It wasn't that I minded Sam spending time with someone else; he needed a life outside of me. I just didn't trust Logan. No matter how hard I tried. But he is the only family Sam had and I was going to keep supporting their relationship no matter how hard it was (or until something happened to prove I had a reason to not trust him). I wondered how much longer I was going to be able to hide my feelings about Logan from Sam.

Besides, I wanted to like Logan and I wanted us to get along. I knew he was having a hard time with everything that's happened to him and what it was like to feel lost in your own skin, to see a stranger in the mirror. Heck, some mornings I still looked in the mirror and was surprised with what I saw. I had gotten used to my scars, had learned to accept them, and now they were gone. I think I could be a help to him if only he wouldn't look at me the way he sometimes did when Sam wasn't looking.

I thought back to the day that Logan had showed up at Sam's old apartment. Sam was outside loading the last of his moving boxes in the truck while I ran back inside to grab one last, forgotten box. Logan appeared in front of me, with a not-so-friendly look on his face. He seemed to enjoy my fear and even took a menacing step toward me. I often wondered what he would have done if Sam hadn't come in the door behind him. From then on, he was the kid brother who worshipped Sam and emulated everything his big brother did. He always treated me like a friend, if not a distant friend. But he always managed to worm his way between Sam and I. Whenever Sam touched or kissed me Logan had an "Ewww gross," or a "Sam, can you help me?" that always drew Sam's attention from me. I understood that Logan was only fourteen and that his life was destroyed the day he turned into a hellhound and he ran away, but sometimes, it felt like Logan liked getting between us.

The doorbell rang and I turned, knowing it wasn't Sam, but hoping to see my replacement behind the counter.

It was Cole, followed by a dark-headed woman.

"I thought you were going shopping with Kimber."

Cole made a face and then pulled the woman forward. "Shopping isn't my idea of a good time. Thought I'd bring my mom for some ice cream. She loves the raspberry chip here."

I studied his mother, someone who, amazingly, I'd never met before. She was beautiful. She looked younger than I knew she had to be and had shoulder-length hair the same dark shade as Cole's. She was shorter than him, thin and dressed nicely, but comfortably, in cropped jeans and a sleeveless blue sweater. Her eyes were not blue like Cole's, but brown and warm.

"A scoop of raspberry chip coming right up." I smiled at her before turning to the cooler to scoop out her ice cream.

"Is this a friend of yours from school, Cole?" his mother asked him.

"I've told you about her, Mom. This is Heven."

As he spoke, I reached out to hand the ice cream to his mother. Cole's mother looked at me, something in her eyes going cold. At the same time, her aura burst with an ugly mustard color with tendrils of brown. It was completely startling because when she first walked in her aura was serene in mostly colors of blue and green. In fact, her aura didn't change until Cole told her my name.

"This is your friend, Heven?" his mother asked, low, her hand going up to her throat.

"Yeah," he said, reaching to take the ice cream I was still holding out. He gave me a small smile before turning to her. His aura, usually full of pure, crystal-clear colors was disrupted by an ugly shade of mustard, signaling he was worried. Clearly, he noticed his mother's odd reaction. "Here's your ice cream," he said, holding it out.

His mother recoiled from the cup like it was poison and then looked up at me, her eyes narrowing ever so slightly. This woman did not like me.

"It's really nice to finally meet you, Mrs. Springer," I said, not understanding why she was staring at me this way. It brought me back to when I had my scars and I felt like I should duck my head and hide.

She opened her mouth to respond then closed it again.

"Mom," Cole prompted, his eyes sliding to me briefly before going back to his mother.

"You know, honey, I don't really feel like ice cream anymore. I think I will walk next door to the bakery and pick something up for dinner."

"O-okay," Cole said, frowning.

His mother pulled out her wallet to pay me for the ice cream and I said, "No charge."

Her eyes flew to my face and the color of mustard, of anger, bloomed around her again. "You don't owe me anything. I'll pay."

"Mom," Cole said, alarmed.

"But you don't even want the ice cream," I said, confused. Why did she dislike me so much?

She put a few bills down on the counter and went to the door, calling Cole behind her. Cole gave me an apologetic look and then went after her.

When they were gone, I leaned against the counter, exhausted. First, the place is practically mobbed by a crowd; then I get slammed by Kimber's jealousy and now by Cole's mother's anger. What else could go wrong today?

Knowing that Sam was probably almost here, I walked into the back to grab my bag from the break room. I couldn't wait to be out of here. While I was in the back, I heard the door chime again and smiled. But then an unfamiliar feeling came over me. My smile fell away as I went out front cautiously.

It wasn't Sam.

It wasn't human either.

The day had finally come. The day that Sam feared above all others.

The day I would be forced to fight off a demon alone.

Chapter Three

Heven

It stared at me without a word. Its eyes were a singular color—muddy brown. They had no depth, no emotion... no *life*. I felt a tremor work its way up my back. It was the first time one of these things had come here and I fooled myself into thinking I was safe at work.

A small nervous laugh escaped me. It tilted its head like it was trying to understand me.

"Go away," I told it, bravely.

It smiled, showing a crowded row of small pointy teeth. It reminded me of a shark. It was really grotesque because otherwise, it could pass for a human from a decent distance away. If you didn't look too closely, you wouldn't notice his pointed ears, craggy sallow skin and the fact that he only had four fingers on each hand. Unfortunately, I was close and noticed all these things. I could also see its snow-white aura.

"I don't have what you're looking for," I said, gripping the strap of my bag a little tighter.

Sam, I need you.

Heven?

There's a demon.

Run!

The demon was blocking the only exit to the place; running was not an option. I looked around for something I could use as a weapon. Too soon, the demon launched itself at me. I screamed and ran, coming up against the ice cream cooler. The demon jumped, landing right on top of the cooler. I grabbed up an ice cream scoop and chucked it at him. It bounced off its head, not even making it flinch. I rounded the corner of the cooler just as it reached out and caught my arm in a vice-like grip.

Just that moment Cole walked through the door. "Heven, I just wanted..."

"Cole! Run!" I struggled to get away, but the thing held on and let out a screech that rattled my eardrums.

"What the hell is going on?" he roared and ran farther into the store. He picked up a chair and swung it at the demon. It was a good enough hit that it was forced to let me go and I lunged toward Cole.

"Let's go!" I yelled, pulling Cole's hand. Cole thrust me behind him and advanced into the store. "Cole, no!" I shouted.

The demon launched itself at him and they rolled. Cole was a good match in size for the thing, but it was stronger. Cole got in a solid punch to its head just before being tossed across the room to land behind the cooler.

I ran forward to see if Cole was all right, but the demon jumped in front of me and grabbed the strap to my bag. "Get away from me!" I yelled and tugged hard. It backhanded me and I fell back, my bag not coming with me.

Cole ran out from behind the counter, jumped on the demon's back, and began punching at its head. It began making the same awful screeching noise as before. I jumped up and ran forward, grasping the broom lying nearby and swung it, hitting the thing in its side. It shrieked and Cole punched it again, causing it to stagger. I seized the moment, grasped my purse, and tugged; the contents of the bag spilled everywhere, and the scroll rolled to my feet. I picked it up and headed for the door, yelling for Cole to follow.

The door to the shop flew open and Sam charged in, sweat lining his forehead.

"Sam!" I rushed towards him.

"Outside," he growled and launched himself at Cole and the demon. They all went down in a tangle of limbs. Logan reached through the door and pulled me outside onto the sidewalk with him and we both stood there and watched as Sam straddled the demon and shoved his hand through its chest. It turned to dust, leaving a panting Sam and a speechless Cole lying on the floor.

"What the hell was that thing?" Cole asked Sam. He was staring at him with awe.

Sam ignored him and jumped up to stalk through the door toward me. "Heven?"

"I'm all right."

Sam reached me and roughly grabbed the scroll out of my hands with a muffled curse and stuffed it into one of the many pockets in his cargo khaki pants. "I told you to run."

"I tried."

"Not hard enough." His arms were shaking.

Cole came up behind him. "You're yelling at her?" His tone was incredulous. "Are you kidding me? That thing was trying to hurt her!" He turned to me, his eyes softening. "Why was it trying to hurt you? Are you okay?" His aura was a wreck and I closed my eyes to spare myself the visual overload. Well, that and the fact I didn't like what was coming through all those colors.

"We're leaving," Sam said, taking my hand.

"I have to wait until my replacement gets here," I said tightly, pulling my hand from his and went back inside and began picking up all the contents of my spilled bag off the floor. Sam followed with Cole close behind, flinging questions left and right.

"What was that thing? How did you make it disappear like that? Have you ever seen it before?"

Sam spun to face Cole. "What are you doing here?" Anger clear in his voice.

"I came to see Heven."

"Stay away from Heven."

"It's a good thing I was here or that thing would have hurt her."

Like a whip, jealousy and rage slapped over me. I was a little stunned at the intensity of Sam's feelings. I shoved the remaining items in my bag and ran to Sam's side. *Please, Sam, calm down. Don't do this. Not here. Not now.*

"Cole, please," I begged.

Cole glanced at me. "What the hell is going on?"

"We'll explain everything," I told him.

Heven, you know we can't.

I ignored Sam's voice in my head to say to Cole, "But not here, not now."

He looked mutinous as I hurried to right the overturned chairs and pick up the mess the demon caused. He was about to start questioning us again as my replacement came in, and we all quickly switched into fake, happy versions of ourselves. Minutes later, we were all on the sidewalk, relieved to be out of the place. Sam wrapped his arm around my waist and drew me into his side. It felt good to be there. Safe. But it also felt gross. I reached into my jumbled purse and pulled out some yummy-smelling hand sanitizer and held it out to Sam.

"Do you know where your hand just was?"

He looked at me like I had lost my mind, but then he held out his hand.

I gave him extra.

"This is so unmanly." He grumbled as he rubbed his hands together. I ignored him.

"We're alone now," Cole said, his eyes meeting mine. Sam stiffened and I felt his muscles ripple. I hooked my arms around Sam's waist, anchoring myself even closer and focused on Cole.

"Later, okay?"

"This is because of him, isn't it?" he said, tossing a look to Sam.

"No!" I gasped.

"I told you he wasn't good for you."

"Cole!" I demanded. "We're friends, but you don't get to talk to Sam like that. Not ever."

"Cole?" From down the sidewalk his mother called for him. He turned and I caught a look at her. She pretended I wasn't even there.

She hates me. I told Sam.

Who is that?

Cole's mother.

"Let's go," Sam said, ushering me away, his body blocking most of mine from view.

"I'll call you later," Cole called to me.

"Don't bother," Sam growled.

In the truck, I was sandwiched between Sam and Logan.

Sam took a moment to rev the truck's engine and stare out the windshield before turning to look at me. "You're bleeding," he said stiffly.

"I am?" I became aware of a sharp stinging in my cheek. I reached up to touch the cut and my fingers came away red. "Oh." I guess that explained why my replacement kept looking at me funny.

There was still anger in Sam's eyes, but he was gentle as he used the hem of his T-shirt to wipe away the blood. To my embarrassment, tears sprang into my eyes.

"It's all right," Sam murmured, tucking the hair behind my ear. His anger seemed to lessen as he studied me. *I'm sorry I was late.* His voice vibrated through my head and soothed away some of my anxiety.

"What's the deal with that Cole guy?" Logan asked over my shoulder.

Just like that, the angry glint was back in Sam's eyes.

"Nothing, he's just a friend," I hurried to say. Couldn't Logan tell Sam was upset enough already?

"He doesn't look at you like a friend."

A quiet growl vibrated Sam's chest and I turned to give Logan a look of disapproval. I swear he smirked without moving his face. I wished, not for the first time, that I could see his aura. But, since he was a hellhound, just like Sam, I couldn't and I was left to wonder what exactly was going on in his head.

I didn't much like the feeling.

It was a little startling to realize that I have actually grown accustomed to my 'supernatural' ability of seeing auras. Somehow, without realizing it, knowing exactly what someone was feeling became a normal thing for me.

Sam lightly touched my cheek with his thumb and frowned. "Does it hurt?"

I shook my head and looked down at my lap. Unfortunately, another normal for me lately was being weak while Sam twisted himself inside out to protect me. I was strong, but fighting off demons with super-human strength was something that I still wasn't able to do.

What happened? Sam asked.

I looked over at Logan. "How about some pizza tonight?"

"Cool," he said giving me a real smile. I smiled back, taking advantage of a moment to hopefully get a little closer to him. Maybe if he began to like me, he wouldn't see me as a threat to his relationship with Sam and he would give trying to get between us a rest.

When we arrived at the pizza place, I reached into my pocket and pulled out the tips I made that day and handed it all to Logan. "Get whatever you want, okay?"

"Thanks, Heven," Logan said, opening up the truck door and jumping out. Sam and I watched as he ran across the parking lot toward the pizza place. As soon as he disappeared inside the door, Sam turned to me.

"So that demon just walked in?"

I nodded. "I walked into the break room to get my bag, and when I came out, it was standing in the center of the room."

"Why didn't you run?"

"It was standing between me and the door. I tried to get around it, but..." I shook my head and a muscle ticked in the side of Sam's jaw.

"How did Cole get involved?"

"He came in earlier to get some ice cream with his mom and she wasn't very nice to me,"

"What do you mean, she wasn't nice to you?" His eyes narrowed. "You said she hates you."

"She does. The intensity of her aura practically attacked me. At first, she was nice, until Cole told her my name. Then everything about her changed; it's like she couldn't stand the sight of me."

"You've never met her before?"

"No."

Sam seemed to find this surprising.

I sighed. "Cole and I are friends, Sam. That's it."

Energy seemed to drain right out of him before my eyes. "I believe you," he said, reaching out and bringing me closer. I rested my cheek against his chest and closed my eyes. "What else?" he prompted softly.

"His mother made some lame excuse about getting something from the bakery next door and ran out. He went after her. I guess he was coming back to apologize for her weird behavior, but when he walked in that demon was there... he was only trying to protect me."

He snorted. "Well I guess he did give that demon someone else to beat up on until I got there. He might be good for something after all."

I smacked him in the ribs. "Not funny."

"You know you can't tell Cole what's going on."

"He's going to want to know."

Sam pulled me back to stare down into my eyes. "I don't think Cole should get involved, Hev. Please."

I nodded, a little lost in his whiskey-colored eyes. He covered my lips with his and I automatically opened further to allow his tongue to sweep inside. We shared too few moments like this lately. During the past two weeks, all we have had time for was settling Sam in his new efficiency apartment, work and, of course, settling Logan into Sam's life. The latter took a lot of effort. Not to mention that every time we turned around, another creepy demon was trying to kill me.

I've missed you, I whispered through Sam's mind. I refused to say the words out loud because I needed the contact of our lips.

Me too.

Too soon, Logan was getting back in the truck and Sam was pulling away. I tried not to pout as Sam steered the truck in the direction of his apartment. I don't think I was successful because Sam hooked and arm around my waist and slid me over so that we were pressed side to side. *You and me, time alone… tonight.*

"I got your favorite toppings, Sam," Logan said.

"Thanks, bro."

"I walked over to the Red Box while you were at work and I rented us an action movie for tonight," Logan said enthusiastically.

I suppressed the urge to groan. Seems our party of two just turned into a party of three.

* * *

Half way through the movie, my cell rang. I jumped up from my seat on the sofa and hurried to dig the phone out of my bag. "Hello?" I kept my voice low, so as not to disturb the boys and walked into only separate room in Sam's apartment — the bathroom.

"What happened today with Cole?" Kimber demanded as I shut the door behind me.

My stomach clenched. Could Cole have told her what happened with the demon earlier? Trying to come up with an explanation for them both would not be easy. Kimber would never let this go. "What do you mean?" I asked innocently.

"He told me that he was too tired to come shopping with me, but then he went out for ice cream, for the *second* time today."

I sighed. "He just brought his mom in for some."

"He brought Christine in for ice cream?" Her voice took on a high-pitched tone and I winced. Had she not known that his mother was with him? "*You* met Christine?"

Clearly, Kimber was on a first-name basis with Cole's mother. I don't know why, but it bothered me. I told myself that of course she would be, she's been dating Cole for years and it's only natural that she would know his mother.

"Heven," Kimber demanded, bringing me out of my thoughts.

I sat down on the edge of the toilet seat. "Yeah, I met her. She didn't like me."

This gave Kimber a reason to pause. "What do you mean?"

"As soon as Cole told her my name, the temperature in the room dropped ten degrees. She couldn't get out of there fast enough."

"Really? Christine is always so nice to me." Was that satisfaction I heard in her voice?

"Do you see her often?" It made me uncomfortable to ask. A lot of things with Kimber lately have felt awkward.

"Sure. I had lunch with her last week." There was definite smugness in her tone.

I didn't like it. I kept my voice nonchalant when I said, "I have to go. We're watching a movie."

"Wait. You didn't tell me what happened with Cole."

"I just did."

"Then why is he acting all weird?"

"Weird how?"

"Distracted, quiet— he keeps staring at his phone like he wants it to ring."

In other words, he wasn't giving her his undivided attention. And, he was expecting me to call him. "I really need to go,"

"Fine."

"I'll call you tomorrow."

She hung up without another word.

I sat there staring down at the little white octagon tile that just a week ago I scrubbed and bleached within an inch of its life. It looked lots better. I got up from the toilet seat and opened the door. Sam filled the doorway. Without a word, I leaned into him, sinking into his warmth and strength.

"Do you understand why I want to keep the scroll now?" His words erased some of the comfort I felt in his arms.

I pulled back to look up into his eyes. "The scroll isn't your responsibility."

"*You* are and having this thing puts you in repeated danger. I'm taking it from you and hopefully taking some of the danger with it." As he spoke he crossed his arms across his chest like he was laying down the law.

I didn't much care for his attitude. "You need to give it back to me." I refused to show how desperate I felt.

He shook his head and started to turn away. I caught his hand and yanked him back. I kept my voice low to say, "I don't want you to have it, Sam. You having this puts you in danger. I can't bear the thought. If anything happened to you..." My voice trailed off as my eyes filled. I didn't even have to pretend because the thought of him being hurt made me crazy.

His fingers tightened around mine. "I understand. I do, but I can't stand watching demons come after you."

"I can hold on to it for both of you," Logan said from behind us.

Sam spun to face Logan and I looked around him to see Logan staring at the scroll.

"No!" I blurted. Sam looked at me and raised an eyebrow. I flushed and looked away. I didn't want Sam to figure out that one of the reasons that he just couldn't keep the scroll was because the thought of Logan around it made my skin crawl. "It would be dangerous," I said, still not meeting Sam's gaze.

"I agree," Sam said. My head snapped up in time to catch Logan frown.

"You mean you don't trust me with it?"

"It's not that. It's just that I can't worry about you *and* Heven all day long."

Logan bristled, his thin chest puffing out. "I am a hellhound too, remember? You keep telling me to act like one—to accept it. Maybe holding onto that would give me a reason to be closer to that side of me." Sam nodded which thrilled Logan, so he said, "Plus, no one would expect me to have it, so it would be safe."

"You make a good case, bud," Sam said, thoughtfully.

He couldn't give the scroll to Logan. I wasn't sure why it bothered me so much, but I really didn't want to find out. "That's really sweet of you, Logan, but I would hate myself if something happened to you because of this."

"I'll be fine," Logan said and I caught a glimpse of the darkness in him that I sometimes saw. I looked up at Sam to see if he finally noticed, but he was busy glaring at me.

"I'll hide it," I blurted.

"What?" Sam's glare softened.

"I agree that I shouldn't carry it around with me anymore. You're right; it's just too risky."

"Finally," Sam muttered.

"But, I don't think anyone else should carry it around, either. It just isn't safe, so I'll hide it."

Sam nodded. "It could work."

"It will work," I said, hope seizing me. This way I could keep it away from Logan, and they would be safe.

"Where are you going to hide it?" Logan asked. Why was he so interested in the scroll all of a sudden?

"I'm not sure," I said, glad it was the truth so I didn't have to lie.

"We'll figure it out," Sam said, pulling me out of the bathroom, toward the couch.

Just as we sat down my phone rang again. I glanced at the screen to see who it was and my stomach dropped to my knees. It was Cole. I knew he had to be going crazy, wondering what was going on. I grasped the phone tightly, considering what would happen if I answered it.

"Don't," Sam murmured, his lips brushing my ear.

I looked up and his face was so near mine. His eyes were tawny and pleading. How could I defy that look? I couldn't. I wouldn't risk another argument or a feeling of hurt between us today so I hit the ignore button on my phone. Tension seemed to melt from Sam's shoulders and he lifted me from the cushions next to him and settled me on his lap, cuddling me close. Logan made a rude noise, but Sam ignored him and brushed a kiss along my forehead.

Thank you. His voice was just as deep and delicious floating through my mind as it was when he spoke out loud. I kissed the underside of his jaw before settling my head in the crook of his neck and shutting my eyes.

It was almost enough.

Still, I couldn't forget the fact that someday soon, Cole would confront me and I was going to have to make a choice: defy Sam and tell the truth *or* lie and drive away someone I cared about more than I probably should.

Chapter Four

Heven

Clink, clink, clink. Tap, Tap, Tap.
The light sounds startled me in the quiet of the house and I jumped. Warily, I glanced over at the window. Something was hitting the panes, making them tremble in the night.

A few disturbing thoughts went through my head with startling force.

I was alone.

Sam wouldn't make sounds at the window; he would let himself in.

The window was unlocked.

Clink, clink, clink.

I swallowed the fear lodged in my throat and climbed out of bed, taking with me the heavy flashlight I had been using to read. I told myself it wasn't a demon. What demon knocks before attacking? I looked over my shoulder at the clock; it was just after eleven. Not awfully late, but not early either.

Tap, tap, tap.

I took a breath, slid the window up and peered out into the night, clutching the flashlight like a bat. I expected some growling demon to burst into my room. I did not expect to hear my name being called from the ground.

"Heven?"

The voice was very familiar, but different somehow and it gave me pause. This was a trick. A trick from a smart demon, it wanted me to come out so it could attack. Still, I said, "Hello?"

"It's me. Can you come down?"

"Cole?" I asked, shining the light down into the yard. It bounced off his face and he cringed.

"Geez, Hev, are you trying to blind me?"

I couldn't stop the smile. But then I frowned at the way he slurred his words. "Are you drunk?" I demanded.

"I had a few," he mumbled. "Are you coming down or what?"

I debated, still wondering if it was a trick. I looked down at his aura, the colors still visible in the dark. It was the same as always, the same magenta color that no one else had. He couldn't fake that. The way his aura pulsed and waved told me that he had more than a few drinks.

"Did you drive here?" I hissed.

He made a noise. "Fine, if you won't come down, I'll come up." He stumbled toward the side of the house, crashing into something in the yard. "Owww!" He howled.

I winced. "I'm coming down. Meet me on the porch." I hurried to close the window and snagged a plush blanket off the bed before quietly making my way downstairs into the kitchen. Briefly, I thought about sending Sam a thought, telling him that Cole was here. I knew that he would drop what he was doing with Logan and come right over because he didn't like Cole, and because he sensed that there might be more between us than friendship. Ashamed, I brushed the thought away as quickly as it came. I wouldn't manipulate him that way. I wouldn't use his feelings against him just to get his attention.

Even if I sometimes wanted to.

There were a few nights that Sam spent with Logan, but mostly he slept here, even if he didn't arrive until very late. I hadn't heard that he was staying at his place so I knew that he would be here soon. The thought gave me pause. I'd better get Cole out of here before Sam arrived and found us both together with me in my PJs.

It wouldn't be good.

I switched on the porch light and opened the door. Cole was there, lounging against the frame, a drunk but very cute smile on his lips. "Hey."

"What are you doing here?" I scowled.

He pushed away from the door and came in, his arms brushing mine as he walked into the kitchen. He bumped into a chair and swore.

"Shhh!" I insisted and switched on the small light over the sink, hoping it would be enough for his drunkenness to see.

He laughed and turned the chair around and sat down in it backward, resting his arms on the back. He looked rumpled with his shirt half tucked in. There was a hole in his jeans at the knee, and one of his shoes was untied. His face was flushed and his eyes were bright, but bloodshot, and I could smell beer on his breath.

"You're a mess." I sighed and wrapped the blanket around his shoulders, pulling it closed. Then I bent and tied his shoe lace, double knotting them both for good measure.

"Thanks," he said, his voice only slightly slurred.

Still bent low at his shoe, I looked up. His face was just above mine and I could see all the different blues that made up the color of his eyes. He reached down and swept my hair out of my face. I pulled back and stood. "What are you doing here, Cole?"

"You didn't answer my calls."

"Do you want some water?" I avoided his questioning stare and grabbed a bottle of water from the fridge. To my surprise the distraction worked. He took the water, gulping it down.

"What's going on with you?" I asked. Getting drunk and showing up at my house was something he had never done before. In fact, he'd never been here at all. Aside from the fact that he walked in on something freaky including me, an ice cream shop and a demon and got no explanation, things seemed a little... different... with him anyway.

He sighed and sat the water aside. "I don't know."

"How are things with you and Kimber?" Given the phone call I got from Kimber and all the jealousy she carried with her, I knew they couldn't be great.

"I don't love her anymore." Cole said matter of fact. It startled me and I looked up sharply.

"You don't?"

He shook his head. "Haven't since we broke up that last time when she used Sam to get back at me for kissing Jenna."

I swallowed down the guilt I felt for that situation because Sam had used Kimber too, which only made her relationship with Cole worse. "But you forgave her."

He nodded. "I always do."

My heart sank. He had always forgiven her and I never once wondered what all those times cost him. Until now. "I'm so sorry." I went over and placed a hand on his shoulder. Being friends with Kimber was difficult so I couldn't imagine what it was like to date her.

"Hell, I'm the one who kissed Jenna in the first place. It had been just a stupid bet, but…" His words trailed away.

"But?" I squeezed his shoulder.

"Part of me wondered what it would be like to be with someone else. Someone less difficult."

"Jenna is not less difficult," I muttered.

He laughed, then looked up at me. "I'm not into Jenna."

My heart began pounding. "That's good," I whispered.

"But I'm not into Kimber anymore, either."

I let out the breath I didn't know I was holding. I wanted to tell him to be honest with her, but Kimber was my best friend. How could I tell her boyfriend to break up with her?

"Things are changing," Cole went on. "And not just between me and Kimber."

"I don't know what you mean," I said, backing away from him. I prayed he didn't hear the lie in my voice. I busied myself by refolding the dish towels by the sink.

"Even my mom is acting weird."

"Like how?" I lied again, even though I knew exactly what he was talking about.

"I don't know." He shook his head. "It's almost like she's hiding something." I looked over at whatever I heard in his voice. His blue eyes speared me with a look so clear I would have sworn he was sober. "Just like you."

I sucked in a breath, wondering what to do. Did I have it in me to make up another lie? To laugh off his words and pretend that it was all in his head? Wasn't he my friend? He was hurting and confused, and I identified with those feelings way more than I wished I did. Yet, if I said anything, I would be betraying Sam. He's given up so much for me and never once asked for anything in return.

I opened my mouth, unsure what was going to come out when suddenly the overhead light came on, startling in its brightness. Cole moved fast, almost like on instinct, coming to block me from whatever entered the room. I blinked in shock before stepping around him. "Gran."

"I heard voices," Gran said, her aura and body relaxing as she realized it was only me.

"I didn't mean to wake you."

"I thought Sam had gone home hours ago," Gran said, looking at Cole. Her eyes rounded as she saw that it wasn't Sam.

"This is Cole, Gran. You've heard me talk about him before." I grabbed his arm and pulled him forward, praying he wouldn't act drunk.

"Of course!" Gran said, staring at him.

We both waited for her to continue with how late it was and that friends shouldn't be visiting at this time of night. She didn't say anything. She just stared at him, her eyes skimming his face over and over again.

Cole cleared his throat. "I'm sorry to have come by so late, Mrs. Uhhh…"

"Just call me Gran, honey," she said, still staring.

Cole nodded. "Gran."

Cole continued to talk, to give an explanation of why he was here so late, but I didn't hear it. Gran's aura was shifting and changing so rapidly that I had a hard time keeping up. Yellows, reds, blues, browns, mustard even some pink bloomed around her. I had no idea what it meant. How could so many colors, a range of so many emotions come into play at once and make sense?

"Gran, are you feeling okay?"

Gran finally pulled her eyes away from Cole to look at me. "Of course. I'm just a little fuzzy-headed because I was sleeping."

Cole stepped forward and grasped her arm. "Would you like to sit down?" He led her over to the table and pulled out a chair. When she was seated, he wrapped the discarded blanket around her shoulders.

"Aren't you a nice young man?" Gran said. I heard the slightest catch in her voice.

What in the world was going on?

Cole didn't seem to notice anything wrong and he took a seat across from Gran. He chatted with her for a few minutes about nothing and they both laughed at a joke he told.

"I really should be going," Cole said, standing. He turned toward Gran. "I'm really sorry to have woken you."

"You're leaving? You can't drive in your state!" Gran said, standing.

Cole and I both stared at her in shock.

She chuckled. "I may be old, but I know when someone's drunk."

A laugh bubbled out of my throat. Cole grinned.

"I'll get some blankets; you can sleep on the couch."

Cole seemed about to disagree, but I cut him off. "You can't drive, Cole. We'll worry." I would worry.

He nodded.

Gran disappeared and came back seconds later with an armful of blankets and pillows. "Here we go." She was almost chipper.

"I'll get that, Gran. You can go back to bed," I said, swallowing and wondering if she would give me that look I would most certainly get from Mom. Leaving me alone at night with a boy…

"Thank you, honey. I'll see you in the morning. I'll make a big breakfast." I nodded, blinking back the tears in my eyes. She actually trusted me. Gran turned to Cole and patted his cheek. "I'll see you at breakfast."

"I'm sorry again," Cole said.

Gran smiled. "I'm not. I'm so glad to have met you."

We both stared after her as she left the room.

Cole spoke first. "I need some air." He opened the door and walked out into the cool summer night.

"Cole?" I followed behind him. He staggered a bit by the stairs and wrapped an arm around the post and pulled back. I heard a great ripping sound.

"Oops," he said, turning to look at me.

I laughed. There was a huge rip in the front of his shirt.

"This was my favorite shirt," he muttered, and in one swift movement, he pulled it up over his head and tossed it at his feet. I averted my gaze, but not before I noted how wide his shoulders were and how toned his muscles had gotten from playing football.

"I'll go make up the couch."

"Heven, wait."

I stopped and turned back. In two great strides he was standing in front of me. "Do you ever think about what it would be like?"

"What?"

"To kiss me?"

"N-no." I shook my head back and forth, backing away.

"Never?" He stepped closer, almost prowling toward me, and lowered his head.

"I'm in love with Sam." There was no hint of doubt in my voice because I did love him.

Cole's lips covered mine, silencing my words. It was a light kiss; his lips were warm and he smelled like beer. I pulled back, stumbling. He reached out to steady me.

"You shouldn't have done that." I raced in the house away from him.

He found me a few moments later in the family room, making up the couch. "Heven."

I ignored him and continued to punch the pillow into a white case.

"Hey," he said, grabbing it from my hands.

"You had no right," I said, hating the tremor in my voice.

"I know. I'm sorry. I'm such an ass." He scrubbed a hand down his face.

"I'm in love with Sam."

"I know. I know," he whispered. "You already said that." He tossed the pillow onto the couch.

"I'm going upstairs. I'll see you in the morning?" I wanted to run to my room and hide.

"Yeah, okay." When I turned away, he grabbed my hand. "Heven, I'm really sorry. I don't want to mess up our friendship."

I sighed. "It's all right, Cole." He hugged me and I let him. When I pulled back, he threw himself down on the couch. On my way out of the room, I noticed that the blinds were still open and went to close them. I looked out into the dark and an eerie feeling of being watched ran up my spine. I pulled them down and took off upstairs, heart pounding.

Once there, I shut the door and sagged against it. Some movement across the room caught my eye and had me straightening in defense.

"It's just me," Sam said, standing up from the bed.

"Sam." I pressed a hand to my chest. "You scared me."

"It was probably hard to hear me come in when you were downstairs with Cole."

Had he seen Cole kiss me? My hands were shaking and I felt sick. How did everything get so messed up? I made a sound in the back of my throat.

"What's going on, Heven? I thought you weren't going to tell him anything. What's he doing here?"

What on earth was I going to say?

Sam

I parked my truck and climbed out, locking the door and stuffing the keys into my pocket. I didn't really think anyone would bother it out here at the edge of Gran's property, practically hidden among the trees and bushes, but I locked it anyway—out of habit I guess. Protecting what was mine seemed to be ingrained in me. It wasn't something that I could turn off; it was automatic, just like breathing. I wondered how I had gotten this way. Well, I *knew* how, but when had it become a *part* of me? It must have been a gradual change, happening slowly over time until it became all I knew.

I walked through the dark, wondering if Heven was asleep by now. I was late, a lot later than I wanted to be, but Logan needed me. Maybe I should have stayed with him like I did the other night but... I really wanted, no *needed*, a break. He had another one of his "fits," as I had come to think of them, again tonight. It was really hard to watch—to not be able to do anything about. For someone who was decidedly protective, not being able to protect my own brother was driving me crazy.

But how do you protect someone from themself?

The night had started out fine. We grabbed some burgers and fries for dinner, rented the new *Transformer's* movie and went to our place. I didn't turn the movie on right away; for some reason, sitting in front of the TV while we ate bothered me. I worked so much and spent a lot of time with Heven. The time that I did have for Logan, I didn't want to spend it with us watching TV and not talking. A memory of my brother and I sitting around the dinner table with Mom and Dad flashed into my head. She never let us watch TV during dinner. She made us turn everything off because it was family time. I guess I learned that from her. Man, it used to make me so mad. I smiled at the memory. "Why?" I would whine, mad that I couldn't watch whatever the latest cartoon was.

"Because I want to hear all about your day. Because I like to see my son's faces."

I brushed away the memory when my chest began to feel tight. Those times were over. But Logan was really struggling to adapt to his new life and I wanted to attempt to give him some kind of normal.

"So I was thinking we could go out to the woods that border the farm this weekend," I told him, tentatively. We wouldn't ever go back to the woods that bordered Sebago Lake again, but even though it had been horrible last time, I still really felt like trying again was something that he needed to do. "Work on how to control—"

And just like that, it was like a switch inside him flipped.

"Would you give it a rest?" he said, cutting me off angrily and tossing down his half-eaten burger to glare at me.

I was momentarily stunned at his tone. Instead of getting angry, I said, "Look, I know that shifting hurts and I hate to see you that way, but it doesn't mean that practice won't help— make it easier."

"I don't care!" He shoved his coke over. The plastic lid popped off and coke and ice went rushing across the table.

I cursed and stood up. Everything was soaked. "What did you do that for?" I snagged a roll of paper towels off the counter and held them out. "Clean this up."

He glared at me, breathing hard, ignoring my outstretched hand. "Don't you get it?" he snapped. "I don't want to be like you. Being a hellhound isn't what I want."

"I get that. I really do, Logan, but you can't change what you are." I tried to keep my voice level.

"You don't get it!" he yelled, jumping up, sending the chair he was sitting in clattering to the floor. "It's all so easy for you. You just walked away from us, from your old life without a second thought. You started a new life."

"I did not walk away from you. *They* kicked *me* out. They told me to go. They couldn't stand the sight of me." My heart was pounding and anger swirled inside of me. He was blaming me. Blaming me for doing what I had to do to survive.

Logan made a sound in the back of this throat and he leaped forward and upset the table, sending it over on its side. There was a huge bang and my food and soda went everywhere, ice slid across the floor, leaving a wet trail behind it.

I lunged at him. He was strong, but I was stronger. My age and honed-hellhound abilities put me at an advantage. I shoved him up against the wall and pinned him there, taking in his wild eyes—I kept a close watch for that flame color to appear.

"Stop it," I said low, not looking away. To my relief his eyes didn't have any of that orange color, but they were still a little off — familiar but not. The hound in him was warring with his human side... hopefully, this time, he would win as there was no wildlife in here for him to take his aggression out on.

Logan sagged against the wall beneath my grip. "Do you know what it's like?" he asked, dropping his stare. "To feel like a stranger in your own body? To not know who or what you are?"

"Yeah, Logan, I do." I didn't lighten the hold I had on him, afraid that his "fit" wasn't over.

He shook his head sadly. "I thought you would make this better."

His words broke something in me. I wanted to be who he thought I could be, but I didn't know how to fix him.

"The hellhound inside you — it's part of you — you recognize it. It doesn't hurt you like it does me. It's not that way for me. Why isn't it that way for me?"

He looked so defeated. It killed me. This was my baby brother. I didn't want this for him. I eased back, no longer restraining him, but hovering close by. "I don't know, Logan, but I'll figure it out. I will."

"Sometimes I feel like..." His voice trailed away and he was silent for so long that I thought he wasn't going to finish his sentence. But then his voice cut through the quiet. "Sometimes it seems like the two parts of me are fighting and eventually one will win." His eyes snapped up to mine. "What if the real me loses? What if the hound takes over, and I'm stuck in a body that I don't want to be in?"

It had never been this hard for me. Being a hellhound was never really something I hated. What I had hated and had to learn to accept was that being a hellhound made me different, that the life I thought I was going to have wasn't an option.

"Logan, listen to me. It's going to be okay. I know it's hard right now. I know you're confused. I don't have all the answers and I don't know what's going to happen, but I swear it's going to be fine. It's not always going to be like this."

He looked up and that wild look had drained away, leaving the look of a scared, vulnerable kid in its place. I swallowed past the lump in my throat. "Promise?" He scarcely said the word, but I heard him.

"I promise." In the back of my mind I cringed. How was I going to make things better for him? What if I couldn't?

He smiled and nodded, all trace of anxiety seeming to fall away. He looked over at the massive mess all over the place and grimaced. "I'll clean that up."

"Yeah, you will." I clapped him on the back with my hand. His shirt was damp with sweat.

"Guess you're pretty disappointed in me," he said while scooping soggy food off the floor.

"It was a pretty good burger." I sighed dramatically.

He laughed. It was such a "Logan" sound that it gave me hope...

I shook myself out of the memory and realized that I was standing in the middle of the yard, hands fisted at my sides in the dark. I started moving again, and seconds later, the house came into view. I expected all the windows to be dark and the house to be closed up. But the lights were on and the back door was open...

I looked across the yard and saw Cole's truck in the spot beneath the tree where I always parked (well when I was supposed to be here).

He was standing on the porch, *without* a shirt, and Heven was just a few feet away — walking toward the door.

"Heven, wait." I heard him call out and she stopped to turn back.

He moved forward so that he was within inches. I held back a growl and the urge to rush over there and knock him out.

"Do you ever think about what it would be like?" Cole said, staring at Heven.

"What?"

"To kiss me?"

I sucked in a breath. He wouldn't dare touch her...

"N-no," Heven said and thankfully began backing away.

"Never?" he challenged, following her retreating form. I ground my teeth together until my jaw hurt. I took a step forward, ready to launch myself in the direction of the porch.

"I'm in love with Sam," Heven said and surprisingly, I felt better. I knew she loved me. I felt it every day. She wouldn't be too happy with me if I raced over there and pummeled Cole into the dirt, which I sorely wanted to do. She would want to handle this on her own.

Cole didn't seem to hear her words because he leaned in and touched his lips to hers. White-hot rage came over me and the thought of letting Heven handle her own life fled my brain.

"You shouldn't have done that." Heven raced from the porch, disappearing from sight.

I ran to the porch, but Cole had already followed, closing the door behind him. I stood there breathing hard, seeing red and thinking of violent ways to hurt him when I realized something...

Heven hadn't liked that kiss.

I had been so focused on my own reaction that I hadn't paid much attention to hers, but I had felt it. When he kissed her, she felt nothing and she had been relieved.

I can't say I was too happy about her relief, because that meant that she had been confused in the first place—but hadn't I already known that? But now I knew that whatever it was between Heven and Cole wasn't romantic, at least not on her end.

Instead of bursting in the house, I went around the side and went through her window into her bedroom.

I liked this space. It was comfortable and filled with Heven. It made me feel like I belonged somewhere. Silently closing the window behind me, I went toward the door and listened for her and Cole's voices downstairs.

She told him again that she was in love with me (I smiled with smug satisfaction), and then I heard her footsteps on the stairs.

I went and sat on the bed, trying to appear as though I wasn't eavesdropping, and knowing I would fail miserably, when she opened the door and sagged against it. She looked exhausted. I moved to stand up and she jumped, not realizing I had been here.

"It's just me," I said, standing up from the bed.

"Sam." She pressed a hand to her chest. "You scared me."

"It was probably hard to hear me come in when you were downstairs with Cole." I couldn't keep out the bit of coldness that crept into my voice. Just because I had kept myself from busting in the house on them didn't mean I wasn't pissed.

She made a sound in the back of her throat.

"What's going on, Heven? I thought you weren't going to tell him anything. What's he doing here?"

"How long have you been here?" she asked.

It was wrong, but I lied. I wanted to see what she would say. It's not that I didn't trust her to tell me because I knew with everything in me that she would. But I didn't want to admit I had been eavesdropping on her and Cole.

"Not long. I can smell him and I heard you talking."

"He kissed me," she admitted, looking down and I smiled because I had been right. But my smile was short-lived because the words were a lot harder to hear than I thought they would be, even after witnessing it. The thought of his hands—his *lips*—on her made me crazy.

Did you kiss him back? I said the words into her mind because I couldn't say it out loud.

No. It was all wrong. It wasn't anything like you. Nothing could be like you. More of that smug satisfaction purred through me and I grinned. But she didn't see it because she was too busy avoiding my gaze.

I walked across the room, stepping right up in front of her. *I heard you tell him you love me.*

"I do. More than anything." She finally looked up and I saw the truth in her eyes.

"I believe you, Hev."

I don't know why, but I feel close to him, she said. *I tried not to, but I can't help it.*

I know. It's okay.

I looked up at him. *You know?*

He nodded. *We have a Mindbond, Heven. I've felt how torn you've been.*

Why haven't you said anything?

I knew you would tell me about it when you were ready. But I also didn't like knowing that some other guy had an effect on her.

She smiled, then tilted her head to the side. *Why aren't you yelling at me?*

I'd rather kiss you. To wipe out any trace of someone else's kiss. I grabbed her shirt at the waist, bunching the extra material in my hands and towed her slowly forward. I wrapped my arms around her and kissed her, urgently at first, like I had something to prove, but then the kiss changed and softened, erasing all thought from my mind.

After a while I pulled away and took in her unfocused and soft eyes. *Let Cole compete with that,* I thought to myself.

There is no competition, Heven replied.

Damn Mindbond.

I guided Heven toward the bed, but she pulled away to go over to the window to pull the curtains closed over the blinds. I lifted an eyebrow.

Did you see anything out there when you came in? she asked.

No. Why? Everything in me went on alert.

She shook her head. *Never mind. I guess I'm just a little freaked out with everything that's been going on.*

I'll go look around. I started for the window, mentally berating myself for being so caught up in my own thoughts and then the scene with Heven and Cole on the porch that I hadn't paid any attention to my surroundings outside. So much for that damn protective instinct.

Heven reached out and grabbed my hand. *No. Stay. I'm sure it's nothing.*

I hesitated as she moved away and climbed into bed. My instincts would have told me if a demon had been close and I was exhausted... I kicked out of my shoes and jeans (I was already wearing basketballs shorts under my jeans) and climbed in next to her. She settled against me with a sigh.

We lay there in silence for a few moments, and as exhausted as I was, I couldn't sleep. *What's he doing here, Heven?*

I think he came to ask me about earlier, but we never talked about it.

No?

We talked about Kimber and his mom. He's just confused... I feel bad for him.

I made a rude noise. *He took advantage of it and kissed you.*

He's drunk. He probably won't even remember in the morning, she said, but I wasn't convinced. Kissing Heven isn't something someone would forget. I couldn't stop from snorting softly. *He'll remember when I punch his lights out.*

She jerked up to stare down at me through the dark. *You can't. Please don't.*

The anger I tried to push away earlier came back. *The guy made a play for you. You think I'm just going to let it go?*

I was hoping you would.

I laughed.

Sam, please. You can't just march in here tomorrow and punch him. Think of Gran. You'll upset her. As soon as she said the words, something in her shifted.

What is it? I asked.

Gran met him tonight. It was weird.

Weird how?

She just kept staring at him.

She was probably wondering what some drunk guy was doing in her kitchen with you.

She shook her head like it didn't make sense. *Her aura was all over the place.*

I sighed. *She was probably just tired. Enough about Cole. I don't want to spend any more time talking about him.*

Me either.

Come here, I said to cover her lips with mine. All this talk about Cole made me want to mark my territory.

Heven seemed to sense my thoughts and pulled away. *You're never going to be able to accept him as part of my life – even if we are just friends, are you?*

I stared at her for long moments. *I don't know.*

I thought she would argue with me, try to make me see reason. But she didn't. Instead, she laid her head on my chest and went to sleep.

* * *

I didn't sleep well that night. After everything that happened with Logan and knowing that Cole was downstairs, I just couldn't seem to find any peace, even with Heven curled up next to me. When the very first rays of dawn began peeking through the clouds, I very carefully slid from the bed, slid off my shorts and shrugged into my jeans. Moving quietly, I slipped through Heven's bedroom door and down the stairs to the living room where Cole was passed out on the couch. I stood over him, staring down, wondering why Heven was so insistent on keeping him in her life. I had the urge to reach

56

down and—his eyes flew open and he jerked up, turning to stare at me.

"What the hell are you doing here?" he said, his voice low from sleep.

He had faster reflexes than I gave him credit for. I lifted an eyebrow. "I'm here every morning at this time to do the barn work," I answered coolly.

"It's morning?"

"You should go."

His eyes narrowed. "I was invited to breakfast."

"Something must have come up," I said, flat.

"Actually, my day is free."

"You're lucky I'm letting you walk out of here after what you pulled last night with Heven," I began and I could see that some of my words took the steam out of his challenge.

"She told you?"

"Did you think she wouldn't?" I smirked. I sat down on the coffee table in front of the couch, making a show of getting comfortable. "Did you really think that one pathetic kiss was going to make her walk away from me?"

"There's something between us." The way he said it didn't exactly disagree with what I said, but there was an absolute truth behind his words.

It bothered me in ways I didn't want to admit.

I stared at him, without blinking, imagining my fist smacking into the side of his jaw.

He got up from the couch and ran a hand through his extremely messy head of hair. "Yeah, I'll go, but not because you're telling me too. Because..."

"Because you showed up here drunk and made an ass out of yourself?" I asked, mildly amused and stood from the table so I could show him the door.

"No. Because I'm sure my mom is freaked out and wondering why I never came home."

"There went your Son of the Year award."

"Yeah, well, at least my parents want me."

His words were like a slap to my face. I stood there frozen for a few long seconds before I jerked forward and plowed my fist right into his jaw. I moved so fast he hadn't even seen it coming and he fell backward onto the couch. It tipped before falling back into place onto the floor.

He looked up at me with wide eyes and slowly felt around his jaw.

"Get the hell out of here before I do it again," I growled.

He went to the door and put his hand on the handle, but then he stopped but didn't turn around. "I deserved that. I shouldn't have said it. But next time… I'm going to hit back."

"Looking forward to it," I said.

His back stiffened, but he walked out the door. I stood there until I heard his truck drive away and then I crept back upstairs. I should've gone straight out to the barn and gotten to work but I wanted to see her. I had come to accept the fact that my parents didn't want me—that I was emancipated at the age of sixteen. Cole's words weren't any surprise. They shouldn't have hurt me.

But they did.

Chapter Five

Heven

Rain was pattering against the roof and window, making me burrow further into the sheets. Sam tried to slide out from beneath me, but I pulled him back in. "Don't go," I murmured.

He groaned. "The sun is already up. I have to leave so I can come back and start the barn chores."

"It's raining,"

"The horses still want to eat."

"Five more minutes."

He pressed his lips to my forehead. "Five minutes."

Five minutes just wasn't long enough because in no time, Sam was climbing out of bed and throwing on his T-shirt and shoes. I watched unhappily as he reached into my closet and pulled out one of the hoodies he kept there. He chuckled when he caught me watching and came to stand next to me.

"I'll be right back."

"But we won't be alone."

His eyes softened. "At least I'm off tonight."

It reminded me. "Ugh, we have dinner tonight with my mother and her boyfriend."

"At least we'll be together."

"Yeah." I pushed the covers back and climbed out of bed. "I'll meet you in the barn to help."

He shook his head. "It's chilly and rainy this morning. You stay inside."

I was about to protest, but he kissed me. "Will you have some coffee ready for me when I'm finished?"

"Of course," I murmured, smiling at him.

After he disappeared into the falling rain, I pulled the curtains closed, gathered up my clothes and went into the bathroom for a hot shower. On my way downstairs, I remembered that Cole was here and I was surprised Sam didn't take me up on my offer to help in the barn, if only to keep me away from Cole. But when I came down the stairs I understood.

Cole was gone.

The blanket and pillows he used were all folded neatly and stacked on the couch.

I wandered into the kitchen, partly thinking that maybe he would be there, eating some of Gran's cooking. But he wasn't and Gran was staring out the window watching the rain fall.

"Cole left?" I asked.

"It seems so." She seemed sad by this.

"He was probably just embarrassed because he was drunk."

Gran didn't turn from the window. "You've been friends with him for a long time?"

"A few years."

"He's a good boy?"

"Yeah, Cole's great. First time I've seen him like that."

"Wonder what's wrong?" Gran said, almost to herself.

"Oh, he got into a fight with Kimber." I brushed it all off and went to make some coffee for Sam. Frankly, I was relieved that Cole wasn't here, even if it meant he was avoiding me. Now *I* could avoid all the awkwardness from last night's kiss and Sam wouldn't have a chance to deck him.

"That's too bad." Gran turned from the window and smiled. "Here, I'll do that." She grabbed the coffee pot and began filling it with water. I relinquished the coffee to her and began pulling out the makings for French toast. I thought briefly about calling to make sure Cole made it home okay, but I thought better of it.

If I called he would ask.

I couldn't tell him.

Sam was still adamant that Cole not know about the demons and the Treasure Map. I managed to dodge the topic last night but luck only went so far. I didn't want to lie to Cole so I figured I would say nothing at all.

* * *

The rain finally stopped, leaving the ground soggy and the air thick with moisture. The sun was out, doing its best to shine rays of light through the lingering clouds. We were standing on the front porch of my mother's house (how odd that I didn't see it as my house anymore), but I couldn't bring myself to ring the doorbell and begin the evening.

Calm down.

I glanced over my shoulder at Sam. *Is it that obvious?*

He caught a strand of my hair between his fingers and tucked it behind my ear. *They won't see it, but I can feel it.*

I don't know what to expect. That was what made me so nervous. All my life I thought I knew exactly who my mother was. Sure, sometimes I didn't always agree with her, but I could always understand her. Until she declared that I was marked by evil. Since that day, I've often wondered if I ever really knew her at all.

And then she threw another curve ball at me.

She's dating.

It's just going to be dinner, sweetheart. Sam's voice cut through my thoughts.

Yes, but, my mother invited me and *you, the boy she has made no secret of disapproving of, and her new boyfriend. She has a boyfriend, Sam.*

His warm, rough fingertips trailed tenderly down the side of my cheek. *Does that bother you?*

My eyes were stinging and I blinked rapidly, telling myself that it didn't. *No. I want her to be happy.*

It's okay to wish it was your dad, Hev.

I turned fully around to face him, his understanding and safety was like a beacon to my dark, uncertain mood. He folded his arms around me and I sighed deeply. This is where I fit, where I belonged, everything else was just details. I squeezed my eyes shut and committed this feeling to memory, certain I would need to call on it later.

Maybe now that your mother has found someone, she'll be more accepting of us.

How close could they be? They just started dating.

One way to find out. He used his oversized hands to spin me around to face the front door and pointed at the doorbell.

I reached out and pressed the button while wondering what was waiting for us on the other side of the door.

* * *

Things were not as I expected. From the second she opened the door, I knew that something was different. What I hadn't decided was if that something was good or bad.

"Well, are you going to come in or stand out there and stare all night?" Mom asked with a smile on her face. She motioned for us to come in and held the door open wide.

"Sorry," I mumbled as I walked in, my eyes searching for a glimpse of Mom's new man.

"It's so good to see you!" she said and pulled me in for a hug. I was caught off guard, but brushed it off and I hugged her back. She pulled back to look at me. "You look wonderful. How has your summer been so far?"

I studied her as I gave some lame response about swimming and hanging out with Kimber. She looked really good. Her brown hair was shining, settling down around her shoulders, and her blue eyes were bright and clear. Her smile was genuine with none of the tension around her mouth that I had gotten used to. She was dressed in a blue sundress that came to her knees. What was most impressive was her aura. It held none of the mistrust and disappointment that usually bloomed around her head when I was near. Things felt like they used to be before I was disfigured, started dating Sam and 'became evil.' Well, maybe not exactly like it used to be.

Even though I couldn't be certain, I had an inkling that her aura now bloomed with more blue and green than *Before*. But that wasn't a bad thing because blue and green were balancing and peaceful. Blue seemed to bloom right out of her head and circle around her. Some of the tension I was feeling about tonight eased because someone with this relaxed of an aura did not have an agenda for inviting me and Sam here. Right?

A deep voice from the kitchen said, "Madeline, where do you keep the napkins?"

I would have turned toward the sound, but I was too interested in my mother. Her whole body shifted toward the sound of his voice. It's like she was drawn to him. "I'll be right there! Heven and Sam are here!"

I knew he was going to come out of the kitchen. I anticipated it, but his appearance was still surprising. It was surprising because he was nothing like I expected.

He was hot.

That thought disturbed me in so many ways. I took a small step backward toward Sam, hoping no one noticed the distance I was trying to create. Sam did and he came farther into the room to stand at my back.

"Heven! Sam! How great to meet you!" he said, sliding into the room. He walked with enthusiasm and grinned jovially. He had short, trimmed brown hair and brown eyes. He was tall, but not quite as tall as Sam, and he was dressed casually in jeans and a white button-up shirt left untucked. The sleeves of his shirt were rolled up and he was wiping his hands on a kitchen towel. He held out his hand as he approached to greet us. I wanted to reach out and take his hand and I understood my mother's earlier reaction to him; the guy was like a magnet. Charm and charisma poured off of him. Instead of reaching out to greet him, I stared. Sam reached out around me and shook his hand briefly. They exchanged pleasantries.

Then he turned toward me.

"Your mother has told me so much about you. It's a pleasure to meet you,"

I placed my hand in his. His skin was cool to the touch, but his grip was firm, indicating confidence and strength. My dad always said that you could judge a man by his handshake. "Nice to meet you..."

"Henry," my mother said, stepping forward. "Heven, this is Henry."

"Henry," I echoed, pulling my hand away and smiling. "Nice to meet you." His aura was a lot like Mom's, laid-back and friendly with no emotion making too strong a point in the curtain of colors that surrounded him. He did have a great deal of clouds of turquoise, a color symbolizing someone with a dynamic, influencing nature. I guess that explained his magnetism.

Mom turned to Sam. "So glad you could make it, Sam. I know we haven't been the best of friends up until now, but I'm hoping that will change."

I clenched my jaw to keep it from falling open. Had I heard her right? Mom was going to accept Sam?

"Well, come on in! Dinner is almost ready. I hope you both are hungry because we made—"

She's going to say chicken. Chicken, eww.
"Steak."
"Not chicken?" The words fell from my lips.
Mom laughed. "I think we've all had enough chicken. Besides, I never could find a recipe that was actually good."

I laughed. We all worked side by side doing what was left to do to get dinner on the table. Henry grilled the steaks outside and Mom and I fixed a salad while Sam poured iced tea for everyone. She asked about my job, the farm and Gran; then she asked Sam about his jobs and what he liked to do when he wasn't working. I waited with baited breath for Mom's reaction when Sam answered "spend time with Heven," but Mom just smiled and told him he was sweet.

Okay, this is why I'm apprehensive about thinking all this was great. Why the sudden change in attitude toward Sam? If something appeared too good to be true, then it probably was. There had to be a catch. I stole a glance out of the corner of my eye at Mom only to see her working happily alongside me. It just didn't seem right. I sighed and swatted away a fly that was buzzing around the salad.

When we were all sitting around the table eating, I took the lapse in conversation to learn a little bit more about my mother and Henry. "So, Mom, how did you and Henry meet?"

"Henry is here with a group of volunteers from our sister church in Portland to help out with our summer humanity project with Habitat for Humanity."

I smiled and batted at the fly that was still buzzing around, wondering if Henry was as involved with his church as Mom was with ours. "That's great. So you're from Portland, Henry?"

"For a while now. I've lived in many different places."

"Henry likes to travel," Mom said, looking adoringly at him. I smiled, resisting the urge to gape. From beneath the table, Sam squeezed my thigh in reassurance.

When dinner was finished, Mom presented the table with a Bee-sting cake that looked perfectly baked and decorated. For some reason, just looking at the sweet concoction turned my stomach and the last thing I wanted to do was eat it. When she turned away to get coffee cups and a knife to cut the cake, I dropped my fake smile for a split second and shifted in my seat. When I looked up, Henry was staring at me. My eyes collided with his and I felt this weird sort of pressure in my head. I wanted to look away, but I couldn't. It was like he was drawing me in. Another fly buzzed in my ear and before my eyes, breaking the trance I was in. I grimaced and shooed it away. "These flies are annoying."

"It's summer," my mother said, returning to the table and began cutting thick slices of the rich cake.

You okay? Sam asked.

Yeah. I felt weird for a minute, but I'm fine now.

Mom slid a huge slice of cake before me and my stomach revolted. Casually, Sam reached over and slid the plate out from under me and placed it in front of him. "No cake for me," I said, patting my stomach. "I'm stuffed from dinner."

Mom frowned.

"But I'd love a cup of coffee," I hurried to say, trying not to wince. I prayed that my rejection of dessert would not lead into a conversation of how I don't eat enough.

"Wonderful," Mom said, her aura never wavering from the tranquil blues and greens. Seconds later, a steaming cup appeared before me. The rich, bold aroma soothed me.

Sam made appreciative noises around the cake and polished off that huge slice before I even added milk and sugar to my mug. Mom seemed delighted and handed him another slice, which he attacked with equal excitement.

You are going to be sick later, I told him.

"There is a reason that I invited you over," Mom said, drawing my focus away from Sam. I glanced up to see Henry staring at me once more. He smiled and something cold slithered down my spine. I shook the feeling and turned toward my mother.

"Yes?" Hadn't I known that this little meal was too good to be true?

"Here," she said sliding an envelope across the table. I stared down at it for several heartbeats wondering what was inside. I wasn't sure I wanted to know. "Open it," Mom urged.

I picked it up and slid my finger beneath the flap. The paper was crisp and I felt it slice into my skin. "Ouch." I drew my finger away and stared down at the welling blood.

"Be careful," Henry said quietly. "Wouldn't want you to get hurt."

I smiled weakly. "It's just a paper cut." I tore the envelope the rest of the way and pulled out a sheet of paper. It was the permission slip for the class trip to Italy. Mom's signature was scrawled across the bottom.

"I don't understand," I said.

"I've decided to allow you to go to Italy," she said as she took a bite of cake. "This cake is just delicious. Thank you so much for bringing it, Henry,"

"It was my pleasure," he said smoothly, running his hand down her arm.

"I don't understand," I repeated. Just like that? For months she had been adamantly refusing to let me go, demanding that I go to Camp Hope instead. So why the sudden change of heart?

Sam gently pulled the form out of my fingers and looked it over.

Mom smiled. "I've been thinking a lot lately and I can see now that I was wrong." Shock must have registered across my face because she said, "I know this seems out of the blue, but really it isn't. You're a good girl, Heven. You always have been and I was punishing you for something that wasn't even your fault." Her eyes scanned the area where my scars used to be.

I resisted the urge to finger my cheek. "You don't think I'm evil?" I whispered, trying not to hope.

"No, honey. I think some bad things happened to you and you did your best to cope."

"I…" I didn't know what to say. This was all so unexpected.

Mom smiled. "I hope you have a wonderful time on your trip. Take lots of pictures and I can't wait to hear all about it."

"Thank you," I said, staring down at the signed form on the table.

"You're welcome," she said, returning to her cake.

I got up from the table and went around to her side and threw my arms around her neck. "Thank you so much."

"I'm so glad you're happy."

I pulled back. "What about Camp Hope?"

She waived her hand in the air dismissively. "I called and gave up your spot. After talking with Henry, it really wasn't that hard of a decision."

My eyes shot to Henry who was sipping his coffee. "You talked to Henry about this?"

Mom nodded. "He is a wonderful listener. He helped me see that I was being too hard on you."

"I..." This was all because of Henry? How much influence did he have over my mother?

"Are you all right, Heven?" Mom said, concern darkening her eyes.

"Oh, yes," I hurried to say. "Thank you, Mom. This really means a lot to me." The last thing I wanted to do was give her reason to rethink her decision.

"I'm so glad. I really hope we can be close again," she said.

I returned to my chair next to Sam and reached for his hand beneath the table. "Me too," I agreed.

I glanced at Henry, wondering if Mom's 'we' included him. He caught my stare and smiled. It transformed his already good looks into something angelic and benevolent. *Maybe having him around wouldn't be so bad*, I thought as I studied him anew. But then, something behind his eyes shifted, and the tiniest flicker of something else emerged, something so small it couldn't really be anything. I blinked and it was gone, making me doubt it had even been there at all. I turned back to my coffee, shaken.

Sometimes looks could be deceiving.

* * *

Despite the summer month, the air was cool and the sun was barely up when we crept into the barn. I was reminded that we weren't as safe as I once might have believed, by the sight of Sam's tense shoulders and roaming eyes. I wondered if there would ever be a time when our lives weren't in danger. Sam slid the barn door closed behind us and I clicked on the flashlight I was gripping. Soft beams of light shone before us, illuminating the yellow hay and dirt floor. A soft nickering to my left made me smile.

"Shhh," I told Jasper through the stall door. "We aren't really here right now."

Jasper didn't seem impressed that he was part of our secret. I handed the flashlight to Sam and reached up to unlatch the door. It made a loud creaking sound when I opened it and I winced. Jasper eyed Sam with the same distrust he always did, but otherwise made no sounds or sudden movements. I was pleased and surprised by Jasper's gradual coming around to Sam. While the horse may not like him, he didn't object to having him around either, which I thought of as some sort of victory.

"There's a shovel over there," I murmured, reaching up to stroke Jasper's nose. It was soft and warm and when the horse breathed out, his breath tickled my fingers.

Sam went and grabbed the shovel, moving so silently it amazed me.

"Let's do it over there in the corner," I said, shinning the light into the right hand corner of the stall.

Sam nodded and stepped around me into the stall. Jasper danced uneasily and eyed Sam. "Hush, now," I whispered and reached into my pocket, withdrawing a large red apple. Jasper promptly forgot about Sam and focused on his treat. Thankfully, I had the foresight to slice the apple into fourths so it would take longer for him to eat. Sam began shoveling the hay out of the corner to reveal solid packed dirt. I fed Jasper a second slice of apple and he chomped happily, ignoring the intrusion. Sam had a deep hole dug in no time.

"That should do it," he whispered, looking up. Even in the dim light I could see a faint smudge of dirt on his cheek. Slipping the last slice of apple to Jasper, I moved over next to Sam, reaching up to brush away the mark. He smiled and caught my hand bringing my chilled fingers to his warm lips. His breath brushed over them when he spoke, sending goose bumps along my arms. "Are you ready?"

I sighed and nodded. I didn't really have a choice. With regret I pulled my fingers away and reached into the front pocket of my hoodie and pulled out the scroll. The bronze tube around it felt heavy and cold in my grasp. "Ready as I'll ever be," I whispered.

"It will be safe here," Sam assured me.

I really believed that it would be. Burying the Treasure Map here, in the barn, literally beneath Jasper, was the only place I could think that it would be safe. Most of the creatures that were coming after me would still assume I would be carrying it or keeping it close. No one would suspect that I would bury it in a barn. And if they did and got close to finding it, I figured that Jasper would freak out the minute any demon came near the barn, giving us enough warning to get out there and save it. Plus, the scent of the horses should cover any other scents that we left here this morning while burying it.

It was a good plan.

So why was I still gripping the scroll like I might never see it again?

Sam covered my hands with his. He made no move to take it, but simply offered understanding and comfort. "It's not forever," he murmured. "We'll come back and get it before we go to Rome in a couple weeks."

I nodded not meeting his eyes. This scroll *had* to be kept safe. It was the only way to keep people from dying. To keep Sam from dying and in a way, it was a repayment to Airis for saving both our lives the night China murdered me. So much depended upon this one map's safety.

Sam exhaled softly. *We don't have to do this,* he told me. *We can take turns holding onto it.*

No. Here. I thrust the scroll at him before changing my mind. We did *have* to do this. I did not want Sam carrying this thing around. He might get hurt. And I certainly did not want to give Sam's little brother the opportunity to get it.

You're sure?

Yes.

Sam turned away and knelt, placing the scroll at the bottom of the hole. I held the flashlight while he shoveled the dirt over it little by little until it was completely covered. Once done, he spread some hay around and sat Jasper's feed bucket back in the corner.

Like we were never here, Sam said.

I looked over my shoulder at Jasper. "Take care of it, okay, boy?" The horse nickered softly like he understood and pushed his muzzle into my hand. "Good boy," I murmured.

Sam slipped out of the stall to return the shovel and then reached through the stall door, holding out his hand. *Ready?*

With a knot in my stomach, I gave the floor one last look before placing my hand in his and allowing him to tow me away. As we crept back toward the house, the sky was lightening quickly. Sam lifted his face to the newly dawning day and smiled.

He was relaxed. The realization sent guilt crashing through me. All these weeks of tension and stress all revolved around the

Treasure Map and my refusal to give it up. Now, just minutes after tucking it away in the earth, I could already feel the difference in Sam. How could I have tortured him for so long like that?

Sam turned from the sky and stared down at me, concern marring his gorgeous features. *What's wrong?*

Nothing. I'm sorry I hadn't done that sooner. Look at you. I cupped his face in my palms. *You seem almost... carefree.*

His smile was quick and devastating. My heart picked up pace and my mind began to feel muddled. *Not quite. But, it is nice to know you aren't carrying that thing around today.*

Not at all until we go to Italy.

He smiled again, his face transforming into the boy I sometimes forgot he was. *I'm going to go get the truck and 'show up' for my morning chores. Help me get them done and we can spend the afternoon together.*

How wonderful it was to see that mischievous, light-hearted smile on his face. *A day of fun?* I feigned confusion.

Think we can handle it?

I rolled my eyes dramatically and made shooing motions with my hands. *Go on, then; let's get the work done so we can play.*

His teeth flashed white when he laughed and leaned in for a swift, hard kiss. Then he was gone, running off to wherever it was he hid the truck at night. Before going inside I couldn't help but turn back, my eyes going to the barn.

The action made me realize that I traded my own piece of mind for Sam's.

It was a trade I would make again in a heartbeat.

Chapter Six

Heven

The water rippled softly against the shore. The grass shuffled in the breeze and the leafy, green trees jutted out of the earth, creating a soft canopy over the water. It was beautiful and peaceful, yet I couldn't stop shaking. Why had I agreed to this? Weren't we supposed to be having fun?

Sam dropped a few towels on the grass and turned to face me, a frown firmly in place. "Maybe this wasn't a good idea," he murmured, almost to himself.

I wanted to agree, but I couldn't because as much as I disliked the idea about learning to swim, it was something I needed to do. "No, we should do this."

He nodded and, in one swift motion, peeled his shirt over his head and tossed it next to the towels. Oh, God what a sight he was. Golden skin pulled taut over lean, corded muscles, his shorts hung low on his hips showing off a stomach that was flat and hard. *Touch.* I wanted—no I *needed* to touch him. I took a step forward, already anticipating the way his muscles would bunch and contract when my fingers slid over his sun-heated skin.

His eyes were golden fire as he watched me approach. My hand started at his shoulder and slowly caressed down his arm and into the palm of his hand where his fingers jerked once, tightening on my fingers before releasing and my hand went over his abs. A purr vibrated his chest. "Heven." His voice was even deeper than usual and the roughness with which he said my name raised gooseflesh along my arms. I looked up at him beneath half-lowered lids, part-shy part-seduction.

"You don't know what you're doing," he warned.

"What do you mean?" I asked a little confused. I knew exactly what I was doing. Couldn't he tell?

He groaned. "You're distracting me."

"I am?"

He blinked a few times then his eyes swept the surrounding area. I guess burying that scroll hadn't been enough to make him forget about protecting me. I sighed and stepped away to strip off my sundress to reveal a simple black bikini.

When I turned back he was staring at me with an unreadable expression on his face. "What?"

"I complain you are distracting me and so you take *off* your clothes..."

I laughed, liking that I might have the same effect on him that he did on me. I bent and picked up the dress. "I can put this back on," I suggested, waving it around.

He laughed, snatching it out of my hands and smacking me on the butt with it. "Don't even think about it."

We both laughed as he lunged for me yet again and began to tickle me. I laughed until I couldn't take it anymore and stumbled away. Sam was laughing so hard his eyes were tearing. It was so good to see him laugh and be carefree this way. After we both caught our breath, Sam looked out toward the water.

"Come on," he said, taking my hand and leading me to the water's edge. Hesitation and fear slammed through me and I slowed my steps.

Sam swung around to face me, his chest and shoulders blocking my view of the lake. "I'll be here with you."

I nodded. Did I really need to learn to swim?

Sam swept me up like a child and cradled me against his chest. I could feel the steady rhythm of his heart against my side and the feel of his skin against mine made everything else fall away. He began walking toward the water as I rested my cheek against his chest. I heard the water rippling as he stepped in and I tensed. His lips grazed my temple and his arms held me tighter and I forgot to be afraid.

"Look at me," he said soft.

I did, quickly getting lost in his whiskey-colored eyes.

I love you. He told me.

I love you. I answered.

Look down.

I snapped back into reality the minute I did as he asked. I was standing knee deep in the lake. I screeched. "You distracted me!" I demanded.

"Are you afraid?"

I waited for the fear to slam into me, but it never came. It just reinforced what I already knew. I would go anywhere, do anything with Sam and nothing else mattered. I shook my head and he smiled, satisfied with himself.

It took a while for him to coax me farther into the water, but soon I was standing with water grazing my shoulders while I kept a death grip on Sam. I couldn't help the shaking of my knees and the pounding of my heart. He was patient and gentle with me as he showed me how to move my arms and legs. I didn't mind the repeated practice because his hands were always firmly at my back and waist. Turned out, swimming was pretty fun. The water was like cool silk against my skin and it was surprisingly easy to keep myself afloat. Splashing Sam was quite fun too.

"I think you're ready to swim on your own," Sam declared.

"I don't know," I murmured, then frowned.

"The last couple times it was all you swimming. I wasn't helping you at all."

I couldn't let Sam be my life raft forever. I was strong. I could do this.

I nodded briskly. "Will you swim nearby?" Just because I was being strong didn't mean I had to drown.

I was rewarded with a brilliant smile just like the one he gave me this morning. It made me want to find other ways to make him like this. I fumbled a little bit at first, but with a few gentle reminders from Sam I was soon swimming, hardly gracefully, at his side.

"I'm doing it!" I exclaimed and was rewarded with a mouthful of water. A coughing fit followed. Sam scooped me up, laughing, and patted me on the back.

"The water isn't for drinking," Sam said, laughing again.

I reached down and splashed him in the face. He sputtered and spit out a mouthful of water that I managed to land in his mouth while he laughed. "That water's not for drinking," I mimicked.

Sam's eyes narrowed and a naughty grin curved his lips. He held me out away from him, suspending me over the water.

"You wouldn't dare," I gasped.

"Oops," he said and then he let go, and with a light splash, I was in the water.

I pushed off the bottom and broke the surface, wiping the water from my eyes to glare at him. "Are you crazy?" I demanded.

"That was good! You pushed off the bottom and found the surface. I thought you would flounder around like a fish." He grinned, his eyes sparkling with laughter.

I growled and splashed him again.

After a while of our water antics, I was feeling much more comfortable in the water and we were having the best time. But I wanted to practice my swimming skills a little more.

"I'm going to swim out there and back," I said, pointing to an unidentified spot in the water. I would go as far as I felt comfortable then turn around.

Sam nodded and I pushed off the bottom and began swimming away. I wasn't a strong swimmer, but I managed to keep my head above water and, for me, that was a victory.

"You're doing great!" Sam said from a short distance away.

With every paddle my strokes became surer and stronger. As I swam, something brushed against my leg and I shivered at the thought of a slimy fish getting that close. I made a wide circle and turned back, smiling.

Sam clapped and hollered at my accomplishment.

The fish brushed my leg again. A creepy feeling raised the hair on the back of my neck. I kicked out, trying to propel myself closer to Sam. Why did I swim so far away? When something closed around my ankle the creepy feeling I had turned to panic, and I knew that whatever was down there was not a fish. "Sam!" I screamed, but only half of his name came out because I was pulled violently beneath the water. I struggled wildly, trying to get away from whatever was dragging me down, but it was no use.

Dark, cloudy water swirled around me, and no matter where I turned, it all looked the same. Water filled my mouth and I sputtered, trying to spit it out. With one last attempt to get free, I turned toward whatever was holding me. I peered through the muddy water and I couldn't see anything.

Except the red eyes.

Those were hard to miss. They glowed with an intensity that shook me to my core. They were inherently evil. I tried to look past the red orbs that stared at me to see who or what they belonged to, but there wasn't anything there. The eyes seemed to belong to a cloud, a cloud that was only slightly lighter than the water surrounding us. It was terrifying. I looked back at the eyes and I wasn't sure if they seemed out of focus – fuzzy – because they were or because I had been beneath the water for too long.

Where is it? a voice inside my head hissed.

I whimpered. This voice didn't belong to Sam.

Tell me…

What do you want? I asked.

The scroll, tell me where it is.

You can't have it.

Blinding light burst behind my eyes and pain seared my head. I couldn't do anything but endure as wave after wave of pain washed over me.

Tell me.

No. No matter how much he hurt me I couldn't tell. I prayed that I would soon pass out.

You're stronger than I gave you credit for little one.

Who are you?

Your future. He laughed, the sound churned my stomach. I felt pressure in the back of my skull, like my head was being squeezed.

I screamed. Water rushed down my throat. The demon gave one final great tug and pulled me further into the depths of the lake,

Cambria Hebert

further away from Sam.

Further away from life.

Sam

The demon had no shape. It was practically without form at all. I kicked through the water toward Heven and the way her body just drifted with the current scared the hell out of me. I watched her die once before.

I would not do it again.

Airis gave us a second chance and I doubted there would be a third.

My lungs burned and felt heavy, and for a brief second, I began to believe that I couldn't breathe. My heart started hammering in my chest. I had to breathe!

But I didn't. And I knew that.

Hellhounds could not drown. We didn't have to breathe to survive. I was feeling Heven's emotion—her pain at drowning. *Focus.*

I wrapped my arms around her torso and kicked with great force toward the surface. How long had we been down here—a minute? More? How long could her brain go without oxygen?

Even with the strength of my kick, we didn't burst through the surface of the water. No. We were jerked violently back toward the lake bottom. I twisted and saw a set of red eyes below, the demon, whose shape I couldn't really see—was holding her at the bottom.

I released her body and attacked it. I wasn't sure where it began and ended, but I threw the hardest, heaviest punch I could. My fist cut through the dark water like butter. I connected with something solid and it shrank back. Then I looked at Heven's ankle where a thick green vine was wrapped. I yanked it from the lake floor and towed Heven to the surface of the water. When my head broke free, I heaved in a huge gulp of air and rushed for the shore.

Heven was pale.

Her lips were blue.

Do. Not. Die.

I pushed back the panic rising in me and began to administer CPR.

If you cannot breathe, I will breathe for you.
If your heart will not beat, mine will beat harder.
If you do not live, neither will I.

After what seemed like endless hours of CPR, she began to cough. I turned her onto her side and water poured out of her mouth onto the ground.

I wanted to collapse in relief. I ran my hands through my hair and took a deep breath as she coughed and coughed.

My throat burned like I had swallowed acid and my entire body was on fire. I allowed her emotions and her pain to pour over me because I was so thankful she had any to feel. Yes, they were horrible and she felt like hell, but at least she *felt*.

"Oh, God, Heven. Thank God."

When the coughing stopped, I was still afraid to put her on her back. Instead, I climbed over her and lay on the ground, mirroring her position and facing her. I reached out my hand and cupped her head where it was lying on the ground, cradling it, trying to give her some comfort.

Her eyes fluttered open and she stared at me. She was confused and disoriented.

"Shhh. It's all right, just rest."

Her eyes closed briefly before opening back up and settling on me.

"Hey. That was scary, huh? It's all right now, though. It's over. You're okay."

"What happened?" Her voice was raspy and low.

I was stupid. I failed to protect you. I failed to realize that we were being stalked from beneath the water. I was so angry at myself that I wanted to punch something. I shouldn't have let down my guard.

"A demon pulled you under the water," I said, trying to keep my voice gentle.

"I almost drowned."

"I'm so sorry." I scooted closer and pushed the wet hair off her face.

"Thanks for pulling me out of the water."

"How do you feel?" I asked, not wanting to accept her thanks because I felt responsible that it happened at all.

"Okay." She tried to sit up but she didn't quite make it that far.

I couldn't help myself. I wrapped my arms around her and pulled her into my chest.

She relaxed against me and we stayed like that for a long time until the shaking in her muscles stopped and breathing seemed easier for her.

I kept my eyes on the water—how deceiving it could be. It appeared peaceful; it appeared beautiful.

It was good at lying.

I had always liked the water, but damned if I wasn't beginning to change my mind.

With every ripple in the current, every jump of a fish, I was certain that the demon was going to rise from its watery camouflage and attack.

I would find pleasure in taking away its life.

The longer we sat there, the more paranoid I became. It wasn't safe. Yes, I could protect us, but I didn't want to have to. She'd been through enough.

I stood, taking Hev with me and walked to where we left our stuff.

"I can walk," she said, turning her face to look at me. She seemed alert.

I set her down, keeping an arm around her waist. "We need to go."

I grabbed up her dress and pulled it over her head and as she finished dressing, I pulled on my T-shirt. I gathered the towels, slinging them over my shoulder, and reached for Heven's hand.

"I'm okay, Sam."

"I'm taking you to get something hot for that throat."

She stopped, seeming to just remember that our Mindbond enabled me to feel her pain. "Oh, Sam. How much of that did you feel?"

She wrapped her arms around me, to comfort me, but I didn't want it. I deserved to feel this way—to carry this memory with me. Hopefully, it would make me more cautious in the future. And I was going to need that caution.

That demon was unlike anything I had faced.

That was saying something because, over the past few weeks, I had faced-off against a lot of evil and vile creatures. But this one was different. More powerful. I know most people would assume that because this demon had no shape, it was weak. How could it be strong when it wasn't even capable of holding its own form? But it was just the opposite. Only a truly strong demon could attack—could take a life like that—and *not* hold its shape. It had to have taken effort to appear so unrecognizable. It had effectively made itself unidentifiable to me whenever I should come across it again.

And I would.

Of that I was absolutely certain.

There wasn't one attribute that I could commit to memory about it. I had been so completely focused on getting Heven out of that water that I scarcely had time to look at it, let alone look for something that would make its identity known.

Well, there wasn't a physical attribute.

Mentally—I think I would recognize it anywhere. It was *dark*. Darker than anything I had encountered.

"This isn't your fault," Heven said, pulling away to stare up at me.

I cut off the noise that rose in the back of my throat and cupped her face in my hands. "I'm glad you're okay." The truck was parked beneath a nearby tree. I was glad that this is where we came, to a spot on the lake that no one ever swam at because there wasn't much of a shore to sit on. I helped Heven into the cab despite her protests and made sure the seat belt was strapped firmly around her. I wasn't taking any more chances today.

I drove down the dirt road toward the area of the beach where everyone else swam, but just before we got there, movement caught my eye and I slammed on the brakes. My hand shot out and pressed Heven back to keep her from jerking forward. Yes, she was wearing a seatbelt, but it was a reflex that I didn't bother to stop.

"What?" Heven gasped, but I was busy staring out the windshield.

There was a woman standing in the middle of road.

She was strapped from head to toe with weapons. Very old, deadly looking weapons. But that wasn't the worst part.

The worst part was that I recognized her.

"She doesn't have an aura," Heven murmured.

What could she possibly want and why was she here? I opened up the door and Heven slid across the seats to follow. "Stay in the truck," I ordered before closing my door in her face.

I will not! she declared, opening the door and climbing out.

Mentally, I sighed. I got that she didn't want to take orders from me, but you would think that, after almost drowning, she might be willing to let me handle this. *Haven't you been through enough today?*

Who is that?

"What are you doing here?" I called.

"You know her?" Heven asked.

It's the woman I got your bracelet from.

She looked down at her empty wrist. I was glad she hadn't worn it today. The last time she almost drowned, she was wearing it and I had to search the sandy bottom of the lake for it.

"She can't have it back," Heven said.

The woman laughed. It was a strong laugh, the laugh of a warrior. Heven and I both turned to face her. "We meet again," she said.

"What do you want?" I asked, suspicion welling inside me.

"I'm not an enemy."

I didn't respond. I simply stood and waited for her to tell me what she wanted.

"I'm here to offer my assistance." As she spoke she walked closer.

I angled my body in front of Heven's because I didn't trust her. Just because I recognized her, didn't mean that I knew her. Heven stepped out around me to stand beside me, rolled her eyes and sighed dramatically. My lips twitched at her display of annoyance at being protected. She was strong. I couldn't complain because, if she wasn't, she would probably be dead.

I looked back at the woman. She had the hair of women on shampoo commercials, glossy and thick. It was a deep, rich shade of brown, so dark it was almost black. She had a heart shaped face with wide, high cheek bones, full, pink lips and wide gray eyes. Her skin was creamy and unblemished. What balanced out all that perfection was the way that she carried herself. She walked like a warrior, with self-confidence and awareness, with grace but purpose, ease but meaning. It made her more than beautiful. It made her interesting and arresting.

You bought my bracelet from her? Heven's voice entered my mind.

Yeah.

"You have a Mindbond," the woman said.

I stiffened, but Heven seemed curious and even a little drawn to her. "How did you know that?"

"Heven," I warned, she shouldn't draw attention to herself.

She isn't here to hurt us. She told me.

How do you know? You can't see her aura.

I just know.

Echoing Heven's silent words she said, "I mean you no harm. As I said before, I'm here to offer my assistance."

"Assistance for what?" I asked.

"I saw what happened earlier, with the demon."

My eyes narrowed. What did she have to do with that demon? "So?"

"They are getting braver, tougher. Word is out that she has protection of a hellhound."

"You know what he is?" Heven gasped.

My head was reeling because it was exactly what I had been thinking too — that demon was stronger than any of the others I had faced up until now.

She smiled, full lips drawing back to reveal perfectly straight white teeth. She turned to Heven to say, "I know everything."

"Who the hell are you?" I asked. I should've known when she sold me that bracelet that she wasn't just a sales lady.

"My name is Gemma. I'm a Celestial."

"What's a Celestial?" Heven asked, her curiosity showing itself again. Although, in her defense, in the past few months her entire world had exploded with hellhounds, angels, demons, Supernatural Maps and Treasures, and now this.

In a gesture so familiar to me, Gemma's eyes swept the trees and areas surrounding us. "A Celestial is a class of Outsiders who are wholly good. We represent the forces of armed justice; we are those who seek out to destroy evil and maintain balance in the world."

"What are Outsiders?" I asked.

Gemma shrugged. "Those of us who are not wholly human. Angels would be one type of a Celestial."

"Like Airis?"

Gemma didn't really react to the mention of Airis, but I sensed one. "Yes, Airis is an angel."

"You don't like her," Heven stated, clearly picking up on the same thing I had.

Gemma's gray eyes widened. "I didn't say that."

"You aren't denying it," she retorted.

"You're very perceptive," Gemma murmured. She looked at Heven with approval. "Can you see my aura?"

"No."

"Can you see Airis's?"

"No. Are you an angel too?"

"Sort of."

"What does that mean?" I asked.

"I'm a fallen angel."

Beside me, Heven frowned. "Aren't fallen angels bad?"

Gemma said that Celestials were wholly good.

"Depends on who you ask." Gemma's teeth flashed.

"Wrong answer," I growled. I didn't trust her. At. All.

"Relax," Gemma said with an eye roll. She glanced at Heven. "Hellhounds can never take a joke."

That caught my attention. Heven gasped. "You know other hellhounds?"

"I've known a few." Something shifted behind her eyes. She covered it by saying, "Fallen angels are angels, who for their reasons, have been cast out of Heaven, usually for a sin of some kind. Some fallen angels are sent here to Earth because we aren't really bad, but we can no longer reside in Heaven. Most of us spend our time doing what I said, acting as armed justice to seek out and destroy evil."

I wanted to scoff at the lame description. Heven seemed impressed though.

"So you're a warrior angel?"

Gemma's eyes widened again and she looked at me. "We've got a smart one here."

"I know," I said, wishing Heven would just be quiet. But then I felt myself asking, "So you're here to help us fight off the demons that keep coming to kill Heven?"

"How did you know they were demons?" Gemma asked.

"I'm a hellhound. I know spawn of Hell when I see it." I was offended she asked. Heven patted my arm.

"I can see why Airis chose you both. You make a surprisingly strong pair."

"And you're here…?" I asked again, annoyed.

"I'm here to make you stronger. I'm going to teach you how to fight."

I barked a laugh. "Seriously? I think I have that part covered."

Without any indication or reaction, Gemma struck out. I felt her coming before she even moved and I leapt in front of Heven just as Gemma reached us, and I spun her kick away. Gemma fell back with my hit and then regained her feet to charge again. I was ready time after time, hit after hit. She wasn't getting the best of me. I wasn't going to show weakness. I was already pissed off over the demon in the lake, and I was more than happy to take it out on her. Gemma must have sensed the willing fight she was meeting because she stopped suddenly and unsheathed the sword that was strapped to her back. I crouched as my body began to shake. I felt a rush of adrenaline and my skin began to hum. The hound was ready to go and I was going to let it out.

Out of the blue, Gemma dropped her sword and pulled something out of the pouch that hung around her waist. She lifted the lid to the metal box now clutched in her hand and something unseen slammed into me. I felt it wrap around me like Saran Wrap. It molded against my body and tightened. I arched my back in pain — caught between the hound and the human, it was all I could do to stay on my feet. This bitch was crazy and whatever she was doing to me was no joke. I wasn't going to show the weakness I felt or the sudden panic about not being able to do what my body was built to do.

The pain went on as the invisible force wrapped tighter around me. I felt my knees buckle and I swore. My skin prickled with sweat and it began to run down my back and temples.

Fight. You have to fight.

"Stop! You're hurting him!" Heven cried and ran at Gemma.

A half-growl, half-shout ripped from my throat as I pushed myself to my feet. I swayed slightly, but found my balance to rush forward and put myself in between Heven and this woman. Gemma struck out with her foot, hitting me firmly in my chest. I fell backwards, slamming into the ground hard, but I barely felt it. I was up and running at her again in seconds, only to be hit again. This was a pattern that I didn't care to repeat a hundred times. I felt exhausted, weak, and trapped and my panic was rising. Whatever was happening wasn't natural.

Heven took off again and made it to Gemma's side, reaching down to pick up her sword.

Gemma arched a single eyebrow at me. I was already calling forth the strength I would need to launch myself in between them again.

Heven, get away from her.

"Lose the box," Heven threatened Gemma, not even looking at me.

That sword was probably a lot heavier than it looked and I wondered if Heven had the strength to swing it.

I couldn't take that chance. With a final burst of speed and adrenaline, I rushed Gemma. *Take the sword and head toward the truck, Heven! Now!*

Gemma held up her hands in surrender. Heven, who once again did not listen to me, reached out and grabbed the box from her hands. Gemma said nothing as Heven slammed the lid closed and tossed the thing into the trees.

Relief surged through me and I was suddenly unbound. My body seemed to swell within seconds and I felt the hound in me roar — a sound that I liked. The next thing I knew, I was completely shifted and completely willing to murder.

Get back. I told Heven. So help me if she didn't listen this time...

She listened and ran backward, putting some distance between us.

I took Gemma down and we rolled across the grass. She was pinned beneath me when I raised my lethal, sharp claws above her.

"I think I proved my point," Gemma said, gasping for breath. "Get off me."

I paused.

"If you kill me you'll never know what just happened."

Damn. She had a point. I hated that she had a point.

Don't hurt her, Sam, Heven pleaded.

I shoved off her and growled. She stayed down on the ground as I prowled toward the truck, never once giving Gemma a backward glance. When I reached the truck, Heven was there, holding out a pair of shorts. I took them in my mouth and went behind the truck. Moments later, dressed hastily, I came around to see Gemma coming out of the woods, tucking that box back into the pouch at her waist.

She tensed a little when she saw us walking toward her. "How pissed are you still?" she asked me, her hand hovering over her belt where there was a dagger.

"Seriously?" Heven exclaimed. "You approach us; you claim to want to help us. Then you do something to Sam and now you're reaching for another weapon? I don't think we want your help. Thanks." She turned to walk away.

I was proud of her.

"I'm not the only one with one of these. Don't you think that he needs to know how to fight when being blocked from shifting?"

Damn.

Heven stopped and turned. "No more games."

"I was only trying to show you," Gemma began.

Heven cut her off to say, "No. More. Games."

"Tougher than you look," Gemma admired.

"You might have that thing strapped to you right now, but if you piss me off again you won't even be able to reach for that thing the next time you need it."

"Agreed," Gemma said and she stuck out her hand.

Heven stepped out to take it and I caught her arm and towed her back. Heven wasn't making any deals. Especially with people I wasn't sure I could trust. With Gemma's hand suspended, I glanced at it and back to her.

"I'm not agreeing to anything until you tell me what the hell you just did."

"As a hellhound you have very few weaknesses," Gemma began and I snorted.

"We don't have any."

Gemma lifted an eyebrow. "You can say that after what just happened?"

Well, damn. Wasn't that like a bucket of cold water dumped over my head? I hated to admit it (and I probably wouldn't out loud), but she had a point.

"Just cut to the chase," I said suddenly, feeling weary. This day was only half over and yet it felt like it had dragged on for an eternity.

"Before hellhounds were cast out of Hell, Satan tried a few ways to control them. He went to Hecate, Queen of Witches, and asked her to create three amulets to bind their powers, making it harder for them to fight. As you just experienced, a hound is more vulnerable when it is trying to shift and cannot. You are very strong and have much fighting ability in your hellhound form but not as much as in your human form. I am sure that whenever a demon attacks you always shift to defeat him. Is that right?"

"Yeah."

"Except for that day in the ice cream shop," Heven reminded me. "When Cole was there."

"Who is Cole?" Gemma asked.

"A friend of ours. He walked in one day when a demon was attacking me," Heven answered.

Gemma nodded. "Does he know, then?"

"No," I said, finality ringing in my ears. I did not want Cole involved in Heven's life any more than necessary. I didn't want him around; then I wouldn't feel like I had to protect him too when he did something stupid and tried to play hero. I might not like him, but Heven would be crushed if something happened to the guy, and I didn't want her to get hurt. I really wished I knew what the heck she saw in him.

"I've been avoiding him," Heven said, and a wave of guilt came over me. I already knew she felt guilty about avoiding Cole, so I did my best to ignore it and not let her feelings get to me.

Gemma nodded and backed up to a tree and slid down until she was sitting, half-leaning against the trunk. Heven seemed grateful and sank down into the grass too, tucking her legs beneath her.

I did a scan of Heven's features. She was still pale and her lips still didn't have enough color in them for my liking. My throat still held an echo of pain, so I knew hers had to be hurting. We needed to get this conversation over with because she needed to get home to rest. I sat down next to her, our knees bumping together. She smiled at me and I ran my hand down her back.

"Hecate created three amulets that would keep a hound from shifting, keeping him vulnerable so he can be hurt or killed."

Gemma's words caused panic to well up in Heven's chest; I felt it like it was my own.

No one's going to kill me, Heven.

"Where are these amulets?" Heven asked, obviously doubting my statement. "Can we get them?"

Gemma shrugged. "I'm not sure where the other two are. Probably still in Hell."

"How'd you get one?" I asked her, curious.

"I killed the guy who had it." Once more something shifted behind her eyes, but I let it go. Her past wasn't relevant to this conversation. Yet.

"Is that what we would have to do to get the other ones?" Heven asked.

"Probably. But since you're a little busy to be off hunting down amulets, I think it's a better idea that you learn how to fight and defend yourself better in human form." Gemma looked at me as she spoke.

"I fended you off, didn't I?" I lifted an eyebrow.

"We were well matched." Gemma allowed and I scoffed. "But we both know that eventually I would have worn you down. And the minute I opened the box with the amulet inside it, you weakened because your body was trying to shift and it couldn't."

She kept having to bring up that damn box didn't she— reminding me of my weakness.

"What would happen to her," Gemma said, hitching her chin at Heven, "if you had been taken down or out?"

Inwardly, I groaned. Point taken. Now wasn't the time to be full of myself. Gemma knew exactly which buttons to push.

"All right, I'll train with you.

Gemma nodded once. "We'll start tomorrow."

"Where do you want me to meet you?"

She thought a moment. "How about at the farm?"

"My Gran's house?" Heven asked, surprised that Gemma knew of the place. I wasn't surprised at all. If she had been around since she sold me Heven's bracelet, then she had been watching us. She knew a lot – probably more than we even did.

"Sure, there's a lot of land there. How about in the woods off the trail where Heven rides Jasper? There's a clearing a little way in."

"I know the place," I agreed. "I'll meet you there tomorrow before I go to work, but after I do the chores around the farm."

Heven frowned, but she didn't say anything. Gemma pushed away from the tree, standing up, clearly ready to end our meeting. I stood up too, equally ready to get out of here. Automatically, I scanned the woods and then looked back over the lake, looking for any strange movements in the water. Everything seemed fine.

For now.

"Wait," I said, wanting the answer to one more question. "You knew who I was back then, who Heven was. You knew that the bracelet had the key to open the scroll."

Gemma waited for me to continue.

"Why didn't you just give it to me? Why didn't you tell me all this then?"

"Would you have believed me?" She didn't wait for him to answer before saying, "You know you wouldn't have. You had to learn about this for yourselves. Besides, I wasn't sure you'd manage to stay alive this long." She shrugged and began walking away only to turn back and look at me. "Besides, the fact that you paid for the bracelet really makes it a gift."

We both watched as she took a few more steps before disappearing completely from sight.

Chapter Seven

Heven

There was one good thing to come out of almost drowning: time alone with Sam. The day was only half over when we left the lake and our meeting with Gemma behind. The undercurrents in the truck were heavy as we were both still pretty shaken up from my near-death experience and from meeting a fallen warrior angel. I wasn't sure how I felt about all of it. Finding out there were three amulets out there that someone could use against Sam was terrifying. The thought of anyone hurting him made me crazy. Then there was Gemma herself. She was gorgeous and strong, and I couldn't help but be drawn to her. I was curious about her, her past, and the shadows that sometimes seemed to pass behind her eyes. I found myself actually hoping she wasn't crazy and that we might become friends. When Sam turned onto the dirt road that led to Gran's, I glanced over at him. He appeared calm, his face smooth and a pair of sunglasses shading his eyes. But I knew that he was still upset about earlier—I could feel it. I ran my thumb over the knuckles of his hand that I was holding and he glanced at me, giving my hand a light squeeze.

When he parked the truck in his usual spot beneath a large tree, I turned to him. "Can you come in before you go to work? I'll make you a sandwich."

He nodded, and instead of releasing my hand, he got out and pulled me along with him, lifting me out of the driver's side door. Inside, Gran was nowhere to be seen and I was glad because I knew that I wasn't looking my best. I left Sam in the kitchen to race upstairs and survey the damage. The worst thing was my hair. It was half dry, frizzing and hanging in scraggly clumps. I grabbed a comb, some leave-in conditioner and got to work. As I combed, I studied the rest of me: my skin was paler than usual, my lips colorless, but otherwise I looked normal. Finished with the comb, I pulled my hair back into a short ponytail and hurried to throw on a pair of jean shorts and a white tank, and then feeling a little chilly, I grabbed a light sweater and threw that on over my tank. Before going back downstairs, I swept on a little pink lip balm, hoping to infuse my face with some much needed color.

Sam was still in the kitchen, staring out the window. When I entered the room, he turned, his hazel eyes sweeping me from head to toe. He said nothing, but pulled me into his arms and held me tightly before releasing me to sit at the table, positioning himself near the door and the window. He wasn't as carefree as this morning. In fact, this morning seemed eons ago.

I went to the fridge and pulled out the makings for roast beef sammies, noting the package of ground beef and package of hotdogs chilling in the fridge. Looks like Gran planned to grill out tonight. I made a mental note to make up a few plates to take to Sam at work and to Logan at home. Then I had a thought. "Sam? Would it be okay if I went and got Logan while you were at work this evening? We're cooking out and he could have dinner with me and Gran."

Sam glanced at me from the window, his eyes turned to liquid honey, mesmerizing me. "You would do that?" He didn't seem surprised but… touched.

"Of course. I don't like to think of Logan alone so much." If he had as many mixed-up feelings as I figured, being alone all the time wouldn't help. Besides, being around Gran would be good for him and maybe he and I could start getting along better, i.e. he wouldn't make me so uncomfortable all the time.

"Thank you," he said, getting up and coming over to where I was slapping some mayo on bread. "But I'm not going to work tonight." He grabbed up a slice of roast beef and shoved the whole thing in his mouth.

"You're not?" I stared at him as he chewed. "I thought you had a shift at the gym?"

"I called in sick while you were upstairs."

"Are you not feeling well?" I dropped the knife and turned, placing my hands on his face and forehead. "This is all Gemma and that stupid amulet's fault."

His mouth kicked up in a crooked smile. "I'm fine. It's you that almost drowned. I'm not leaving you alone today."

My hands fell to my sides. "You're skipping work for me?"

"I won't be able to concentrate anyway." He grabbed up the sandwich and took a huge bite. He groaned in appreciation. I couldn't blame him. I made a good sandwich.

I couldn't say that I was sorry he was skipping work. I would get to spend an entire day with him—something that had only happened once or twice since we met. I was sorry, though, that the reason was because he was afraid for my life. "Maybe Gemma could teach me to fight too."

He paused in chewing to look down at me. "No."

I rolled my eyes. "It's a good idea. Then I would be able to take care of myself. You wouldn't have to do it."

"It's my job." He shoved yet another insanely huge bite into his mouth. He was going to have that sandwich gone in like three bites. I shook my head and began to make him another one.

I knew that Sam loved me. I felt it every day but how much of his love came from responsibility? How long before he tired of me and all the trouble I caused him? "I'll ask her tomorrow." I went back to finishing the sandwiches.

"You'll get hurt. Gemma's tough. The answer is no."

"You're not the boss of me." *Why did he think he could tell me what to do?* I muttered beneath my breath while I shoved everything back into the fridge and slammed the door. When I turned, I ran right into a solid wall of Sam.

"You scared me today," he said quietly. "When I pulled you to shore you weren't breathing, your lips were blue…" I laid my palm against his chest. "All I could think about was that if it weren't for me, none of this would have happened."

"This is not your fault."

"I've brought a lot of evil into your life."

I wrapped my arms around his waist. "You've brought a lot of love."

"I have to do this. I have to be the one to train with Gemma. I'm the one who brought the evil. I'm going to be the one to take it away. Your job is to stay alive."

Learning how to defend myself would make that a lot easier, but clearly he wasn't going to listen, especially after I almost drowned and was standing here wanting pain relievers. I tipped my head back to ask, "Want to walk up to the orchard?" Maybe a change in scenery would do us good.

He pressed a kiss to my forehead. "First, make some hot tea for your throat. We never did get anything."

Hot tea did sound good so I heated the water and added a generous amount of honey. Sam offered me a bite of his sandwich but the thought of eating made me queasy. When he wasn't looking I quickly downed a few pain relievers because my head was still pounding. The pressure on the back of my skull was uncomfortable. A vision of beady red eyes flashed before me and I gasped, dropping the bottle of pills.

Sam was at my side immediately. "What?"

"Nothing," I said, scooping the pills up and shoving them in the cupboard.

"Maybe you should lie down."

"No! I'm fine. I want to walk with you."

The orchard was showing promise for bountiful apples in the fall. Sam and I worked hard these past couple of weeks to get it where it needed to be and the work was paying off. The twisting apple trees were full of leaves and blossoming fruit. This spot was special to Sam and me, our haven where we could come to be alone and get away from all the drama in our lives. But right now, it was hard to appreciate its full beauty because Sam was scanning everywhere with his eyes. I hated that we could never relax, that danger seemed to stalk us at every turn.

"We should talk," I said, stopping at the top of the hill to look out upon the rows of trees. The only way I knew to make things any easier would be to come up with some sort of plan. If I could convince Gemma to train me, then it would be one more line of defense.

"Don't want to," Sam murmured behind me, his hand releasing the band that held back my hair. Soft strands fell around me, brushing my cheeks. He took my hand and we walked farther into the orchard. About halfway in, he stopped and sat beneath a tree pulling me down with him.

"This has to stop, all this worrying," I whispered. His warm breath against my neck was intoxicating, making it hard to think.

"I'm not worrying right now," he breathed the words against my neck, his lips grazing me ever so lightly.

I had to stay focused.

"I want to train with you and Gemma." My voice wavered, not sounding as strong as I wanted it to.

I was tucked as tightly as possible between his thighs with every inch of my back pressed against his front. His knees were drawn up, making a cocoon for me and his arms were wound tightly around me just beneath my breasts. Sam drew one hand up to brush the hair farther to the side, exposing even more of the sensitive flesh on my neck. "Sam." I tried to be firm.

"No," he said, like that was the end of it. Then he pressed a gentle kiss just behind my ear. "You're the one that said we need to relax more; that's what I am doing…"

"You can't turn my words around on me."

His hair had grown longer these past short weeks and now the messy locks tickled my cheek. He pressed his face into my neck and inhaled. When he blew out the breath, he scraped his teeth over the back of my neck.

I groaned, frustrated that he wasn't really listening to what I was saying, but was briefly distracted because I sensed a small rush of anxiety and adrenaline pumping through him, but then it was gone, and he turned my face to the side and began kissing me. I turned completely around, folding my knees into my chest and faced him.

"Closer," he urged, tugging me even closer.

When our lips met again, he moved suddenly, grabbing me, swiftly tucking me beneath him and lowering his body to brush against mine. The grass was soft against my back and it was warm, heated from the sun. The scent of him, strong, heady and deep mixed with the fragrant sweet, budding apples overhead acted as a balm to everything that had happened that day.

I loved this boy. More than myself. More than life. More than anything. Tears leaked from beneath my lids because my feelings were so intense that they had nowhere else to go, there just wasn't room in a single body for how I felt for him.

He kissed me fiercely, his lips slanting over mine with deep hungry aggression. Our bodies moved against one another… searching. Just as Sam was relaxing, his head snapped up. He was breathing hard, his chest rising and falling rapidly. He rose above me with his eyes closed and jaw locked.

"Hey," I murmured, stroking the side of his unshaven jaw.

He tilted his head down and his eyes popped open. They were pure gold, flashing brilliantly.

I gasped.

Before I knew it, he was beneath the apple tree next to me, and the breeze from the trees was brushing against my fevered skin. I watched him blink several times and take a deep breath before looking up at me. The shocking gold of his eyes was gone.

"I'm sorry." He sounded like he swallowed gravel.

"What happened?" My heart was still thundering in my chest.

"I—That was intense. I didn't mean..." He swallowed. "My emotions and your emotions were bleeding together and..."

"It's all right." I held my hands out palms up. I wanted to go to him, but I was unsure if that's what he wanted. "A lot has been going on."

He shook his head as if he was trying to clear it. He looked up at me, puzzled. "You're feeling all right?"

I nodded.

"You'd tell me if anything was wrong?"

"Yes." Like I'd have to. He would sense it, just like earlier with my throat.

"Your throat is sore–that's all?"

"I have a headache too."

"Heven? Did that demon..." His jaw clenched and anger swam over me. "What did it do to you?"

Red eyes flashed before my face. *Where is it...* it had spoken to me. I hadn't remembered that until now. It wanted to know where the scroll was. It hurt me, tried to make me tell it. I shuddered.

Sam took me by the shoulders. "Heven!"

I looked up, my thoughts clearing at the sight of his whiskey-colored eyes. "It didn't touch me, except to drag me down..."

Sam's face drained of fear. "That's good."

"It talked to me, though. Asked me where the scroll was."

"Did you tell it?"

"No."

He nodded and settled himself next to me once more, but seemed reluctant to pull me into his arms. I tried not to show my hurt and settled beside him, reaching for my mug and cradling it in my hands. I sipped at my tea while we watched a few squirrels running through the grass. A short while later I asked, "Sam? Why would you ask me that, about the demon hurting me?"

His brow creased and I knew his mind was turning, trying to formulate an answer that I would understand. "When we were close—just now, our emotions were bleeding together and I felt something... sensed something."

"What?"

He shook his head. "I don't know. I just felt a jolt of darkness."

I took stock of my body. I didn't feel any different than before.

"Forget it." He scooted closer and laid his hand on the back of my neck. Pain shot through my skull, but I ignored it. "I probably just sensed some left over fear from when you were... drowning. Add that to the hot and heavy kissing we were doing, and I guess the hound in me got a little too worked up."

I let it go like he asked. It was probably nothing and I wasn't about to let anything get in the way of our afternoon together. I snuggled closer and he accepted me without reserve into his arms. I tried to dismiss it, except my brain wouldn't let it go. Sam and I were no strangers to danger, and our make-out sessions got hotter every time, but this was the first time that the hound in him couldn't handle it. In fact, sometimes he seemed too good at separating the hound from the human. So why not this time?

Sam possessed good instincts, so if he sensed darkness in me, maybe it was there.

* * *

When we entered the kitchen, Gran was there cooking up a storm. "What's all this?" I asked, surveying all the food.

"I thought it was a good day for a cook out," She said, not looking up from the fruit she was slicing.

"Great! Sam actually has the night off from work."

Gran paused and looked up, a strawberry plopping onto the mountain of already cut fruit. "Well, that's wonderful. The more the merrier." Her cheerful words and voice did not match her aura, which was suddenly flaring with a shade of brown I rarely saw around her. She was worried... which I thought was very odd.

"Gran, do you mind if we went and picked up Logan to join us?" I asked, trying not to give away that I was staring a little too hard at her.

"Sure, honey." Again another brown cloud. It was so unlike Gran to be unsettled or worried about anything. And why would she be worried that Sam and Logan were coming to dinner? Clearly, she was making enough food and they ate here a lot anyway, but was she starting to tire of having us all around so much? Was I wearing out my welcome?

"Can we pick anything up at the store while we're gone?" I asked.

Her aura smoothed back out as the usual blue, green and yellow bloomed around her. Still, she seemed somewhat distracted. "No. But thank you. Hurry back so we can eat."

I glanced at Sam who was standing in the door. He lifted an eyebrow at me. I shrugged and followed him out the door.

"Something wrong?" he asked as we slid into the truck.

"Nope." Why voice my thoughts when it was probably nothing anyway?

Logan wasn't upstairs in the apartment. But that wasn't unusual. Logan made friends with the landlord's son Brent, and they spent a lot of time downstairs playing an Xbox in the back room of the consignment shop that the landlord ran during the day. It was really great that Logan had already made a friend, and I know that Sam felt a lot less guilty about working so much since Logan had someone to hang out with.

Sam cast a quick glance around the little efficiency before turning to me. "Ready?"

I shook my head. "I saw that longing look you gave the bathroom. Go take a shower. I'll go get Logan."

"I can wait."

"You could, but you don't have to." I walked over to the single dresser near the bed and pulled out a clean orange T-shirt and a pair of khaki cargo shorts. "Here." I held them out.

He hesitated, then sighed, taking the clothes and reaching around me to grab a pair of boxers. "I'll be quick."

"No hurry," I said, straightening the blankets on his bed and fluffing the pillows.

As Sam passed through the bathroom door, he paused and looked over his shoulder. "Hev? Will you wait for me before you go downstairs?"

"Yeah, sure."

He didn't say anything more as he pushed the door around without latching it. I sighed and tackled the dishes in the sink. I hated that Sam worried about me so much. How awful it must be for him to carry such a heavy responsibility. I didn't want it to be that way with us. I didn't want to be someone he had to take care of all the time, a hindrance to his life. I couldn't really be part of his life if he spent all his time protecting me. Where would his life be? There had to be a way that I could somehow, someway, ease some of the pressure on him, some way that I could make him see that I was stronger than he thought.

I was so deep in thought that I didn't hear Logan come in. He just appeared right beside me out of thin air. I jumped and a small shriek escaped my lips. The bowl I was washing landed in the sudsy water with a hard thump.

"Logan, you scared me!" I gasped, sliding a look to the bathroom door as I calmed my racing heart.

"Sorry," he said innocently, however, his eyes were anything but. It's like he did it on purpose.

"It's all right." I fished the bowl out of the water and rinsed it off. "We were going to come down to get you in a few minutes. Gran is having a barbeque tonight we wanted you to come."

"Great," he muttered.

I looked over at him sharply. "What?"

He stared back at me and I fought the urge to shudder. There was something about him that just didn't seem right sometimes. "I said it sounds like fun."

"That's not what you said." Why did I feel the need to argue? Keeping the peace with him was important.

Logan stepped closer, so close that his shoulder bumped mine. "Maybe not," he whispered, "but we both know it doesn't matter. You won't tell Sam anyway."

I stared at him in shock, forgetting about the dishes. I chose not to tell Sam about my concerns about Logan. I didn't want to get between him and his brother. But, maybe, by not telling Sam the way I feel about Logan, I was actually giving Logan more power over us. While I thought about that I said, "I want us to be friends, Logan."

He smiled, but it was not friendly. The hair on the back of my neck actually stood up. "You only want to be friends because you know that if it came down to it, Sam would pick me over you."

His eyes, a hazel color similar to Sam's, were not the eyes of a fourteen-year-old boy. Sometimes they looked so old and so *wicked*. It wasn't often that I saw the look he was giving me right now because when Sam was around he was completely different. At those times, he *was* the fourteen-year-old boy who worshipped his big brother, the love he held for him was clear. Sometimes, he stared at Sam with a desperation that I found alarming. It was those times that Sam spent extra time with Logan, sensing the boy needed to know that he was there for him.

I cleared my throat, not looking away. "I wouldn't ask Sam to choose."

"I might."

My heart began thumping again as I considered his words and the malevolent way he said them. I didn't want to antagonize him and make our relationship worse, but I didn't want him to think he could threaten me this way, either. Turns out, it didn't matter because Sam came out of the bathroom. I stared at Logan, wondering if he would show his bad side to Sam for once.

Of course he didn't. He transformed himself in seconds. It was like flipping a switch inside him. He turned into the sweet, devoted brother in a flash. It almost made me wonder if I had been imagining the cold way he looked at me.

Almost.

"Everything okay?" Sam asked, his eyes going between Logan and me. Could he feel the tension in the space?

I turned back to the sink, finishing up the dishes.

"Sam!" Logan said. "Gran's having a cookout."

"Cool, huh? Hey, why don't you go grab the football? We'll bring it with us and throw it around."

"Awesome." Logan went over to the far corner of the room and began digging through a plastic laundry basket filled with odds and ends.

Sam came up next to me, his eyes appraising as I dried my hands on the dish towel and hung it to dry. *Are you okay?*

I'm good. I wondered if I should tell him what Logan said.
You can tell me anything.
I know. Really, I'm fine. Instead of staring into his sincere honey eyes, I wrapped my arms around his neck and hugged him. The feel of his arms was reassuring and I closed my eyes. When I opened them again I saw Logan standing there, staring at me. The innocence in his eyes once again vanished. In fact, I thought I saw a shot of an orange color— kind of like the first lick of a flame.

I looked away. *I love you, Sam.*

I love you, too. He pulled back and looked into my eyes, searching.

I smiled.

"Ready?" Logan asked, jogging to the door, clutching the football.

"Let's go," Sam said.

"Let me just put this away," I said, stacking the dried dishes and opening the cupboard.

"You don't need to do that," Sam said, coming back to my side.

"I don't mind." I lifted the bowls and slid them into the cupboard. For a split second, my vision seemed to change and instead of the inside of the cabinet I swear it looked like I was reaching into a nest of snakes. I jerked back my hands and a bowl crashed to the floor, shattering.

"Crap!" I swore and bent to pick up the broken shards.

"Be careful," Sam cautioned, bending down to help. But it was too late and a piece of glass stuck my finger and blood welled to the surface. Sam swore and grabbed the dish towel and wrapped it around my finger.

"Let me get this," he said.

I looked back up at the cabinet and it looked exactly as it should. My head was pounding and I knew it was the headache that was making my eyes play tricks on me.

"Let me see," Sam said, holding out his hand.

I removed the dish towel, tossing it in the sink and looked down. "It's just a scratch."

Sam took my hand in his and studied the cut. A muscle in his jaw ticked once. Twice. Then he looked up. "All right?"

"Yes. Sorry about the bowl."

"It's nothing." He shrugged and clasped my hand in his, being careful of the new injury. Logan was standing in the open doorway, watching us. I had the sudden urge to tattle on him like a school girl. But I didn't. I held my breath. I swear I thought he smiled before turning and racing down the stairs toward the truck.

He was so positive that Sam would chose him if forced to pick. I never intended to allow things to go that far. Someone who really loved Sam wouldn't ask him to choose. So what did that say about Logan?

Chapter Eight

Heven

Summer air rushed through the windows and pushed against my skin, forcing the uneasiness I felt about Logan toward the back of my mind. It was the warm breeze coupled with the blue cloudless sky that made me want an afternoon of summer fun filled with hot dogs, fruit salad and football in the grass. I wanted to enjoy this rare, work-free afternoon with Sam. Who cared if the only reason we got it was because I almost drowned this morning? I didn't and we were here. What was wrong with wanting a little summer bliss?

I was feeling pretty relaxed by the time we arrived back at Gran's, energized by the idea of such a wonderful afternoon. Even Logan seemed a little more laid back. With Sam's hand wrapped around mine and his solid thigh pressed alongside my own, the day's drama was almost out of my mind.

Unfortunately, my positive mood was short-lived.

When the house came into view so did the cars parked beside it. The steering wheel jerked in Sam's hands and he glanced over at me before driving on.

What the hell is he doing here? he said.

What on Earth is she doing here? I said.

This day keeps on getting better.

Logan seemed oblivious to our drop in mood. As soon as Sam parked, Logan made a beeline for Gran and the food in the kitchen. I watched him disappear and thought about how nice disappearing might be.

The door banged and I looked up. Cole was standing on the porch, staring at me through the windshield. My stomach tightened and guilt assailed me, guilt for avoiding him, for promising an explanation, then refusing to give one and even guilt for not feeling something when he kissed me.

But there was guilt worse than that.

Most of all I felt guilty because I had *missed* Cole. I knew that he was angry with me. How could he not be? I knew that there was going to be an intense conversation and probably more anger, but it was just really good to see him. *But* by missing Cole, I felt as though I was betraying Sam. I pushed those thoughts away, fearful he might pick up on them.

More people came out onto the porch, my mother and her new boyfriend. The ache that had been slowly lessening in my head intensified. Sam opened his door and, at the same time, reached for my fingers and gave them a squeeze.

Sam was my strength. Some days it felt like he was the only reason I could put one foot in front of the other. I reminded myself that those feelings were wonderful but I couldn't allow myself to lean on him so heavily. I was stronger than that. Even without Sam, I could get through this. But it sure was nice to have him around. Sam lifted me out of the truck, blocking out all the eyes on me and I let myself use the moment to compose myself. As soon as my feet hit the ground, I held my chin up and faced everyone.

"What a surprise!" I said, injecting enthusiasm into my voice. "I didn't expect to see you all here."

My mother was the first to come forward. "I was missing you and Henry suggested we come and visit. When we got here, Gran was cooking up a storm and invited us to stay." To my intense surprise, she came down the steps and hugged me. It took me a minute to comprehend what was happening, but then I hugged her back. It felt good. It was a hug from the old days, from *Before*. *Before* I was attacked and disfigured. *Before* I met Sam and my entire life changed. *Before* my mother accused me of being marked by evil.

I couldn't help but notice that, while we embraced, I was enveloped by her aura. She loved me and she was happy. She didn't seem the least bit upset by Sam's presence. Maybe she really was trying to accept him as a part of my life. A little bit of the tension in me eased.

From up on the porch Henry said, "Great to see you, Heven. Sam. Thanks for having me at your barbeque."

"Oh! That reminds me! We were just coming out to get out the grill and light it for Sylvia." my mother exclaimed, looking up at Henry.

Henry came down the steps and held out his arm to my mother. "Lead the way, my lady."

My mother giggled like a school girl and a funny feeling slid down my spine. I pushed it away. I wanted her to be happy. My dad would want her to be happy. I smiled, hoping it looked genuine and watched them go off toward where Gran kept the grill.

That left me, Sam and Cole.

"What are you doing here?" Sam demanded in low tones.

I pinched his side and pulled away from him to go up the stairs toward Cole. "Hey, Cole, it's really good to see you." At least with Cole I didn't have to fake my emotions like with my mother.

"You've been avoiding me," he growled.

I stopped short, teetering on the top step. "I'm sorry."

Sam came up behind me, gently pushing me up on to the porch away from the stairs. "What are you doing here?" he repeated.

"Be nice," I snapped.

He ignored me.

"Sylvia invited me." Cole directed his answer at me.

"Gran invited you?" I echoed. Why would she do that? Her reaction to him the other night was a little odd.

He shrugged. "I thought maybe you asked her to."

My heart constricted. I hadn't. I kind of wished I had.

"Why would she do that?" Sam bristled beside me.

I sighed and prayed that this meeting didn't come to blows. From across the yard, Henry called, "Seems we need a lighter to get this grill going. Sam, could you bring one out here and give me a hand?"

I caught a flare of gold in his eyes and I reached out and laid a hand on his arm. *You okay?*

I don't want to leave you alone with him.

I should to talk to him.

He still seemed torn about what to do.

"Sam?" Henry called.

A muscle in his jaw ticked, but he called, "Be right there!" Then I was being hauled against his hard chest and his lips were rough against mine. It wasn't the way he usually kissed me, with passion and love pouring from his every pore. This was a kiss that stamped me as his; it was the kind of kiss that told Cole what his place was.

It made me uncomfortable, even sparked some anger within me, but I allowed it. If I pulled away or protested, how would Sam perceive it? How would Cole? Then Sam pulled away and went inside for a lighter, seconds later, brushing past Cole and down the steps to help my mother and Henry.

Then it was just me and Cole.

His deep blue eyes studied me. "You look tired. Pale." His aura was flaring the magenta tones, a mix of purple and pink that was so unusual to see. Beneath the magenta was his usual blue and green, but there was also a bit of a dirty-brown color. He was worried about me.

"So do you." His clothes were rumpled and he had circles beneath his usually bright blue eyes. At his side his hand flexed like he was trying to hold himself back from saying more.

"What's going on, Hev?"

"I can't tell you."

"You said you would."

I shook my head. "I know. It's just..."

"He doesn't want me to know." His voice was flat.

"He has reasons, Cole. Good reasons. And..."

He folded his arms across his chest. "And?"

"It's better you stay out of it. You could get hurt."

"You're worried about me?" His voice dropped.

"Well, yeah. We're friends." I felt the need to point that out.

"About the other night," he said taking a step closer, closing the distance between us. "I—I'm sorry. I shouldn't have come here."

"You needed a friend. I'm your friend." I pointed it out one more time.

He frowned. "Yeah, we're friends."

"Look," I said, realizing this conversation wasn't going that well. I glanced over my shoulder at Sam who was helping Henry light the grill. "I told Sam about... what happened..." I looked at him, praying he knew I meant the kiss.

He nodded. "So he wants to deck me, right?"

"There will be no decking," I said firmly. "I asked him to try and be nice and I'm asking you the same."

He regarded me with a look of serious concern and did not agree to my request. "Are you in trouble, Heven?"

I shook my head. "Please, Cole, just stay out of it."

"I'm not sure I can do that." His aura flared, magenta shooting out around his head in flames. I was momentarily distracted by the explosion of brilliant color.

He put a hand on my elbow. "Are you okay?" he asked, leaning down in my face.

"Of course."

Sam appeared, slipping his arm around my waist and knocking away Cole's hand. *Okay?*

Yeah. His aura is just so... overwhelming.

Sam steered me toward the back door and inside, where Gran was piling condiments on the table. "There you are!" Gran said. "Would you boys be a dear and take those platters outside to the grill?"

Sam dutifully picked up the first platter heaped with hamburger patties and some chicken and went out the door. Cole picked up the other platter filled with hot dogs and buns. Gran came over and patted his cheek before he disappeared from view.

"I didn't know you were inviting Cole," I said casually.

"I thought you two were friends." Her aura was flashing with colors that were not her usual. What was going on?

"We are."

"Good. I hope that he will be spending a lot of time here."

My head was aching with renewed force as I struggled to make sense of how she was acting. I found the pain reliever, shook a few out into my hand and dug around in the fridge for a bottle of water. My hand was about to close over a bottle when the fridge and its contents fell away. I was left staring at a black stone wall. My fingers brushed over the rough cold stone and my hand snapped back in shock. I blinked several times, trying to clear my eyes and trying to see in the sudden darkness. I heard a sound behind me and I spun, barely seeing the trickling water dripping down the stone to splash at my feet. I was surrounded by stone with barely any light to see. I looked up. There was a circle of light beckoning me from far above.

I was in a well.

How was this possible?

One minute, I was standing in Gran's kitchen, and the next, I'm trapped in a well. Panic began to build, tightening my chest and making my breathing shallow. I reached out, turning in a circle, my hand scraping over the rough sides, and finally, getting caught on a sharp edge.

"Ow!" I pulled my hand back and saw the puncture, blood trailing down my wrist. I cradled the hand against my chest as another sound at my feet caught my ears. I looked down. Even in the dim lighting I knew what I was looking at.

I screamed.

The snake slithering across my shoe reared up and bared its surprisingly long fangs.

I screamed again.

Hands grabbed my shoulders and I struggled.

Heven, it's me. Calm down.

Sam?

Yes.

A sob caught in my throat as I collapsed against him. The well melted away and I was once again in Gran's kitchen encased in Sam's arms.

The door swung open and Cole charged in. "I heard a scream."

Gran was following behind him, both staring.

I forced a laugh. "I'm sorry. I saw a spider."

Gran chuckled, moving around Cole to place spoons in the baked beans and potato salad. "You never have liked spiders. Close the fridge door, honey."

Sam pushed the fridge door shut as I peaked over his shoulder to stare at Cole. He was frowning. When he saw me looking, he scowled. Clearly, he didn't believe my story. I shut my eyes tight, willing away the images. Seconds ticked by and I forced myself out of the comfort of Sam's arms.

He bent down and picked up the pills that I dropped and handed them to me. Then he reached into fridge and pulled out a water bottle. I couldn't help but peer into the fridge with fear.

What happened?

I looked down at my hand where I had cut it against the stone. There was nothing there. It was like it never happened.

Just then, Henry poked his head in the back door while Logan entered from the living room, carrying a brightly colored vinyl tablecloth.

"You found it!" Gran exclaimed, taking the cover out of his hands. "I wasn't sure it would be where I told you."

Logan beamed under her happiness. "It was right where you said."

"I don't want to alarm anyone," Henry said. "But we need some ice out here."

"Is someone hurt?" Gran asked, turning away from Logan.

Henry nodded. "Madeline stumbled into the grill and burned her hand."

"Goodness!" Gran grabbed a huge ice pack out of the freezer and raced outside calling behind her, "Heven, get the burn cream!"

Logan followed Gran outside, still carrying the tablecloth. I hadn't realized he had been in the house before.

I ran forward toward the cabinet with our medical supplies. "I want to know what is going on." Cole demanded as I dug through the cabinet.

"Cole, please," I begged. "Not now."

He stared at me for a long moment then nodded tightly and stalked out of the room.

What's going on?

"Cream must be in the bathroom," I said and rushed out of the kitchen. Sam kept pace along with me easily. Once I had the cream, he grabbed my hand to stop me from rushing by.

Stop for a second. What happened back there?

I thought I saw something. It's like my mind is playing tricks on me.

Your headache still hasn't gone away. He touched my forehead. It wasn't a question. He could probably feel my headache. I nodded in response anyway and prayed the pain reliever would start working.

Still have a sore throat?

I forgot about my sore throat with all the other drama going on around us. "Not really." I made a move to walk past him. "I really need to go see about Mom."

"Of course." He towed me along with him outside where everyone was gathered around my mother who was at the picnic table with an ice pack on her arm.

"Mom, what happened?"

"Oh, honey, I'm fine. Clumsy me stumbled and my arm caught the grill." She lifted the ice pack and showed me an angry red welt already raised on her arm.

I gasped. "That looks horrible! We should go get it checked out."

"It looks worse than it is," Mom said, shaking her head. "With the ice, it hardly hurts at all."

"Did you get the cream?" Gran asked me. I looked at her for some back-up about taking Mom to the doctor. Her aura was smooth and unruffled. It was like she wasn't worried at all.

"It's right here." I held out the tube.

"Here. I'll put some on you," Gran said, uncapping it to smooth a thick layer of the stuff over the burn. Mom didn't even wince.

I did. I looked at Henry who was watching the scene with mild interest. He saw my stare and looked fully at me. "What do you think, Henry? Think Mom should get looked at?" It was almost a challenge.

He smiled. "I think if your mother says she's all right, then she probably is."

Mom beamed up at Henry, her aura not even displaying the slightest bit of pain. "I'm just fine. Let's not ruin the afternoon with this. Shall we eat?"

I seemed to be outnumbered. I looked at Sam and he shrugged.

"At least let me wrap the burn," I tried, not ready to give up.

"That would be wonderful. But let me keep this ice on it while we eat; then you can wrap it."

I stopped arguing. She really didn't seem to be in any pain. Her aura was clear and auras didn't lie. So I let it go.

Everyone took a spot around the table, but I was slower to sit down. My stomach still revolted at the thought of food, but I couldn't avoid at least sitting with everyone. To my utter dismay, the only empty spot at the table was right next to Cole. Rather than allow Sam to slide in next to him, I hurried over and Sam sat down on my other side, frowning. Inside I winced, thinking that it probably didn't look too good when I hurried to sit next to Cole.

Gran said a short blessing and everyone dug in. I couldn't help but notice the apprising looks she was giving Cole and I. Was Gran trying to set me up with Cole? No. She couldn't be. She loved Sam, and I knew it. I saw it in her aura. Yet, there was love in her aura too every time she looked at Cole. I prepared myself for a long dinner, but it ended up not being as uncomfortable as I thought.

Henry was a captivating storyteller. He possessed a magnetism that drew you in when he spoke, and all throughout dinner, he told us stories about the places he had traveled to and the people that he had met. I found myself unable to relax, but at least the pressure in my skull was easing. Because of Henry's talent for speaking, no one seemed to notice that all I did was push the food from one side of my plate to the other. Finally, I gave up even making it look like I was eating and looked up, brushing away a fly that was swarming around the table. My mother was clearly happy, staring at Henry with a sort of awe in her eyes. I just couldn't believe that her arm didn't bother her at all.

Not long after eating, my mother announced that they needed to be going. I had to make an effort to seem disappointed. It made me feel guilty, and I insisted on applying more burn cream to her nasty-looking burn and wrapping it lightly in some gauze. That burn was going to turn into one nasty blister. After I had her all bandaged up, Sam and I walked Mom and Henry to his car while I tried one last time to convince her to get her arm looked at. She still insisted she was fine. I tucked the burn cream into her purse and kissed her cheek. "I'll call you later," I promised before Henry ushered her into a very black sedan with very dark tinted windows.

"Heven, promise me that we will see each other again before you go off to Italy," Mom said before Henry could close the door.

I was still a little shocked that she was so willing to let me go after months and months of her insisting that I go to a Bible camp to exorcise the evil out of me.

"Sure, Mom. I'll come by next week and we can have lunch together."

"Great. I had a great time today. I love you."

I swallowed past the lump suddenly in my throat. "I love you too, Mom."

She said a short, but nice, goodbye to Sam, and then Henry shut the door. The tint was so dark that she disappeared from view. On his way around to the driver's side he touched my hand and said, "Thanks for the wonderful day."

Red beady eyes swam before me. My lungs squeezed. I swayed a little on my feet. Sam was there, his body coming up against mine. Henry looked at me with concern in his eyes. "Are you all right?"

I forced a smile. "I'm great. Just a little headache is all."

"Well, get some sleep tonight. I'm sure you'll feel better in the morning."

"I will. Thanks."

We watched until they were out of sight, and then I turned to lay my head on Sam's chest. The sound of his heartbeat made me feel stronger.

"Are you going to tell me what's going on with you?"

"It's nothing," I insisted. "I just got a little dizzy."

"Yeah, and your mind is just playing tricks on you," he muttered.

Gran stuck her head out the back door. "Heven, could you come in here please?" Her aura was flaring nervous energy.

Something is going on with Gran. I told Sam.

She does seem a little preoccupied.

Inside, Cole was sitting at the table in the kitchen with a plate of cookies in front of him. Gran was standing at the sink washing dishes.

"Let me help you," I said, going over to the sink.

She waved me away and picked up a towel to dry her hands. "Sit down. There's something I need to tell you."

"What?" I plopped into a chair next to Sam and across from Cole.

Gran patted her pocket before saying, "I debated on whether or not to say anything, but I think you both have a right to know."

I didn't understand who or what she was talking about. "Me and Sam?"

"No, you and Cole."

Cole and I looked at one another. He shrugged.

"I don't understand," I said.

Gran nodded. "When you first came here, Cole, I am sure that you thought I acted a little strange."

He shook his head. "I wasn't really myself the other night." His cheeks turned pink with embarrassment.

"Don't think anything of it," Gran replied and patted her pocket before continuing. "It's because you remind me of someone. Two people actually."

"Who?" Cole asked.

"My late husband and son."

My heart stuttered. I groped for Sam's hand beneath the table.

"About seventeen years ago, my son Jason met and married your mother, Heven. But what you don't know, what no one knows, is that before he met her, he was involved with someone else." Gran looked at Cole.

"Your mother's name is Christine? Christine Matthews?"

"Christine Springer, used to be Matthews until she married my Dad when I was two," Cole said as the color leeched from his skin.

Gran nodded. "My son Jason is your biological father, Cole."

I gasped and I felt the blood drain from my face.

Cole stood, the chair clattering to the floor behind him. "No."

"Yes." She pulled a photograph from her pocket and laid it on the table in front of Cole. It was a photograph I knew well. It was my dad and grandpa smiling into the camera with their arms thrown around each other. It was an old photograph from when Dad was about my age and my grandpa was what age my dad would be now. I never realized it before because the memories of my grandpa were from when he was older, but Cole looked a lot like him when he was younger.

Cole stared down at the photograph on the table. "So I look like him." He pointed at my grandfather. "But not that much. And not like him." He pointed to my Dad. His aura was all over the place. Disbelief, hurt, curiosity...

"I had a DNA test done," Gran said quietly then she pulled another sheet of paper from her pocket and laid it next to the photo.

We all stared at her. "That night you stayed here, I — I snipped a piece of your hair off and took it to the hospital for a DNA test. The lab ran it against my blood since Jason isn't here. It matched. You're my grandson."

We all sat there stunned.

"Please understand. I wanted to be sure before I said anything."

Cole picked up his chair and dropped back in it. "Then that means..." He looked up and our eyes met. Joy flowed through me. Joy and relief.

"Heven is your sister." Gran said.

Sam started laughing. I brought my eyes away from Cole and I looked at him. He was happy. This news thrilled him. I focused on the feeling swirling through me, pushing past my own to find his. He was relieved. He didn't have to feel threatened by me and Cole's relationship anymore. I was shocked he had felt that threatened before. I must not be the only one who could push down my feelings.

"I'm sorry," he said, noticing everyone staring. "It's just really great news."

Cole jumped up and stormed out the door.

"Cole!" I yelled and went after him. Sam got up to follow, but I stopped him. "Give me a minute with him, okay?"

Sam sat back down.

Cole was at the far end of the porch, staring out toward the orchard. I approached him and leaned my back against the railing next to him, facing the opposite direction. We stood like that for a long time, not saying anything.

Finally, Cole cleared his throat. "I could never figure it out."

I looked up. "What?"

"What it was that I felt for you. At first I thought I was attracted to you... but it was different somehow. I always wanted to protect you, to watch over you and be close to you, but the other night, when I kissed you, it didn't feel right."

"I felt the same way."

"Really?" His aura flared magenta, mixing with the blue and green.

"I think that might be why Sam doesn't like you. He could feel how much I cared about you and knew I was confused." He thought I was torn between the two of them, but really I couldn't figure out my connection to Cole.

"The guy sure is relieved," Cole muttered, the side of his mouth picking up.

"So do you believe her?" I asked timid.

He was quiet a moment. "I'm not sure. Why would she lie? I should talk to my mom."

"Yeah." I wondered how that would go.

"I should go." He pushed away from the railing and went toward the stairs then turned back. "You think she would let me take the DNA results with me?"

I nodded and he disappeared inside. When he came back he was clutching the paper and the photo of my dad and grandpa. When he saw me staring at the photo, he cleared his throat and shoved them into his pocket walking quickly toward the steps.

"Wait!" I stumbled after him.

He turned back.

"You'll come back, won't you?" Now that I knew who he was to me, I wanted time with him. I wanted to know him better than I did.

He smiled. "Yeah."

I took a hesitant step forward and watched him mentally debate something until he opened his arms. I hugged him hard, my arms wrapping around his torso as I buried my face in his shirt. All the feelings that confused me clicked into place and settled with certainty inside me. Cole closed his arms around me and rested his chin on the top of my head.

Kimber chose that moment to drive up.

Cole swore beneath his breath and pulled away. I spent a moment hoping that maybe she hadn't seen. Then I looked up and quit fooling myself and braced for the fireworks. Her aura was on fire with red. Jealousy and anger. There was hurt mixed in there too and I regretted that.

"I guess I know why neither one of you are answering your cells," she said stepping out of her red Bug and slamming the door.

"Kimber," I began, but she cut me off.

"Save it, Heven. I don't want to hear your excuses."

Sam came out the back door followed by Logan.

"Do you know that she's cheating on you right under your nose?" Kimber asked Sam.

"Kimber," Cole said. "No one's cheating on anyone."

Kimber snorted. "You are such a liar."

"Kimber, we can explain what you just saw," I hurried to say, but Cole put a hand on my arm and squeezed. I glanced over at him and his aura. He didn't want her to know about his father-my father-*our* father.

"Go ahead. Explain." Kimber spat.

"I can't," I whispered.

Kimber gave a humorless laugh. "Of course you can't. There's no excuse for you."

"Please believe that I wouldn't hurt you like that." I went down the steps to stand in front of her. "Cole and I are just friends."

"I wanted to believe that too, but the evidence is too hard to ignore," she muttered.

"What?" I asked, confused.

"Don't see him anymore," she said, lifting her chin to stare into my eyes.

"What?"

"I mean it, Heven. If you really are my best friend, then I don't want you to hang out with Cole anymore."

Was she really asking me to choose?

"Kimmie, quit being dramatic. Heven told you we're just friends," Cole said, coming to stand at my side.

"Don't Kimmie me," she snapped. Then she turned back to me. "Well?"

I fished around for some kind of excuse. "We can't all just avoid each other. We're going to Italy together next week."

"Don't go." She shrugged.

I didn't have a choice. The Treasure Map had to be returned and this was our only opportunity to do it. "I finally got my mom to agree. She already paid. Sam and I have plans."

"How you have managed to get two guys to trip all over themselves for you I will never understand," she muttered.

Her words hurt.

"That's enough." Cole growled.

I shook my head. Defending me wouldn't buy him any points with her.

"Tell your mom you changed your mind about Italy. Stay away from Cole," Kimber repeated.

"I can't do that," I said, standing my ground.

Kimber's eyes widened in disbelief for a fraction of a second before narrowing, her hands fisted at her sides. She was used to getting her way, used to me caving. I wouldn't this time. There was too much at stake.

"You're making a mistake," she hissed, turning back to her car.

"Kimber, wait. Can't we talk?"

"I knew this would happen eventually. I've always known what kind of person you are. It's why I befriended you in the first place. Keep your friends close but your enemies closer and all. I thought maybe your accident had changed you, but it was an illusion. You used those scars on your face to your advantage, and when you got what you wanted, you got rid of them."

Shock vibrated through me. She believed what she was saying. Her aura vibrated with truth and anger. How had I thought we had been best friends all these years? How had I never realized that she never really liked me, only liked the popularity I brought her?

"Leave. Now." Sam growled from behind me.

"Whatever." She tossed out her window before speeding away.

My shoulders slumped when she was gone from sight. I expected fireworks from Kimber, but not casualties. I wasn't sure that our friendship would survive this.

I wasn't sure I wanted it to.

Chapter Nine

Heven

That night as the stars twinkled in the sky and the cool Maine air drifted through the window, I drifted off to sleep all too easily. Unfortunately, peaceful sleep was elusive.

I dreamt of dark, choking water and red beady eyes. My lungs burned as I struggled to breathe while I panicked as I searched the darkness for Sam. The only thing I could find was the demon, slowly dragging me into the depths of the lake.

Where is it…

I knew I was dreaming; I tried to wake myself up. But, like the demon, the dream dragged me further under.

Show me where you keep it…

The demon beckoned me to reveal where I kept the Treasure Map. I forced my mind to stay in the present with the burning pain in my lungs and the knowledge I was drowning, the pain and fear was preferable to telling the demon anything. Even if it was only a dream, I refused to give him the upper hand.

I swear I felt myself die in the dream. The life drained right out of me.

Suddenly, the lake was gone and so were the greedy hands of the demon. The icy water was replaced by a golden sun and a sprawling meadow of wild flowers in shades of amethyst and yellow. I spun in a circle, the flower petals tickling my ankles and the sun's rays kissing my skin. But then I noticed that no birds sang and the breeze did not blow. It was as if everything was still, not really real, but a façade.

A man appeared at the other side of the meadow. He was wide and tall and he was dressed impeccably. Even though I couldn't see his face, I knew that he was the biggest façade of all. He held out his hand to me and I knew exactly what he wanted.

"You can't have it!" I screamed.

Around me the flowers wilted and died; their brilliant colors turning a putrid brown. The sky, once a clear blue turned stormy and dark. Wind whipped around me and threatened to lift me off the ground.

You cannot resist me forever, little one.

Pain splintered my head and I sagged to the ground. My eyes sprang open and I wanted to weep with relief. I was awake and everything was fine. I rolled toward Sam, reaching for him, craving his comfort.

He wasn't in bed.

Alarm filled me and I pushed myself into a sitting position, fighting the pressure in the back of my skull. "Sam?"

I heard a sound across the room and peered through the darkness. Sam was there, wedged in a small space between the wall and the dresser. I tripped, trying to get free of the covers and stumbled across the room, falling to my knees on the floor beside him.

"Get back," he said roughly, pushing himself even farther into the corner.

"What's wrong?" The sight of him trying to get away from me was worse than the choking depths of the lake.

His head snapped up and he stared at me with pure glittering gold eyes.

I gasped and fell backward onto my bottom. I scrambled back up scooting as close as possible and reached out a hand.

"No," he protested weakly as I closed my fingers around his wrist.

His skin was burning up as I tugged him away from the wall. I used my other hand to push the hair off his forehead. He took a deep breath and his body shook with effort.

"Please get back, Hev." His voice was strained.

I released his wrist and scooted back so that there was a little more than an arm's distance between us. I sat there, watching him as his breathing evened out and the tremors shaking his body slowed.

Finally, he looked up at me, his eyes no longer gold, but the warm honey color they usually were.

"Come back to bed," I whispered, holding out my hand. Suddenly, his hand shot out and grabbed mine, yanking me so that I practically fell into him. My face was mere inches from him as his eyes bore into mine. My heart beat rapidly, threatening to come right out of my chest. His eyes were intense, like he'd never seen me before. Something inside me whispered that maybe I should be afraid.

But I could never be afraid of Sam.

"What happened?" he whispered. His voice was raspier than usual.

"I should ask you the same thing," I said, twisting my hand from his grip.

He frowned and let go. "I didn't mean to be so rough,"

I nodded.

"I tried to wake you."

"I was having a nightmare."

He stood, reaching out a hand to help me and I slid my fingers back into his. Once I was on my feet, he released me, moving across the room.

"Why were you in the corner like that?"

He stopped by the window to glance out into the dark. "You were sleeping, but I was restless. I was afraid of waking you, so I got up to surf the net."

Next to me the laptop was still open on my desk.

"You began tossing and turning. You cried out and I tried to wake you, but it was useless. I couldn't get you to wake up. I just... snapped."

"Your eyes were gold."

His face drew into a frown like he was trying to work out a puzzle. "It's like someone flipped a switch inside me and all of the sudden I was fighting the urge to shift. Right there in the bed with you." Clearly, the idea horrified him.

"Sam, you wouldn't have hurt me."

He didn't say anything, like he wasn't convinced.

"I was dreaming of what happened at the lake this morning, drowning. I was afraid," I said and his back stiffened. "Maybe my fear was so strong it bled to you and triggered your protective instincts."

"Maybe." He allowed. "I wanted to jump out the window, but I was afraid to leave you alone."

"You've shifted in the same room with me before," I said, thinking back to when he first told me he was a hellhound. He hadn't so much as told me, but *showed* me instead. "And you didn't hurt me then, shifting around me now wouldn't be any different."

"I wasn't in a bed with you, Hev. I am usually in control when I shift. I bring it on myself. This was different. One minute I was fine, and the next, my body was shifting, trying to fight some threat it was sensing. Except the only other person in the room with me was you." He looked up and his eyes were bleak.

So instead of jumping out the window, he got as far away from me as he could to not only protect me from outside dangers, but from himself. I couldn't stand the distance between us anymore and moved across the room to stand next to him. "You thought you were going to attack me?"

"No!" he denied adamantly, but then doubt crept over his face. "I don't know what to think."

"You're exhausted. You need to get some sleep."

He glanced warily at the bed. I sighed. "Nothing else is going to happen tonight."

He still seemed wary of touching me, so I went to the bed and climbed in, pulling the covers around me, trying to ignore the pain in my head. The back of my skull was squeezing my brain and now the front part of my head was hurting… it was like both parts of my brain were warring with each other.

I watched as Sam stood, debating on whether or not he trusted himself enough to get in the bed. A few moments later and with a heavy sigh, the mattress dipped beneath his weight. A smile played on my lips.

"I knew you couldn't resist me."

Sam grinned. "Yes, well, it was either the bed or the floor, and the floor is pretty hard."

I hit him with a pillow.

He choked back a laugh and grabbed the pillow and stuffed in under his head as he stretched out on the bed.

"You're a bed hog," I grumped.

"And you like it," he said, his voice practically a purr. He rolled onto his stomach and turned his face away. A deep sigh lifted his back.

He still had yet to touch me and it was beginning to drive me mad. There was no way I was going to let him start thinking that the hellhound in him was about to attack every time we touched.

I reached out a hand and ran my fingers over his back. The muscles beneath my hand bunched, but he didn't say anything. We laid there in the silence as I rubbed slow circles over his back. Eventually, he relaxed into a soundless sleep.

I knew that I wouldn't sleep the rest of this night, but it didn't matter. For once, I could give a little bit back to the boy I loved more than myself. Tonight, Sam would finally get some peace and I would watch over him as he slept to make sure that no one tried to take it from him.

Sam

Gemma was already in the orchard when I arrived. She was leaning against a tree, a large bag at her feet. She gave off the impression of relaxation, but I had a feeling that she never relaxed. She was always on guard and the way she presented herself, the way she allowed people to perceive her was all very calculated. It wasn't that I didn't trust her – actually I did – I just thought that she was a woman who had seen a lot in her years and it hardened her. She seemed to have a wall built around her that hid the real her from everyone else. I would like to say that perhaps we could be friends, but I really didn't know if she would let anyone that close.

I thought back to when I first met her. The day she sold me Hev's bracelet. I hadn't perceived any of those things then. Maybe because I hadn't been looking, maybe because she was hiding more of herself that day than she was now, or maybe it was because I was getting better at reading people.

Yeah, it was that last one. I'm just getting better. I smiled to myself, putting a little swagger in my step.

"Feeling pretty confident?" Gemma asked, her lips lifting as she pushed away from the tree.

"Maybe."

Before I could even blink, she was ramming into me, her fist catching me just beneath the ribs, stunning me and sending me into the ground with a sickening thud. Breath whooshed from my lungs as I stared up at the blue cloudless sky.

Gemma stepped into my sight, blocking the sky. Her dark ponytail cascaded over one shoulder and she smirked. "This is no place for confidence."

Clearly. Nothing like getting knocked over by a girl to ruin a man's mojo.

"You held back, that day by the lake," I said, thinking back to the day she pulled out that amulet and we fought. She hadn't moved that fast then.

"You weren't exactly in top form, and since Heven all but drowned, I figured beating up her one and only wasn't really appropriate."

"You can't beat me up," I said annoyed, jumping up from the ground and turning to face her. Just how weak did she think I was?

She tilted her head to the side. "Maybe not. But you could definitely use some improvement. You need to learn to fight as you are now, not just as a hellhound."

"I'm here. Are we gonna do this or stand around and talk?"

She walked over to the bag that lay beneath the tree. She was dressed in tight blue jeans and brown leather boots that reached her knees. Her white T-shirt was snug and she was strapped with weapons, the most interesting being a dagger that was strapped to the outside of her thigh. She moved with ease and grace. Clearly, she was comfortable in her body. Her dark brown hair was pulled up in a ponytail that swung when she walked. She was a beautiful woman.

I preferred blondes.

Gemma dumped out the bag and I laughed. Weapons of every kind littered the grass. Daggers, knives, a sword, some ancient-looking things I had no clue as to what they were and even a bow and arrow.

"Pick your poison."

I reached down and snagged a dagger. It was all steel and gleamed in the sunlight. I liked the weight of it in my hand.

"Good choice," Gemma said, pleased. "Although, I think we better get in the basics before we move on to weapons."

"Seriously? Why would you show me a bag of toys, then tell me I couldn't play with them?"

She grinned, enjoying my annoyance. "Just giving you something to work toward. First, you have to prove to me that you are strong enough to play with the big-boy toys." She patted my cheek as she spoke.

I slapped at her hand. "I passed the big-boy test a long time ago."

Gemma smiled. "Prove it."

I shrugged and tossed the weapon back with the others. "Let's do this."

"It's important you learn to fight in your human form, without weapons, because you never know when a threat might present itself. You won't always have the freedom to shift, to pull out a weapon – so you need to become your own weapon."

I nodded. What she said made sense. I wanted to be as strong as humanly possible in both my forms. I had to protect Heven. I had to protect Logan and this was the best way to do it.

"I think the best way to learn is through actual fighting," Gemma said, walking a few steps away. "Are you ready?"

I smiled.

"Oh, and one more thing," she said and looked over her shoulder. "Don't hold back because I'm a girl. I might be a girl, but I will kick your ass."

I laughed and as I did she charged. She was fast, impossibly fast, and part of my brain wondered if it was because she was a fallen angel. The other half of my brain was busy anticipating her moves, calculating what she was going to do before she did it.

I managed to throw off her first hit, but didn't expect her to practically snap back and come at me with a well-formed kick. She sent me sailing into a tree, a branch snapping when I hit it. I picked up the branch and launched it at her and she barely moved in time. I charged her, feeling the familiar quiver in my body–the need to change. It pounded through my blood — begging to be released.

"Don't do it," Gemma called. "Shift your focus. Use that desire to shift and put it toward your fight."

It was harder than it seemed. To deny your body something that came so naturally was nearly impossible, but I held onto my human form and the force of the effort took away my concentration and she headed off what I meant to be a solid hit and sent me flying backward into the tree again.

I jumped up with a loud roar, and instead of heading for her head on, I changed my strategy. I ran off to her right, away from her in a wide arc, cutting back toward her at the last possible second. Then I jumped up and caught a low hanging branch and swung myself up and around, sending myself at her feet first. I hit her in the shoulder and she fell. I took advantage of her moment of vulnerability to grab her legs and flip her over so that her face was in the dirt. I shoved my knee into the center of her back, my fingers pinning her shoulder down.

"He learns fast," Gemma said.

"Hope you like dirt, you're going to be eating a lot of it today." She did some kind of maneuver that I had never seen and I ended up on my back, once again staring up at the cloudless sky. A dagger came crashing down inches from my skull. I reached for the dagger, but she kneed me between the legs—just beneath the place that would have had me crying, but I reacted instantly, curling my body up to shield myself.

"I never took you for a girl to land a low blow," I said, my voice slightly strained.

"No one touches my dagger but me."

I made a rude noise and jumped up.

"You're not tired yet, are you?" she taunted.

I answered by charging her and landing a series of punches and kicks. She laughed as she deflected the final blow. The fighting/training went on for a long time, until I thought my body would drop, but somehow, I found the energy to keep going. She never once treated me like I couldn't do it. When I started dragging, she would say something to make me mad or indignant, and I discovered that I could push further than I realized. I was stronger than even I knew.

Turns out I was lousy with a bow and arrow, so-so with a knife and lethal with a dagger.

Gemma was good at all three. It made me try harder.

Finally, we called a truce long enough for me to gulp down an entire jug of water. I'd long since shed my shirt and the sun was hot against my back. I ran my hands through my sweat-soaked hair and took a deep breath. Gemma was standing a few feet away, drinking water of her own. I walked over and she eyed me warily—waiting for me to dish out a hit.

"Why are you doing this?" I asked, curious.

"I told you, I want to help."

"But why do you care?" She didn't strike me as the kind to get involved with anyone, especially people she hardly knew.

She avoided my stare as she capped her water jug and sat it on the ground. "I might be a fallen angel, but that doesn't make me a bad person. I saw what was going on around here. I didn't like it. You two got a bad deal and I was tired of watching you both fight so hard."

"You think we are going to lose? You think that one day I'm not going to be strong enough and we're both going to die."

"It's happened before."

"To people you know?"

"I don't know anyone. Not anymore."

I stuck out my hand. "I'm Sam. Nice to meet you." She looked at my hand then back up at me. I grinned. "Figured if I was going to keep kicking your butt, we should at least be properly introduced. I want you to *know* where your butt kicking is coming from."

She rolled her eyes but then she put her hand in mine and shook. "Gemma," she murmured.

Then she yanked and I was sailing through the air again, taking out yet another one of the tree limbs. For a moment I laid there, marveling in the fact that just being a hellhound made my human form stronger... if I were only a human, I would probably be dead.

The sound of running feet caught my attention and I looked to my left and saw Heven running through the orchard toward us. I jumped up and turned to face her.

Gemma took that moment to strike out again. She was ruthless! Heven was yelling as I face-planted. I rolled onto my back and sat up. Gemma came to my side. "Never let your guard down."

I grunted.

Heven stopped just feet away from us, placing her hands on her hips. Her hair was windblown from her running and her cheeks were flushed. "Are you two still fighting?"

"Training," I corrected.

"Aren't you exhausted?"

Actually, I was, but I wouldn't admit it. I was going to be sore tomorrow.

"We're done here," Gemma said, getting to her feet. "You did a good job."

I stood and swept Heven up in my arms, inhaling the sweet scent of her hair. She squealed and pounded me on the shoulder. "You smell and you're all sweaty. Put me down!"

I made sure to run my sweaty forehead against her cheek and she laughed. "You are so gross."

I laughed and sat her down. Gemma began gathering weapons and tossing them in the bag and I helped her.

Heven's eyes widened. "Did you use all this stuff?"

"Some of it."

"So when are you going to teach me how to fight?" Heven asked Gemma who stopped picking up weapons to look at her.

"You really want to know how?" she asked.

"I really do," she said. "You probably don't know what it feels like to be weak."

Something passed over Gemma's face, but then it was gone. She looked down at Heven and I could almost see her giving in.

"She can't train you and me at the same time," I said, interrupting the conversation. It wasn't that I wanted Heven to be unprotected, to not know how to defend herself, but I didn't want her to get hurt and Gemma was not the person to be training her. Heven wasn't strong enough for the kind of fighting Gemma did, which was so far advanced that Heven would only get hurt and frustrated. Besides, we were leaving for Italy in a few days and we didn't have time for this.

My comment was enough to break whatever Gemma was thinking. "He's right. You're not ready."

Heven growled in frustration. "Why does everyone want to treat me like I'm weak and helpless? I'm not."

"No one said you were weak and helpless, Hev."

Heven turned her back and began picking up more weapons. I was about to give in, to offer to train her myself when Gemma launched herself at me, thinking to catch me off guard.

This time I was ready.

I sent her flying backward and she grabbed the nearest weapon, a knife and threw it at me. I caught it before it buried itself in my chest.

"Nice," Gemma said.

"Are you two crazy!?" Heven yelled. "What if he hadn't caught that?"

"He did." Gemma said, shrugging.

Heven opened her mouth to say more when another voice called out. "What the hell is going on here?"

All three of us whipped around to see Cole striding forward between rows of budding fruit trees. I was surprised to realize that I didn't hate him as much as usual. Knowing that he was Heven's brother softened some of the anger I had toward him. At least this way, I wouldn't have to worry about him trying to kiss her again. On the other hand, there was no getting rid of him now. He was family, a permanent fixture in her life. I knew how important family was — especially brothers, so I had to figure out a way to get along with him.

"You came back!" Heven exclaimed, running to him. She hesitated for a few seconds when she reached him — not sure if she would be accepted by him. Is that how Logan felt when he first got here? Had he been afraid I wouldn't take him in?

Cole opened up his arms and pulled Heven in for a hug. I still didn't like when he touched her. "I told you I would," he told her. "What's going on out here?" Cole asked again, pulling away from Heven.

She pretended not to hear him ask. "Want to go to the house and see Gran?"

"I already saw her."

"Oh."

Cole stepped away to toe the now half-empty bag of weapons on the ground.

"Who's this?" Gemma asked, appearing beside me.

"This is my friend Cole we told you about," Heven responded, probably afraid of what I would say.

"*This* is Cole?" Gemma's wide gray eyes appraised him.

Cole took notice and stood a little taller, turning toward us. His blue eyes narrowed on Gemma. "Who are you?"

"Cole, this is Gemma. She's a friend of ours," Heven said.

He took in her snug, curve-hugging outfit and knee-high brown leather boots. He noted how every inch of her was strapped with some sort of weapon and his eyes settled on her hand, which was clutching a bow.

Cole reached over and tugged an arrow out of a tree. "I think you lost something."

Was he fighting a smile?

"Nope. I put it there," Gemma retorted.

Cole's lips lifted.

I stepped between the pair to tell Cole, "You should go back to the house." He'd already seen way too much.

Cole's eyes hardened when he looked at me, taking in my missing shirt, various scrapes and bruises and my grass-stained jeans. "What have you got my sister involved in?"

Beside him Heven beamed because Cole acknowledged her as his sister.

"Sister?" Gemma said, sharply.

Heven turned toward her. "We just found out that Cole and I have the same father."

"That would explain it." Gemma nodded.

"Explain what?" Cole asked. All three of us looked at Gemma.

She shook her head and muttered. "Mortals."

"What?" Cole asked.

Gemma turned toward Heven. "Isn't his aura different than everyone else's?"

"Yeah," she answered, her eyes widening.

"Aura? What is she talking about, Hev?" Cole was becoming alarmed. Great, the guy was probably going to start asking a million questions.

Heven didn't seem to notice and kept talking to Gemma. "It always has a huge balloon of magenta. Pink and purple swirled together. No one else I've met has that color permanently; it's only in short bursts and the color rarely mixes together."

"Somebody better start explaining." Cole said and grabbed Heven's wrist.

Something in me snapped. He might be her brother, but he needed to keep his hands to himself. I yanked him away and we went rolling in the grass. Cole landed a solid punch to my jaw and Heven called out. We ignored her and continued fighting. I had been wanting to hammer this guy for months now. I tossed him off me, enjoying the sickening thud his body made when it hit the ground, and then I pounced on him, landing a punch to his jaw.

"Sam! Stop it!" Heven yelled. Her fear slammed into me and it drew me up short. Pummeling her brother in front of her wasn't a good idea.

I got off him and began walking away, but Cole got up and charged me, hooking his arms around my waist only for me to flip him back on the ground. "Don't make me knock you out," I snarled close to his face.

"If you aren't going to do something, then I am." I heard Heven say to Gemma.

"Let them get it out of their systems. Clearly, they have been waiting for a chance to fight."

Heven snorted. "Since they met."

"It makes sense." I saw Gemma shrug when I pushed away from Cole. Like an idiot he came at me again.

Heven made a sound and jumped between us. Cole wasn't expecting Heven's sudden appearance and he tripped, trying not to plow into her and fell to the side. He lay on his back staring up at me breathing hard, his dark hair falling onto his forehead. I smirked. Heven smacked me in the stomach.

"Are you okay?" she asked Cole. He sat up and nodded.

He had a bloody lip.

Heven whirled on me. "You could have hurt him! I thought that things were better since we found out he's my brother!"

"Don't ever get in the middle of a fight like that again," I said mildly. She glared. But I smiled and said, *Things are better. I don't want to kill him anymore, just punch him.*

Heven was not amused. "Better be careful or I might punch you," she muttered.

I grinned. I liked a feisty woman.

"You fight well," Gemma was telling Cole as he got to his feet. "You should train with us."

"Are you kidding? He kicked my ass."

The guy got points for taking it like a man.

Gemma laughed. It made Cole smile. Gemma turned to Heven. "You should tell him."

"I agree." Heven nodded and glared at me practically daring me to argue.

They were right. He'd seen too much for him to just accept some generic explanation. Plus there were other advantages of letting Cole in on the secret.

It's a good idea. He can watch out for you when I'm not around. I might not like him, but I know I can trust him.

Heven beamed with happiness and I figured this would get me out of kicking Cole's butt a few minutes ago.

"I'll come back tomorrow. We'll meet here. Bring Cole," Gemma told us. She began tossing the weapons into the bag she brought. Cole bent to help her, picking up *her* dagger. The one that no one was allowed to touch but her. I waited for her to react, but she just smiled, plucked it out of his hand, slid it into some sort of strap on her thigh, then tossed the bag of weapons over her shoulder and began to walk away.

I got a threat and Cole got a smile. Interesting.

"We can't tomorrow. We have a meeting at school about our trip to Italy," Heven hurried to tell Gemma. A meeting I forgot about until now. I wanted to train. I needed to. Today taught me how much I had to learn and I needed to learn it ASAP.

"I'll meet you later, after the meeting," I said, hoping she would agree. Hoping she would forget about Cole coming along.

"I'll see you both then, late afternoon."

So much for that idea.

"Wait," Cole called after her.

"See you tomorrow," she called without looking back.

Then she was gone.

Literally vanishing from sight.

It took us all a minute to recover from her abrupt disappearance, but then Cole was looking at Heven. "You have major explaining to do."

Heven was staring after Gemma with a frown on her face.

What is it? I asked.

Gemma left before giving a few explanations of her own. Like, why exactly my brother's aura isn't like anyone else's.

I stared at the spot that Gemma disappeared from. That was a good question, something I wouldn't mind knowing the answer to either.

*   *   *

My muscles were screaming. I knew I would be sore after that training session with Gemma yesterday, but I didn't know I would be this sore. My legs protested as I stepped down from my truck and I stood there on the sidewalk, stretching out my back muscles before climbing the stairs to the front door. The meeting at the school for the Italy trip was later this morning, but I wanted to come home and see Logan before I had to be there. My keys jangled together as I pulled them out of my pocket and lifted them to the lock on the door. But when I went to insert the key, the door swung open. It hadn't been latched. It hadn't been locked. What the hell was Logan thinking not closing and locking the door at night?

Why would he even need to open the door? It was late when I left to go back to Hev's last night and I made sure it was shut and locked behind me. He had been sleeping...

"Logan?" I said, stepping inside the apartment, pausing to close the door and turn the lock.

There were no lights on and nothing looked disturbed. It didn't take me but a glance to know he wasn't in the apartment. There were no rooms to search except the bathroom, which I ran to and threw open the door. Empty. I looked around for some kind of note—some kind of sign about where he might be. There wasn't one.

The entire apartment was empty.

My stomach twisted. I sank down onto the couch and stared at the floor. Where was he? Did I leave him alone too much? Was he mad because I didn't "fix" him like he thought I could?

Did he run away?

I had to find him! I raced to the door, throwing it open and rushing down the stairs. It was still really early so the streets would be empty. If he was still in the area, he wouldn't be too hard to track down.

I debated whether to go on foot or by truck... I could move faster on foot, my senses able to pick up his scent if he were nearby but what if he was hurt? I might need the truck.

I rushed toward the truck when something caught my eye. The door to the second-hand store I lived above was ajar. It was too early for the store to be open.

Logan.

Instead of bursting through the door like I wanted to, I pushed it open and stepped in, calling out. "Is anyone here?"

Then my eyes fell on the contents of the store and I froze.

It was completely destroyed.

A swear leaked from my lips as I took another step inside, stepping over a busted mirror and lamp. A noise from the back of the store caught my attention and I pivoted toward it. "Hello?"

I couldn't see anyone because the destruction was so great. Overturned furniture, racks of clothing and broken glass were everywhere. The glass case that used to be at the front of the store was now shattered, its steel frame was tilted and leaning against the wall in the back.

I stepped over an old television set with a busted screen, glass crunching beneath my feet as I made my way to where I heard the noise.

"Who's there?" I said again, my voice coming out hushed.

A shuffling and strangled sound followed and I *knew*. I rushed behind a wooden armoire tilted on its side and stopped.

Logan was there and it wasn't pretty.

He was tucked against the wall, his knees pulled up against his chest as if he were trying to make himself as small as possible. He wasn't wearing a shirt and his arms were up over his head, covering his ears and he was rocking himself back and forth.

My chest tightened and emotion welled up inside me. He looked so... so... broken. "Logan," I whispered, hoarse.

He looked up, his face was streaked with tears and his hair was wild, standing on end. "Sam?"

I knelt down in front of him, ignoring the way the glass cut into my knees. "Bud, what happened?"

"I don't know what's wrong with me."

"There's nothing wrong with you," I said, reaching out toward him, grabbing his wrist. "Who did this... did they hurt you?" My eyes scanned the store for traces of the people responsible.

A sob caught in his throat as more tears leaked from his eyes. He nodded.

Rage and adrenaline burned through me. Whoever hurt him was going to pay... I was going to see to it personally. I yanked him forward and wrapped my arms around his shoulders. "Hey, it's all right now."

Logan took a shuddering breath and wrapped his arms tightly around me. Guilt, sour and heavy, draped over me. This was my fault. I left him alone, unprotected, and now he was hurt.

I pulled him back to look at his tear streaked face. "Which way did the thugs go, Logan?"

His eyes dropped to the floor. "You don't understand,"

"Understand what?"

"There were no people that did this."

"Of course there were, Logan. Look at this place. You said you saw them. You said they... hurt you."

"It hurts now... after..." he said, sobbing again.

"Logan," I said firmly, giving him a shake. "What the hell are you talking about?"

He looked up, straight into my eyes. "It was me, Sam. I did this."

"No," I said, gripping his arms. "You couldn't have."

"Yes. I did. And it isn't the first time."

"What are you talking about?" I released him and stood.

"Before I came here... before I shifted I would get so mad sometimes... I just wanted to destroy something. To rip it apart. I thought once I found you, it would stop. It *did* stop, until now."

I knew that Logan was prone to having "fits." I knew that he was angry that he was a hellhound but this... I looked around me at the massive destruction. *This* went beyond being angry. I was about to ask him why he didn't tell me about this when he said,

"I guess you're going to kick me out now." The way he said it, so defeated, so lost, made a rough sound lodge in the back of my throat. I swallowed it down, ignoring it.

I knelt back in front of him once again. "I'm not kicking you out, Logan."

"You aren't?" He wiped at his eyes and blinked up at me.

"No. You're my brother. I'm here for you. There's nothing that you could do to make me send you away." Like they did to me. Like our parents.

He stood and, in his haste, he tripped over debris and fell forward. I caught him and he wrapped his arms around me again and squeezed. "I'm so sorry. I don't know what happened. I was asleep and when I woke up I was here... in this mess."

My body stilled. "You mean you don't remember doing this?"

He pulled away. "No."

"Then how do you know you did?"

"I just do, okay?" He turned away.

My eyes went straight to a set of scratches across his lower back. They were red and swollen and matted with dried blood. "What happened to your back?"

He shrugged.

I grabbed his shoulder and turned him to face me. "No, it's not okay. What aren't you telling me?"

His shoulders drooped. "Sometimes I go to sleep in one place and wake up somewhere else... I can never remember anything."

I nodded, slowly trying not to show my extreme alarm. This wasn't normal. I never heard of another hellhound behaving this way before.

"Sam?"

"I'm not sending you away, Logan. We're going to figure this out. Me and you."

It looked like he might cry again so I started moving to the front of the store. "Come on, I gotta call the landlord."

Logan gasped. "You can't! He'll know I did it!"

I pivoted in the wreckage. "No. He won't. I'm gonna call and tell him we heard some noise and when I came down here, I found the place like this."

"You're gonna lie?"

"Yeah. You weren't here. You stayed upstairs in the apartment the whole time. You didn't see anything. Got it?"

He nodded.

"Stick to that and everything will be fine." I started walking again. "Now, come on. You need to get upstairs before people start to wake up and begin moving around and I need the phone." When Heven and I formed the Mindbond I ditched my cell because there was no point in having it anymore, but now, I really needed to think about getting a pair of cell phones so Logan and I could keep in contact when I was at work and with Heven. I sighed. One more bill to pay.

The landlord Mr. Cartney was here within minutes after I called him and the police showed up just after. Logan had showered, put on clean clothes, and was sitting in front of the TV with a bowl of cereal when I went downstairs to meet them. I made sure the door was latched this time.

The police and Mr. Cartney were already standing amongst the damage, shaking their heads when I walked in the room.

"Who did this, Sam?" Mr. Cartney asked when he saw me.

"I wish I knew. I wish I had seen them," I lied; the regret in my voice wasn't hard to fake because I wasn't faking. I felt immense regret.

"You're the tenant upstairs?" one of the officers asked.

"Yes, sir." I looked him straight in the eye so he could see that I had nothing to hide.

"Can we ask you a few questions?"

"Of course, I didn't see much. I was upstairs asleep when I heard some noise. At first I didn't think anything of it, but then I heard something shatter and I decided to get up and look. This is what I found."

The officer nodded and scrawled notes in his note pad while his partner walked around with a camera snapping pictures. He asked about a million questions, but it was about the same ten, just asked in different ways. I gave the same answers every single time.

I was asleep. I heard noises. After a few minutes I came downstairs. We were in our apartment all night, me and my brother, who is visiting. He didn't come downstairs when the noises started because I wouldn't let him. He knew nothing. He saw nothing. I wished I could do more.

No one seemed to doubt me. After the officers were satisfied, they gave me a card and told me to call if I thought of anything else. I wouldn't call. I pretended I would. Then Mr. Cartney laid his hand on my shoulder and thanked me for calling him and the police. He thanked me for "scaring off the intruders with my presence."

"I wish I could have done more," I said, looking over the damage with regret. "You don't deserve something like this."

"It's okay, son," Mr. Cartney said. No one had called me that in a long time. It made me feel guilty about my lies because he was a nice man that didn't deserve to be lied to.

But it was him or my brother.

It wasn't a hard choice.

"I have insurance. Once I get this place cleaned up and new inventory to sell I'll be back in business."

"If there is anything I can do, please let me know."

"Thank you, but you've done enough. Most people would have ignored it and not even called the police. I can't thank you enough."

I didn't say anything else as I let myself out of the store and into the morning sun. He was right. I had done enough. He just didn't realize that none of it was good.

* * *

Just before I let myself back into the apartment, Heven's voice floated through my mind.

Everything okay where you are?

Yes, everything is fine, I said, lying again.

Sorry.

Don't be sorry, I get it. And I did, I mind dialed her all the time just to make sure she was okay. It was exactly why I lied to her about what was going on. She didn't need any more to deal with right now. Besides, she was already uneasy around Logan and this would just make it worse. It was hard to juggle things—responsibilities—and I was tired. I let myself back into the apartment and Logan looked at me with stricken eyes.

"Everything is fine. They don't suspect you."

He let out the breath he had been holding. "I'm so sorry."

"I know you are." I sat down next to him on the couch. "How long has this been going on, Logan?"

"Since before I ran away from home."

"You didn't tell me."

"I thought that it had stopped. I thought that being here with you would make it better. It did for a while…"

He thought I had the answers to everything because I was a hellhound. I didn't want to tell him that I had been figuring it out as I went, and that the things he was doing didn't seem normal to me.

"There have been times that you remember, uh, getting mad?" Maybe he was just sleepwalking, maybe he thought that he was responsible and he really wasn't.

"Yeah. I trashed the bathroom at home before I left. I got into a fight at school and I trashed the place you first lived when you moved out of our house."

I swallowed, trying to show no reaction to the things he was saying. I wanted him to feel comfortable talking to me.

"The kids at school deserved it," he muttered.

"What kids?"

He looked away, ashamed.

"Logan," I pressed, grabbing his shoulder.

He shrugged me off. "Brent and his crew."

"The jocks? They were giving you problems? They never had before."

He looked at me and then it hit me. The reason he never got picked on was because of me.

When I was there, I must have been protecting him. No one ever messed with me. Well, one kid did once… but he never did again. I never realized that it was me that kept the bullies away from Logan too.

And then I left.

And he was fresh meat.

I didn't think I could feel any worse than I had earlier when I found him crying in the mess. I was wrong. I failed my brother. My parents might have stopped loving me. They might have abandoned me, but Logan never did. He was a victim in all this, just like me.

My emotions must have been clear on my face because Logan said, "Don't worry about it. I taught them a lesson."

"Oh yeah?"

He smiled. It was a smile that reminded me he was only fourteen.

"I flushed Brent's head in the urinal." He laughed.

I grinned. "Awesome." I held up my fist and he bumped his against mine.

But then Logan's face fell and he looked away.

"Is there something else?" I pressed.

He glanced up at the television which was playing the news. The woman on the screen was talking about the weather. "Think what happened downstairs will be on the news?"

"I don't know," I said, watching him watch the news.

"Sometimes, I hear voices," Logan said, not looking at me.

"Voices?" How many more surprises was this kid going to lay on me today?

"Well, really only one. I used to pretend it was you."

"Used to?"

"It started saying things that didn't sound like things you would say…"

"What kind of things?"

"Forget it."

"No, Logan. What kind of things?"

"Bad things," he whispered.

I stood up from the couch, not wanting him to see the horror on my face and not sure enough that I could hide it. Anger, rage, voices…

What the hell was wrong with my little brother?

"Listen to me," I said, pushing his empty cereal bowl out of the way to sit on the coffee table in front of him. "You aren't alone anymore, okay? We are going to figure this out. I'm going to help you."

He nodded, relief on his face.

"I know I work a lot, and I have responsibilities and a girlfriend, but I want you to know that you are important to me, okay? Don't doubt that."

He nodded again. "I know. Thanks, Sam."

I stood and went across the room to grab some clean clothes and set them in the bathroom. "I'm going to take a shower. I have somewhere to be in a bit. You can come with me."

"Cool." All the intensity and fear from our conversation seemed to vanish and he looked like a normal kid on the couch, channel surfing.

But he wasn't normal.

"Crap. I left something in the truck I need. I'm going to run down and get it and I will be right back."

He nodded, absorbed in whatever he found to watch. I slipped out the door, avoiding the police still in the store and went around the side of the building in the alley. My brother needed help. I needed help to help him. I only knew of one person that might be able to help me. I stared up at the sky and prayed that she would listen, that she would come to me.

"Airis!" I said her name as loud as I dared, not wanting to draw attention.

Nothing happened.

"Airis!" I yelled louder this time, not caring who might hear.

Still nothing.

I began to pace. Why wouldn't she come? Didn't she care? Wasn't it her job to care?

I let out a frustrated growl when a white light appeared off to the side and Airis floated through. She was dressed all in white like always and her blond hair was around her shoulders.

"You came," I said, rushing toward her.

"Technically, I shouldn't be here. But your intentions are good."

"Why shouldn't you be here?"

"Because Heven isn't here, so this obviously does not involve Heven — the Supernatural Treasure you are meant to protect."

"Heven is fine. I'm protecting her."

Airis inclined her head. "Yes, you have done well."

I didn't say thank you because I got the feeling it wasn't a compliment. "Look, you said to protect her at all costs. I've had to kill some demons—"

She held up her hand. "This isn't about you and the demons after Heven."

"Then what's this about?"

"You are getting caught up in your lies. Be careful, Sam. Do not stray from your path."

Lies? What lies? "If you mean what I told the police, I was protecting my brother. I think he's sick, there's something wrong with him. I need help to figure it out. You're the only one that can help me."

"Perhaps a doctor would help?"

I let out a frustrated growl. "You know I can't take him to the doctor. He's a hellhound. I think his body is rejecting the hellhound gene... it's the only thing that makes sense. It's supposed to be only one hound every other generation. I already turned; he wasn't supposed to."

"You need to focus on your responsibilities, on the scroll. On Heven. You are getting distracted."

"Then help me!"

"I am helping you. You aren't listening."

"You're telling me to forget about my brother—my only family, to just leave him alone when he is sick!"

"I'm telling you that you are straying from your path—your job. Don't let the darkness around you cloud the way you think—the way you behave."

"The darkness. You mean the hellhound in me. That's why you won't help Logan. Because he's a hellhound and he hasn't passed any of your 'tests.'"

"Not every hellhound has your ability for good."

Maybe they would if they weren't treated like they were lepers. Like they were evil. It was obvious that Airis wasn't going to help me and this was a waste of time.

"Thanks for the help," I said sarcastically and turned my back on her to walk away.

"Remember what I said, Sam. Remember who your first priority is."

She made it sound like Heven was a job, an assignment. Like she forgot that the whole reason any of this happened was because I'm in love with Heven, that I would die for her... I didn't like being made to feel like this was a job. It wasn't. This was my life.

And my brother was part of my life whether Airis liked it or not.

If she wanted to spew her riddles and half-answers then she could, but I wasn't going to listen. I was just about around the corner when Airis called out to me. I stopped and turned, hoping she changed her mind.

"Remember if you or Heven need me just call."

I snorted. She meant if Heven needed help because, just now when I asked, things went so well. I walked around the corner without another glance. She made it clear where I stood with her but it didn't matter. I would find a way to help Logan without her.

Chapter Ten

Heven

It seemed a little strange to have a quiet, uneventful morning in the middle of an extremely unpredictable summer. It almost made me wary to relax so much.

Everything okay where you are? I asked Sam.

Yes, everything is fine.

I sighed and concentrated on my cereal bowl. I wished Sam were here instead of spending the morning with Logan at his apartment. A few moments later, there was a loud clatter and a bang. I leapt from my chair, sending it crashing to the floor, and looked for the demon that probably just broke in.

"My goodness!" Gran said. "I didn't mean to startle you. You're about as jumpy as a cat this morning, Heven."

I took in the tray at her feet and the upset tin of coffee on the counter and felt like a complete idiot. "Sorry, Gran," I muttered, righting my chair and sinking back into it.

"It's all right." She began to clean up and bent to pick up what she dropped. "I know the last few days have been very stressful."

"You do?"

"Of course, finding out you have a brother isn't something that happens every day."

She thought all of this was about Cole. I nodded and allowed her to think that, even though Cole was about the only thing that seemed to be going right these days.

"Did he find you yesterday morning?"

I nodded. "Sam and I were in the orchard." And Cole got quite an eyeful. After Gemma left Sam and I sat Cole down and did our best to explain everything to him. It took a while because we had to go all the way back to last year when I was injured (I didn't think of it as disfigured anymore because I wasn't disfigured. There had been nothing wrong with the way I looked. The problem had been with the way I felt.) It was such an unbelievable tale I thought for sure he would think I was crazy and declare he didn't want anything to do with me ever again. But he surprised us by believing everything we confessed. Thinking about it now, I guess it isn't *so* hard to understand why he accepted everything. Cole had seen too much to discount everything we told him. The abrupt disappearance of my scar, the demon attacking me added to what he witnessed with Sam and Gemma made a very impressive case.

"I thought that's where you might be," Gran said while she finished cleaning up the spilled coffee grounds.

I made a noise of agreement while I wondered if the orchard was the best place for the boys to be training. What would happen if someone saw us like Cole did?

"He seems to be accepting everything fairly easily," Gran said, drying her hands on a towel and coming to sit across the table from me.

Embarrassment heated my cheeks. We had been so busy explaining all the supernatural aspects of our lives that I completely forgot to ask Cole how he was doing. "Did he say how his mother was handling things?"

Gran grimaced. "I don't think she's very happy with me right now."

"I met her once. She wasn't very happy with me, either." At least I finally understood why she seemed to hate me so much that day at the ice cream shop. She knew who my father was. Of course she felt angry and hurt that he essentially chose me and my mom over her and Cole.

"It's been hard on her. Jason could have handled the situation better."

"Why do you think he did it, Gran?"

Gran sighed. "I don't know. I think he wanted to be part of Cole's life, but his mother wouldn't allow it after he chose your mother. I think Jason decided not to fight her and keep Cole a secret like she wanted, so he didn't upset your mother too."

I shook my head, trying to imagine what the situation would have been like and what I would have done in my dad's shoes. But it was no use. I had no clue what I would have done and I can't imagine having to choose between your children. Looking at it that way made me wonder why Cole wasn't angry.

"Do you think Cole is angry?" I asked quietly.

"I asked him, told him it was okay if he was," Gran said, taking a sip of coffee. "He said he wasn't angry because he already had a father who loved him and he never felt abandoned."

I nodded.

"I think he's upset that his mother is so hurt by all this, but I think he is glad to know."

I thought of how relieved I felt when I found out. It made sense of so many feelings that I didn't understand. "Thank you for telling us."

"It was a hard decision, but in the end I thought you had the right to know and... with Jason being gone..." Her eyes turned sad, but then cleared and she smiled. "I really wanted to know my grandson."

I reached out and grasped Gran's hand. We sat quietly for a while, Gran drinking her coffee and me drinking my orange juice until Gran cleared her throat and said, "It's been really wonderful having you here."

"I love it here too."

"You and your mother are really getting along these days."

My eyes went up to Gran's face. What was she trying to say? Did she want me to leave? I didn't want to leave. I liked it here. "She did agree to let me go to Italy," I said, glancing at the clock, making sure I wasn't running late for our meeting at school.

"She stops more often to see you," Gran pointed out, like she was trying to remind me of the other good things Mom was doing of late.

I nodded. "I like spending time with her, but I'd really like to stay here, if that's okay?" What would I do if she didn't want me here any longer?

Gran smiled and her shoulders seemed to relax. "As long as that's what you want."

"It is," I confirmed.

"I don't want you to feel like you can't go home when you want."

"I am home."

"It's settled then." Gran smiled and grabbed up her mug and took it to the sink. She seemed lighter than before. Had she really been worried that I would want to go back home? Sure, things were going great with my mother lately, but only for like a week. Then, there was Henry. How much time was he spending around Mom's house? I suppressed a shudder. For whatever reason, the thought of seeing him anymore than I had to was more than I could handle.

* * *

Sam was leaning against the side of his pickup when I pulled into the school parking lot. My heart lifted at the sight of him. He had my door opened and was reaching in to grab me before I even had the engine of Gran's car turned off.

He hugged me tightly, his nose pressing into the side of my neck. Something was wrong; he was upset about something, sad. *What's the matter?* I spoke with my mind because when I tried with my mouth his lips covered mine. I didn't have much (okay, practically none) experience in the kissing department, but even with my lack of knowledge, I knew that Sam was an expert kisser. But even with his expert kissing, I couldn't forget that something was bothering him. *Sam, what happened?*

He pulled away, reluctantly, with a sigh and leaned his forehead against mine. His whiskey-colored eyes were heavy-lidded, but they were also clouded. Behind him the door to the truck opened and I glanced over Sam's shoulder to see Logan jumping down from the cab of the truck.

My eyes flashed back to Sam, searching for an answer, searching for something because I knew this was why he seemed upset.

"Hey, Heven," Logan said as Sam pulled back from me.
We'll talk later.
"Hey, Logan! I didn't know you were coming to the meeting."

He seemed a little self-conscious like he didn't know what to say, so instead of pressing for an answer, I hooked my arm through his and pointed us in the direction of the school. "I'm glad you came. You can sit next to me."

Sam shot me a grateful look and I smiled. "I told Logan that he and I could go out for pizza after the meeting. You know, have some guy time and I figured there was no harm in him coming to the meeting."

"The teachers won't even notice." I laughed as we approached the doors. Sam stepped ahead of us and held open the door and we stepped inside. The meeting was being held in the gymnasium and Mrs. Britt was already seated on the bottom bleacher of the room with a stack of papers beside her. Students talked in low tones around her, all clustered into several small groups. Kimber was sitting a few rows up by herself and she glanced at me, but her eyes strayed to Logan who was walking beside me. I stepped toward her and she glared at me, but I ignored it and sat next to her anyway with Sam taking up the space on my right and Logan right next to him.

"Hey," I said, trying to sound like nothing was wrong between us.

"Come to gloat?" Kimber sniffed.

"Gloat?"

I guess my confused tone sounded true because it got her to turn and look at me. "Like you don't know."

"Know what?"

Her eyes narrowed on my face as she studied me, but she found nothing because I really had no idea what she was talking about. After a few minutes of her scrutinizing me she gave up and looked at her feet. "I figured the first place he'd go was to you."

"What are you talking about, Kimber?"

"Cole dumped me."

My breath caught. Why would he do that? Now, it would absolutely look like he was interested in me—at least to Kimber anyway. "I had no idea."

She laughed. It sounded hollow and bitter at the same time. "Right."

I caught her wrist and squeezed. "Really. I didn't know. I'm sorry." But I can't say that I wasn't surprised.

She looked down where I grasped her and then back up at me. For a minute, I thought I caught a glimpse of the friend I used to have. Her aura seemed to shift, ready to change but then the same old colors bloomed back around her. They were the same colors that filled the space around her every time we saw each other anymore: red, brown and some orange. I sighed and released her at the same time that Mrs. Britt stood up and called the meeting to order. The bench we were sitting on vibrated as Cole walked across to slide in next to Logan. He offered his fist to Logan who smiled and bumped his against Cole's. I smiled. Guys were so strange sometimes.

He gave me a little wave, which I returned and then scowled, motioning at Kimber with my head. He grimaced and turned his attention up front. Out of the corner of my eye, I glanced at Kimber who was glaring straight ahead. If she believed me at all before, she didn't now.

The meeting seemed to drag on forever with Mrs. Britt going on about what time to be at the airport and how important it was to be on time. She went over all the airline regulations on security and packing and passports. She handed out info sheets for our parents and packing lists for us along with an itinerary and hotel information. I didn't care about any of this. I only cared about returning the scroll, everything going back to normal, and the chance for Sam and me to be alone.

Sam nudged me in the ribs. *You aren't paying attention.*

It's boring and Kimber's aura is attacking me.

Sam's shoulders shook with his silent laughter and I felt my lips crack into a smile. Logan looked between us, trying to figure out what we were laughing about. When Sam caught him looking, his smile fell away to be replaced with a pensive frown.

What's going on, Sam?

What am I going to do with Logan when we leave for Italy? How can I just leave him alone?

I didn't have a response for that. I hadn't really thought about it, but it was a long time to leave Logan all by himself. *Don't worry. We'll think of something.*

Sam nodded, but I don't think my lame response made him feel any better.

I did my best to pay attention, I really did, but the closer we got to Italy, the more nervous I became. What if something went wrong? What if we got caught trying to sneak away from the class and were unable to return the scroll? From what little research I did online about the Catacombs, they were pretty big with different sections… What if we got lost?

My thoughts were interrupted when Mrs. Britt introduced the teacher's assistant that was coming along on the trip to help chaperone. She was a tall woman with strikingly sharp features and dark brown eyes. Her dark hair was long and curled down her back. When she walked in, most the male students sat up a little straighter.

"This is Ms. Merriweather, everyone. She will be assisting us in our studies abroad." Ms. Merriweather gave us all a wide smile and a small wave. "We are very lucky to have her," Mrs. Britt continued, "because she speaks perfect Italian and has actually lived in Rome for a time. She will be very helpful in getting us around."

The new lady stepped forward and spoke up. "Please, call me Tabitha, and I am very excited to have this opportunity. I'm very sure that we will all have such a wonderful time together."

"What happened to Mrs. Malone?" Cole whispered toward Sam and me.

I shrugged. Mrs. Malone was supposed to be the chaperone with Mrs. Britt. She was the home economics teacher. "I don't know," I whispered back.

As if she heard, Ms. Merriweather's eyes snapped up to where we were sitting. I fell silent and slumped a little in my seat.

"Way to go," Kimber muttered. "Pin us as the bad ones before we even take off."

I didn't bother to reply because Ms. Merriweather was still watching us. I focused on her aura, but it wasn't anything unusual or even stunning. In fact, it looked a lot like my mom and Henry's the last few times I saw them: calm and cool, relaxed and happy with a lot of blues and greens. I hoped that meant that she would be easy to get along with. She looked up at us again and I smiled, hoping to impart the message that we wouldn't be problem students.

From beside me, Kimber groaned then cursed beneath her breath, and without warning, a clipboard slammed across my lap. I jerked and both Sam and Cole whipped around to see what was happening. I focused down on the paper in my lap. It looked like some sort of chart... for hotel roommates.

Uh-oh.

Never mind the fact that we had to share a room, which meant Sam and I weren't going to be able to sleep in the same bed, but I had a sinking suspicion that I wasn't going to like my bunk mate. I scanned the list for my name and used my finger to go across to the next column to see who my roommate would be... Kimber.

Great.

I glanced at Kimber and offered her a tentative smile and she practically sneered at me. "Prepare for a memorable trip, roomie."

My stomach knotted. No way were we going to be able to share a hotel room for two weeks and not kill each other. Just as I was about to raise my hand and request a change, Mrs. Britt announced, "There will be no changes to the roommate roster. I expect everyone to get along and cause no problems... or else."

Wonderful. I glanced at Sam and he patted my leg while pulling the clipboard from my lap. I looked over his shoulder to see who he was paired with. He let out a snort and handed the clipboard across Logan to Cole.

Who'd you get? I asked.

Your brother.

I snickered. That should be interesting.

Finally, the meeting ended and students began filing out. Sam and Logan made their way to the stairs. Kimber stood and gathered her bag and turned to walk away. "Kimber." I reached out and grasped her hand.

Her shoulders tensed, but she turned. "What?"

"Can't we put all this behind us and be friends again?"

"Are you serious? You stole my boyfriend, you've been a lousy best friend, and to top it off you're a liar."

"I've never lied to you," I protested, hating myself. In a way, I *had* lied to her by omitting many things about myself, Sam and even Cole. But those things were only done to protect her, not to harm her.

She snorted. "So you're telling me that Cole didn't dump me because of you?"

"No, he didn't." I turned and looked at Cole for some back up.

He sighed and stepped forward. "Come on, Kimmie."

The use of his nickname for her seemed to anger her more. "Don't call me that."

"Fine." He gritted his teeth. "But, I told you, this is not Heven's fault."

"So you said," she snapped. "But yet every time I turn around, you're at her house, or at her work, hell, you even sat with her today!"

"I thought we were all friends," he said.

"Not anymore," Kimber said, yanking her hand from my grasp and rushing away.

I turned on Cole. "What happened with you two?" I demanded. "You should have told me you broke up."

"It just happened last night."

"Why?"

He shrugged and scrubbed a hand over his face. "It's just things are different now. I *feel* different and Kimmie just…" He sighed and sat down on the bleacher.

"Yeah, I know. You feel different." I reminded him of our little conversation the night he came over and was a little drunk.

"Damn beer," he muttered, shoving a hand through his hair. "It's for the best anyway. I don't want her involved in everything that's going on."

"I get it," I said sadly, sitting down next to him and laying my hand on his shoulder. "Did you at least tell her about our father?"

"No," he said. "I told my mom I wouldn't tell a bunch of people. She isn't dealing with this so well and the idea of word getting out..."

"Yeah. Okay." I stared forward, trying to think of something to say, to do, anything to make any of this easier. Ms. Merriweather was dawdling at the bottom of the bleachers. When I first looked her way, she was staring at us with a thoughtful expression on her face. When she noticed me looking, she turned away, but I had a feeling she was listening to our conversation. Sam and Logan were already standing down at the bottom behind her, waving at me to hurry up.

"Come on," I said, standing. "Let's go."

The four of us walked outside, none of us speaking until we made it to our cars. Cole was the first to climb in his truck and back up, but before driving away, he stopped and rolled his window down. He didn't look at me, though, but at Sam. "So I'll see you later on at the farm... for training?"

Sam's eyes widened like he forgot, but then he nodded. "Yeah."

"Training?" Logan asked. "What kind of training?"

"I'll tell you about it in a few," Sam answered quickly.

I wondered again what was going on with Sam and exactly what it had to do with Logan.

"Cool." Cole nodded at Sam and then gave me a wave before driving away.

"He seems awfully eager to get his butt kicked," Sam mused, watching the truck pull out of sight.

"I don't think he's thinking about getting his butt kicked so much as *who* is going to be kicking it," I murmured.

Sam whistled between his teeth. "Gemma and Cole?"

"He's interested—that much I know. It's all over his aura."

Sam laughed. "Something tells me Gemma would be a handful."

I didn't think it was very funny. Cole already had his hands full with an angry ex-girlfriend hell bent on revenge.

* * *

Maybe what I did next wasn't the most intelligent thing ever, but still. I *had* to see if my friendship with Kimber had any chance of survival. I felt bad for the way things had been going and for the fact that she was hurt. And I knew she was hurting. I have been friends long enough with Kimber to know when she was putting up a front and she definitely was. Kimber was really good at making people see what she wants them to see: a spoiled daddy's girl whose only worry was what to wear the next day and what flavor coffee she was going to drink. She's gotten so good at the charade that even, I, her used-to-be best friend, bought into it.

With Sam spending a few hours this afternoon with Logan (I still didn't know what was going on) and then his training session with Cole and Gemma (a training session he didn't really want me around to watch), I figured that now was as good as any time to see if our friendship was salvageable because, deep down, I still hoped it was.

I turned onto the street that led to her house and drove slowly past the huge lake-front homes while I wondered if she would even let me in.

See, the real Kimber feels as alone and insecure as the rest of us—if not more. Her parents ignore her and barely notice when she is around. She's come to think that having money and popularity is the only way she'll ever get noticed. In a sad way, it's worked for her. But there is a price for popularity, which I learned too well last year after my accident and was left scarred. The more popular you get, the more you have to hide because if one thing gets out that goes against that perfect image you crafted for yourself, then it's all over. Kimber may not realize it, but high school friends are fickle and only looking for the next thing (or person) that can make them feel like somebody. I'd guess that right about now, Kimber's perfectly crafted world is tumbling around her, and her only 'real' anchors (me and Cole) were gone.

I pushed away the niggling thought that maybe Kimber had been using me all those years to gain her popularity and maybe we just weren't that good of friends. I didn't want to think that way. Kimber and I *did* have some great times before my life took a wild turn. I wasn't ready to believe that those good times were all for the sake of her popularity.

I took a deep breath and knocked at the front door, waiting to see who would answer. I was beginning to think no one was going to answer when the door cracked open, and through the small space, I could see Kimber's green eye staring at me.

"Go away." She started to close the door, but I threw my palms against it and pushed.

"I want to talk."

"I'm busy."

"I brought you a mocha with whipped cream..." I sang, dangling the cup in front of the crack.

The door opened and I suppressed a smile. She snatched the cup from my fingers and started to close the door again.

"Hey!" I yelled and pushed myself inside.

"What are you doing here?" she asked.

"Are your parents home?"

"No." With that, she turned on her heel and disappeared from sight. I knew where she was going and followed, making it through her bedroom door just before she slammed it.

"Look," I began, feeling a light breeze from the window and turning. "Why is your window open?"

"Huh?" She placed her coffee on her dresser and went to the window and closed it. "I felt like some air."

"You never open the window. You don't like bugs and your parents run the AC."

"You came all the way over here to discuss my window?" She lifted a brow.

"I wanted to apologize for hurting you. I was hoping we could come to some sort of truce before we leave for Italy."

"You mean so I don't make you miserable during our trip?"

"No," I said, working to hold onto my patience. "I thought we were friends."

"Well we aren't. Not anymore."

"There are things you don't know about Cole," I began. "And when you find out, you'll understand everything. I swear."

She crossed her arms over her chest and glared. "So you know about all of these things that Cole is 'going through?'"

Oh, boy. That didn't really come out right. "Sort of."

She laughed. "You have some nerve. You sure are full of yourself since you got rid of those scars."

The barb stung, but I refused to let it show. "I need you to trust me. When you find out..."

"Tell me now then!" She flung the words at me in challenge.

"I can't. It's not my information to share."

"You can leave now. I have packing to do." She went into her bathroom without looking back.

I looked up at the ceiling and sighed. Coming here had been a huge mistake. Kimber was too angry and hurt to listen. At least I could leave knowing I did everything I could to repair our 'friendship.'

Maybe she was right. Maybe we never had a real friendship to begin with.

Just as I was about to leave, I noticed something sitting on her dresser. I'd been in this room a million times and I had never seen it before. It wasn't very large and looked like a box you might get a bracelet in. It was wood with a small silver clasp on the outside. I found myself moving forward and reaching out to pick it up. My fingers closed over the smooth surface and I realized that it wasn't wood at all-but metal made to look like wood. My fingers itched to open it and see what was lying inside...

"Snoop much?" Kimber snapped and grabbed the box out of my hands, tucking it into the pocket of the fluffy pink robe she was wearing.

"Where'd you get that?"

"That's none of your business."

"What's inside?" I knew she wouldn't answer, but I had to ask.

"Geez, can't you take a hint? Get out!" she yelled. The bathroom door behind her slammed shut as if to punctuate her scream.

Her eyes went wide and she jumped, looking over her shoulder at the door. When she turned back, her face was pale.

"Are you all right?"

"Like you care." The cloud of worry around her dissipated and red took its place.

"I do." I reminded her.

"You need to leave," she said, much softer this time. Another cloud of brownish-yellow surrounded her head.

"You can talk to me, you know."

For a minute, I thought she might say something, but then the walls around her went back up and she said, "I'll talk to you when you talk to me."

"I can't tell you Cole's business." *Or mine.*

Her shoulders slumped and she shoved her hands into the pockets of her robe. I imagined her hand closing tightly over that mysterious box. "Please, go."

I went without looking back. Clearly, she was agitated, and my presence only made things worse. I climbed into Gran's car with a heavy heart. I came here for answers and I got them. Kimber's and my friendship was dead and there was nothing I could do to resurrect it.

Chapter Eleven

Heven

I hated sleeping alone. Without Sam, the bed felt too large, the room too cold. Even though he said he would be here, I watched the minutes turn to hours on the clock. Still no Sam. I tried not to be upset with him because I knew that he wanted to be here.

So I blamed Logan, instead.

But really that wasn't fair, either, because even though Sam hadn't told me yet, I knew that there was a lot going on with Logan. Something must have happened this morning—something that Sam needed to be with Logan for. Still, I couldn't quite ignore the nagging feeling that Logan was trying to keep Sam away.

But why would he want to do that?

Something didn't make sense. I just didn't know what it would be.

I rolled over and punched my pillow, letting out a frustrated sigh and resisted the urge to reach out to Sam and find out what he was doing. Doing so would only distract him and cause him to worry that something might be wrong here. I sat up, taking a sip of water and squeezing the back of my neck with my free hand. The pressure was back, sending small sparks of pain through my brain. I rubbed at my temples next, but nothing I did lessened the pain.

I flopped back onto the pillows and pulled the covers to my chin. With one last look at the clock, I rolled over, putting my back to it. Sam would be here when he could. Until then, I would sleep. I closed my eyes, forcing myself to concentrate on my breathing, taking long, deep breaths. Finally, I drifted into slumber.

I should have stayed awake.

As soon as my body surrendered to sleep, I felt like I was being sucked through a tunnel, all the air being sucked right out of my lungs. My stomach was tossed up into my throat right before I landed forcefully on a hard surface, flat on my back. With a groan, I opened my eyes. It wasn't quite dark, but the lighting was dim and murky. Almost like a terrible storm had just passed, but the black, heavy clouds still hung low in the air, sucking out the life and creating a sallow, depressing cast to everything.

I stood up, noting that I was still dressed in the black shorts and white baby tee I wore to bed. My T-shirt was smudged with something that looked like soot. The back of my head throbbed as I took stock of where I was. The landscape around me was colorless and barren. The rocky, uneven ground consisted of dirt and chunks of shale that cut into my bare feet. It appeared that there once might have been trees, but now they were nothing more than broken limbs and stumps jutting out of the ground. All of them looked like they had burned in a fire. It would explain the soot on my clothes and the ash in the air. It would explain the desolate, dead way everything appeared.

Come to me.

I felt the power in his voice. It was raw and strong, and before I could think better of it, I was walking forward. I knew I should be frightened, part of me was. The other part of me knew that I was dreaming. People couldn't get hurt in their dreams, could they? I didn't think so. I walked on, curious about this place and the pull of the power that summoned me.

As I walked, the world around me changed very little. I came upon a river flowing alongside where I walked; its water was thick and black like oil. And it smelled. It smelled of sulfur and death. I veered away from the water, feeling a little sick, and came upon a valley. Before venturing down, I stopped on the hill and studied the scene below me.

There were demons. Lots of them. Some were fighting with one another, screaming and biting, causing pain where they could. Others were raiding the few shacks that scattered the area. The tiny broken buildings would shudder under the attacks, but none fell down. A few small fires burned around them, but no one seemed to care. I took a step backward, wanting to get away from the horrible scene. Unfortunately, my movement caught their attention.

Every demon below stopped what they were doing and turned toward me. I felt the hatred and excitement from their beady, soulless eyes burn right through my core.

Screw this dream. It was time to wake up. *Please, wake up.*

Bring her to me, the powerful voice ordered and the demons tripped over themselves to comply. I ran, the sharp shale and rocks stabbing into my feet, but I didn't care. I just wanted to get away. The demons followed me, all of them much bigger and faster than I, and I was quickly trampled from behind. I didn't stay down long, though; I was pulled up by various rough hands. I screamed and fought, kicking and scratching when I could, but they were too strong. One demon thought I was funny and began laughing in a high-pitched wheezing noise that hurt my ears. I looked over and immediately regretted it.

He had sharp, pointy teeth that were grotesquely small for his large gums and mouth. His eyes were far apart and tiny, black pin pricks in his head. He stuck out his tongue, which was a long, black thing that seemed to have a mind of its own. When it reared up in my direction, I saw the red eyes and screamed. His tongue wasn't a tongue; it was a snake. The snake hissed and shot forward. I tried to knock it away, but my hands were pinned and so were my legs as the demons carried me forward.

Do not harm her!

The demons grumbled and moaned, but the snake retreated back into the demon's mouth and I shut my eyes and prayed. The demons grew quiet, their steps slowed and they dumped me onto the ground. I sprang up, catching them off guard and lashed out with my fist, connecting with something solid. The thing screamed and grabbed me. After watching Sam fight so many times and hearing Gemma's recent instructions about fighting, I struck out with a solid fist.

It felt like I was pushing my hand through sand.

I pushed harder.

The demon fell to the ground at my feet and did not move.

All the other demons stared at me in shock. I was a little shocked too. I could defend myself! I just killed a demon.

Warm, rich laughter filled my ears. *I knew you had it in you.*

I shuddered. It was not Sam who congratulated me.

A loud, shrieking sound came from behind and the demons began running, leaving their dead comrade at my feet. What could possibly scare away a demon?

Fear threatened to incapacitate me when a huge dark shape floated through the gray sky. It was so big that if there had been a shining sun, it would have completely blocked out the warm rays. It had a wingspan unmatched in size and I was momentarily reminded of the dinosaur museum we visited in third grade.

Except dinosaurs were extinct.

Right?

Its head was wide and square with a snout that stretched its face, elongating its intimidating looks and turning them to frightening. Thick, pointy teeth in several rows met like knives in the center of its mouth. The teeth were so large that its lips could not cover them even though it appeared to have its mouth closed.

As it lowered itself closer to the ground — and to me — large, vein-filled wings flapped almost lazily but still with enough power to blow my hair into my face, which I pushed away to stare at the creature.

I had been right. Dinosaurs are extinct.

But apparently, dragons existed.

It landed with a thump just feet away.

The dragon had a fat, protruding belly and sharp spines along its back and tail. Horns seemed to rip right out of its head and curve possessively toward the sky. Its eyes were small compared to the rest of its head, but they found me and stared, drilling a hole right through me. As it stared it tilted its head to one side.

I took a step backward and it hissed.

I stumbled and fell. Strong arms wrapped around me from behind.

The dragon swooped forward, hunching over the demon I just killed. It sniffed the body, then looked back up at me. Could it tell I was the one responsible?

Its eyes were gold like Sam's. They were not nearly as hypnotizing or beautiful and the gold color was not pure, but there was something in them that made me pause.

"Come, little one, The Devourer is not a pet."

I paid little attention to the man hauling me away, but kept my eyes locked on the dragon. Finally, it snorted and looked down. Its huge jaws opened and I expected it to bite. Instead, a whirring noise filled the air and everything around us began vibrating and pulling forward. My hair whipped forward as did my clothes. The dragon was sucking in air?

"We must go," the voice said and began to tow me faster. The sucking seemed to have no effect on him.

My last sight before being pulled completely away was a white shape being dragged out of the dead demon and float into the dragon's mouth. The demon then turned to ash and settled into the blackened earth.

The sucking around me stopped.

The dragon flew away.

I was dragged onto the drawbridge of a very creepy looking castle.

* * *

"What do you think?" the man asked, gesturing to the castle.

I was busy studying him. Power radiated from every pore. It was the kind of power that you could get drunk on; it pulled you in and made you want more. I took a step back. He chuckled.

He had hair the color of midnight and lips the color of blood. His skin was pale, like it hadn't seen the sun in years. Looking at the sky, it probably hadn't. He wasn't handsome; his features were too rough for that. His nose was a little crooked and his front tooth was chipped. His frame was large, corded with muscle, but on a closer look, he was not as large as he first appeared. The power he radiated made him look and feel bigger. The one thing that did not radiate around him was an aura. He was without one and I wondered what it meant. His looks were not unpleasant, some might find him appealing, but I was used to seeing a sun-kissed golden boy with steel in his back and love in his heart. I was certain this man did not know about love.

"I asked you, how do you like it!?" he roared, his voice stinging my ears. I forced myself not to cringe and turned my attention to the castle.

It was impressive. If you liked Goth architecture. The place was incredibly large with walls that were made of black, unpolished granite. There were iron bars for windows and a gloppy moat of that thick, gross water all around. There was a tower to the right that rose out of the structure and jutted into the sky. From inside the walls, I heard screaming.

I shrugged, trying to seem bored. "It's okay."

Anger, strong and hot, burned through his eyes, which were an alarming shade of blue. But then they flashed red. "You dare speak to me that way?"

My stomach cramped. Show no fear. That's what Sam would say. What I wouldn't give to see him right now. I lifted my chin. "Yes."

With a roar, he reached into the oily water and pulled out a demon. It was the same kind that tried to kill me before: half crocodile, half man. He ripped its head off without pause and threw the head at me. It whizzed by, making all the hair on my arms stand on end. The headless body fell back into the water. With his show of temper gone, he laughed, chuckled actually. I wanted to run. "Your defiance surprises me."

"I'm leaving," I stated, having no clue how to get myself to wake up. This dream was so real I would have sworn I was in this place.

He laughed. I took that as a no to my previous statement. "Where am I?"

"Learn the place well, little one. Someday you will call it home."

Never. I would die first. "Do you live here?"

"When it suits me."

I began to feel detached from this place, like I was viewing it from afar. I welcomed the sensation.

He screamed and punched the ground. "You will not go until I allow it!"

My head began pounding, the front and back warring with each other again. "What do you want?" Although I already knew.

"Tell me where you hide the Map. Give it to me. I will make you my queen and you will rule here." Power rushed toward me, calling me forward. I denied it.

I still didn't know where here was. "Never." I took a step back as the world around me began to fade. I wanted to go home.

He screamed, his eyes turning red and I knew he was going to hurt me. I squeezed my eyes shut.

Nothing happened.

When I opened my eyes, I was in bed. I gasped and sat up, pressing myself against the headboard, and glanced at the clock. I had only been asleep for an hour. It felt like eternity.

"I'm sorry I'm so late, baby."

My eyes snapped over to the foot of the bed where Sam was sitting, pulling off his shoes. God, my head hurt.

"Sam?" I whispered, hoarse.

His eyes flashed up to mine, gold sparking the hazel depths. "Someone was here?" He leapt to his feet and prowled around the room. He stopped at the window, making sure he had locked it behind him, then paced around, looking for someone to kill.

"No one," I rushed out. "I had a bad dream."

Was it really a dream? It felt so real. My head wouldn't stop pounding, leaving me feeling exhausted and weak.

"Again?" He rushed to my side.

His quick movements made me dizzy and I leaned over the bed to retch. Thankfully, my belly was empty so nothing came up.

"Oh, Hev." He scooped me up, making the world tilt again. My stomach heaved.

"Head hurts…" A tremor stole through my body. I knew the feeling. It was exactly the same from when my aura reading ability exploded into my head. Was a new supernatural power trying to assert itself?

He looked me over, panic seeping into his golden eyes. "Your clothes are filthy,"

"It wasn't a dream?" I groaned, my head hammering. My limbs began to shake uncontrollably.

The next thing I knew, Sam was leaping out the window with me in his arms, landing in the darkened yard.

Another tremor licked through my body, making me moan.

Sam tilted his head to the sky and roared "Airis!"

My eyes fastened on a star that was shooting from the sky. It looked like a tear, trailing through the clouds. Everything went white.

* * *

"Something is wrong with her," Sam said urgently. His loud whisper only irritated the pain shooting through my skull.

"Bring her to me," I heard Airis say from a short distance away, but I didn't lift my head from Sam's chest to look.

I felt a soothing hand touch my cheek and peace and light flowed through me. The warring sides of my skull called a truce and left me peacefully alone. I let out a sigh.

"Thank you," I told her, feeling better than I had in days.

She inclined her head.

"How did you do that?" Sam asked, his voice holding a trace of bitterness.

If Airis noticed the bitter tone Sam spoke with, she pretended she hadn't. She looked down at me serenely and smiled. "Celestials have the ability to heal, but I am afraid that it is only temporary."

The thought of another round of skullboxing made me want to cry.

"What's going on?" Sam demanded.

"It is good you came to me," Airis continued, her eyes glancing at Sam. "There is something you need to know."

"I'll do anything for Heven," he said, and there seemed to be some type of warning to his voice. Now wasn't the time to ask him about it, so I pushed it away and wiggled out of his arms. When I was on my feet, I faced Airis. I knew whatever she had to say was not good, but I couldn't run away.

"Something's gotten into my head," I said with certainty.

Sam's eyes widened.

Airis nodded. "I'm afraid so. There are a few very powerful demons that house a very rare ability. When a person loses consciousness, their mind becomes vulnerable. Dream Walkers forge a path into your mind and leave behind a thread so that they may find their way back. They can then come and go as they please, but the person must be asleep."

"Why would they do this?" Sam asked.

"In Heven's case, the demon must be trying to discover the location of the Treasure Map."

"The demon from the lake," I began. "It must have happened then. He tried to get me to tell him where the scroll was, but I wouldn't. He's been looking around in my head ever since."

"How do we get him out?" Sam demanded.

"It is very important that you do it quickly," Airis explained. "The longer he is there, the more power he gets. If left there long enough, you won't have to be asleep for him to get in your mind."

I thought of the place he dragged me to and of his anger and power that he gave off, and I shuddered. I thought of him demanding that I be his queen.

Sam jerked like he'd been slapped and stared at me. *Queen? It's never going to happen.* I assured him.

"You've already begun trying to destroy the thread." Airis told me.

"I have?"

"Yes. The headaches," Airis began, but I cut her off.

"The two parts of my head fighting with each other."

"Your newest supernatural ability is trying to assert itself, but first, it must rid your mind of what doesn't belong. If your new power asserts itself too early, then the demon could use it to gain knowledge that you don't want it to have."

"How do we get this thing out of Heven's head?" Sam asked, pacing around in front of me. I was busy trying to wrap my head around the idea of another new ability.

"Destroy the thread," Airis said simply.

I laughed. Like it would be that easy.

"How?"

Before responding, Airis glanced behind her like she heard something that we could not. She turned back around to say swiftly, "Use your Mindbond."

Sam nodded, grim.

"I must go," Airis said.

A muffled, far away voice carried to me. "Please, Airis, let me in."

There were no doors in the white space that surrounded us. I couldn't understand how someone would be kept out or why. Airis glanced at me worried, and I was confused.

"Please," the voice said again. Something familiar stroked over me.

"Goodbye," Airis said, stepping forward to lay her hand upon us to send us home.

I couldn't allow it. I jumped back. "Wait! Who is that?"

"You must go," Airis said, looking more flustered than ever.

"Dad?" I asked, whispering his name in awe.

Airis became alarmed and grabbed me.

"Dad!"

But it was too late.

Everything went white.

* * *

The soft pad of Sam's thumb brushed over my cheek to catch a tear and carry it away. I watched as he brought his thumb to his lips and sucked. *No more crying, sweetheart.*

I couldn't stop. So close to my father, yet so far away. I replayed his voice over and over again in my head. The voice I thought I would never hear again. Renewed sadness swept through me and fresh tears fell. Why was he there in the InBetween with Airis? Why wouldn't she let him see me?

I stared up at the clear blue sky and considered screaming again. Sam knew my intention and tightened his arms around me, trapping me in his embrace. "Screaming will not get you anywhere. Airis is stubborn when she decides she's done helping someone."

"You seem mad at her," I said, momentarily forgetting about screaming to the heavens.

"When Airis makes up her mind not to help, there isn't anything that can change it."

"What?" I said, wiping the last of my tears away.

"We can talk about Airis later. It isn't important right now."

"If it's important to you; then it is to me."

He smiled. "I know. But the day has been long enough already."

I looked back up at the sky. Sam was right. Screaming for Airis wasn't going to bring her back. I could beg and demand all I wanted, but nothing would make her come back. My father was gone. I lost him again.

We were quiet as we went back into the house and up into my room. I looked at the bed with a mix of longing and fear. I was so tired, but it seemed like sleep was the enemy now. Who knew what that Dream Walker would do next? Sam kicked off his shoes and unfastened his jeans with a yawn and yanked them down over his hips, tossed them on the floor with his shoes and climbed in bed without a word. I stood there a little shocked, staring at him. When he caught my stare he frowned.

"I wasn't thinking. I'll grab some shorts." He made a move to toss the covers back.

"No," I protested, moving forward, recovering from my momentary shock. It wasn't that I was all naïve and embarrassed, I mean, we had been sleeping in the same bed for a while now, but this was the first time he hadn't put on a pair of shorts. "It's okay. It's not like I haven't seen your boxers before."

He yawned widely. "I'm so damn tired."

Something inside me warmed. I liked that he was comfortable enough to just toss his pants on the floor without thinking about shorts. I liked the fact that he would admit to being exhausted. It was a new side to him, a *closer* side to him. He wasn't just an invincible hellhound who could deal with everything. He might be rock solid, he might be heroic, but he was *real*. He might be able to dish out an ass kicking, but it made him tired. Part of me was secretly thrilled he felt comfortable enough to show me that side of him.

"There are a couple hours till morning. Try to sleep."

"Oh, there'll be no trying. But then I gotta head home, *after* you are awake."

I didn't bother to tell him I wasn't going back to sleep. "Aren't you training with Gemma again in the morning?"

He made a sound I took as a yes.

"What happened with Logan, Sam?" I knew his brother was the reason he was late and needed to get home. I wondered if it had anything to do with Airis.

"Sam?" I asked again, after he didn't respond.

The soft sound of a snore reached me through the dark. He hadn't been kidding, he was exhausted and he was also asleep.

*   *   *

I gotta go. Sam said, and I felt brief kisses on the tip of my nose, my temple and then both my eyelids. I smiled and stretched out like a cat. I was too comfortable to get up. I didn't want to. Then reality came bubbling to the surface and I realized I had been asleep. After I swore I wouldn't sleep the rest of the night.

I fell asleep. I said, my eyes popping open. Sam had already tossed his legs over the bed and was pulling on his jeans. He paused to look over his shoulder.

You were exhausted. Besides that, the Dream Walker knew he better stay out or I'd clobber him. He held up his fist and shook it at me with a grin.

I giggled.

That's a nice sound to wake up to.

I let my eyes stray down his bare back. I think I had the better view.

He stood up and shoved his feet into his shoes. I glanced at the window. There was barely any light filtering in around the blinds. *It's early.*

I gotta go check on Logan. He paused and looked at me. *I'm worried about him, Hev. Something isn't right.*

I stilled. Did he finally seem to grasp what I had been feeling all along about his brother?

I think he might be sick. I think his body is rejecting the hellhound gene.

Is that even possible? I asked, sitting up and pushing my hair behind my ears. So Sam wasn't thinking what I was, but if he was right, then I felt incredibly guilty for ever thinking anything bad about Logan.

I don't know. He shook his head, his face grim. *I need to keep an eye on him. I'm going to bring him back here with me this morning. Do you think you could stay here at the house with him while I go train with Gemma and Cole?*

Of course. He can have breakfast with us.

Sam visibly relaxed. *Thanks, Hev. That makes me feel better.*

I smiled. He pressed a quick kiss to my lips and then went to the window, pulling up the blind. *You'll be able to stay awake?*

Yep. Wide awake. I peeled my eyelids back with my fingers and stared at him.

He grinned. *I'll see you in a little while.*

I blew him a kiss and watched as he jumped out of the window. I hadn't exactly planned to spend my morning with Logan. I had planned to follow Sam and Cole to training and make Gemma include me. I climbed out of bed and gathered some things for a long, hot shower. Maybe it would be good to spend some time with Logan. Maybe it would give us a chance to get to know one another better.

I just hoped I liked what I got to know.

* * *

Gran was already in the kitchen when I went downstairs. She was drinking a cup of coffee and reading the newspaper.

"Wow, I thought I would be the first one up," I said, heading for the coffee.

"You were, but I didn't have to do my hair." Gran laughed.

Normally I wouldn't have either, but I felt like looking nice. "I have to work this afternoon."

"Well, you look wonderful."

"Thanks," I said, taking a sip of hot, sweet coffee.

"It's such a shame," Gran said, gazing at the newspaper.

"What is?" I asked, leaning back against the counter while I thought about making something special for breakfast.

162

"There seems to be a rash of vandalism in town lately. Did Sam say anything to you about it?"

"No... should he have?"

"Well, no, but it says here that the second-hand store that is below his apartment was one of the victims of the vandalism. Everything in the store was destroyed. All the money was missing too."

"That's awful!" I exclaimed. "Maybe he doesn't know."

Gran nodded. "That wasn't the only place vandalized and robbed either. Just two blocks over, that little bakery was destroyed too." Gran made a tsking sound. "She made such good cupcakes."

"Did the police find who did it?"

Gran shook her head. "No. There was one eyewitness who said that, around the estimated time of the bakery vandalism, they were driving on the street next to it and saw a man with a mask run into an alleyway."

A shiver raced up my spine. "People can be so cruel."

Gran made a sound of agreement and flipped to a new page. "Enough with that. I think I will enjoy the crossword puzzle."

I handed her a pencil, added more coffee to my mug and sat down across from her as we tried to solve some of the harder clues. A little while later, there was a knock on the door. Before I got up to answer it, the door opened and Cole stuck his head in. "I smell coffee."

"Cole!" Gran said, smiling and waved her hand. "Come in, come in."

I gave him a wave and motioned for the coffee. "Coffee's fresh."

He headed straight for it.

"What brings you by so early this morning?" Gran asked.

The coffee pot froze halfway to his cup. Clearly, he didn't think about needing a cover story for training. Then he seemed to recover and as he poured he said, "Woke up early and decided to come see two of my favorite ladies."

"Well, let me get some pancakes and bacon cooking," Gran said, jumping up from her chair. Cole passed her and laid a kiss on her cheek. Her aura flared with pink, a shade so pure and clear that my breath caught. It meant so much to her to have her long lost grandson—the child she thought she would never know—here.

I smiled at Cole when she turned away and mouthed *thank you*.

He shrugged like it was nothing. I don't think he realized what he meant to her. To me.

But maybe he did because his aura was blooming with pink too.

Before the pancakes were even finished, I heard footsteps on the porch and I got up to open the door for Sam and Logan.

"Well, Logan!" Gran said. "So good to see you! Just in time for some breakfast."

Logan smiled as I looked him over, trying not to be obvious. He looked okay. He didn't look sick.

"Why don't you come over here and help me flip," Gran said, holding out a spatula to Logan. He grinned and grabbed the utensil.

Logan was still putting down the pancakes when Sam got up from the table. "I need to get to the chores. Lots to do and I have to work this afternoon." He put his plate in the sink and turned to Logan.

"You go on, Sam. Logan can stay here and finish eating."

"I'll keep him company." I smiled.

"I'll give you a hand," Cole said and got up from the table. "It'll go faster."

Sam nodded. "I'll warn you. I have some stuff in the orchard that I need to do. Think you can handle it?"

Nice, he just gave them both a reason for going out there.

"Bring it on," Cole said cheerfully and I wondered if he was thinking about Gemma.

"I'll feed the horses," I told Sam as he was heading out the door.

He winked.

After the dishes were done and put away, the crossword filled in, and the coffee was long drunk, I slipped on some shoes and grabbed the door handle. "I'm going to go feed the horses."

Gran had Logan busy chopping up strawberries for a strawberry pie, so I figured it was a good time to get away. After I volunteered to feed the horses, I realized that I didn't really want Logan in the barn because that's where the Treasure Map was buried. Not that I thought Logan would know it, but it still made me edgy to have him in the same place that it was.

After the horses were fed, I was in the tack room, putting away the bag of carrots that I fed the horses for treats when I heard the horses begin to stir. Jasper made a sound that he only made when he was distressed. I slammed the refrigerator door shut and rushed for the door, only to run right into Logan.

I gasped and stepped back. "Logan! You scared me." I laughed.

"Sorry, I didn't mean to. I just wanted to see the horses. Sam says you ride." He looked young and eager and it disarmed me. He wouldn't know that the Map was here, so what was the harm?

"Yes, I've been riding since I was little." I brushed by him and headed toward Jasper's stall. "This is my horse, Jasper."

"He's big," Logan said, staying in the doorway.

"He's uneasy right now because you're a new person. Animals are sensitive to new people." To hellhounds.

"How do you know? Can you see their aura's too?" Logan asked, staring at me.

I shifted beneath his gaze. "You know I can see auras?"

He nodded. "Of course. Sam told me when I first came to town." He smirked like he finally had gotten one up on me and managed to catch me off guard.

I shrugged, faking that I didn't really care. "It's really no big deal, seeing people's auras." But for some reason it felt like a big deal that Logan knew about it. I never advertised my ability. It was something that I kept close so I could use it to my full advantage. I mean sure, even if people knew about it, they couldn't lie about their aura, but they could make it harder to read by throwing all kinds of other feelings at me that I would have to dig through to get to the real stuff.

"So what's mine look like?" Logan asked, taking a step closer.

I wanted to step back but I didn't, instead I held my ground. "I can't see yours. Or Sam's. I can't see any animal's aura."

"But I'm a person," Logan said, confused momentarily and looking like a fourteen -year -old.

"Of course you are. But best I can figure, the hellhound in you is an animal, which masks your aura."

"Stupid hellhound," Logan muttered. He seemed to become agitated and began tapping his foot.

"I was just about to turn them out into the pasture. Want to walk with me?" As I hoped, the distraction seemed to work, seemed to pull him back from whatever was going on in his head. I showed him the lead line that I used to escort each horse and how to hook it to their bridles. He walked with me as I took out each horse, one by one, to the green pasture and turned them out. He seemed interested, asking all kinds of questions about the animals and I found myself relaxing and enjoying the time with him.

After the last horse was turned out, we walked back into the barn to put away the lead line.

"Sam's learning how to fight in his human form," he said.

"Did he tell you that?" Sam seemed to be telling Logan a lot.

Logan nodded. "Those demons just keep attacking you."

Something cold slithered down my spine.

"I bet you're scared you're going to die."

I looked at him. He seemed older than he had about five minutes ago. "I try not to think about that too much," I said slowly.

"So where did you put the scroll?"

"It's a secret."

"I won't tell anyone. You can trust me."

Could I? "Are you feeling okay, Logan? Maybe we should go inside so you can get some water." Maybe he was sick and it was causing him to have mood swings.

"I'm fine," he said and smiled.

I went about closing and latching the stall doors then headed for the barn doors. "You know you should tell someone where the scroll is, that way if something happens to you, we'll know where it is."

I stopped and turned. "I don't think anything will happen to me. Besides, Sam knows where it is." Maybe the mention of his brother would cut the weird.

"You never know." He took several steps toward me, like he was prowling. "Sam can't always be where you are."

I took a step closer to him. *Show him you aren't afraid.* "Are you threatening me?"

His eyes glinted, the color of burnt orange. "Tell me where it is."

"No."

"Is it here?" He looked around, up toward the loft. "Up there?"

"It isn't here," I said firmly.

He took another menacing step toward me and I held my ground. I would not let him threaten me. I wouldn't.

Even if he did scare the hell out of me.

Chapter Twelve

Sam

My teeth snapped together and pain shot through my jaw when I hit the tree and bounced off. Automatically, I gained my balance and dropped into a fighting crouch, but my heart just wasn't in it.

My thoughts kept straying to my brother and to Heven—who I left alone with my brother. My brother who just wasn't well. I knew Heven was uncomfortable around him. I could feel it. I pretended not to, but pretending something wasn't wrong didn't make it go away.

If anything pretending made something worse.

Gemma appeared at my side and I sprang into action, kicking out my leg, knocking her feet out from beneath her and then pouncing. We rolled across the ground and I delivered a few hard hits. They were harder than I usually delivered—even though she told me not to hold back because she was a girl—sometimes I did. Except for right now.

I was suddenly angry. Angry at everything, angry at Airis for not helping me, angry at myself for not knowing what to do, even angry at my brother for being sick.

Gemma went with my fight, matching it, challenging it. We ended up near a pile of weapons and I chucked a few daggers into a nearby tree just because I could. She deflected my kicks but she wasn't able to spin me or herself away.

I kept coming.

"What the hell?" Cole said, coming over to where we were.

I spun on him and advanced. He dropped into a crouch, not a hint of fear on his face.

Stupid.

Gemma inserted herself between us, blocking my path to Cole. "That was good. Why don't you take five?"

I was breathing heavy, my chest rising and falling rapidly, but as she spoke, some of my anger drained away and I grimaced. "Sorry, I didn't mean to attack you like that. You okay?"

She lifted a brow. "Do I look injured? Are you doubting my skills?"

"You are most definitely the toughest fallen angel I know."

She rolled her eyes. "I'm the only fallen angel you know."

Cole stepped around Gemma. "What's up with you?"

I sighed. "Nothing. I guess I'm just not feeling this right now."

It's a good thing Gemma stopped me when she did because Cole just wasn't as strong as she was, and then I would have had to explain to Heven why I creamed her brother.

"Why don't you go back to the house? That's where you want to be anyway. Maybe we can meet up tonight for one last session before you leave tomorrow?"

I nodded. "I get off work at seven. I'll meet you here."

I didn't waste any more time, but headed to the house. Behind me I could hear Gemma and Cole still training.

I couldn't stop thinking about Logan. I was leaving for Rome tomorrow and he couldn't come with me. But I didn't want to leave him home alone, either. What if something happened? What if he had one of his "fits" and trashed something or hurt someone? What if he hurt himself? But I couldn't stay home with him. I had to go with Heven and return that scroll. Once the Map was in its rightful place, hopefully the demon attacks on Hev would stop and I could focus more on helping Logan.

I rapped lightly on the kitchen door and heard Gran call out, so I let myself in. She was standing at the small island making what looked like a pie crust.

"Chores all done?" she asked with a smile. She had a smudge of flour on her nose.

"Yes, ma'am."

"Wash up there and get yourself a drink. You must be thirsty."

I went to the sink and did as she asked, watching the grime on my hands from my training flowing down the drain. When I was done, I grabbed a bottle of water from the fridge.

"Where's Heven and Logan?"

"Heven went to feed the horses. Logan just went out there a few minutes ago to join her."

My eyes strayed to the door. I wasn't sure how I felt about Logan and Heven being alone together. "I'll go see what they are up to."

"Sam? Before you go, is everything all right? You seem worried."

I stopped halfway to the door and turned. "I'm worried about leaving Logan here by himself while I'm in Italy."

"Ahh," Gran said. "He's not going home?"

I felt my shoulders slump. I was so tired of lying and making up stories. "No. My parents... they can be kind of hard to live with. It's the reason I'm emancipated. When I left home, things got a lot harder for Logan. He doesn't want to go back there and I can't make him."

It wasn't the whole truth, but it was some of it. Just that little bit of truth actually made me feel better.

Gran picked up a kitchen towel and began wiping flour off her hands. "That must be very hard for you. Caring for a younger brother must be tough, considering how young you are yourself."

I nodded.

"Sam, I want you to know that you are always welcome in my home. Logan too. I see how you look at Heven..." She turned to grab two pie plates, and with her back turned, she said, "I know how you take care of her."

It almost seemed for a moment that she understood more than we thought. But then she turned around with a smile and began assembling two pies.

"Why don't you bring Logan here to stay while you are gone? I'll watch over him."

It would be the answer to my worry about Logan. Unfortunately, it would give me new worry. Gran was like the family I never had. She was unbelievably kind and loving. The thought of leaving Logan here and him accidently hurting her in one of his "fits" left me feeling cold inside.

"Thank you for the offer but Logan is... he's been hard to deal with... I think he's having a hard time adjusting and he can be a real handful. I don't want to put that on you."

She didn't seem the least bit concerned. "I think I can handle one sullen teenage boy. I used to be married to a police officer, you know. And my son was one too. They taught me a thing or two."

She winked as she poured what looked like a strawberry mixture into the pie shells.

Even so, her strength would be no match for Logan's. If he went into a rage, there would be no stopping him. "Heven's grandfather was a police officer too?"

"Oh, yes. Best cop on the force." She smiled fondly.

"How… how long has he been gone?" My curiosity got the better of my manners as the question tumbled right out of my mouth.

"A long time, almost seventeen years ago. He died when Heven was just a baby." She looked up from her work and seemed lost in a memory. "He loved that girl more than life itself."

Then her thoughts seem to clear and she glanced at me then back at her pies.

I shouldn't have asked. Really it wasn't my business and I didn't want to upset her. "I'll go check on Heven and Logan now."

I pushed open the door and stepped out onto the porch.

"Sam? Think about it. Logan is welcome here anytime."

I thanked her and then walked toward the barn. I was tempted to leave Logan here at the farm, but something inside me just couldn't say yes. I wanted to protect Gran from all of this, and what would happen to Heven if something were to go wrong with Gran? Yes, Heven and her mother's relationship was a lot better than it used to be. Even I, who thought I would never forgive her mother for telling Heven she was evil, could see the genuine good in her. But even still, I knew that the farm was where Heven belonged. This was her true home.

When I reached the barn door a skittering of fear ran over my body. I wasn't afraid, so that meant that Heven must be. I resisted the urge to burst through the door to see where the threat was because along with her fear I was also feeling her effort to control it, to make it go away.

A very bad feeling that Logan was behind this sunk into me.

I stepped up to the door and listened, focusing on the voices just inside the barn.

"You never know," Logan said, his voice sounded different than usual, deeper somehow. "Sam can't always be where you are."

What was he saying? Why would he speak to her like that?

"Are you threatening me?" Heven's voice sounded strong, but I knew that she was frightened.

"Tell me where it is."

"No."

"Is it here?" There was a slight pause; then he said, "Up there?"

"It isn't here," Heven insisted and I had enough.

I grabbed the barn door and opened it, trying not to just fling it, trying to hide the simmering frustration beneath my skin. *Remember that he's sick. He doesn't mean what he's saying, the way he's acting,* I told myself.

"Hey guys, what's going on?" I tried to sound casual.

"Sam! Heven was showing me the horses!" I could sense the change come over him and I suddenly understood why Heven was always so uncomfortable around him. He acted different when I wasn't around—who knows the things he has said and done to her.

And she never said a word. She never complained.

"Cool, huh?" I answered Logan.

"Yeah. I wish you would have let me train with you."

"Maybe next time." Maybe training would teach him control. Maybe it would help.

"Are you guys done already?" Heven asked, moving closer to me.

"Almost. Gemma and Cole are just finishing up."

Heven nodded. "Let's go back to the house. I was just offering Logan some water."

Heven hurried outside to close the door. I looked at her. *Something wrong?*

No, everything's fine.

Once again she covered for my brother. I realized that she was trying not to put me in the middle. She wanted me to have my brother in my life even if it was hard on her.

At the porch Heven stopped and said, "Why don't you guys go ahead in. I want to walk out and say hi to Gemma before she leaves."

I wanted to say something, but I couldn't. I didn't know what to say. Even if Logan was acting strange, I couldn't abandon him.

"Sam, are you coming?" Logan asked, going up the steps.

I looked back at Heven, wondering if she just wanted to get away from my brother.

I want to ask Gemma about my dad.

Ahh, so maybe not all of this had been about Logan. She was worried about her dad. Heven started off toward the orchard, and I heard her sigh.

I stuck my head into the kitchen where Gran and Logan were. "I'll be right back,"

I didn't wait for Logan to answer because I knew — I knew that he would act like he wanted me to stay. I wanted to be there for him, but I wanted to be there for Heven too, and even though she wasn't asking for my attention, I wanted to give it to her.

I caught up to her easily and reached out for her arm. "Hey."

She stopped walking and turned. "Hey." She looked over my shoulder for Logan.

"I left him in the house with Gran."

I slid my hand from her wrist to wrap my fingers around hers. "What did I walk in on back there?"

"I was showing him the horses and barn."

"You're upset, scared. Tell me what happened."

She sighed. "It was nothing. Logan and I... It's just taking longer to bond with him than I hoped." Before I could say anything she continued. "But I won't give up. He's your brother and that makes him family. We'll get there."

I lifted her hand to my lips. "If he... treats you bad, scares you... You can come to me, okay? He's my brother and I won't abandon him but you... You're my heart and I won't let him hurt you."

Her fingers tightened on mine and seconds later, Gemma and Cole came into sight. Gemma was smiling at something and Cole looked pleased with himself.

I think she likes him. I said, thinking about the way she put herself between us. *She's easier on him than me.*

Heven poked me in the ribs. *You have an advantage over him in the strength department.*

I laughed. *She doesn't look at me the way she does him.*

Thank goodness.

I looked over at her, admiring her shining blond hair and the way it fell over her blue eyes. "I've been thinking about the Dream Walker."

She winced like just the mention of it made her head hurt. It probably did. "What about him?"

I pulled her close, my lips hovering just above hers as the chemistry between us spiked... there... I snapped my eyes up to hers and she gasped, her hand coming up to her throat.

"It's him," she said, realizing what I was showing her. "The Dream Walker is what you have been sensing inside me. It's why you have the urge to shift when you're with me sometimes."

I pulled back and nodded. "I think so."

"It makes sense." She laughed.

"Why are you laughing?"

"Because it means that it wasn't me!"

"I never thought it was you in the first place," I answered, shaking my head. I should have realized she would think that it was her.

She wrapped her arms around my neck, bouncing with her happiness. I hugged her back with a chuckle. Gemma was waving at us and Heven pulled back and walked over. She didn't waste any time on small talk.

"Can you go to the InBetween?"

Gemma didn't seem to mind the abrupt question. "Sure."

"Could you take me with you?"

"Yeah. Why?"

"I think my dad's there."

Gemma shook her head, and beside her, Cole stiffened at the mention of his father. "Can't be."

"Why?"

"The InBetween is a temporary place that people who die pass through. No one ever stays there."

"But I heard him." Tears swam in her eyes and she blinked them back. Cole crossed his arms over his chest, frowning.

"Did you see him?" Gemma asked.

Heven shook her head and I took her hand, offering quiet support.

"He was probably on the other side. In Heaven. He wouldn't be able to get to the InBetween unless a Celestial, like Airis, brought him."

"Could you bring him?"

"I can't go into Heaven. Fallen angel, remember?"

"Oh."

"Ask Airis to bring him."

"She shipped us out of there fast when she realized I heard him yelling. She doesn't want me to see him."

"Then she must have a good reason. You can trust Airis."

It was hard to accept that.

"You saw him?" Cole asked Heven, his voice low. "Why were you there, in the InBetween?" I was a little surprised he didn't want to know more about their father. Of course, Cole has kind of made it clear that he didn't consider Heven's father his true dad.

To spare Heven a drawn-out explanation that would only upset her; I gave Cole a quick, but thorough, overview of everything that happened from the last time we last saw him, even explaining about the Dream Walker. When I explained about their father, he drew Heven in for a hug.

"Sorry you had to go through that," Cole whispered.

"I would have loved just a few minutes with him." Heven's voice was muffled against his shirt.

"At least you know he's safe and well somewhere," Cole told her.

She pulled back and studied his face. "You're not upset?"

He shrugged. "I'm upset you're upset."

Heven pulled back and straightened her shirt and hair. "I'll be all right." Obviously Heven had been hoping for a little more reaction from Cole.

"I'm sorry," he said, frowning, realizing that his reaction wasn't what she was wanting.

Heven shook her head. "It's okay, I should have realized…"

"So you have a Dream Walker in your head?" Gemma asked, changing the subject. I was glad for it.

I nodded. "I'm going to try and get it out."

"You should do it soon. The longer it's there, the stronger the hold."

I could practically hear a clock ticking in my head with urgency. "Considering we are leaving for Italy tomorrow, I'm going to do it tonight."

Heven seemed a little green at the idea and I felt a twinge of pain in the back of my skull, so I knew that her head was throbbing.

"Good luck," Gemma said.

Yes, tonight. I had no choice but to get that thing out tonight. I might not know what to do to help my brother, but this, this I could do.

I would do it. Failure was just not an option.

Heven

Another training session. Two in one day. I guess I should have known there would be another one when this morning's seemed so short. Both Sam and Cole didn't seem to mind at all. They even appeared to enjoy it and put all they had into it. They were covered in sweat and dirt by the time Gemma was done with them. I paid attention, trying to learn something, but it seemed like an arduous session and as we were packing up I asked her why.

"It's because you are leaving for Italy tomorrow," Gemma explained.

"You think there is going to be trouble?" I whispered, putting my back to the boys and looking squarely at her.

"You don't?"

My shoulders slumped. "Yeah, I do."

Gemma nodded. "Just keep your eyes open and your guard up. You'll be all right."

"Thank you," I said, sincerely and laid my hand on her arm. She paused in packing up her bow and arrow. She looked down at my hand on her arm.

"Sorry," I said and pulled it away.

"I haven't been close to anyone in a very long time."

"Then why would you help us?"

"Because you remind me of me a very long time ago,"

"Me?" I choked. I couldn't imagine Gemma as ever being as weak as I.

She smiled, but then turned serious. "I'd like to see things turn out differently for you than they did for me."

"Who'd you lose?" I asked.

Something shifted behind her eyes and I knew that I was right. I knew that if Gemma hadn't always been the strong warrior that stood before me today then, only one thing could have turned her into one. Loss. Loss of someone that meant much to her.

Cole chose that moment to jog up to us, something clutched in his hand. "Ladies," he said grinning.

And just like that, the moment between us was gone. I knew better than to try and ask her about it again, her guard was back up and it wasn't coming back down anytime soon. "What do you have there?" I asked Cole, pointing to his hand.

"I found it over there beneath a tree. It's Gemma's." He held it up for us to see. It was a dagger. The silver blade gleamed in the sunlight and looked deadly sharp. The handle was silver with a few jewels encrusted on it, the center one being large, circular and it held all the colors of the rainbow. It was the first time I had seen it up close and I thought it was awfully beautiful to be a weapon.

"Keep it," Gemma told him.

His eyes widened. "This one is yours." He glanced down at the sack of daggers at our feet then reached for one of the simple ones.

"And I want you to have it," Gemma said, pushing it back toward Cole. "You might need it."

"Thank you," he said, holding the dagger to his side.

Gemma seemed flustered by the second thank you that day. "It's no big deal." She shrugged and turned away.

I looked at Cole who lifted his eyebrow at me. I shrugged. Gemma might not be ready to admit how she feels about my brother today, but someday she would be. And until that day I was keeping my mouth shut.

* * *

When training was finished, Sam, Cole and I walked back to the house and I was surprised to see my mother's car parked beside the house.

"That's my cue to leave," Cole said, looking at her car.

"You don't have to go, Cole." Then I realized I had no idea if my mom knew that Dad had another child or not.

"I gotta get home anyway, finish packing. Tell Gran I said later." He jogged over to his truck and got in. He was driving down the driveway when Sam and I walked into the kitchen. Logan was at the table, devouring a plate of pork chops, mashed potatoes and green beans while Mom and Gran were talking over hot tea.

"There you are, Heven!" Mom said, getting up to hug me. "I came to see you before your big trip!"

"Thanks, I'm glad you came."

"Sam," Gran said, getting up from the table. "You must be starving since you worked through dinner. There are plenty of leftovers. I'll make you a plate."

"I am hungry," he admitted and I laughed. Sam was always hungry.

He went to wash up and I helped Gran put a plate together for him. When he came back, we all settled around the table, Logan and Sam with their full plates and I, Gran, and Mom with our tea.

"Are you looking forward to the trip, Sam?" my mother asked, cradling the mug in her hands.

"Yes, ma'am."

"I've been getting to know your brother here. He says he's visiting you for the summer."

Sam nodded and reached for his water. "It's been good to have him here."

"You must be worried about leaving him alone while you are gone."

I glanced at Mom, wondering where this was going.

"I would feel better if I knew he was taken care of."

"Sam, honey, I told you. Logan is welcome here," Gran reminded him.

Sam nodded and I could see him considering her offer, even though I knew that he didn't want to leave Gran alone with Logan. He was too unpredictable. But we were leaving tomorrow and we had no other option.

"Well, I would just love to have Logan stay with me," Mom said, shocking us all.

"Mom?"

"Sure! It's been too quiet without you there. It would be fun. We could watch movies and Henry could take him fishing." She glanced at Logan. "Logan, do you like to fish?"

He looked up from his plate. "Yes, ma'am."

Sam looked at me and I shrugged. Mom really meant it when she said that she was going to accept Sam as part of my life and this offer was her way of proving it.

"I don't know," Sam said.

I looked at my mother's aura. It was filled with blues and greens. She was calm, comfortable and I knew that she meant what she said. I would see if she was only offering out of guilt.

"I think that's a wonderful idea!" Gran said, her aura looking a lot like Mom's.

Gran's acceptance seemed to put Sam at ease and he looked at Logan. "What do you think? Want to stay at Hev's Mom's?"

Logan nodded. "Can I eat candy when I watch movies?"

Mom laughed. "Sure."

I just hoped she didn't try to cook him some chicken.

"Okay, then." Sam nodded. "Thank you. I really appreciate this."

"You are most welcome, Sam." She turned to Logan. "Bring your things over tonight and you can stay, that way you won't have to get up so early to come over."

Logan nodded.

"Wonderful!" Mom said, happy with her plans. She gave me a warm smile and I smiled back.

Our relationship was getting stronger every day. I prayed it stayed that way.

Chapter Thirteen

Heven

When the sky darkened and night fell, the back of my skull began to scream. The pain was intense and distracting, but at least I understood why I was feeling this way. There was a demon in my head. This pain was that demon's—the Dream Walker's—way of trying to get inside my brain and manipulate me.

I glanced at the bed and groaned. I did not welcome sleep tonight. I prayed Sam would soon be here, so that the idea of sleep wouldn't be so bad. Turning my back on the bed and doing my best to ignore the pain, I looked at the door where my suitcases sat packed and ready. Tomorrow, we were leaving for Rome.

Tonight, all across town, my fellow classmates were packing their final items, pouring over the itinerary and texting excited messages to their friends. The anticipation of going abroad would fill their dreams with adventures and fun. I couldn't remember the last time my dreams were full of adventure and fun.

And this trip to Italy wouldn't be, either.

While everyone else was going for culture and learning, Sam and I had a much broader agenda. Saying we could possibly be saving the world seemed very melodramatic, but saying we could be helping to keep the world as we know it seemed much more manageable. And a little less frightening.

I heard a light sound and turned to see Sam slipping through the window.

"Did you get Logan over to my mom's?" I asked, still a little surprised that she was being so supportive of Sam and this trip.

"Yeah, she seemed really excited to have him there. She rented movies and made popcorn for him. And, of course, she had candy." Sam laughed and shook his head.

I smiled. "We used to do that a lot." It made me sad that we didn't anymore. I decided right then, that after the scroll was returned and we got home, I was going to do everything I could to put my relationship with my mother back together. She was making a great effort to accept Sam and now his brother, and I vowed to make a bigger effort as well.

"He'll be okay," Sam said, taking a breath and sounding like he was trying to assure himself of that fact.

"Yeah, I really think he will. At least this way he isn't alone."

He nodded and I glanced down. In his hand he grasped the bronze case that protected the Treasure Map. My breath caught. Sam held out the scroll and I took it, pulling it close to my chest.

"You dug it up without me."

"I figured you had enough on your mind." He brushed his fingertips across my forehead.

"Can you feel it too?"

He nodded. "Just an echo of it through the back of my head, so I know it's got to be hurting you."

"It gets worse the later it gets." I glanced at the clock.

"I've been thinking about that."

"You have?"

He lifted a golden-brown eyebrow. "Of course."

Sam sat down on the edge of the bed and pulled me down alongside him. "Your dreams, the ones the Dream Walker manipulates, seem to only happen when I'm not sleeping with you. Is that right?"

I thought a moment, having to relive the few dreams that I have had. Slowly, I shook my head. "The first time it happened, you were here."

"Yeah, but I got out of bed and was over there at the desk." His eyes flicked to the corner where I remembered waking and finding him.

I gasped. "That's why you're body was trying to shift! You sensed the Dream Walker."

He nodded.

Charade

It all made complete sense. Except for one thing. "Who is this Dream Walker?"

Sam cleared his throat and the area around his eyes tightened before he asked, "Have you seen him in your dreams?"

I nodded, the face flashing into my mind, pale skin and dark hair. Mostly, I recalled the power and pull he exuded. Someone wanting power and control could easily be drawn to someone like him. I felt something warm on my thigh and I looked down to see Sam's hand lying in my lap.

"Tell me about him."

I shifted uncomfortably and got to my feet to pace the small room. "Why?"

"So I know what to look for when I go in your head to get him out."

I stopped in my tracks and stared. "You're going to go in my head?"

His lips curved. "I'm already there."

I resumed pacing. "True, but…"

"But?"

"You have access to some of my thoughts and feelings because of our Mindbond, but the Dream Walker is different than that."

"I know. I'm going to try and get in like he did."

"But I was unconscious then."

"I should be able to get in while you're sleeping."

I couldn't help but shudder. My head was just too crowded these days. I didn't like feeling like my head was a playground.

"Hey…" Sam caught my hand and drew me forward, standing to look into my eyes. "It's the only way I can think of."

"I understand."

"I won't take advantage of you."

"I know you won't," I said, tilting my head down. I felt ashamed that he thought he had to tell me that.

He placed his finger beneath my chin and lifted. "I promise."

I placed a finger to his lips. "I trust you."

"You'll let me try?"

"Of course."

Sam fell quiet and I was reminded of his request to tell him about the Dream Walker. "He's very powerful, more powerful than all the others who have come after me," I said quietly.

Sam's movements stilled and his head cocked to one side, so I knew he was listening. "He calls me 'little one' and says I belong with him… in Hell."

Sam catapulted away from me and began to pace. I shot him a worried look and lapsed into silence.

Go on, he urged.

"He pulled me into Hell." I paused, realizing that Hell was exactly where I had been. I just hadn't realized it until I said the words out loud. "He showed me his castle. When I didn't swoon all over it, he became very angry… angrier than anyone I've ever seen. The others are scared of him… it's almost like he rules them."

Sam stopped pacing and stood with his back to me, staring out the window into the night. He said nothing as I told him about what I saw when I was there and gave him a description of the man we call the Dream Walker. He barely moved at all throughout my descriptions and my stomach flipped a little at the dark mood I could feel beginning to cloak him.

"He wants the scroll and demanded that I give it to him. Sometimes he seems amused when I tell him no; other times he gets angry and screams."

I fell silent for a few minutes. Sam still said nothing and just stared out into the dark yard. Surely, he didn't need any other details? I did not want to talk about my dreams anymore and I didn't think he wanted to hear any more. Tentatively, I approached Sam and laid a hand at his side. His T-shirt was soft and worn against my skin. "Sam?"

"I hate…" he murmured very low.

"What?" I turned my body slightly, trying to wedge just a portion of myself between him and the window.

"I hate that I couldn't protect you from him." He didn't look at me when he spoke the words.

"I don't blame you."

"I want to *kill* him." His voice was so low I had to strain to hear. My heart began to thud slow and heavy.

"To rip him apart and scatter the pieces."

I remembered the power and control that the Dream Walker exuded and knew deep down that this wasn't an ordinary demon — he was something more. Something that Sam might never have had to encounter before. It scared me to the bone. How angry would this demon be when Sam broke the thread into my mind? What would his punishment be?

A small sound caught in the back of my throat and I swallowed it, pushing down the panic. Sam turned his head and looked at me, eyes wild and golden. "Let's do this." His gaze shifted to the bed.

"I don't want to," I blurted.

He sighed, but his voice was hard when he spoke. "We have to try, Hev."

"Maybe the Dream Walker will go away when we don't have the Treasure Map anymore."

"Maybe he'll be angry and punish you."

I tried not to react to Sam's harsh words outwardly, but inside, I was shattering.

Sam's shoulders slumped and he sighed and hauled me against him. His chin rubbed against the top of my head as he spoke. "I'm sorry. I don't mean to be an ass. But we have to get this thing out of your head."

He was right and I knew it. I pulled away and climbed into the bed. Sam stood, watching me with a haunted look in his eyes. I lifted the blankets in silent invitation. He was beside me in seconds.

"I'm never going to be able to sleep," I told him.

He brushed a kiss along my hairline and forehead while his hand came up to rub slow circles across my back. "I'll wake you when it's over."

"What are you going to do anyway?" I asked around a yawn. It amazed me that his touch was able to calm me this way.

"Protect you," he murmured. His deep, raspy voice vibrated my ear.

Just like that, I fell asleep.

Sam

I stared up at the ceiling, frustration welling up inside me. How the hell was I going to get into Heven's mind, find the thread the Dream Walker used, and destroy it? Earlier, Airis had been so busy trying to conceal Heven from her father that she didn't stop to answer any of my questions. She just flung "use your Mindbond" at me and that was all. I snorted, not that I was that surprised. Airis wasn't much help at all for anything these days. I wanted to be Heven's guardian; the job filled me with purpose and pride. I knew that it wasn't going to be easy, but I couldn't help but feel like Airis was just using me as a means to an end. As someone to protect her asset and that she didn't really care about how I went about it.

I brushed the thought away. It didn't matter what Airis thought of me. What mattered is that I was supposed to be protecting Heven, and right now, there was a demon—a Dream Walker—in her head that was causing her pain.

Hate churned inside me. I felt the darkness that was part of the hellhound rising up, trying to take control. I wasn't lying when I said I wanted to rip him apart. I hadn't felt this violent since I faced off with China for the last time. The time I killed her.

Just like I would kill the Dream Walker.

But I had to figure out how to get to him first. I had to figure out how to sever the hold that he had on Heven's mind.

Carefully, I slid my shoulder out from beneath her head and rolled to the side, looking down at her sleeping face. Blond hair fell over her forehead and I brushed it away, noting that even in sleep, she did not look relaxed. *I'm going to fix this.* I told her. If I hadn't insisted she learn to swim, that demon wouldn't have gotten a hold of her at all.

But that wasn't true. This would have happened one way or another. I had a feeling that I wouldn't have been able to stop this. The hound in me has been restless, unsettled, knowing that there are undercurrents at play that we didn't understand. Knowing that there is a charade somehow going on around us—I just haven't been able to see past it. Not yet anyway.

But before I stripped away the charade, I had to first tear away the thread that was left in Heven's mind. I looked back at her sleeping face. She had been through so much that I didn't have the heart to tell her I had no clue how to get that thing out of her mind. She depended on me, trusted me.

I blew out a breath and forced my body to relax. Being angry and hateful wasn't going to help me get to sleep or even get into her mind. The Mindbond gave me a great deal of access to her, but I didn't think the bond we shared would allow me to walk straight into her mind.

Yet, that demon had done it.

How?

Heven had been unconscious. Airis said that she had to be for him to get in. So I guess it would be easiest for me now as she slept. I felt like I was taking advantage of her as she slept, but I had no choice. Besides, she knew what I was doing, so I wasn't exactly busting in uninvited.

I would just have to trust that the Mindbond we shared was enough of an opening to let me in.

The only way I would know was if I tried it.

I exhaled and wrapped my arms around her, something inside me easing at the way she shifted toward me, completely trusting me, even in sleep. I closed my eyes. She smelled good... like strawberries. As I relaxed, I opened up the Mindbond as far as I could, dropping any barrier that I might hold up to keep my thoughts my own.

Let me in, Heven. Open up, I urged with my mind.

I felt her mind give way, and instead of pushing in, I backed out slightly. The last thing I wanted to do was scare her or hurt her. That would only make this harder.

So I lay there, taking even breaths and counting her heartbeat, feeling her chest rise and fall as air moved through her lungs. After a short while, I began to talk to her, murmur thoughts from my mind to hers. She sighed and snuggled closer and I knew that this was the moment I needed to act.

With closed eyes, I pushed my mind and my thoughts out toward her, feeling the bond we shared and the invisible wall where it stopped. I kept pushing—gently—continuing to tell Heven that she was safe and that I loved her, and I felt the wall give way as I entered a part of Heven's mind I never had before.

I was assaulted.

* * *

The human mind is a complex thing. I always thought that our Mindbond was something extremely unique. Something that completely opened up Heven to me. And in so many ways, it was. But I had no idea how much of her mind was still closed off. I almost felt like I was tangled in a spider web in the dark. I resisted the urge to shake, to fight off the spidery threads that brushed against me, afraid that I would somehow hurt Heven.

I never imagined the inside of Heven's mind to be a dark place. She's such a bright spot in my life, and while I knew she faced a lot of challenges and had been through so much, I never once believed that it hampered who she truly was.

I still didn't.

I focused and tried to make out what was in the darkness. There was nothing there.

Heven. I spoke her name, a mere whisper from my mind to hers, testing her response.

She didn't make a sound; she didn't speak a word, yet I was overwhelmed.

Assaulted by feelings, by thoughts, and by images. Suddenly, the darkness gave way to a curtain of light and I felt as if I were watching a movie. A movie in which I was the star.

It was a memory.

We were at Bubble Maineia, sitting in a corner. I knew the place had been packed, but seeing this from her side, I hardly noticed anyone else but... me. I watched myself lift the chocolate drink to my lips and take a pull from the straw and the feeling of longing with a touch of lust swept over me. She wished that my lips were on her instead of the straw. I saw my lips moving, but didn't hear the words; then I laughed. Joy and happiness rained over me and I felt the breath leave my chest a little.

I knew that Heven loved me. I felt it every day. I saw it in her eyes. But this. This was more than I imagined. To see myself through someone else's eyes, to feel what she felt without her emotions mixing with mine was... it was the purest feeling I have ever known.

The memory died away and I was once again left in the dark. I stood there, the threads of her mind brushing against me and feeling extremely precious. Something caught my eye... a glint of gold. There, where the memory had replayed in front of me, was a shimmering golden thread.

Our thread.

I recognized it immediately. It was part of me too, and as I watched it grow and elongate, it stretched toward me. My first instinct was to move away, to not disturb the thread that helped to bind us together. What if it broke? But the closer it got, the warmer I began to feel and I couldn't help myself. I reached out and wrapped a finger around the thin gold.

It was much, much stronger than I thought it would be. It looked fine and delicate, shimmering gold in the dark, but it felt like steel. I tugged at it and it didn't so much as move. On instinct, I moved closer until I felt a warm glow pour throughout my mind and spread to each of my limbs.

Our connection was growing, solidifying.

She was *mine*.

The hellhound in me growled in possession and satisfaction. The human side of me realized that I was being archaic, but the animal in me didn't care.

As the connection of our thread washed over me and strengthened, a million other threads and chords revealed themselves to me. Every single one was a color of its own. It was beautiful. They illuminated the darkness and revealed to me who I always knew Heven was.

Absolutely stunning.

But I wasn't here to be in awe of her true inner beauty. I was here to get rid of what didn't belong. I began to make my way through the millions of sparkling threads, carefully navigating them, only touching them when necessary and with the utmost care. When I did touch one, I got a sensation of what the thread was for.

The blue thread seemed to store the words to all her favorite songs. The green thread was for her love of nature. I came to a thread that was duller than the rest; it didn't glimmer like the others. My adrenaline surged. I found it! To be sure, I reached out and wrapped my palm around it.

It wasn't the thread the Dream Walker left behind. But it was the thread that seemed to hold her physical pain. The minute my hand wrapped around it, I got an intense pain in the back of my skull. I dropped the thread like a live wire and swore.

Is that what he was doing to her? Is that the kind of pain she has been walking around with?

It ended now.

As stunning as they were, I tuned out all the other threads. I stopped thinking all together and I *felt*. Heven's mind was a pure place, so I searched until I felt a glimmer of something that just didn't seem to belong. I moved in that direction, no longer needing to watch out for the other threads. It's like my mind knew where to go and how to get there.

When I reached the spot where I felt the thread should be, I expected to see it, looking like an intruder, sticking out like a sore thumb.

But the space was empty.

I made a sound of frustration. It should be here!

I felt as if I was standing right next to it. My skin prickled with the sickness of it. The hound in me was restless, urging to get out, to defeat the presence it had detected all along.

I knew it was here. It must be camouflaged.

How did you destroy something you couldn't see?

I began to move forward, not giving up the search when a humming sound filled my ears. My insides began to vibrate and I cringed. Suddenly, I felt as if I was being electrocuted and I was blasted backward to fall through the darkness.

* * *

Damn it. No matter how hard I tried, the thread was just out of reach. It was there, yet invisible. I sat up in the bed, pushing at the covers, irritated that I had been so close only to be knocked out of her head. Not only was the Dream Walker's thread camouflaged, but it was somehow protected.

If I could only see it, I knew I could take the pain of tearing it away. And there would be pain. The hairs on my arms and legs were still standing from being blasted only moments before. There was a fine tremor in my hands and I felt slightly sick.

I turned back to the bed and looked down at Heven. I would endure just about any pain to take away what was being done to her.

I knew what I had to do. I didn't like it, but it was the only way.

I leaned down and pressed a kiss to her temple, then stood, moving away from the bed. It made me sick to know that with every step I took away from her, the easier it would be for her mind to be invaded. But the only way I was going to destroy that thread was to see it, and I knew that I would be able to see it if the demon was using it.

I backed away from the bed, toward the opposite side of the room. Heven shifted and made a small sound. I kept moving until my back pressed against the wall. I slid down slowly to sit on the floor and rest my head in my hands.

I did everything I could to relax, to open up my mind. When Heven made a strangled sound, my muscles clenched, but I stayed where I was and pushed my mind out to hers. I had no problem getting back to the place I had been before.

But this time something was different. I felt it the moment my mind touched hers.

He was here.

Heven

Thick, oppressive air made me cough. My eyes sprang open and I knew instantly where I was. There could only be one place as desolate as this.

It could only mean one thing.

Sam was having trouble finding or breaking the thread that allowed the Dream Walker into my head. I wondered where he was, because if our theory was right, in order for me to be here, Sam was not in bed with me. It was useless to try to wake up. So I began walking. The land was dry and unfertile, depressing and crass. I knew now why those sentenced here were like they were. *A product of their environment.* It seemed like such a waste. I understood the meaning of Hell, the point of it. Hell was a place for sinners unrepentant for their deeds and a punishment for those that didn't believe in God and Heaven. But sending those kinds of souls here wasn't really solving anything, was it? Wasn't it like encouraging the behavior that sent them here in the first place? Like, 'you don't deserve to go to Heaven, so go to Hell and continue to act in sin.' How did that solve anything? Should the demons here really be allowed to just wreak havoc at all times and cause pain and suffering to those on Earth? Where was the leadership — the rule?

My thoughts were interrupted when the ground beneath my feet began to rumble. Something was coming. I looked around for somewhere to hide, knowing that anything that made the ground shake like this was *not* something I wanted to see me, but there was nowhere to go. It didn't matter anyway because it appeared beside me in a matter of seconds.

"We meet again," the Dream Walker said, acting as though I was out for a morning stroll and he just happened upon me while out for a ride. I would tell him how ridiculous he was if I wasn't so afraid.

He wasn't alone.

He was riding a huge horse. Only it wasn't really a horse. It was half horse, half man: a centaur. Something that I thought only existed in folklore and legends. You would think by now I would have known better. Apparently, anything was possible these days.

The centaur was outrageously huge with the body and legs of a giant stallion, but where the head should be was the torso of a man. He was the size of an ogre with a muscled chest and thick arms corded with veins. His head looked human, but he had long, black hair that flowed behind him like a mane. His jaw was large and jutted out, matching the way his forehead did. His eyes were small, beady and too far apart. They looked upon me with hatred and lust and I struggled not to squirm under the venom directed at me. How had the Dream Walker conquered such a vile beast and tamed it enough to ride?

"Come with me," he said and held out his hand.

"No." I took a step backward. The back of my head squeezed and the muscles knotted until I thought I might cry out, but I stood tall. The front of my skull began aching and my eyes filled with tears.

He laughed and nudged the evil beast closer. I screamed as it reached out its strong arms and grabbed me. It held me out in front of it while it looked me up and down, making my skin crawl, while it licked its lips. Hadn't I read somewhere that centaurs liked to rape women?

I kicked out a shoeless foot, not even connecting with the monster, but the act still enraged it. It yelled a deep roar and squeezed my arms until I thought they might break.

"Enough!" he roared, power emanating from his voice. The squeezing stopped as the centaur pitched me over its shoulder. The Dream Walker caught me and planted me in front of him between his thighs. I wanted to retch.

"You're disgust makes this better," he whispered in my ear as he urged the centaur forward. The creature took delight in giving us a terrifying, bumpy-as-hell ride. At the castle he let me go and I fell to the ground, hitting hard. Both he and the centaur enjoyed laughing at me as I got up and dusted myself off. *Wake up. Please wake up. Sam, where are you?*

"Come," he snapped and walked over the drawbridge to the castle door. Behind me, the Centaur leered and I decided to take my chances with the Dream Walker rather than him. I didn't hurry to catch up. The idea of making him wait on me was somehow satisfying. When I at last sauntered to his side, he lifted a brow at my little act, then swiftly threw open the castle door and shoved me inside ahead of him. I landed against something, but couldn't tell what it was because it was so dark. Whatever it was made a noise, a cross between a growl and a screech, and I jumped back in surprise.

The Dream Walker walked through the room and disappeared from sight. I hurried to catch up to him. "Who are you?" I called.

Of course he didn't reply. I found him in a room, standing with his back to me in front of a large, curtained wall. The curtains were blood red and I prayed that it was their original color and not the leftovers of people who had done this man wrong.

I stood there, unsure what to do, and considered my options. The idea of running crossed my mind, but I wasn't feeling very well, kind of fuzzy-headed and heavy. My limbs were shaking from what I assumed was fear, yet I didn't feel afraid. I felt detached, like this was happening to someone else and not me. All of a sudden, the Dream Walker flinched and then went rigid, spinning to look at me. He scrutinized my face as if looking for some sort of answer to an unasked question. Seconds ticked by and nothing happened. I shifted my weight from foot to foot and waited. *Where are you, Sam?*

I'm here. His voice slid through my brain like thick, warm honey. It coated all the edges of worry and gave me sweet hope. *I've found the thread.*

"What are you doing?" the Dream Walker demanded. He stalked over beside me.

"I'm not doing anything."

He didn't believe me, yet he couldn't prove otherwise. "Look," he demanded, then pressed a button on a small remote and the curtains began to slide open. The darkened room lightened some and I was able to see more of my surroundings. The room was large with black walls and a massive black desk in the center. There was a chair behind the desk that was made of black leather. The only color in the room came from the red curtains and a red rug beneath the desk. There were chains hanging from one wall that made me wonder what a person had to do to get chained there.

"I said look," he yelled right in my ear. With my eardrum ringing, I walked over to the windows and looked out. It was a panoramic view of depressing proportions. I could see for miles and miles until the dark rock earth blended with the gray smoky sky. The terrain was completely flat with nothing but broken, dead vegetation for life. I could see demons milling about fighting, screaming, and torturing one another. There were buildings, some large and some small. They all looked on the verge of caving in or falling down. A long and winding black river flowed, snaking through the terrain and looking like a stream of tar.

"This could all be yours."

"This is nothing."

I thought he might yell, but for once, he didn't. Instead he said, "This is power. I know you can feel it. I know it calls to you."

I thought the power I felt came from him, and before I could stop the words, they tumbled from my mouth. He laughed a loud, unfriendly laugh. "I command this place. The power here *is* mine because I *take* it."

Was he Satan then? Somehow, this wasn't how I pictured the devil, and this wasn't how I pictured Hell, but there was no denying this place. My gaze went back out the window. I guess evil came in many forms.

"Why are you offering me this?" It didn't make any sense.

"I want the scroll."

"If you're so powerful, how come you haven't taken it from me?" I didn't say the words to taunt him. I wasn't trying to anger him. But I did.

The slap hit me fast and hard, ricocheting my head back off my shoulders, causing pain to explode behind my eyes. I fell backward, falling on the cold, unforgiving floor, heat searing through my face. He stood over me, panting, eyes blazing like he wanted to kill me. Somewhere inside my head, Sam roared. An angry, powerful roar. And I knew that he was so deep in my head now that he knew what just happened.

"You can't get it open, can you?" I said, lifting my chin with a challenge. I was done being afraid of him. He might be scary, but I would only be scared if I allowed myself to be.

He snarled and lifted his fist.

"You know I can get it open. Something no one else has been able to do. It's why you haven't killed me. You *need* me."

"You little bitch," he growled. The strong features of his face twisted into something ugly and sinister. He grabbed me by the arms and hauled me up, making my teeth slam together. My head began hammering and I felt dizzy. Still, I looked straight into his frigid stare.

"None of your minions have managed to find the scroll," I taunted. "I still have it hidden and soon it's going back to where it belongs and you will never have it!"

His face came close, so close that I could smell his rancid breath and see the white spittle forming in the corners of his mouth from rage and desire to cause me harm. "When everyone around you is dead, we'll see how brave you are, *little one*." He tossed me backward and I hit the desk before sliding to the floor.

I pushed him too far. Now everyone I loved was in danger.

"It's true. I may need you alive," he said, stalking forward, pushing up the sleeves of his dark sweater, "but I can still find ways to cause you agony."

Another wave of pain and dizziness came over me as he raised his fist to the sky, preparing to strike. I brought my arm across my face for protection, but then thought better of the action and lowered my arm, lifted my face up and waited for the blow.

It never came.

"No!" he screamed, reaching out to grab me.

But he couldn't. His hands went right through me. Sam must have found the thread and destroyed it. I looked up at him and grinned, lifting my hand in a wave.

Right before I disappeared, I heard him say, "This isn't over."

When I opened my eyes, Sam was leaning over me. His usually sun-kissed face looked drawn and pale. "Hi," I whispered.

Tension drained right out of him, leaving him looking exhausted. I pushed myself up, tossing away the covers to wrap my arms around his neck. He was warm and solid, so I pressed myself closer and willed away the words that still bounced around in my head. *This isn't over.*

"Are you all right?" Sam asked, pulling me back to look me over.

"I'm fine. You broke the thread?" I reached for the glass of water on the bedside table.

He sat down beside me on the bed; our legs pressed together all the way down until our feet touched the floor. "Yes. I'm so sorry you had to go back there. I was hoping you wouldn't have to." I heard the regret in his voice and the restraint from finishing his thoughts.

"I thought he couldn't get inside my dreams when you were with me."

He looked pained and guilty when he said, "I left you alone for a few minutes."

This surprised me and I lifted my brows.

"I had to. I couldn't find the thread; it was well hidden. I figured the only way I would find it was if he used it to get to you."

"It's all right." I took his hand and pressed my lips to his knuckles. I pretended not to notice the slight tremble in his fingers.

"He hit you." Sam's eyes glittered with gold.

"Could you hear all of it?" *Even the part where he threatened you and my entire family?*

He nodded, his eyes turning to liquid honey. "Don't be afraid."

"I'm not," I lied.

"Tomorrow, we're going to Italy and the Treasure Map will no longer be ours to worry about."

I nodded. It was a relief to know that I was taking it far away, away from the people I love who are innocent in all of this. But I couldn't help but worry about the trip. Something told me that getting that scroll where it needed to be was not going to be as easy as we might have believed.

"Hey," Sam murmured, touching my cheek. "Does your head still hurt?"

I shook my head. "He's gone." What a relief it was to know. We lay back down in bed and I settled in Sam's embrace, ready for a few hours of peaceful sleep and painless rest.

Just before I drifted to sleep, a tremor ripped through my body. Beneath my cheek Sam stiffened and his voice was heavy when he whispered, "Was that what I thought it was?"

"Yeah," I said miserably as my temples started squeezing my brain.

"I'm sorry, sweetheart." His lips brushed my forehead.

Was one night of peace so much to ask for? Another tremor began at my toes and traveled all the way up to my head. I pressed myself closer to Sam. The Dream Walker was gone and now my new 'supernatural' power was going to assert itself.

I couldn't help but wonder what this one was going to be like.

Chapter Fourteen

Heven

It wasn't even light out when Sam slid from the bed. I groaned and reached for him.

"I have to go," he whispered, leaning down, his breath feathering against my skin. "I have to run home and get my suitcases and the truck. I'll be back so Gran can drive us to the airport."

Why did the plane have to leave so early? I pushed myself up too fast and the room tilted.

"Hey? You okay?" Sam slipped his arm around my waist for support. I let my head fall onto his shoulder.

"I'm all right," I groaned.

"How's the head?"

"Okay." It wasn't anything a few pain relievers wouldn't take care of.

"I'll be back soon." He pressed a too-quick kiss to my lips and then disappeared out my window.

Rather than burrow back into the covers like I really wanted, I got up and headed for the shower, hoping it would wash away my grouchy mood. I slept without invasion from the Dream Walker and his sick games. I didn't dream at all, but truly restful sleep still seemed just out of reach. Tremors kept me from completely relaxing and the worry of a new power crowded my head. What if it was something that would be hard to hide? What if it was something that was hard to use?

What if it was something stupid?

Having the ability to see people's auras isn't exactly what I would call a cool 'supernatural' power, so maybe this new one would be something silly too.

I took time to blow my hair out smooth and flat ironed it until it was straight and shiny. I didn't bother with make-up, except for a little pink blush and some cherry lip gloss. I dressed comfortably for the long plane ride in wide-legged, black knit yoga pants, a white tank top and a blue cardigan. I added a few last-minute items to my suitcase and grabbed my bag from my desk. The scroll was sticking out of the top and I pulled it out and held it in my hand. As attached to it as I felt, I was somewhat relieved that it was time to take it home. This thing had brought a lot of trouble into my life. Gran called to me from downstairs, and I shoved the scroll back into my purse and took care to zip it closed. Before leaving my room, I stuck my hand beneath my mattress and pulled out the chain that I put the key on. I pulled it over my head and tucked the key under my tank and hurried from the room.

Sam wasn't here yet and Gran was brewing a pot of coffee. The rich aroma filled the dim kitchen. "Are you ready for your trip?"

"Yes, although I'm not sure about the plane ride." I'd never been on a plane before.

"You'll do just fine," Gran assured me. "Make sure you take lots of pictures."

"I will."

When she went out of the room for extra batteries, I hurried to the cabinet and got some pain reliever for my head and swallowed them down with a glass of orange juice. Gran came bustling back into the room and handed me a pack of batteries, which I shoved into the front pocket of my suitcase.

"I have something else for you as well," Gran said, holding out a white envelope.

I took the envelope and turned it over in my hands. My name was scrawled across the front in beautiful script. My eyes seemed to focus in on the letters and take in every detail and curve. I blinked at the sudden focus I seemed to have.

"I thought you could use it on your trip," Gran was saying.

I glanced inside and saw a neat row of twenty dollar bills. "Oh, Gran, you didn't have to do this."

"I know that. I wanted to. You and Sam help out around here so much and you work so hard in school and work. Get something nice to remember this trip, Sam too."

As if the monetary gift wasn't enough, she slid something else across the table as well, a small package wrapped in brown paper with a beautiful yellow ribbon tied around it. "What's this?"

Gran motioned toward it, so I carefully ripped the paper and took the gift in my hands. It was a journal, brown and leather bound. It was soft against my fingers and I flipped through the blank, white pages.

"Keeping a diary of your trip and the things you see and do there will help you remember it years from now. I think you will find that as you grow older, memories are very important. When you are old like me, you will enjoy looking back on this and remembering."

It was perfect. I threw my arms around her and hugged her tight. "Thank you so much! I love you, Gran."

She laughed. "I love you, too."

Suddenly, the horrible threat that the Dream Walker made whipped through my mind. No one I loved was safe. I swallowed and stepped back, feeling nauseated. My being here put Gran at risk.

Where was Sam? We needed to leave. The faster we got on that plane, the faster everyone here would be safe. *Sam?*

He knocked lightly on the back door and I ran to open it. He was there, suitcase in hand and a duffle bag slung over his shoulder. He was wearing scuffed-up jeans and a gray and white striped T-shirt.

What took you so long? I demanded, pulling him inside and closing the door. The morning sky was just beginning to show signs of day and the cool air came rushing in with him.

I was just making sure Logan was okay. His eyes narrowed on my face.

How was his first night at my mom's?

He said it was fine. I think he'll be okay.

That's great. Now you won't have to worry about him.

Sam didn't seem completely convinced about this.

"Good morning, Sam," Gran called, setting a large plate of muffins on the counter.

"Morning. Thank you for letting me leave my truck here while we're gone."

"Have some breakfast; we should be going," Gran said, looking at the clock.

My stomach revolted at the thought of food, but I grabbed a muffin from the counter and pretended to eat it. When Gran wasn't looking, I handed it to Sam. He frowned, but took it and ate it in one bite.

The ride to the airport was quiet and uneventful. I could feel some tension from Sam and noticed the way his eyes swept the streets and road behind us. Did he think that we might get ambushed on the way? The scroll felt heavy in my bag and the closer we got to getting rid of it, the more anxious I felt.

When we finally said good-bye to Gran, I felt a little guilty for the relief I felt. Maybe now she would be safe and I wouldn't have to pretend so much to be excited for this trip. Cole was already here, sitting at the gate with most of our class. After Sam and I checked in with Mrs. Britt and her odd assistant Ms. Merriweather, we went and sat next to him.

"Ready for this?" Cole asked in low tones.

I nodded. Sam was busy watching the people around us, looking for signs of danger. I slumped in the seat close to Cole and resigned myself that this is the way the trip would be. Asking Sam to relax would be pointless. He would be wound tight until this Treasure Map was no longer in our possession.

Another tremor decided to run through me, shaking my arms even as I tried to hold still. "Whoa," Cole said. "Are you okay?"

Sam turned to glance at me.

"I'm good." The overhead lights seemed harsh, not really hurting my head, but not really helping either. "I'm going to go to the bathroom."

Cole jumped up to escort me at the same time that Sam appeared at my side. I stifled an eye roll. "It is right over there. I'll be fine."

"We'll walk you," Cole said.

I didn't say anything and tried to ignore the glances of my classmates as I was 'escorted' to the ladies room that was only feet away. *Are you going to burst in there and search it too?* I asked grumpily.

"Call for me if you need help," Sam said, ignoring my barb and tapping my head before I could walk in the restroom.

In the bathroom, the lights weren't any dimmer and I did my best to ignore them. I had a sinking feeling that whatever this new power of mine was had to do with my head and eyes again. I turned on the taps to let the cool water slip through my fingers and dampened a paper towel to blot over my eyes and forehead.

"What's wrong with you?" a voice from behind me asked.

I jumped and spun around toward the voice. "Gemma? What are you doing here?"

She shrugged. "I wanted to talk to you."

"About what?"

"Cole."

"What about him?"

"He's special, you know?"

I nodded; my brother was very special. His aura proved it with the unique shade of color that he carried around him permanently. Is that what this was about? Gemma did say that she knew why Cole's aura was different than everyone else's. "You never did tell me about Cole's aura. There's something about him I should know, isn't there?"

Gemma nodded. "You said you heard your father the last time you were in the InBetween?"

"Yes. Airis wouldn't let me see him." The memory left a small pang in my chest. "But what does that have to do with Cole?"

"Your father must be a Supernal Being."

"What's that?"

"It's a step down from an angel."

"My dad never had any powers," I said, head reeling.

"Supernal Beings usually don't. But if he did, they probably would have been easy to hide. They are humans, kind of like angels on Earth. They are inherently good people, people that don't have any kind of malice within them. They can't be influenced by Satan's darkness. These people tend to take on armed-justice roles, to keep peace and balance here."

"My dad was a police officer," I murmured.

Gemma nodded, her wide gray eyes expressive. "They have an inherent need to help and protect others, especially those they care about. A police officer would have been a natural career choice for him."

I was surprised by this, but honestly, I wasn't shocked. Too much had been happening to me since last year that my dad turning out to be some angel on Earth wasn't a huge revelation. In fact, it just made all my memories and feelings about him feel validated. He was truly a good man and if anyone could be considered an angel—a Supernal Being—it would be him. "Did my dad know what he was?"

Gemma shook her head. "Probably not. Most people have no idea that they might be more than just a good person. But I think that's why you could hear him. He must still have his complete form."

"What do you mean?"

"When you die, your soul leaves your body. You go to Heaven as a spirit; there's no need for your complete form. Supernal Beings tend to keep their form and all their memories. Sometimes God calls upon them to spread his word or do certain acts."

My father could be sent back to Earth by God? I pushed the thought away, terrified of getting my hopes up of someday seeing him again, knowing how bad it feels when you get so close and then nothing. "But demons have bodies. Aren't demons sinners who have died and went to Hell?"

Gemma nodded patiently. "Think about it, Hev. Demons don't really look like humans, do they?"

I thought back to the half-man, half-crocodile and shivered. "I guess not."

"Their souls are just twisted into different evil forms."

The Dream Walker didn't *look* like a demon. What did that mean? "Why are you telling me this now? And what does this have to do with my brother?"

Gemma shifted and glanced away.

"Cole's a Supernal Being, isn't he?"

Gemma nodded. "It's why his aura is different than everyone else's. Your father's would have looked a lot like Cole's."

"Why are you telling me now?"

She was silent a moment before she spoke. "I have a feeling that this trip is going to be rough. The people, if you can call them that, who want that scroll aren't going to give up. Just be careful, okay?"

"Why can't you come with us?"

"This is your journey to take, but don't worry, I'll be around. Watching."

I had a feeling she would be watching more of Cole than of me and Sam. She cared about him and couldn't admit it to herself. "You think Cole is going to put himself in danger."

"It would be his natural instinct. If he sees something dangerous or threatening, he's going to go after it."

"You think he'll get hurt?" I chewed my lip.

"No!" She denied the idea fiercely, but I saw something different in her eyes: fear. "I've been training with him. He's strong and a good fighter, but I haven't had enough time with him…"

Did she mean enough time to train him or time to be with him?

"He doesn't have your dagger," I murmured, beginning to worry too. "No way he could get through security with it."

Gemma pulled it out of a holster around her waist. "I brought it for him." She held it out. "Give it to him for me."

"No."

"Why?"

"*You* give it to him." Why was she hiding from him?

"I can't." Her voice cracked.

"Why not?"

She stared at me silently.

I shrugged and turned away.

"Wait."

I turned back. "Thank you for telling me this. I've been wondering. I don't get why you haven't told him yet?"

Gemma remained mutinously quiet.

I sighed and turned away once more. Her quiet words stopped me, but this time I didn't turn around. I recognized that it was easier for her to admit her feelings when I wasn't looking right at her.

"He's not as human as we all thought."

I waited, praying she would explain herself.

"It was easier before... to deny how I felt... when he was just human. A human and a fallen angel together is laughable. But now..." Her voice trailed off and I understood.

Gemma was totally falling in love with my brother and trying like hell to fight it. A human and a fallen angel was a good excuse to deny her feelings, but a fallen angel and a Supernal Being must be a lot more plausible in her world.

"It's okay to love him," I told her quietly, my back still turned.

She said nothing, but I knew she was there. Her absolute silence was clear enough. Gemma the warrior fallen angel was scared of loving someone. "What happened to you?" I whispered.

I waited for her answer, and just when I thought she might say something, a head poked around the corner.

"Geez, Heven, Sam's practically wearing a hole in the carpet out here. What's taking so long?" Cole asked.

I stiffened as his eyes went past me to Gemma. His whole aura and body shifted. If Gemma could see his aura like I could, then she wouldn't be afraid he didn't feel the same as she did.

"I'll see you later," I said to Gemma, giving her a little nod, trying to tell her that what we talked about would stay private.

For now, anyway.

On my way past Cole I whispered, "Talk to her."

I went out the door where Sam hurried to my side, questions in his eyes. "Gemma's in there." I leaned against the wall, acting as look out as my brother disappeared a little farther into the bathroom. Several minutes later, the announcer came on to tell us to board the plane. Cole appeared at my side silently.

"Thanks," he murmured as we all went forward to line up. I stared at him, willing him to give me some clue as to what was happening, but Mrs. Britt began counting us all and taking last-minute attendance. From the front of the line, I caught a glimpse of Kimber glaring at the three of us as we took our places in the back of the line. My stomach knotted at the thought of sharing a room with her for the trip.

Ms. Merriweather stopped in front of us and smiled with a clipboard in her hands. "I have your room number assignments here."

I glanced down at the paper on her board and my focus went right to the list of names and numbers. My eyes did that focusing thing again and I felt an odd click in my brain. I blinked and looked up, shaking my head slightly.

"Don't forget your room number; you'll need to know it as soon as we get to the hotel," Ms. Merriweather said and then moved off down the line.

Sam placed his palm at the small of my back. "Want to write it down, Hev, so you don't forget?" He held out a white card and a pen.

"Uh, no, but thanks."

He gave me an odd sort of look and I just shrugged and pulled out my boarding pass. I wouldn't forget my room number. It appeared I wouldn't forget anyone's room number. I closed my eyes as if to prove what I was thinking. A crystal clear image of the paper appeared behind my eyes. I could see every single person's name and coordinating room number with ease. No, I wouldn't forget my room number.

I had a feeling I wouldn't forget anything I didn't *want* to forget ever again.

Chapter Fifteen

Heven

I couldn't help but get caught up in the fun of the trip. The excited laughter around us on the plane, the tiny bags of peanuts and headphones for a movie… It was all pretty cool. And it made it easy to forget this high up in the air that our lives were in danger. I had no problem at all filling in the very first page of the travel diary that Gran gave me. It felt good to have some fun, to write out something that I would look back on and enjoy.

Our first stop in Italy was Tuscany. We were driving by bus to Florence, the capital of Tuscany. As we drove, I watched the rolling hills, the green expanse of grass and the brilliance of the clear, blue sky. It was all so gorgeous I had an entire notebook page filled in minutes, detailing the scenery that stole my breath.

I felt a warm stroke down my arm and reluctantly pulled away from the window to look at Sam. His eyes were like warm sunshine and his mouth was curved up in a smile. *Having a good time?*

Oh, yes. It's so beautiful here, so different. Don't you think?

"It's a little hard to see with a window hogger sitting next to me."

I gasped. "I'm sorry."

He laughed. "Don't be. I actually like seeing your excitement more than anything out the window."

I laced my fingers with his and tugged him closer. "Look."

We came upon a vineyard and we all cheered when the bus turned in. Of course, the teachers were quick to tell us sternly that we would not be sampling any of the wine. But we did get a tour of the rooms where they made and stored the wine, and we got to see the miles and miles of open land where rows and rows of grape vines grew, sun-kissed with the leaves swaying slowly in the warm summer breeze.

Too soon, it seemed we were back on the bus, heading once more for Florence and the hotel that we would be spending our first two nights in. It was like a whole other world existed outside of mine. You'd think that the events of the past year would lessen the shock I felt when presented with new and exciting places and people, but I guess it hadn't. It relaxed me. Beginning the trip this way gave me hope that maybe we would have more fun than we thought.

* * *

My original good nature faded when we arrived at the hotel. Because we were a school group, traveling with teachers, we did not have to check in at the front desk. Instead, we were to go directly to our assigned rooms. The keycards were passed out on the bus — one for each student — and no more. Sam and Cole were roommates and were staying on the first floor. My room was on the second floor with Kimber. I managed to avoid her on the plane, in the vineyard and on the bus, but I knew our moment was coming, and I knew it probably wouldn't be very pretty.

I dawdled on the bus, allowing everyone to go before me, trying to stall for time before Sam and I would have to part ways. Eventually, we were the last ones to file from the bus. Ms. Merriweather stood at the bottom of the steps with a checklist in hand, making sure all the students were accounted for. She smiled at us as we disembarked and I had to force myself to smile back.

Inside the hotel was nice. It looked a lot like the chain hotels back home with a large lobby, a reception area, and a mini kitchen to the right where they served coffee and tea all day long. A small sign by the coffee service advertised free cookies every evening at seven o'clock. At the bank of elevators, Sam and I were finally forced to say good-bye.

"I'll see you at dinner," Sam said, giving my fingers a light squeeze.

"Okay." The elevator doors chimed open and students began filing in. I noticed they were all girls. Girls must be bunking on the second floor while the boys were on the first.

Unable to kiss me under the watchful eye of our chaperones, Sam settled for tapping my forehead with his fingers, reminding me that we could always talk. Then he turned on his heel and met up with Cole, who was waiting just yards away. I gave them a little wave and got on the elevator; no doubt my roomie was waiting.

She took over the room and decided on the rules before I even got there. From the minute I opened the door, she made it clear she thought she was in charge. She chose the bed closest to the windows and a small wingback chair and table (which all her stuff was draped across), her stuff took up more than half of the closet and her shower bag cluttered the only available space on the counter in the bathroom. Kimber even went as far as to turn the TV in her direction and put the remote on her bed.

I would have laughed at her incredible childishness, but if I had, she would have found ways to make me even more miserable.

I chose not to comment on her actions and, instead, placed my suitcase on the floor between the wall and my bed, leaving it unzipped (I could live out of a suitcase, I didn't *need* a closet) and left my shower bag beside it. I took more care with my bag containing the scroll, placing it on the shelf underneath my bedside table. When Kimber went into the bathroom, I hurried to stuff the Treasure Map between the mattresses on my bed. When Kimber came back in the room, I made myself look busy by digging out a *Seventeen* magazine from my suitcase and pretending to read.

How's your room? I asked Sam.

Not bad. How about yours?

So far so good. I wasn't about to outline all of the little ways that Kimber planned on making me uncomfortable. Besides, it didn't matter anyway. We wouldn't be spending that much time in here.

"I hope you don't plan on leaving your stuff all over the place," Kimber sniffed, sitting down on her bed.

"No," I said, not glancing up from the magazine. "If I do anything to bother you, *please* let me know. I wouldn't want to annoy you." I resisted the urge to laugh.

I was saved from her smart comeback because Mrs. Britt knocked on the door. "Attendance, ladies!"

I tossed the magazine down and got up. "I'll tell her you're here."

I went out into the hall, pulling the door behind me. "We're both here, Mrs. Britt."

"Good, Heven. Did you enjoy the flight?"

"Yes."

"Wonderful. Now, we are meeting downstairs in the conference room in an hour for a meal; then we will do some light sightseeing on the bus before calling it an early night."

"Yes, ma'am."

"See you girls downstairs," she called, but stopped and turned back around. "Oh, Heven, I don't think I need to remind you that this is the girl's floor *only*. There are to be no boys in your room."

"Yes, ma'am. I understand."

"Good. See you at dinner."

I sighed and pushed the door open. It hadn't latched all the way, so I didn't have to use my keycard to get back in. When I walked in, I saw Kimber scurry away from my side of the room. Saying nothing, I glanced at my suitcase, the clothes were askew and the lid was open. I gaped.

Kimber had been going through my things.

"What do you think you're doing?" I asked, putting my hands on my hips.

"I don't know what you're talking about."

"You were going through my stuff!"

"Why would I want to do that?" she asked, sounding bored and trying to play it off.

But I could see her aura. She was lying through her teeth.

I sighed. "Look, I don't like this situation any more than you do, but we are stuck with each other until this trip is over. Do us both a favor and you stay on your side of the room and I'll stay on mine."

"Whatever."

I went to my suitcase and began straightening the clothes. What had she been looking for anyway? I couldn't possibly have anything that she would want. My stomach sank when I thought of the scroll. Since I was already on the floor beside the bed, I carefully slid my hand between the mattresses in search of the bronze tube. It was there. I breathed a sigh of relief. Kimber didn't even know about the scroll, so I wasn't sure why I was even worrying.

I watched her gather up a clean change of clothes and storm into the bathroom, angry at me for reasons I really didn't understand. Kimber could go through my things all she wanted, she wouldn't find anything. Even if she did happen to see the scroll, she wouldn't have the first clue as to what it was.

* * *

Sleeping without Sam was not something that came easily. Sleeping right next to your best-friend-turned-enemy was even worse. Kimber insisted on sleeping with the bathroom light and TV on. It was beyond frustrating. I was enjoying the time here in Italy so far, but our days were full of people, places and noise. It would be nice to have a break at the end of the day. For my head and eyes to have a break. Even though I hadn't told Sam yet, I was pretty sure what my new 'supernatural' ability was. If you could call it that. I closed my eyes and called up an image from the Sistine Chapel's famous ceiling. It came easily, quietly. The images took perfect shape in mind with the slightest of clicks. I had been practicing this since I caught on to my brain's newest ability. Every time it became easier and clearer.

I had a photographic memory.

Why this would be considered a 'supernatural' ability was beyond me. It seemed kind of lame and was one of the reasons that I had yet to tell Sam. I mean, gheesh, he turns into a super-powered animal with super hearing and strength. Fire doesn't harm him, water cannot drown him, even ice cannot freeze him.

Those are superpowers.

Using my brain as a camera just seemed lame.

It didn't stop me from practicing and seeing how much my mind could hold. Airis seemed to think that this 'power' would be useful, and considering that we are being hunted by demons for the Treasure Map, I figured that it couldn't hurt to use everything available to me. Who knows when this little ability might come in handy.

From the bed next to mine, Kimber snored lightly. Moving slowly, I got up and tiptoed to the TV and shut it off. The room plunged into darkness except for the light shining from the bathroom. I went to the door and pushed it closed so that only a slim ray of light shone into the room. Relaxing already, I slipped back beneath the covers and thought about Sam. I reached out to him with our Mindbond, which had seemed to grow stronger since he broke the Dream Walkers thread, to know that he was already sleeping.

I closed my eyes and willed myself to relax. A while later, a sound roused me from my half-sleep and I lay there, unmoving with my eyes closed, trying to figure out what I was hearing. It sounded like someone was ruffling through a bag or a box.

And whomever it was… was right next to me.

My suitcase! Someone or *something* was searching my things. On impulse I threw out my fist, while yelling, "Kimber, wake up!" My fist connected with something solid. I turned my head and gasped at the large figure looming over me.

I heard Kimber moving. "Turn on the light!" I ordered as the intruder began to scramble backward.

"What the hell is wrong with you?" Kimber demanded, but she switched on the lamp beside her bed.

We both gasped.

There was a demon at the foot of my bed.

It seemed familiar somehow with its long, black hair, full of twigs and leaves. He was naked and I wanted to gag. His hands were deformed and twisted… I strained my memory for this demon and what he could do… and suddenly I cursed the fact that I hadn't always had a photographic memory.

The demon jumped on the foot of the bed, causing the mattress to dip. When it opened its mouth, I remembered exactly what this thing could do.

"What the hell is *that?*" Kimber cried, clutching the blanket around her.

Sam! I shouted. *Hurry, Sam!*

A strange mist began floating out of the demon's mouth, a heavy curtain of fog. I bounded off the bed, trying to stay out of its reach, knowing that if I got lost in it we would be in trouble.

"Run, Kimber! Get out of here!" I said, reaching between the mattresses and pulling out the scroll.

The demon made a sound, the screech of an angry bird and more mist began filling the room, reaching toward us.

Kimber gasped, but made no move to flee. I looked at her to try to reassure her that this thing wasn't going to hurt us. She must be scared out of her mind at seeing something like this.

Only she wasn't looking at the demon.

She was staring at the scroll in my hands.

"Kimber, we have to get out of here," I insisted, stumbling toward her, grabbing her arm to make her understand. The mist was getting closer, beginning to curl around us. I coughed.

Then something strange started to happen. The mist continued to fill the room, reaching for us, but it couldn't get close. It wrapped completely around us, but it was like we were standing in an impenetrable bubble.

I looked at Kimber for some sort of an explanation, but she was focused on the demon advancing toward us, angry that his mist wasn't working.

The door slammed open, smacking the wall with a bang and Sam stormed in the room. Cole followed behind and began coughing at the stuff that filled the room. Before I could say anything, Sam was driving his fist through the demon's back, his hand coming out of its chest. Instantly, the demon disintegrated and vanished, taking the weird, choking mist with it.

Sam reached for me, pulling me close. I breathed a sigh of relief. I guess giving him my room keycard every night before bedtime was a good idea, because without it, he would have had to break down the door. He was wearing a hoodie sweatshirt with a kangaroo pocket in the front. Without second thought, I slid the scroll into the pocket.

"What the hell was that?" Kimber asked.

"I have no idea," I lied, hoping I sounded convinced.

Kimber's aura flared with disbelief, but there was curiosity there too, which seemed a little strange to me. She glanced back down at my hands and frowned. "Where did it go?"

"I guess Sam scared it off." I knew full well that she was talking about the scroll, but I played dumb.

"Yeah, sure," she agreed.

"Are you okay, Kimber?" Cole asked, reaching out to place a hand on her shoulder.

She shrugged him off, angry. "I'm fine."

Why wasn't she more scared and surprised? Why did she seem interested in the scroll?

Cole flipped on the lamp between the two beds. He whistled between his teeth. "You girls are messy."

The room was trashed. Both our suitcases had been overturned, our clothes scattered everywhere. My shower bag had been dumped, its contents littered the floor. Kimber's shower bag was also emptied all over the bathroom. My eyes collided with Sam's and he nodded.

Guess they've figured out we're here.

Take the scroll with you tonight. As soon as we get to Rome, we have got to get it to the catacombs.

He nodded and turned to meet Cole's stare. Something seemed to pass between them. When had they started working together? Did they actually *like* one another? Cole looked at me and smiled. "Want some help picking up?"

He knew that we didn't do all this; he was just playing along for Kimber's benefit.

Kimber huffed beside me.

"No, thanks. You guys better go back to your room before you get caught in here," I said.

"Wouldn't want you to get in trouble for breaking the rules," Kimber snapped.

I wouldn't put it past her to call our chaperones herself.

If you need me... Sam said, pulling me close once more.

I'll be fine. They won't come back tonight. At least I hoped they wouldn't.

When the boys were gone, I looked at Kimber. "How did you do that?"

"Do what?"

"Stop that mist from surrounding us."

Her arm froze, just briefly as she bent to pick up her clothes, but then she said, "I have no idea what you're talking about."

She was lying and her aura told me so. I watched her as she went around the room, picking up clothes and it dawned on me that she wasn't picking them up. She was searching for something.

"What are you doing?"

"Uh, hello? Some creepy man broke in here and trashed our stuff. I'm picking it up."

My eyes narrowed. She was taking this awfully well. And she was lying. I didn't stop that mist from surrounding us. It had to have been her. She made a small sound and I looked over in time to see her slipping a familiar box into her shower bag. It was that same box I saw sitting on her dresser in her bedroom. What was in there? Why was it so important?

Kimber caught me staring and turned around, hands on her hips. "What?" she demanded.

"Nothing," I mumbled and began to pick up my stuff.

Something was going on with Kimber and I had a feeling that whatever it was wasn't going to be good.

Chapter Sixteen

Heven

After days of sightseeing in Florence, Venice and Pisa (the leaning tower of Pisa was so cool), finally, we arrived in Rome. The places we had been to were stunning, and we had such a wonderful time, but the constant strain of looking over our shoulders was wearing on us. Thankfully, no more demons had attacked, but I couldn't shake the feeling that we were being followed *and* watched.

After breakfast at our hotel (even though we changed hotels we still had to stay with the same roommate), we were heading out for another day filled with sightseeing and activities. I was looking forward to the main attraction of the day: the Colosseum.

From the minute we pulled up on the bus, everyone was enraptured. The place was enormous, and even in ruins, it was amazing. I could only imagine what it had looked like when it was new and not crumbling. We spent the morning with a tour guide who filled our heads with stories of the history of the things that went on here. Executions, gladiatorial combats and classical mythology drama were just a few of the things that the walls of this place had seen. It was a great distraction, almost enough to make me forget about what we were to do while we were in Rome.

Sam, you brought the scroll, right? After the demon attack and Kimber searching my things, I decided that the scroll would be safer with Sam and he's been keeping it close since then.

It's in my backpack.

I tried not to stare at the dark green pack slung over his shoulder too much, but it was hard. Lunch time came and we all gathered to get the bagged lunches that the teachers kept in big coolers and then spread back out to find places to eat. Having lunch at the Colosseum in Rome was not something one could do every day. Sam, Cole and I found a spot away from the others where we could talk.

"We have to get this scroll where it belongs," I whispered, looking around at the crumbling travertine walls.

Cole pulled a copy of the itinerary out of his back pack and looked it over. "I've got it all figured out," he said. "We're supposed to go to the Via Appia Antica tomorrow. There's an entrance to the catacomb of San Sebastiano on that road."

I nodded. "We'll have to figure out a way to slip away from the group."

"I haven't figured that out yet," Cole said, taking a huge bite of his sandwich.

I closed my eyes and called up the information I read about the Via Appia Antica in the tourist book I had. "Via Appia Antica is a national park now. There's a long road that runs through it. It is super popular with cyclists and runners. There are a bunch of cafés and shops along the road until you head out into the countryside. The catacomb entrance is south on the road."

When I opened my eyes Cole and Sam were staring at me. "When did you memorize all that?"

I blushed. "I didn't. It's my newest 'super power.' I have a photographic memory."

"Cool!" Cole replied.

Sam frowned. "How does it work?" *Why didn't you tell me?*

I was embarrassed. "I just look at something once, and I can recall it exactly."

Does it hurt? Sam asked. He didn't seem put off that I kept it from him.

Not at all. No more headaches either.

"This might come in handy," Sam said aloud, covering the fact we were having a conversation of our own.

I'm sorry I didn't tell you right away.

"You'll never flunk a test again!" Cole laughed.

I get it, but you don't ever have to be embarrassed with me, okay?

I nodded and leaned into his side, feeling a little guilty. Sam reached out and snagged the itinerary from Cole.

"It says on the itinerary that we can rent some bicycles and ride along the path. Maybe we could do that and pretend to get separated from the group for a while," Sam suggested.

"Sounds good," Cole said.

I nodded. "Now we just have to keep the scroll safe until then."

"What's the deal with Kimber?" Cole murmured, his gaze going past us.

I didn't have to look to know he was watching her, just as she was probably watching us. "I'm not sure yet, but it might be good to stay clear of her. She's acting weird."

She stopped that mist from wrapping around us.

How?

"Nuh-uh, no brain talking without me," Cole said, realizing what Sam and I were doing.

"Sorry," I mumbled. "I get the impression that she knows more than we think."

"Like about the Map?" Sam asked.

"Yeah," I said, slowly. But how could she know anything? Suddenly a sense of anger filled me. Why did everything have to be so confusing all the time? We were here in this beautiful place and I wasn't able to enjoy it completely because I was so preoccupied with everything else. I probably wouldn't get the chance to come here again and I wanted to look back with good memories. I reached into my bag and pulled out the travel diary Gran gave me. It was filling up with notes and drawings. I couldn't wait to add the pictures that I had been able to take.

As we finished our bagged lunches, I pulled out my camera and began snapping pictures. I smiled to myself because I knew that my brain was now kind of like a camera and these sights wouldn't be forgotten. Still, having a photograph for my book was special.

There were a lot of missing stones and marble from the structure creating holes and crumbling windows. It was in one of these crumbling spaces that something caught my eye. A movement. Someone was sitting in what I assumed was once a window. When he caught me looking, he leaped off the other side and disappeared from sight. I gasped and looked at Sam and Cole to see if they had seen him too.

"What is it?" Sam asked, his hand moving to my back.

I blinked and looked back up to where the person had been. He was gone.

"Heven?" Cole asked, worried.

I shook my head and forced a smile. "Sorry, guess my eyes are playing tricks on me."

Sam frowned. "What did you see?"

I laughed lightly. "Thought I saw someone sitting up there." I pointed to the empty space.

Cole laughed, but it was a little strained. "Maybe you've had too much sun."

"You're probably right." Except now all three of us were wondering if something was actually there. We all knew that it wasn't out of the realm of possibilities.

I sighed. Isn't this what I was trying to avoid? Now, instead of just me not enjoying the trip, it was all of us. "I'm sure it was nothing. Let's try and have a good time."

Students were moving around, exploring for the little bit of time we had left until we had to board the bus. By unspoken agreement, our conversation ended. I looked out over the Colosseum, entranced by its beauty.

In the center of the arena, the floor was missing and you could see down to the underground passages where the gladiators once awaited their fates. It looked like a complex stone maze with walls running in every direction. Across the center of the arena was a modern walkway.

"Let's go get a closer look at those passages," I said, tugging Sam along with me.

The walkway was long and went directly from one side to the other. We walked across, pointing out the hidden passages and tumbling travertine walls. I tried to imagine what it had been like for a gladiator, waiting down in the narrow stone rooms, hearing the roaring crowd and the clanking of armor and weapons. Had he been scared? Terrified that he wouldn't live to see another day or had he been anxious to get above and show everyone what he could do?

I thought I heard a sound from the shadows below and peered down, but saw nothing.

"Hey, come on. We have to be back at the bus soon," Sam called from a few feet away, pulling me away from whatever I thought I heard.

Most of the students were heading back toward the entrance already and I rushed to catch up with Sam and Cole, who were walking back toward the exit. I stumbled a bit as I moved forward because my pant leg had gotten caught on something. I looked down to see where I was caught and I saw that I wasn't caught at all. Something was holding me.

"Sam," I whispered fiercely. He spun and I pointed at the gnarled hand grabbing my ankle.

I did my best to yank my leg free, but the demon was strong and yanked back, causing me to pitch forward. I caught hold of the railing, trying to stop myself from falling, but it was no use. I tumbled right over, down into the dark stone passageways below.

* * *

It was darker down here than it seemed from above. It was also narrower and it was cold. The walls were rough and the floor was packed dirt. I didn't hurt myself when I fell because the demon caught me. I screeched and jerked my elbow, connecting with its face. It dropped me with a hiss and I scrambled to my feet and took off running. When I came to the end of a passage, I slowed to turn, but another demon jumped out in front of me. I looked over my shoulder to see the other one advancing. I was caught between them with stone walls boxing me in.

Sam and Cole appeared behind the demon and Cole used the dagger that Gemma must have given him to take off its head. I didn't even bat an eye at the head rolling across the floor. In fact, it was a welcome sight as it meant there was one less demon to fight. The demon in front of me grabbed my arms and I kicked out, connecting, but it wasn't a strong enough kick to make it free me. So I kicked again, harder this time. The demon shrieked and released its hold and I took advantage of my freedom to kick it in the shoulder as it doubled over. It fell backward on its bottom and its hollow eyes flared with menace as it jumped to its feet and cracked its neck, no doubt considering how to make me pay.

"I've got what you want," Sam taunted it. I turned to see him holding up the scroll.

The demon shoved me aside and ran at Sam, who threw the scroll behind him to Cole. The demon screeched and dove, but not before Sam caught it in the chest with his fist. It disintegrated before our eyes.

"Come on. Let's get back," Sam said, motioning for me to join him and Cole. We walked forward to where the walkway was, but we were stopped from climbing back up because two more demons jumped in front of us. Sam and Cole started fighting and Cole tossed me the scroll. Before I knew it, a large demon grabbed me from behind and began dragging me away.

I grunted, struggling against its grip, causing Sam to look my way and take a hard punch to the side of his head. He went down just as I was dragged around the corner and out of sight.

* * *

I was *totally* right when I thought that these passageways looked like a giant maze. It is exactly what they were, and I was lost. They all looked the same: dark, cold and winding.

Or maybe, I couldn't find my way out because I was busy being chased by demons. Just another typical day for me. After that demon dragged me away, I managed to fight my way free and tried to find my way back to Sam, but I couldn't. These passageways were filled with demons, and everywhere I went, there was another. So, I figured the safest thing for me to do was to take the scroll and run away from Sam and Cole to give them a chance to get out. I had no idea if Sam was hurt, if Cole was hurt.

But I kept running.

Glancing over my shoulder for the hundredth time, I confirmed what I already knew; demons were hot on my heels. I picked up the pace and turned to my left, praying it wasn't a dead end. It wasn't and there was a small crumbled section in the wall off to my right so I jumped through and started running in the opposite direction. I heard a great thump and a crumbling sound and knew that one of them saw where I had gone, and they were destroying the wall so they could follow. It made me mad that this ancient place would be damaged for something like this. I took a right and ran smack into the rough stone wall.

"Dammit," I swore and turned to go back the way I came. I had no idea how deep in this place was or how big it actually was. It couldn't be that big... could it?

There was a small alcove in the wall. I squeezed myself in and doubled over to catch my breath. Maybe I should start carrying a weapon like Gemma. I heard a scuffling sound and peered out to see a demon run by. I waited a few minutes and left my hiding place and ran in the opposite direction. There was a light up ahead and I ran toward it, hoping it wasn't a trap.

It was an old door that was open and led to stairs that went up to the ground floor. I could hear the traffic go by on the street.

Sam! There's a door to the outside. It was close now. I was almost there.

No, Heven! It's a trap! Turn around!

Too late. A demon rushed me from the side and sent me crashing to the floor. The scroll fell out of my hands and rolled away into a shadowed corner.

The demon that sent me to the floor landed on top of me and was scrambling off me to get to the scroll. I dug my nails into its arms, trying to keep it from getting away. It looked down, annoyed, and I brought up my knee between its legs. I had no clue if that was even a good defense against creatures like this, but it was worth a try. It hissed and rolled to the side.

Note to self: it is good defense to knee demons in their 'man parts.'

I pushed off the ground and raced toward the scroll. The demon recovered from his groin injury and grabbed me by the foot, yanking me off my feet. I used my free leg to kick it in the head as Sam lunged, ramming his fist right through its back; it disintegrated right on top of me. Gross.

I rolled over and grabbed the scroll, hurrying to shove it inside my bag as I stood. Sam helped me to my feet and we both turned when we heard scuffling.

Cole was being ambushed by the two remaining demons.

As he was fighting, he was hit from behind and Cole slumped to the ground.

"Cole!" I screamed as Sam ran forward at the demons.

But he didn't have a chance to do anything to them.

A super strong gust of wind blew in from the door and knocked the demons to the ground. Sam hurried to send them to dust. I crouched beside Cole. "Cole!"

He groaned and looked up at me. I grabbed his hand and squeezed.

"Is he all right?"

All of us whipped around at the new voice. Kimber was standing in the doorway looking torn.

"Kimber? What are you doing down here?"

"Mrs. Britt sent me to see what was taking you so long."

What had she seen? How would she even know we were down here?

"Oh, uh—I accidently tripped and fell off the walkway above these passageways. Cole and Sam came after me and we got lost down here."

"Cole?" Kimber asked, taking a few more steps inside. I could see her aura even in the dark and I could see that she was genuinely worried about Cole.

And that she still loved him. Nothing like a demon attack and threat of death to bring out someone's true feelings.

"Heven?" Cole groaned, grabbing my arm.

"Everything's okay," I told him as he sat up, holding his head. I felt around for blood, but there wasn't any. Thank goodness.

"You need to hurry up," Kimber snapped.

My show of concern for Cole angered her. If only she understood...

"Kimmie?" Cole asked, getting to his feet.

Kimber, who was on her way out the door, stopped and turned. The red in her aura gave way to pink. "Yeah?"

"What are you doing down here?"

Kimber huffed and her worry turned back into anger. Keeping up with her aura was like watching exploding fireworks. "Hurry up!" she barked and disappeared from sight.

"How much did she see?" Cole asked as we walked toward the door.

"I don't think anything," Sam said.

I remained silent because I wasn't so sure. I think Kimber saw a lot more than they thought. I also thought that she pretended to buy my excuse about being down here, because if she started asking questions, then I would too.

Like how exactly she knew where to find us and why that gust of wind flattened those demons right as they were threatening Cole, the guy she still loved.

Chapter Seventeen

Heven

The rest of the day seemed to drag on endlessly. I was filled with dread, waiting for the next demon to attack, expecting something in every corner or shadow we passed. Sam and Cole were wound just as tight, and wherever we went, they flanked my sides, closing in and making it harder to breathe than it already was. My bag felt like it held ten heavy stones when, really, all it held was a cherry lip gloss, some money, a student ID and the scroll. But what weighed me down most of all were the questions. They swirled through my brain like snowflakes in a winter storm, clouding every other thought I had.

Something was going on with Kimber.

I knew.

She knew I knew.

When I wasn't staring at shadows and corners, I was staring at her. She avoided my gaze like the plague. I might have brushed it off before as her just being angry and thinking I stole Cole, but not anymore.

Her eyes betrayed her, the way she hunched her shoulders betrayed her, but most of all, her aura betrayed her. Lies and uncertainty cloaked her wherever she went. And it seemed to me that her skin became paler every day.

What did she have to do with that wind back at the Colosseum? What is in that box she is carrying around? Why do things seem to happen when she's around—*odd* things, like slamming doors and blocking that mist? What bothered me most of all about Kimber is that she seemed to hate me. Sure, she was angry and sure, she turned out not to be the friend I thought she was, but I never believed she hated me. Maybe she did begin to hate me when she began thinking that I was after Cole, but deep down, I think she knows that Cole and I are just friends. I think she uses it as an excuse to cover up something else, an excuse to hate me.

And I let her.

Because I have secrets too. Secrets that I don't want her to know because it would put her in danger by knowing. Isn't there enough danger already? I would rather Kimber hate me than be my friend and be hurt because of it.

An echo of the Dream Walkers last words echoed through my head. *When everyone around you is dead...* I shivered and Sam pressed even closer to me.

Is everything okay?

I have to talk to Kimber. As much as I wanted to protect her, I needed answers because I had a terrible feeling that something was wrong and only getting worse.

He nodded. I leaned around him to look at Cole. "Cole, I need to tell Kimber."

Cole stared back at me for a long, quiet moment. I prayed he would agree because, even if he didn't, I was going to tell her anyway. Telling Kimber that Cole was my brother would take away her excuse to be angry at me for stealing her boyfriend; she wouldn't have an excuse to 'hate' me anymore. Maybe then I could get her to talk to me.

"Yeah." Cole sighed, scrubbing a hand down his face. "She needs to know."

"Thank you," I whispered, reaching out to squeeze his hand. He didn't respond, but returned the pressure with his fingers.

The bus pulled up in front of the hotel and I wanted to weep. It seemed silly to be happy to see a place that wasn't really safe. I mean, hadn't a demon already attacked us at a hotel? Yet it was kind of serving as my temporary home, and at least inside my room, I could relax a little and not have to worry so much about watching everyone around me.

At the bank of elevators, Sam hesitated, his fingers clasped tightly around mine. I knew from our Mindbond that he did not want to let me go upstairs alone. He was my guardian, my protector, and he wanted to be with me, but rules were rules and Mrs. Britt was standing by the elevator doors, watching everyone like a hawk. I sighed and leaned forward, pressing my lips to his, not caring that the teacher was watching. Sam's lips were gentle as was his caress to my cheek, which was a complete juxtaposition to the urgent intensity that he carried within.

I'll be fine. I promise. I tried to soothe him.

It's only an hour until dinner, he said, the words like a mantra.

I tapped his forehead, reminding him like he always did with me that we are connected even when we are apart.

I'll rip this place apart if I get one bad feeling.

I'll see you in an hour. I tried to reassure him before turning toward the elevators, ignoring Mrs. Britt's glare. I'm sure I'd be reminded about the no-touching policy later. Whatever. Sam was still watching as I climbed on the elevator and the doors began to close.

During the short ride to my floor, I prayed that my talk with Kimber went well because, if it didn't and I couldn't control my emotions, Sam might not be able to keep the tight lid closed on the already tenuous grip he had over himself.

I stepped off the elevator and into the empty hallway. I was behind everyone because I lingered in the lobby with Sam. I took a deep breath and relished the single moment when I was blissfully alone. It was one of the few times since arriving here in Rome that I had one second to myself. I walked slowly, trying to draw out the time, if only for a second. When I rounded the corner, my heart sank because there was someone in the hall and I was no longer alone. The person hurried in the opposite direction towards the stairwell and didn't even give me a glance.

It was Ms. Merriweather. When she reached the door, she paused to look left, then right... to make sure she was alone? Hadn't she heard me come around the corner? I slowed my steps even further, trying not to make a sound as I watched her. She always seemed off somehow. Just before she stepped into the stairwell, something happened that shook me to my core: her usual blue and green aura blinked out and the space around her was replaced with a cloud of black.

I had never, not once, seen black in a person's aura before.

I blinked, thinking my eyes were playing tricks on me, but when I looked back, the black cloud was still there, hanging over her like an angry thundercloud... I blinked once more and the blue and green aura was back, surrounding her like it had never been gone. As if the black had never been there at all.

The shower was running when I let myself into the room and I heard the beat of music from behind the bathroom door as I passed.

As anxious as I was to speak with Kimber, I was glad that I had a moment to think. What could it mean about Ms. Merriweather's aura? Had I really seen that burst of black or was I just imagining things? Black was not a color I associated with an aura and I didn't know what it could mean. Aura's always surrounded people with certainty, clarity and truth. Was Tabitha Merriweather somehow able to mask her aura? Or change it? Influencing an aura wasn't something I'd ever even considered before. To me an aura was true; they didn't lie. It unsettled me to think what I believed to be a constant truth was somehow being manipulated.

I went over to my suitcase and ruffled around for something clean to wear to dinner and settled on a cotton sundress and sandals. Laying my choices out on the bed, I reluctantly removed my bag and placed it beside my suitcase. Kimber took a long time in the shower and I began to worry that we wouldn't have time to talk. Finally, the shower turned off and moments later, she came out of the bathroom wrapped in a towel. She walked right past me without even glancing in my direction.

"Hey," I chirped, trying to sound friendly.

She ignored me and turned her back, reaching into her suitcase and pulling out some clothes.

"I was hoping we could talk."

"I don't want to talk." Her voice was low and muffled as she pulled a dress over her head.

"Great minds think alike," I said, motioning toward the dress I had chosen as well.

She turned toward me, glancing in my direction briefly. "We are nothing alike."

Her cheeks were splotchy, her eyes were red and her voice was thick from crying. I gasped. "What's the matter?"

"Nothing." She turned away again.

It didn't look like nothing. Kimber hardly ever cried, so whatever made her cry had to be bad. "Did something happen back home?"

"I said I'm fine!"

"You don't look fine."

She huffed and went back into the bathroom, shutting the door in my face. I was about to yell through the wood, but the hairdryer came on and blocked my words. With a sigh I picked up my brush and went to the mirror on the wall and began brushing. It looked like I wasn't going to be allowed in the bathroom anytime soon, so I did my best to clean myself up out here.

Is everything okay? Sam asked.

Yeah. Kimber doesn't want to talk.

I'm sorry, sweetheart.

For some reason tears sprang to my eyes. I sat the brush aside and blinked them back as I checked my reflection one last time before changing into my sundress. The deep purple material was soft and cool against my skin. It was slightly long and it brushed at my toes when I moved. Instead of being annoying, it was comforting. The dress was strapless so I couldn't really hide the necklace with the key on it beneath my shirt. I shrugged and allowed it to fall forward down over my chest. It was pretty and no one would know it was anything other than an accessory. I decided to grab a light sweater out of my suitcase in case I got cold and bent down to search for the one I wanted. When I stood, Kimber was there behind me, mere inches away.

"Gheesh!" I gasped. "You're going to give me a heart attack."

Her eyes were alarmingly blank and I wondered if she heard what I said. Suddenly, she moved, taking a swift step toward me, her eyes still strangely vacant.

"Kimber?"

She blinked, her eyes clearing. "What?" Her voice was defensive, but her aura flared a muddy brown shade, telling me that her actions confused her.

"I wanted to talk to you."

Her gaze dropped down to the key on my necklace. I had the urge to curl my hand around it out of view, but that would give away more than I wanted, so I ignored her stare to say, "It's about Cole."

"What about Cole?" She forgot the key and looked at my face.

"Remember how I told you that something was going on with him and I couldn't tell you?"

She crossed her arms over her chest and nodded.

"He said I could."

"He did?" I hated to see the hope come into her eyes. Kimber still loved Cole, but his heart wasn't hers anymore.

I nodded. "It's confidential, but you're my friend and I want you to know."

Her eyes softened and her aura smoothed out into the vibrant hues that were normal for her.

I opened my mouth just as there was a loud knock on the door. "Girls," Ms. Merriweather called on the other side. "We're going downstairs for dinner."

Kimber stiffened and took a step back. Her face hardened and became a mask. I sighed.

"We'll be right there!" I called. "So about what I wanted to tell you,"

"Kimber, you don't want to be late," Ms. Merriweather said.

Something passed behind Kimber's eyes and her aura bloomed a shade of gray. I suppressed a shudder at the unsightly color. She didn't seem to notice my obvious distress as she grabbed her bag and slung it over her shoulder, walking to the door.

"Kimber."

She stopped and turned.

"About Cole—"

"Forget it. There isn't anything you could say that would take back what you've done."

"This isn't about me. It's about Cole."

She paused with her hand on the knob before whispering so low I had to strain to hear, "Then tell him to come to me."

She rushed out the door before anything else could be said. My stomach turned. Why did it suddenly seem that whatever was going on with Kimber might have something to do with Tabitha Merriweather?

Just who the hell was she?

Kimber never came back to the room after dinner. I waited and paced, looked at the clock, and waited some more. When midnight rolled around, it became clear she wasn't coming. I glanced at her empty bed and wondered what to do.

The first thing that popped into my head wasn't the most honorable thing, but it *was* a good idea. I rushed across the room and began pawing through her stuff. I was looking for anything that might give me a clue as to where she could be or what had been going on with her lately.

I was also looking for that box.

I found nothing.

I sighed and sat down on the edge of her bed. How could eagle-eye Mrs. Britt not have noticed that she wasn't on the bus? Because she *had* been on the bus. Could someone have grabbed her when she was getting off the bus? What if she was hurt or lost?

I got up and ran out into the hall, down the corridor, stopping in front of our chaperones' room. Just as I raised my fist in the air to knock, the door swung open and Ms. Merriweather stepped out.

She didn't seem very surprised to see me.

I took a step back and cleared my throat. "I came to see Mrs. Britt."

"She's with a student. Is there something I can help you with, Heven?"

"Ummmm..."

She crossed her arms over her chest and waited patiently. Her aura was strong and clear, shades of soothing blue and green. "Kimber hasn't been in our room since before dinner," I blurted.

Ms. Merriweather's face softened. "Oh! I'm sorry. I thought Mrs. Britt told you. I guess she hasn't had time yet. Kimber isn't feeling well, so we thought it best if she was in her own room tonight, so you don't get sick too."

"She's sick?"

The teacher's aide nodded emphatically. "Poor thing can't hold anything down."

Is that why she seemed out of it earlier, because she was sick? It would explain her lack of color. But still... could I trust this woman?

"She's sleeping now. Mrs. Britt gave her some anti-nausea medicine so she should be able to join the group tomorrow." Her words were sincere and her aura didn't waver at all when she spoke. It was already after midnight and morning wasn't far off, so waiting until then didn't seem so terrible.

"Okay," I said. "I'll see her then."

"Good night, Heven."

"Night." I went back to the room and let myself in and leaned against the back of the door.

Kimber is sick, so she's staying in another room. I told Sam.

You're alone?

Yes. I knew he would come to me. *Be careful, Ms. Merriweather is trolling the halls.*

Thanks.

I didn't waste time or linger by the door. Instead, I went to bed, climbing between the sheets and switching off the bedside lamp. The room plunged into darkness, but I wasn't scared. I faced down demons almost daily and had been sucked into Hell through my dreams. No, the dark didn't scare me.

The door opened quietly, slowly and I smiled. He moved through the room lithely and confidently, without so much as a misstep. I heard the rustle of fabric and felt his T-shirt land at the foot of the bed.

His skin was warm, as it always was, and it felt like silk against mine. I snuggled up against him, pressing close and rested my cheek on his chest. His arms encircled me, and while I hadn't been scared before, I hadn't felt safe until now.

I missed this, he said as I felt a long sigh exit his lungs.

Me too. I haven't slept well at all.

Rest now. His voice was like a lullaby through my mind.

Before I could drift into a thoughtless slumber, my mind returned to Kimber. Was she really sick or was Tabitha Merriweather lying?

There's something off about Mrs. Britt's TA.

Shhh. Whatever it is will be there in the morning.

Sam was exactly right, and it scared me more than anything. No, I wasn't afraid of the dark. But I was afraid that when day arrived and the sun came out, it would shine light into all the shadows from the night before, revealing all that the darkness had hidden.

I woke to the sound of my cell phone ringing inside of my bag and struggled to untangle myself from Sam and the sheets to reach over and haul the bag on top of the bed. The contents spilled everywhere and I sifted through them to grab up my phone and silence the annoying ring.

"Hello?" I mumbled glancing down at the scroll in my lap.

"Heven! I didn't wake you, did I?"

"Mom?" I glanced at the screen on the phone at the clock. It was barely seven a.m. "Isn't it like one a.m. there?" I guessed, struggling to remember the time difference between Maine and Rome.

"Yes, but I wanted to speak with you and I figured before you left for the day was the best time."

"I tried to call a few times, but you were never home," I said as the early morning cobwebs evaporated from my head. "Is something wrong? How is Logan?"

Behind me, Sam sat up and I felt his arms wrap around my waist. I knew he was listening for my mother's answer.

"Everything is fine. We're really enjoying our time with Logan. He's a wonderful boy." I couldn't help but focus in on the "*we*" and the "*our*" in her words. She didn't notice my silence and said, "I just wanted to see how you are enjoying your trip so far. I miss you."

"I'm sure Sam will be glad to hear that Logan is doing well. He's been worried about him," I said as I leaned back into Sam. "And so far the trip is great. Rome is beautiful and the people here are so nice."

"What's your favorite place you've visited so far?"

I spent a few minutes going into detail about the museums and the Leaning Tower of Pisa telling her all about the art and history. It was so easy to describe everything thanks to my new photographic memory. She seemed interested asking about places and people. I found myself relaxing into Sam and enjoying the conversation. We hadn't been able to talk like this in so long… I realized how much I missed it.

"It sounds like you're having such an experience! The memories you will have will last a lifetime!" she said.

"Thanks for allowing me to come, Mom." I shuddered at how close I came to not being here.

"Of course. Henry was right in suggesting that you go."

I paused. "Yes, I remember you saying Henry suggested that I come." It still seemed odd to me, but I didn't say that.

I could almost see Mom frowning on the end of the line. "Did I say that?"

I sat up, out of the circle of Sam's embrace. "Mom? Are you all right?" I turned and looked at Sam, who was frowning. I knew he could hear our conversation.

"Yes. I guess I'm just tired—it's so late here." Her voice was back to normal and it was like the last few words never happened.

"Are you sure that's all it is?"

She gasped and I heard a clatter, which I assumed was the phone falling to the floor.

"Mom!"

I heard the phone being picked up and expected to hear my mother on the line. But it wasn't my mother. It was Henry.

"Sorry about that, Heven. Your mother tripped and dropped the phone." For some reason I shivered.

"Is she hurt?"

"Oh, no. She's fine. Just stubbed her toe on the coffee table."

I relaxed a little, but still wanted to hear her voice. "Can I speak with her please?"

"Sure! Oh, hey," he said, sounding like he was talking to an old friend. "Glad to hear you're having a great time in Rome."

"Thanks," I mumbled, wondering what Henry was doing at my mother's house at one o'clock in the morning. The thought was so disturbing, but it kind of described her "we" comments.

"What great place are you visiting today?" he asked.

I didn't want to talk to him. I wanted to talk to my mother, so I told him quickly about the planned visit to Via Appia Antica.

"Can't wait to hear all about it when you get home!"

"Sure," I said impatiently.

"Oh, and, Heven?" Henry said, annoying me yet even more. "Be careful today, those catacombs are dark and very old. Your mother and I would be very upset if you were hurt."

He said the words good-naturedly, if even fatherly, but something inside me tightened. Before I could respond, my mother came back on the line laughing. "Sorry, about that, honey. I'm just so clumsy anymore!"

"Did you fall?"

"Oh, no. I just stubbed my toe on the coffee table. It wasn't even my big toe, just the little one." She laughed.

I smiled. And because I knew Sam really wanted to talk to his brother, I asked Mom, "I know it's late there, but is Logan awake? Could I speak with him?"

"Oh, honey, he fell asleep hours ago. He spent the day with Henry and he was exhausted." Sam was thinking so loud that I blurted out what he was thinking. "He is there, right?"

Why Sam would think Logan wouldn't be there, I wasn't sure, but he was clearly worried about it, so I wanted to be sure he got an answer.

"Of course, Heven."

Sam relaxed and I turned to face him to be sure that's all he wanted to know. He nodded. "Okay, well you should probably get to bed. It's late there."

"I plan to. I'm so glad we got to talk!"

"Me too. When I get back, maybe we can have dinner? I got you a present I want to give you."

"Sounds wonderful. I'll talk to you soon. I love you, Heven."

"I love you too." I disconnected the phone and dropped in on the bed next to me.

"I wish I could have at least said hi to Logan," Sam said, looking down at the phone. Worry etched across his face.

"Do you want me to call her back and have her wake him up?"

He shook his head. "If he's sleeping, then its best to let him rest." Then almost to himself, he said, "I should have gotten that cell phone."

"Even if you had, the international rates would be outrageous. I can only imagine what my mother is paying for that international plan. He was okay when you talked to him the other day, right?"

"Yeah. He did seem good."

"See? Everything is fine. We haven't really had much time to talk about things. How is everything with Logan? You seemed to not want to leave him alone much."

He sighed. "He loses time, Hev. He goes to bed some nights and wakes up in a different place—not even in the apartment and he can't remember anything."

"Wow. That must be really scary." I didn't know what to say. I felt sorry for Logan, so young and to have all this happening to him. He must be so confused. It's no wonder Sam is so worried about him. "You think it's because his body is rejecting the hellhound gene?"

"I don't know what to think anymore."

He seemed weary, with worry lines crinkling his forehead. I reached out and fisted a handful of his hair, right in the front and lifted his head a little. "What can I do to help?"

The side of his lips raised in a lopsided smile. "You're already doing it."

"Pulling your hair?" I grinned and tugged his sun-kissed locks a little harder.

He laughed and grabbed my hand and held it against his chest. I liked the feeling of his heartbeat against my palm. "Being with you like this, it makes the hard times easier, you know?"

"Yeah," I whispered. "I know."

He tipped my chin up with his knuckles. "Hopefully, after today we will be able to concentrate on just having a good time here and when we get home, I'll concentrate on Logan."

I looked down at the scroll and nodded. Today we would go into the catacombs and return the scroll to where it belonged. Our promise to Airis will be filled and Sam and I could get on with our lives. So why did I feel a little sad to see it go?

"It's been a stressful couple months. It's normal to feel nervous," Sam murmured, brushing the hair back from my face.

I *did* feel nervous.

Sam pulled me against him and kissed me thoroughly, completely and thrillingly. When he pulled back, I could barely think at all. "I have to go," he whispered.

I nodded.

"I'll see you…" He glanced at the clock. "In thirty minutes."

I nodded, staring at his mouth.

He laughed. "Did you hear anything I just said?"

I blinked. "Uh, yeah. Breakfast."

He shook his head, got up, and threw on his T-shirt. Before slipping out the door, he kissed my forehead.

When he was gone, I looked over at the empty bed where Kimber should have been. I hoped she was feeling better and I would see her at breakfast. If I didn't, I was going to have to find a way to sneak into her room so I could see her for myself.

I grabbed my shower bag, the scroll and some clean clothes and took advantage of the fact I actually got to use the bathroom. Halfway there, a thought speared me and I stumbled. I told Henry about our visit to Via Appia Antica today and the planned bike ride. I *hadn't* told him about the catacombs. How did he know we were going there… and why did he tell me to be careful?

Chapter Eighteen

Heven

Kimber wasn't at breakfast. I watched the door the entire time we were eating, pushing the oatmeal around in my bowl, my heart leaping every time someone walked in the room, only to be let down when I realized that it was not her. Mrs. Britt sat a few tables away with Ms. Merriweather, and neither teacher acted as if anything was wrong. All the students chatted and laughed, no one seeming to notice Kimber's absence.

Because of this, I noticed it more.

That and the fact that everyone's auras were all very good-natured and peaceful this morning. It wasn't a bad thing, but it wasn't right either. An entire room full of people, rarely — if ever — has the same general feelings. It hadn't been this way at all during the trip till now. Usually, there were lots of different feelings flooding the room: homesickness, jealousy, curiosity, even nervousness at being somewhere so foreign without a parent. Of course, good-natured and happy auras were always present also.

But today, it was almost as if they felt fake.

It wasn't something I had really thought about before.

"How are you feeling today, Cole?" I asked, leaning toward him.

He shrugged and sat down his glass of orange juice. "Fine."

His aura looked like it always looked, which *was* usually filled with blues and greens. Of course, the magenta was there, a burst of vibrant color around his head. "Never mind." I sighed. Even if everyone's mood was being influenced, who's to say it would work on Cole? He is a Supernal Being, after all. Plus, if everyone else's auras were being manipulated, wouldn't that mean mine would be too? Wouldn't I be feeling calm and happy like everyone else?

I didn't feel like I was being influenced, so maybe I was just being paranoid.

"What is it, Heven?" Sam murmured.

I pushed my oatmeal away, done with even pretending to eat. "Everyone's aura looks a lot alike this morning."

Sam frowned. "You think it's a charade?"

An interesting way to phrase it. Could an entire room full of people's aura's be disguised and replaced by something more favorable? I shook my head slowly. "I don't know."

Without thinking about it, my eyes went back to the teachers' table and I remembered what I saw when Ms. Merriweather thought no one was looking. Her aura blanked out to be replaced with a cloud of black for a few moments...

"I'll be right back." I pushed away from the table and walked across the room.

Mrs. Britt looked up from her plate. "Heven? Is something wrong?"

"No, Mrs. Britt. I was wondering about Kimber. Is she all right?"

"She's still under the weather, I'm afraid. Ms. Merriweather checked her this morning."

I turned to the teacher's aide. She smiled up at me and I couldn't help but notice that the smile didn't reach her eyes. "Kimber vomited until the early hours of this morning. She is just too weak to join the class today."

Her aura remained exactly like everyone else's.

"I want to see her."

Tabitha Merriweather narrowed her eyes just a fraction at my words, but otherwise remained still. Mrs. Britt drew my attention away. "We have to be on the bus in just a few minutes, Heven. Kimber's probably sleeping. I will take you to her room this afternoon when we get back from the Via Appia Antica and you may see her then."

If I put up a fit, then Ms. Merriweather would know that I suspected something. There was nothing I could do but agree and go back to where we were sitting.

"Hev?" Cole asked when I sat back down.

"Something isn't right," I murmured, hating the fact I didn't know what it was.

Sam covered my hand with his. "You're just nervous that we're returning the scroll today. Once it's where it belongs, you'll feel much better."

234

I nodded, threading my fingers through his. I sincerely hoped he was right.

Deep down, I knew that he wasn't.

It was a beautiful day in Rome. The sun was shining, filling everything it touched with light and joy. The sky was a cloudless blue, brilliant and perfect. Yet, I couldn't shake the feeling of impending doom and it darkened my mood. I wasn't sure what to expect at Via Appia Antica because I had never been there, so when we pulled up, I climbed off the bus feeling a little nervous. It was unnecessary. The place was beautiful and I understood its tourist appeal even though it didn't seem like much. It was green and lush with trees and plants of different shapes and sizes. There was a long road that ran through it and people of every age were running, walking or cycling along the path. Others were picnicking on blankets and soaking up the sun's rays.

"Feeling better?" Sam asked, his hand rubbing my back.

"Yeah."

We all gathered around while Mrs. Britt outlined the activities that were available. A group would be formed for those who wanted to walk and explore, stopping at the shops that lined the street. Another group would be formed for those that wanted to cycle along the path and explore.

The cycling group would be led by Ms. Merriweather.

How would we manage to get away from the group to 'get lost' with her leading us? She seemed to have an eagle eye trained on me at all times. But we had to try because this was our only shot at getting the scroll into the catacombs.

Luckily, the cycling group was larger than the walkers. Being on a bicycle allowed us to cover more ground and see more of the attractions, so most wanted to do that. Ms. Merriweather led us to the rental place and we were all given a bike and a map, highlighting the main attractions and best eateries along the road. It also boasted a lot of history and trivia. I noted where the catacombs of San Sebastiano where located, then shoved the map into my bag. I didn't need information about anywhere else.

We started the tour in the center of the group, then gradually fell back until we were the last three, trailing behind. It was good that Ms. Merriweather headed south because we could travel that way with the class and then "accidentally" separate later.

Butterflies fluttered in my stomach and I ignored the fine shaking of my hands as the time drew closer for us to go off on our own. What if she saw us? What if she kept us from doing what we needed to do?

Turns out, separating from the group wasn't as difficult as I thought it would be. Small groups of students began going to the attractions that they wanted to see most. We fell in with a bigger group that was heading toward where we wanted to go. They all passed where we stopped, probably because it didn't look like much.

The small two-story church told of its age. It was made of stone with three great arches and large columns at the front. The church had a pitched roof and windows along the second story. There were tourists here, of course. Inside was a marble slab with the impression of Christ's feet. It was said to be the original with a copy housed somewhere else in Rome. Most people were studying the marble, so it was easy to find the staircase that led down into the catacombs without much notice.

The Catacombs of San Sebastiano is one of the smallest cemeteries, so it wasn't preserved very well. The stairway that led down was dark and murky. The stairs were covered in dust and dirt and very steep.

Sam went first and I was next with Cole bringing up the rear. We each had a flashlight, but none of us turned them on because while it was pretty dark, we could still see due to what lighting there was. At the bottom of the staircase was a restored crypt. It was the crypt of San Sebastiano that held a table altar. On top of the altar sat a bust of Saint Sebastiano. Underneath were platforms which were the tombs. I shivered, knowing that people were buried there. It seemed like such a desolate, creepy place for such revered men to be buried. The platforms were covered in paintings; some were faded because of their age.

Tourists were down here as well. Everyone was hushed out of respect or maybe fear. We stood amongst the people, pretending to study the paintings. Most people did not linger down here long and soon Sam was tugging me across the crypt and pointing down a narrow hall. I nodded and the three of us began walking. We were alone here, probably because the crypt had been creepy, but this narrow, dark stone hall was downright scary. As soon as we rounded the bend, all three of us clicked on our lights. The walls were dark stone, and when I say stone, it isn't the pretty kind that people put in their kitchens and bathrooms. It's little more than rock. Black rock that appeared to have been chipped away with old-style tools to make room for the burial places. The walls were jagged and uneven, dusty and dark. The place smelled musty and old… A scent I was beginning to associate with death.

"This place is scary," I whispered.

Sam stopped walking and turned. I ran right into his chest. Cole bumped into me from behind.

"You can go back. I can do this."

I shook my head and he sighed, and the three of us started walking again. Paintings and drawings lined the walls here too. They were of crosses and men dressed in robes. There were a few that I thought might be of God and Jesus. Wine and fish, angels and men also made up many of the drawings. The next corner we rounded brought Sam to a halt. Built into the stone walls were arches with ledges. Upon these ledges rested corpses dressed in dirty brown robes with hoods. One of them clasped a giant silver cross in his hands.

"Wow," Sam said, hushed.

"I hope those aren't real mummies," Cole murmured.

"I really don't think they are props." I said, goose bumps racing along my arms.

"Where are we supposed to leave the scroll?" Cole asked.

I looked up to shine my light around, looking for a sign. The rays of my flashlight fell upon another drawing. This one wasn't as faded as the others and I was drawn to it. I stepped away from Cole to study it.

It was of a dagger with gems on the handle. The dagger had great white wings that jutted from behind and it was surrounded by yellow, representing a bright shining light. Beside the image was another of a man lying on the ground with another dagger sticking out of his chest. The man's eyes were yellow as well as his mouth and ears. His face was full of pain and I imagined his screams.

"Stop," Sam said, gently turning me from the sight. "Come away."

I allowed him to lead me away and I tried to banish the sight from my thoughts. It didn't matter though because my mind would hold onto the picture and it would haunt me forever.

It was cold down here. Without windows or light, warmth could not get in. There was also no sign of life and I had a feeling if a person stayed here long enough, this place would suck the life out of them too. I never imagined that crypts were so sad.

"Maybe we should go. Maybe we are in the wrong place," I told Sam, my steps faltering.

He pulled me against his body, wrapping his arms around me. Warmth from his skin seeped into me and I sighed.

"Up here!" Cole called from ahead of us and we went running.

Cole was standing in some sort of alcove in the crypt. Like everything else, it was made of rough, dirty rock. Inside was another archway, but there was no body resting on the ledge. The feeling around this little corner was different than the rest of the catacombs. It wasn't depressing or sad. I felt better in here, like this place really was blessed and was the resting place of the most sacred of men. The air wasn't warmer here, but it didn't have the chill of the other areas, and it brushed against my skin in welcome. "This is the place," I murmured.

Sam and Cole looked at me. I stepped further in the room, as if being called. Along the top of the archway were words written in script in what I assumed were Italian or maybe Latin. "I wonder what they mean." I said, studying the words.

Here lies hope. The words drifted into my mind and settled. I repeated them out loud and knew it was right.

"How do you know that?" Cole asked.

"This place told me."

"Let's leave the scroll and go," Sam murmured, unzipping his bag and pulling it out. I grabbed it and felt it begin to vibrate in my hand.

"It knows it belongs here," I said.

"Where do we put it?" Cole asked, looking around.

Why were they in such a hurry? Couldn't they feel the power and peace of this place?

"Heven, we need to go. It isn't safe here," Sam said, tugging my arm.

"Of course it is," I said. He gave me a little shake and I looked up. His eyes were filled with concern and maybe a little fear. I reached into our Mindbond and felt his anxiety.

"I'm all right," I promised. "We're fine."

He didn't look convinced.

"Okay, let's get this done."

We spent the next several minutes looking for a place to leave the scroll. There weren't many places in this tiny alcove. "Just leave it on the ledge and let's go," Cole said restlessly. "People are going to start looking for us."

It felt all wrong. We couldn't just lay it there and go. "Maybe there's a trap door in the stone," I said, walking to the arch.

All three of us began tapping on the stones and feeling for loose ones. I pushed on one in the center of the archway. I heard the softest of clicking sounds before the stone came out, falling to my feet. From the wall a blinding white light shone out. It illuminated the space and infused us with warmth.

"Here," I murmured, reaching my fingers into the light.

There was a great cracking sound behind us and we turned. The alcove was empty, but as we looked, the floor began moving and crumbling. From beneath the floor rose a demon. Its eyes were red and its teeth were black. It crawled out of the floor, bringing with it thousands of black bugs. The bugs began scattering everywhere, up the walls, across the floor and onto my shoes.

I screamed and began stomping on them.

The demon launched itself at us, teeth barred. Sam and Cole attacked it, sending it backward, only to have it come at us again. In one swift move, Sam hit the demon, sending it backward into the hole it climbed out of. It didn't appear again.

Cole walked over to the hole and looked down. "That's a long way down." Sam joined him and they both stood staring down into the pit.

"I wished it had taken these bugs with it," I screeched, stomping on another. "Come away from there," I ordered, bending to pick up the scroll, which I dropped in the chaos. A large black bug was crawling on it and I flicked it, sending it into the air.

It morphed and turned, landing as a snarling demon. I swore and turned to run, but the demon was fast and caught me around the waist and hefted me up to rush out of the alcove. Bugs all around us began turning and twisting into demons, blocking Sam's path and keeping him from following.

I fought as hard as I could as the demon ran through the crypt. In one swift move, I hit him upside the head with the very scroll he was after. He screamed and dropped me. I landed hard, but scrambled to my feet. I was trapped against the wall and he came at me. I backed up, bumping against something. I turned to see one of the robe-wrapped men fall to the ground. He hit with a sickening thud and I watched as his head detached from his body and rolled away. Thinking fast, I scooped up the head and threw it at the demon; my aim was good and the head smacked into the demon's face.

The demon stumbled as Sam appeared behind it, clutching a dagger in his hand, and rammed the demon through. It dissolved into ash before us. "Did you just throw a *head*?"" Sam asked, shock in his voice, but there was also a hint of amusement.

"Well, no one will give me a dagger, so I had to be creative," I said, trying to rush past him and back into the fight.

Before I could get very far, he grabbed my arm and pulled me around. Without saying another word, he handed the dagger to me, handle first.

I looked up at his face. "I was wrong to keep you from trying to protect yourself."

"Yeah, you were." I took the dagger. It was heavy. "But I forgive you." I smiled.

"Remember that next time you think about throwing a head."

I laughed and held up the scroll. "Come on, let's get this in there and go."

His smile fell away and we rushed back toward the alcove.

The place was crawling with demons. Some more dangerous than others, and there were still so many of those bugs, promising even more if we fought too hard. The bright white light was like a beacon in the dark, leading us back to where we needed to be. When we rounded the corner, what I saw made my blood run cold.

Cole was covered in demons. He was throwing punches and trying to shake them off, but there were too many. I watched in horror as one bit him. His scream echoed around us.

I felt the familiar tremor course through me as Sam prepared to shift to save my brother. He ran forward and leaped, only to fall out of the air onto his knees. I watched him writhe in pain.

"Sam!" I screamed.

Run, Heven!

I looked down at the dagger in my hand. I wasn't running anywhere but into the fight. I turned to go help Cole and ran right into Kimber.

"Kimber!" I gasped. I didn't have time to be shocked. "Help us!"

Her eyes were vacant and she stared into me without any real emotion. "Kimber!" I screamed, shaking her.

Then I noticed her aura.

It was black.

The same exact color I saw briefly surround Ms. Merriweather at the hotel. It hadn't been my eyes playing tricks on me. The color was real and it meant something. I didn't have time to figure it out, but I knew it wasn't good.

She blinked and looked down. I followed her gaze. In her palm lay an amulet identical to the one Gemma had. I gasped and grabbed for it. She snatched her hand back.

"You have no idea what you're doing!" I yelled. "Get that thing out of here!"

"I am not here to help you," she spat.

I heard a scream and turned back. Sam had gotten to his feet and was fighting as best he could to free Cole of the demons. Sam was a great fighter, even in this weakened state, but he and Cole were outnumbered badly.

They needed help.

"Kimber, please," I begged.

"Give me the scroll," she said, reaching for it.

I stepped back automatically, holding up the dagger in warning. "How could you betray us like this?"

She laughed.

A flash of light ran by and Kimber screamed. I turned to see Gemma picking her way through the mountain of demons.

Oh, thank God.

Turning my back to Kimber, I ran forward and did what I could to fight off the demons, trying to help my friends. I wasn't very good with a dagger, so I wasn't much help. I did manage a few good swipes and was proud to take out a couple of demons.

Gemma managed to get to Cole and lifted him in her arms. I didn't like the way his body seemed to just collapse against her. Thank goodness she had the superhuman strength of an angel.

"Cole?" Kimber said with more emotion than I heard all day. I turned, taking a hard kick to the side and fell, the scroll falling out of my hands and rolling away.

"No," I moaned, reaching. Black bugs covered my hands and arms.

Sam picked me up from the ground and I fought him. "Not me, the scroll."

Suddenly, the demons around us fell to the ground and lay there, unmoving. The black bugs fell from my arms and legs. Sam pulled me up and we all turned to Kimber. She was staring at Cole, who was now leaning heavily against Gemma. His breathing was labored and he had bite marks along his arms.

"Get the hell out of my way," Gemma growled.

"Cole, are you hurt?" Kimber said, seeming not to hear Gemma.

He made a sound in the back of his throat. Gemma kicked out her booted foot at Kimber, but the hit was deflected by some sort of invisible shield that surrounded her. Harsh, high-pitched laughter filled the tiny room and someone rose out of the hole in the ground.

It was Ms. Merriweather. This time she didn't bother to disguise her aura — that had to be what she was doing before. Black completely surrounded her, no hints of any other color. We watched as she walked to Kimber's side, the demons and bugs seemed to part, giving her a cleared path in which to walk. Once there, her façade of the teacher gave way to someone else entirely. Kimber was the only one who didn't seem surprised. The woman had long, flowing hair of onyx that reached the backs of her legs. She was wearing a dress, more like a robe of the darkest black. A blood-red belt cinched her waist. Her face was unlined, yet I somehow knew she was thousands of years old. Power sparked from her finger tips and sizzled around the room. Her evilness was palpable in the thick air. I noticed how she avoided standing directly in the bright white light that still shone through the room from the wall.

"Hecate," Gemma hissed.

This was Hecate, Queen of Witches, who was aligned with Satan? Now I knew exactly what the black meant. It was the color of a witch.

"Kill them," Hecate ordered Kimber.

Still gripping that damn amulet in one hand, Kimber lifted both her arms over her head and began chanting in some weird tongue. The black in her aura pulsed around her.

Gemma turned to look at me.

"Go!" I yelled.

Gemma ran forward, with Cole firmly in her arms, but Kimber stepped in her path. Gemma tried to fight, but once again was blocked by the invisible shield that seemed to surround Kimber.

"Kimmie," Cole groaned.

Kimber paused and looked at Cole.

"Please," he said. "Don't do this."

Kimber stepped aside and Gemma ran out, taking my brother to safety. I breathed a deep sigh of relief. Cole had gotten through to Kimber. Maybe together we could take down Hecate. Beside me, Sam stiffened and I felt him try to shift again. He made a sound deep in his throat in frustration, but squared his shoulders. I looked up.

I had been wrong.

Kimber had spared Cole, but she was coming directly at us. I lifted the dagger, preparing to stab my used-to-be best friend if I had to.

Just as she was about to attack, Hecate stopped her. "Come!" she yelled. We all turned to see Hecate standing in triumph near the hole. The bronze scroll was gripped in her hands.

"No!" I screamed and ran forward. Hecate flung her hand and I was tossed against the stone wall. The dagger flew from my grasp and hit the ground with a loud clatter. I slid to the ground in pain. Sam ran to my side.

Hecate laughed and jumped into the hole. Kimber went to the hole and looked down. She turned back and looked at me.

"Why would you do this?" I whispered, my voice cracking with hurt.

"You betrayed me," Kimber spat.

"I never betrayed you, not like this." I couldn't keep the tear from rolling down my cheek.

I thought I saw a flash of the Kimber I knew somewhere in her eyes, but then it was gone. Kimber turned her back on us and jumped, disappearing from sight.

Pain wracked my body, but failure weighed me down. How could I leave this crypt, knowing that I allowed the scroll to fall into the wrong hands?

So close. We had been so close.

Up, sweetheart, Sam said, lifting me from the ground.

We failed Sam.

I'm sorry.

I felt the weight of his apology, the regret. He felt responsible for the way things turned out. I turned to him. "This was not your fault."

"It wasn't yours either."

"No," I agreed. It still didn't lessen the fact that we failed.

I lifted my hand, letting it pass into the white light. It was still warm. It was still brilliant and filled the alcove. *Didn't it know we failed?* I asked myself.

Would it still wrap my fingers in warmth if it knew it wasn't getting what belonged here?

"Let's go," Sam said, his voice exhausted.

"Are you hurt?" I turned to him, searching his body for injuries.

"I'm fine."

"I didn't know she had that amulet." It must have been what she was hiding in that box. If only I had known, everything might have been different.

"I know, sweetheart. This isn't your fault." He kissed my palm before stepping away to replace the stone in the wall, covering up the last of the brilliant light. The room was plunged back into darkness. It seemed even darker than before.

"Watch your step," Sam cautioned as we began to leave. The hole in the floor sealed back up as soon as Kimber jumped in. The demons and bugs disappeared as well, but it didn't mean that something couldn't jump out at any moment.

Before the alcove disappeared from sight, I turned back once more and shone my flashlight over the words written above the archway.

Here lies hope.

A sob caught in my throat as Sam led me away.

Not anymore.

244

Chapter Nineteen

Sam

I failed.

It was a thought that pounded through me stronger than my heart beat.

I failed.

I failed to get that scroll back to where it belonged. I failed Heven. I failed Airis. I failed God himself. Hell, I even failed Cole, who seemed to take the brunt of the fighting. I should have held my ground and refused to tell him our secrets. I should have refused to let him train with us because deep down hadn't I known that he wouldn't be strong enough?

Yes. I'd known.

But I had also known that Cole would be one more person between Heven and harm if things went bad.

And they had gone bad. They went from *this might go all right* to *someone's going to be really pissed.*

That someone was Airis and I prayed she didn't take her anger out on Heven. What would her reaction be? Would she take away the life that she gave back to Heven when she died? Would she offer my life in exchange for Heven's again?

Thoughts of Logan speared my brain. What would happen to him if I gave up my life for Heven? Who would watch out for him? Who would figure out a way to help him?

Beside me, Heven squeezed my hand. Her thoughts of failure mirrored my own. She was scared, nervous and confused and I couldn't blame her. I couldn't offer her any comfort either, because there wasn't any to give. All we could do now is face the consequences of losing that scroll.

I would bear as many of those consequences as I could. I would bear them all if Airis allowed it.

We knew something wasn't right when we got back to the bus. My first thought was that someone realized we weren't where we were supposed to be. When we got closer to the group, one of the girls came rushing over, wide eyes on Heven.

"What's going on?" Heven asked, her voice surprisingly light.

The girls eyes widened, clearly thrilled to be telling the gossip to someone who didn't yet know. "Ms. Merriweather had a family emergency and had to leave."

Heven exhaled a breath. "That's it?"

The girl looked at me and I shrugged, relieved this wasn't about us. She seemed disappointed that we weren't impressed by the latest gossip. "Mrs. Britt is freaking out because she has to handle all of us now by herself."

That would explain why she was yelling for everyone to get on the bus. I pulled Heven along and we slid past her and into our seat.

Do you see Cole anywhere? Heven asked.

No. No sign of Gemma, either. I hoped they got out safely and that they would meet us at the hotel. I was worried about Cole. He took quite a beating, and if he was seriously injured, it would be hard to explain and Heven would be upset.

Or Kimber. Where do you think she went?

I don't know. No where good. I had no idea she was involved in this. Something else I failed at. I should have kept a closer watch on her these past couple of weeks. I knew she was upset with Heven and I knew why, but that bit of drama didn't seem important in the grand scheme of things.

Lesson learned.

Heven lowered her head, a guilty look marring her features. *If I had explained better and tried harder to be friends, then maybe she wouldn't be working with Hecate.*

I wouldn't let her blame herself for something she had nothing to do with. *Heven, did you know Kimber was involved?*

No. I knew something was going on with her. She's been able to do stuff…

Stuff? What else had I missed along the way?

Heven nodded and looked out the window of the bus. *Like slam doors when she's angry and I think she's responsible for the wind that knocked over those demons, you know, in the Colosseum. And the other night, that demon with the mist… she kept it from surrounding us.*

You think she's a witch? That would certainly explain things, and at this point, I wouldn't be surprised.

She's been working with Hecate. What else could she be? Besides, her aura is black, just like Hecate's and black is a color I haven't seen in an aura until now. That has to be it.

She's in trouble, Heven said after a few moments of us just sitting in silence, and I felt her misery like it was my own. In fact, it was. It was *our* misery and it was — well, miserable. We didn't speak the rest of the way back to the hotel. Thankfully, we were spared from making a bunch of excuses for our roommates' absence because Mrs. Britt hadn't taken attendance.

When the bus stopped, Heven didn't seem to notice and I nudged her. We exited quickly before someone could stop us and ask too many questions. Once again, we took advantage of Mrs. Britt's distraction and hurried down my hallway. I had the keycard in my hand ready to use when the door popped open and Gemma looked at us through a small crack.

"Thank Goodness!" Heven said as we hurried into the room. "Cole?" she said before the door was even shut.

"He's in the shower," Gemma said quietly, pacing across the room. She looked tired and paler than usual.

"How is he?" Heven asked, staring at the bathroom door.

"He'll be fine."

"Thanks for coming today," I said, sinking down onto the corner of my bed. If she hadn't shown up to help me fight off that swarm of demons, who knows what might have happened.

Gemma nodded. "I figured things would get messy."

"Have you been here this whole time?" Heven asked.

She nodded again.

"Why wouldn't you say something?" Heven blurted and her eyes met Gemma's. Something passed between the two and they seemed to come to some unspoken agreement.

What's going on? I asked.

Gemma is just fighting her feelings for Cole and is trying to keep distance between them, but now she can't.

Girl stuff. That wasn't my department. "Hecate took the scroll," I told Gemma, changing the subject far away from girl stuff.

She nodded. "The odds were stacked against you."

Gloom settled over the room and we all lapsed into silence. Soon, the bathroom door opened and Cole came out. He was wearing a pair of gym shorts and a pair of socks. No shirt. But judging from the bruises and marks all over his chest, it was no wonder he didn't want to wear a shirt. It probably hurt too much. Heven rushed over, stopping short of throwing her arms around him after she quickly took notice of his appearance.

His arms and chest were covered in swollen, angry-looking bite marks and scratches. The bite marks were red with some sort of black substance oozing from the wounds. He had a split lip and more scratches on his neck. One of his knees was swollen with another bite and his skin was unnaturally pale. His lips were cracked like he was dehydrated, and when he breathed, he took shallow breaths like it hurt.

"How bad are you hurt?" she asked timidly.

He gave her a smile and my respect rose for him a notch. Clearly, he was not okay, but he cared enough about her not to make her feel any worse. "I'm good. You okay?"

The back of her head bobbed up and down with her nod. "I'm so sorry." Her voice was hoarse and I hated to hear it so full of pain.

Cole made a noise in the back of his throat. "Don't be sorry. I knew what I was getting into."

"Kimber..." Heven's voice trailed away.

His eyes darkened. "I didn't know she had it in her."

Heven sniffled and shifted from one foot to the other and Cole held out his arms. Heven hugged him carefully, and over her shoulder, Cole winced.

Gemma shot up from the chair she was perched on and began pacing the room once again.

"Scroll's gone?" He mouthed to me.

I nodded.

Heven pulled out of his arms. "I'm glad you're okay," she said, but looked down at one of the worst-looking bites, which was also next to one of the worst looking scratches. I frowned.

Gemma cleared her throat. Cole forgot about Heven and looked at her.

"I have something for you to put on those bites. The sooner the better." Her voice bordered on a whisper and she avoided looking at Cole. For a warrior she sure seemed squeamish about his injuries.

"I'll be fine."

Her eyes snapped to him. "Those bites are going to start burning and the poison in the saliva is going to make you sick. You need this." She held up a small silver jar. Suddenly, I recognized the look in her eyes. If I looked in the mirror right now, I would probably see the same look. It wasn't his injuries that bothered her. It was Cole's pain. She was upset because she felt she failed the person she cared most about.

He nodded grimly. "They're already burning." He turned toward his nightstand to switch on the light. I caught the swear in my throat. He had a huge bite on his back; the skin was practically hanging from his body.

Gemma made a sound and Heven stumbled back. I reached out and pulled her toward the bed, pressing her down to sit.

"I'll help you," Gemma said, unscrewing the lid of the cream she brought.

"Yeah, okay," he said, swaying a little on his feet. Heven jumped up, but I beat her to his side and helped him sit on his bed. "I hope that stuff works," he mumbled.

Heven was white and a little green. I knew she wanted to be here for her brother, but I thought she might need a breather before being faced with Cole's downward spiral into pain. "You should probably get upstairs. Mrs. Britt didn't take attendance on the bus. She will probably be coming around to our rooms."

I turned to look at Gemma. "I'm going to walk her upstairs. Will you stay with him?"

"Sure."

"I don't think you should be around Kimber," Cole said to Heven, a fine sheen of sweat was breaking out on his forehead.

"I'm sure she won't be there. She disappeared with Hecate."

I went to the door, opened it and looked out into the hall. It was clear. Once Heven said her good-byes to Cole and made Gemma swear to watch over him, I ushered her out into the hall and into the elevator.

"He looks really bad," Heven said, leaning against the wall.

"He's tough. He'll be okay." My thoughts flashed to those scratches all over his body. They somehow seemed familiar.

Heven brushed away a stray tear and straightened as the elevator doors opened. I went out first, making sure nothing or no one was in the hall. Someone was at the far end, but they let themselves in their room and then there was no one.

Sam? What will happen now that the Treasure Map is gone? Will people on the list start dying?

I wished I could say no. I wished that I could deny her fear, but I couldn't. Because I really didn't know. *I hope not.*

All those innocent people. All slaughtered because…

I failed.

Heven stopped and turned to face me. *You didn't fail. You're the reason we all lived. You and Gemma. Yes, the scroll is gone, but this isn't your fault. I guess that means it isn't my fault, either.*

I dropped my forehead to rest on hers. *We'll make it right. Somehow.*

I know we will. But first let's take care of my brother and get home.

I don't want to leave you here alone.

It's only for an hour. Then I'll meet you downstairs for dinner. She pulled away and used her keycard to open her room. I pushed past her to search the room, making sure it was clear.

Heven waited patiently by the door and then wrapped her arms around my neck when I came back.

I'm fine. She isn't here. Try to relax.

Kimber was the least of my worries. The people she seemed to align herself with are another story.

I'll see you at dinner.

I pressed a kiss to her lips, lingering longer than I should have, but it felt so good and I couldn't make myself back away. Finally, I did and I waited until I heard the lock on her door before I went to check on Cole.

Now that Heven wasn't in the room, I would find out just how much he had been faking and how hurt he really was.

* * *

Before I even got to the room, I heard him retching. When I opened the door and stepped inside, I was greeted (if you could call it a greeting) by an awful stench that made me want to gag.

"What the hell is that stuff you put all over him?" I asked Gemma, who was busy rushing to the bathroom to empty Cole's puke bucket.

She stopped in front of me to glare. "It's not the salve. It's what the salve is pulling out of him. It's the poison from the demon's saliva. He was bitten almost twenty times."

She was more rattled than I had ever seen her as she hurried away.

"You search Hev's room?" Cole asked, his voice hoarse as he turned to face me. How he was sitting up at all amazed me—he looked like death.

"Of course. Shouldn't you lay down?"

He grunted then looked toward the bathroom where the water was running. "It hurts too much to lay down."

I bet it did. That bite on his back was nasty. All of them seemed more swollen than before and I said as much as I walked across the room.

"It's that crap she smeared all over me. She says it's supposed to do that."

I sat down on the side of my bed, facing him. "You fought hard today. You did good."

He looked up at me, dark circles ringing his red-rimmed eyes. "You're a bad-ass fighter. I'm sorry I ever doubted your ability to protect my sister."

Gemma came back to Cole's side with a clean bucket and a few wash rags. She leaned back and looked at his back. "It's definitely working. I'm going to clean it again."

Cole winced, but steeled himself. "Do it."

Gemma climbed on the bed on her knees behind Cole. She looked at me briefly before turning to Cole's back and placing one of the cloths over the bite wound. Cole's jaw flexed, but he said nothing as she gently wiped away black ooze.

"So are we calling a truce?" I asked Cole and stuck out my hand. He looked up at me. "I figure any guy who can manage to get a fallen angel in bed with him is a guy I can respect."

He laughed out loud. Gemma took a final wipe to his back, and his breath hissed between his teeth. Then abruptly, he lurched forward and I shoved the bucket under him as he retched again. Gemma was biting her bottom lip, jar of salve in her hand.

Cole looked up, wiping his mouth with the back of his hand. "You guys don't need to be here for this."

"I've seen worse—no worries," I said.

"I need to get this on you," Gemma said quietly.

Cole nodded and she smoothed a thick layer on his back. He didn't seem to mind that and I thought maybe the stuff made him feel better. When Gemma was done, she climbed off the bed and glanced at me.

"I need to go and get some more of this salve from where I'm staying. And I want to get him something else that should help. Can you stay with him until I get back?"

"Sure."

Gemma looked over at Cole and it looked like she wanted to say something, but she didn't.

Cole felt her stare. "I'll still be alive when you get back."

She made a face and walked out of the room. Just as the door was shutting, I heard words that I was sure were only meant for her. "You better be."

It was silent for a few long moments and then suddenly Cole thrust out his hand. "We never did get to shake on that truce."

I put my hand in his and shook. I couldn't help focusing on the long scratches on his forearm. He seemed to notice my stare and pulled his arm back. I cleared my throat.

There was a knock on the door and I jumped up. "Attendance," Mrs. Britt called from the other side. I grabbed up a small blanket that was on the end of the bed and draped it around Cole's shoulder's to hide the worst of his injuries and he let out a low swear.

"Sorry, man," I whispered and went to the door opening it, only partway.

"Cole and I are both here," I told the teacher, hoping she would go away.

"What is that awful smell?" she asked, recoiling from the room.

"Uh, Cole caught that stomach bug and he's been throwing up."

She tried to look past me into the room so I opened the door a fraction and looked over my shoulder. Cole was still on the bed with the blanket around him, head bowed and the bucket in his lap.

"Would you like to move to another room?" Mrs. Britt asked me, clearly convinced.

"Nah, I hardly ever get sick, and besides, I've already been exposed." I pulled the door back around once more.

"Well, all right. Cole…" she called out, but I didn't bother to open the door again. He made a sound and she took that as a response and she continued, "You're excused from dinner. If you are better tomorrow, you can join in the last day here, if not, get some rest so you won't be sick on the plane home."

"Yes, ma'am."

She moved off down the hall and I shut the door. Cole tossed the blanket away like it was on fire.

"Did Gemma say how long you would be sick?"

"Depends on my body, I guess."

I sat back down on the bed and wondered if he was going to be able to sit during the very long flight home.

"I guess Heven told you about my angel status?"

"On the plane." Cole was a Supernal Being — not technically an angel, but not quite a human either. "Think that will help your body heal?"

"I sure as hell hope so." He made a motion like he might vomit again and I snatched the bucket and held it out. He swallowed back his illness and took a deep breath.

I kept the bucket ready.

"Guess my almost — angel — status and your hellhound status is the reason we instantly disliked each other."

I hadn't thought about it that way before, but he was right. I guess we should be natural enemies if you consider where we both came from. Still, it bothered me that he would be the "good" one and I would be the "bad" one. "You know, I'm not really from Hell. God created me, it's just that part of me was… twisted by Hell, by Satan, but I try to be better than that."

Cole looked up at me. "I didn't want to believe that at first. I wanted you to be the bad guy. But now I know that I was wrong."

His words meant more to me than I thought they would. I always told myself that what Cole thought never mattered. But I think maybe it did. I didn't need his friendship, but it would be nice to have. "Once you stopped hitting on Heven, I realized you weren't as bad as I thought either." I grinned.

He grimaced. "I knew there was a connection there, with her. I just couldn't figure out what it was and the only thing I could think of was that we were… well, you know. I never in a million years thought she could be my sister."

He didn't just get a sister, though. He got pulled into an entire supernatural world. His life would never be the same. "You cool with everything that's been going on? It's been pretty crazy."

He sat there for a minute, his breathing slightly ragged, and I figured that while he was battling his pain and sickness, this wasn't the best time to talk about this stuff. I got up and grabbed a clean change of clothes out of my bag, a pair of shorts and a dark-colored T-shirt, thinking a quick shower before dinner would help wash away some of the day's worst.

"It's kind of strange. Even with everything that's happened, I still feel like I am where I belong, you know? Like this life was meant for me."

I turned back to him. "Yeah, I do know."

It was a little strange to realize that the person I've been hating for months turns out to have a lot in common with me. But what would happen now? "Now that the scroll is gone..." I said, "who knows what will happen."

"What do you mean?"

I turned away from my suitcase. "I mean, Heven died. Airis gave her life back and in return we had to return the scroll, only we didn't."

"You think Airis will take Heven's life back?" Cole said, alarm making his eyes wide.

"I won't let that happen." But if Airis wanted a life debt, she would take one. "I need you to promise me something."

Cole's eyes narrowed. "What?"

"If something happens to me, you'll take care of Heven."

"You're going to make Airis take your life instead," he said flatly.

"If I die, she won't be the same. Our Mindbond... when it's severed, it might be too much for her." I didn't say what might happen. She might die anyway, and if she didn't, she might go insane. Mindbonds weren't made to be severed.

Cole's chin lifted. "I'll take care of her."

I didn't expect him to talk me out of what I planned to do. I knew he would sacrifice me for his sister, just as I would sacrifice him for her. I turned away, the answer I wanted mine, but instead of making me feel better, it made me feel worse.

The idea of being separated from Heven left me with an ache in my chest.

"What if we got it back?" Cole said quietly.

I turned around.

"If we got the scroll back? No life debt would need to be paid."

Was it possible that I could correct what happened down in those catacombs? For the first time since we got back, I felt a surge of hope instead of just trying to accept what was.

Cole must have seen the change come over me and puffed up with excitement. "They probably took the scroll to Hell, right? Isn't that where that witch lives?"

I nodded, thinking. "Hecate most definitely lives in Hell." She reeked of evil.

"Going there might be hard for some people, but not for a *hell*hound."

My eyes snapped up to Cole's. "Exactly." I might try to be better than the darkness in me, but it was still there and I would let it out if it meant saving a life. It wouldn't be the first time — or the last.

I felt a smile curl my lips. "You're pretty smart for an angel."

"Supernal Being," he corrected.

I waved his words away with my hand. "How will I get into Hell?" I said, already trying to formulate a plan in my head.

The door opened and Gemma came in carrying a small sack and a plastic water bottle. Her eyes went straight to Cole, but she didn't waste time butting into the conversation. "Find a portal."

"A portal to Hell?" I asked.

"They're all over the place. How do you think those demons get around?"

I vaguely remember Airis mentioning the portals to Hell a while ago, but with everything going on, it had slipped my mind. The demons started coming around and I became too busy trying to rip their heads off. "But where?"

Gemma sat the small bag she was carrying on a small table in the corner and pulled out a white water bottle and unscrewed the cap. "I can't see them. You should be able to *feel* them though, being a hellhound and all."

"Here, drink this," she said, handing the water bottle to Cole.

"What is it?" He eyed the bottle dubiously.

She rolled her eyes. "It will speed up the healing."

Cole grabbed it and took a long swig then began coughing. "That shit is nasty!" He spat, setting the offending substance on the bedside table.

Gemma snatched it up and sat down across from him on my bed. "Don't be a baby."

"What do you mean *feel them?*" I asked her.

"Just think about it," she said, holding the drink back out to Cole. "Haven't you ever been anywhere that you have been drawn to for no apparent reason? That's where it would be."

Cole reluctantly took the water bottle then glanced at me. "Looks like we got ourselves a plan."

I grinned. It might be a crazy plan, but I was good with crazy. "I'm taking a shower. I'm supposed to meet Heven at dinner in a few."

"Fine." Cole lifted the bottle and began drinking, my attention once more caught by the nasty scratches on his arm. Why were they so familiar?

I shut myself in the bathroom, but left the door unlocked in case Cole needed in here for something and submersed myself under scalding-hot water. I thought about our new plan, about getting the scroll back. It was my only hope to keep Airis from taking back a life—my life. I would still be here with Heven. With Logan.

I froze.

Oh. My. God. Logan.

Cole's scratches. They were familiar because they were exactly like the ones I had seen before… that day in the second hand shop.

On my brother.

* * *

I chose a table away from the Mrs. Britt in the hotel dining room just as Heven walked in. I took a minute to enjoy the view, how truly beautiful she was to me. She was wearing a long, dark blue cotton dress that brushed her toes as she walked. It was sleeveless and her slender arms were tan from all the sun we had been out in. Her hair was down, brushing against her collar bone, and my skin tingled with the memory of how it felt when it brushed against me.

She caught my stare and smiled.

Hey, beautiful.

Handsome. But then her face cleared of the moment. "Where's Cole?"

"He's not doing so good, Hev," I said, taking her hand and pulling her into the chair next to me. When I came out of the bathroom after my shower, Gemma had finally gotten him in a comfortable position lying down, but I knew he was still in pain.

"I should go see him." She got up from the table.

"Gemma's with him. He needs to get some sleep." She still seemed torn so I said, "I told Mrs. Britt he must have caught whatever Kimber had."

"If Gemma's with him, I guess he'll be okay." She sighed and sat back down.

"She made him drink some nasty drink. He complained like a girl."

Heven laughed. "You two are getting along better."

"He's not so bad." I got up and snagged her hand. "Come on; let's get some food before it's all gone."

After we filled our plates at the buffet overflowing with Italian goodness, we sat back down and began eating. "I've been thinking," I said, leaning closer to her and lowering my voice. "What if we went after the scroll?"

Heven blinked. "We have no idea where it is."

"Hecate probably took it to Hell with her."

"You want to go to Hell?" She dropped her fork in her plate of pasta.

"I want that scroll back." I didn't go into the whole life debt thing, but I realized that it was something she probably already thought of.

"He wanted me to open it," Heven whispered, her voice far away.

"Who?"

"The Dream Walker. He doesn't know how to open it and he thinks I can."

I glanced at the necklace hanging around her neck. The key that opened the scroll.

Of course! "So they haven't gotten it open." A smile spread across my face.

Heven smiled back. "You really think we could get it back?"

"Oh, I'm going to get it back, baby." I said it with renewed energy and attacked my pasta.

"Might be worth a shot," she said, digging into her food as well.

I didn't want to spoil the mood with my thoughts, so I kept it to myself.

Getting that scroll back was our *only* shot.

Heven

By the time I fell asleep that night, Kimber was still a no-show. I was saved earlier when we got back from explaining why she wasn't here because once I opened the door to the room, Mrs. Britt assumed Kimber was inside, marked us both off on her sheet and kept moving. But that was hours ago and now I was beginning to think that maybe she wasn't coming back. I wondered how I would explain her absence tomorrow when we got on the bus for the airport, but then I remembered that I didn't have to. Kimber and I weren't friends anymore. She betrayed me. Because of her the Treasure Map was gone, Cole was hurt and people were in danger. I didn't sleep well, tossing and turning, unable to find a comfortable position that didn't hurt my back. I was lying in the dark, thinking about getting some pain reliever from my bag, when I heard the lock on the door click. My entire body tensed and I lay as still as possible, listening. The door creaked open and then swung closed. A shadow swept across the wall as the person moved farther into the room.

I sat up and switched on the lamp.

Kimber stopped sneaking toward her bed.

"You're back," I said.

"Yep." She didn't turn around to face me, but her shoulders tensed the minute I spoke.

"You're a witch now?"

She shrugged. She didn't have to say anything, the black cloud around her said it all.

"You have no idea what you've done," I spat.

She turned, her face livid. "Me? What about you?"

"I'm not working with Hecate."

Kimber tossed her red hair over her shoulder. "She's been honest with me. She's taught me stuff."

"Like how to betray your friends?"

She jerked like I slapped her. "You stopped being my friend the day you slept with Cole!"

This time I jerked. "Slept with Cole?"

She rolled her eyes. "Don't play stupid with me. I know."

I laughed. "You don't know anything."

For the first time, her confidence wavered. "I saw you."

"I don't know what you saw, but it wasn't me *sleeping* with him."

"So he wasn't at your house a few weeks ago in the middle of the night?"

I thought back to that night he came by, half drunk. "You were there too?"

Kimber turned smug, like she caught me. "Of course. I was with Cole; then he ran off and I followed him… right to you."

"If you had told me you saw us, I could have explained."

"Spare me your lies, Heven." She went across the room to her bags.

"He's my brother."

Kimber stopped in her tracks and looked at me. "You're lying."

I shook my head. "He couldn't say anything because his mom isn't handling it all very well and she doesn't want anyone to know."

Kimber didn't say anything, but sank down into a nearby chair. I pulled the blankets up over me, covering my legs. "My dad is his dad. Gran kind of freaked the first time she saw him and had a DNA test ran without anyone knowing. That night you came out to the house and we were on the porch hugging? That was the night that she told us."

"Sam knows," Kimber said.

"Yeah, he was there when Gran told us."

She looked up at me. "You didn't sleep with him."

"No. I would never have done that to you." I let the unspoken accusation come through in my words.

"You still lied to me," she said coldly.

"I couldn't tell you about Cole. He asked me not to."

"I'm not talking about Cole."

I shoved the covers back and stood, angry. "Yeah?" I spat. "You're right. I didn't tell you that my boyfriend turned out to be a hellhound and his crazy old roommate is the one who messed up my face. I didn't tell you that an angel came to us and asked us to return a sacred document where it belonged. Sorry for my omission, Kimber, but none of that was about you and it was dangerous! I didn't want you to get hurt."

"A sacred document?"

"Yeah, you know that thing you helped Hecate steal?"

"She said it belonged to her."

"Of course she did. I guess I wasn't the only one who lied." I began gathering up a few things to shove in my bag.

Kimber rushed across the room and grabbed my wrist. "It wasn't hers?"

"Of course it wasn't!" I yelled. "But now she has it and innocent people are going to die!"

"No."

I don't know why, maybe it was the disbelief in her eyes or the complete chill in her aura that wrapped around us both, but I took a minute to tell her about the Treasure Map. I explained how we got it and what it was for. I told her about the training that Sam had been doing to be able to fend off all the demons that had been attacking us. Finally, to drive the point home, I told her how Cole interrupted me getting attacked and it was the only reason we told him. I didn't tell her that Cole is a Supernal Being. I already told enough of his secrets for one night.

"I had no idea," Kimber said, almost to herself, when I was finished.

"You're right. You didn't. And maybe I should have told you, but I was trying to protect you. I tried to tell you that I was still your friend and things weren't what you thought. But you didn't believe me. Instead, you aligned yourself with Hecate, Queen of Witches."

Kimber's eyes rounded. "*Queen* of Witches?"

"Yeah. She works with Satan, you know."

"No," Kimber said, backing away. "I knew she was someone powerful, but she didn't say…" Her voice faltered and I almost felt sorry for her. Almost.

I arched an eyebrow. "Let me guess. She left that part out? How convenient. Maybe you should have asked more questions before jumping into bed with the Devil's henchwoman." I paused to let my words sink in. Then I took a step toward her, advancing, and said, "How could you? You went against everything, even goodness."

"I—I didn't know."

"Like you didn't know that damn amulet you have hurts Sam?"

She didn't say anything, but her eyes dropped to the floor.

"You could've gotten him killed. You could've gotten Cole killed." Her eyes filled with tears, but I was beyond caring. I turned and grabbed my bag, slinging it over my shoulder.

"Where are you going?" Kimber asked.

"Anywhere away from you."

"Heven," she called, but I didn't turn back. I went to the door and pulled the handle. It didn't budge. I yanked on it again. Still, it wouldn't move. I turned and looked at Kimber. She was staring at me with her arms crossed over her chest.

"Let me out," I demanded. Frustration welled within me. I would not yell for Sam to get me out of here. I would get out myself. Somehow. How come everyone else got cool powers and I didn't?

"I'm not done talking," Kimber said.

"Well I am. In fact, I don't ever want to talk to you again. We aren't friends anymore." I turned my back on the hurt I saw spear through her aura.

Several seconds ticked by in which I began formulating a plan that involved screaming for Mrs. Britt in order to get out of here, but then I heard a soft click and the door popped open. I wanted to ask her how she did that. But I didn't. Like I said, we weren't friends anymore and as far as I was concerned, Kimber was the enemy. I rushed out of the room without looking back.

Chapter Twenty

Heven

The view out the airplane window made me think of my dad. Up here, the sky was limitless, filled with floating, fluffy white clouds and shades of blue that I never saw from the ground. Is this what heaven was like? Was my dad happy there? Was he at peace? I pressed my forehead against the cool glass of the window and remembered the sound of his voice that day in the InBetween. It was exactly as I remembered it being. I missed him.

"Hey, whatcha thinking about?" Cole asked.

I watched the sky for a moment longer before turning. "Where's Sam?"

Cole was sitting where Sam had been only moments before. "He went to the bathroom."

I nodded.

"Well?" Cole asked. He looked a lot better. Most of the color in his face had returned and there were only mere shadows beneath his eyes instead of severe black and blue smudges. I knew that the bite marks were still healing, but his long-sleeved shirt covered them. I was actually surprised that he was doing so well, but he said that Gemma's cream really helped along with that nasty drink. I had a feeling it wasn't just her cream and nasty drink, but I kept that bit of thought to myself.

"Uhh," I searched my mind for what he asked.

"You looked awfully intense staring out that window."

"I was thinking about Dad."

Cole's lips flattened.

"I know you're angry at him. I understand it, but he was my *dad*."

"I get it," Cole said, his shoulders slumping. "I have a *dad* too."

"Of course you do," I agreed, thinking of the man who raised Cole. From what I knew, he was a good man. "I wish you could have known him, though."

263

"He didn't want to know me."

I jerked. "No. Gran said that your mother told him to stay away."

"Yeah and he listened. If he had really wanted to see me, he would have."

My shoulders slumped this time because I didn't have an argument. I had no idea what my father had been thinking when he agreed to stay away. "I'm sorry," I whispered.

"Don't be." Cole put an arm around my shoulders.

We sat there for a minute without saying anything until I looked up at him. "Cole? I know that finding out about our dad was a huge shock and I know it hurt you and your family, but... I'm really glad Gran told us. I really like having a brother."

He smiled. His blue eyes were a truly beautiful shade and I realized that the color I saw out my airplane window was one that I had seen on the ground before... in Cole's eyes. "You're pretty cool for a sister."

I glanced back out the window. "So you think getting the scroll back is a good idea?"

"Yeah, I do," he answered quickly. "Do you?"

It was risky, but really leaving it down in Hell was riskier. "Yeah, but... the idea of going to Hell is scary."

Sam came up the aisle and took a seat on the end next to Cole. He smiled at me momentarily, making me forget the conversation.

"Tell me the time and place and I'll be there," Cole said, reminding me.

After what just happened to him in the catacombs, I wasn't so sure that it was a good idea. He seemed to read my thoughts and he speared me with a look. Determination and a hint of embarrassment bloomed in his aura. "I can handle it."

"Of course you can," I agreed.

And really, we needed him. We had to get that Treasure Map back. Now. Who knew what was being done with it right now? How much time did we have until someone got it open? If the names on that list became known, the world as we know it would change forever. The balance between Heaven and Hell would be tipped in Hell's favor. Everyone would be in danger.

Sam would be in danger.

If Airis tried to claim the life she gave back, he wouldn't allow her to take it from me.

I couldn't allow Sam to sacrifice himself for me again.

In that moment, my wavering thoughts solidified. We had to at least try and get that scroll back before it was opened. We had no choice. Maybe it wasn't the hopeless effort as I thought before. We had a hellhound, a Supernal Being, a fallen warrior angel and my knowledge of Hell from the Dream Walker to help us through.

Yes, getting that scroll back was looking more and more like something that we could do.

* * *

Crowds of people pushed against me and their auras all blended together in one crushing mass of color. The air was hot from so many bodies and my mouth felt dry. Warm hands encircled my waist and drew me backward, away from the worst of the crowd to a less condensed area off to the side.

"I hate the airport," I declared, turning my back and trying to focus on only Sam. And his blissfully aura-free form.

He smiled. "Let everyone else grab their bags first. We can wait."

Who knew that baggage claim would be worse than going through customs? I sighed and settled in for a wait. "Where's Gran?" I wondered for the tenth time.

"Maybe she's stuck in traffic. Looks pretty crazy out there."

I looked out the huge glass doors to the loading and drop off zone, which was definitely packed with cars. "Yeah." I agreed, but it didn't feel right. Gran would have gotten here early to beat the traffic. I expected her to be standing at the gate.

But she wasn't.

But Cole's mother was.

The minute we entered the airport, I knew she was here. I could feel the hate radiating off her and melting around me. When she saw Cole walking with me, her eyes narrowed. Cole's steps faltered and he looked between us.

"It's all right," I told him. "Go. Call me later."

He seemed relieved to avoid a scene and hurried to his mother's side. Sam and I hung back until they began walking toward baggage claim. I glanced over to see if Cole was having better luck claiming his stuff and saw that he was. He and his mom were already heading toward the exit. Through the doors I could see his dad at the loading zone, waving and smiling, taking his bags and stuffing them into the trunk. Cole was laughing and talking animatedly. This was Cole's father. Seeing them together made me understand even more why Cole wasn't that accepting of our dad. He didn't need to be.

They drove away and a sleek black car pulled in taking their place. It was some sort of sedan with four doors and a boxy shape. The windows were so dark I wondered how they got away with driving around town without being pulled over. I watched in fascination as the trunk popped open, but no one got out. The windows remained closed tight and there wasn't a hint of movement from inside. Someone approached the car.

She had red hair piled high on her head. Kimber.

The window opened just a crack and she leaned forward and spoke. Several seconds later, she went around and threw her bags in the trunk and slammed it closed. Then she opened the back door and slid inside. The car pulled away from the curb before her door was even fully closed.

I did not know that car.

It was not her parents.

Who could it have been?

I was afraid I knew.

I turned to Sam, to see if he saw. He was looking over my shoulder, face pale.

"What is it?" I asked.

He seemed to shake himself, yet the color remained absent from his cheeks. It disturbed me to see my golden boy looking not-so-golden and I turned to see what on earth could upset him so much. Gran was hurrying toward us. She was trying to smile, but I hardly noticed the attempt because her aura was screaming out in shades of worry and pain.

"Gran?" I said, running forward, not caring who I had to bump out of my way. I reached her and she stopped, pulled me into her arms for a quick hug.

"I missed you!" she said and pulled back to look me over. "How was your trip?"

Why was she pretending nothing was wrong when there clearly was? "What's wrong?"

She dropped the happy charade and looked at me. "I didn't want your homecoming to be like this."

"Gran, tell me." My stomach began to knot.

"There's been an accident. Your mother's in the hospital."

I gasped. Sam's arm came around my waist for support. "What happened?"

"I'm not really sure, honey."

"How bad is it?" I whispered. "When did this happen?"

Gran nodded, she expected these questions. "Just last night. I figured there was no use in calling with you arriving today."

"Gran, how bad?"

"Not so bad," she said, her aura saying otherwise. "She's unconscious right now."

I gasped. "No."

"But," Gran hurried to say, "the doctors are very hopeful. They say she'll wake up soon."

Then why was Gran's aura such a wreck? "We have to go." I turned, looking at the crush of people still crowding the baggage claim area.

"I'll be right back," Sam murmured. "Come help me?" he said to someone just behind Gran.

Gran shifted, turned. "Oh, Logan, I'm sorry. I didn't mean to keep you from saying hello."

Logan was here? Of course he would be. I'm sure he was anxious to see his brother. Logan murmured something to Gran and she smiled. He went to help Sam, who clapped him on the shoulder before they disappeared in the throng of people.

When everyone around you is dead... the Dream Walker's words were like a snake slithering up my spine. I shook myself. He couldn't be responsible for this. He got what he wanted. He got the scroll. The threat to my loved ones wouldn't be necessary anymore.

What happened to my mother was just an accident. That's all.

With the Dream Walker out of my head and out of the picture there was no one left that would want to hurt me like this.

Right?

Sam

"What is it? What happened?" I said in a fierce whisper.

I suspected that something was wrong the minute I saw Gran enter the baggage claim area. She was pale and grim-faced and then I saw Logan trailing behind her. That's when I *knew* that whatever was wrong was going to be bad and I prayed that he had nothing to do with it.

He opened his mouth to answer and I clapped him on the shoulder once more to turn him toward the conveyor as luggage started slowly moving around. "Heven's mom," Logan began and his voice cracked.

"We just talked to her on the phone the other night. She said that you were fine. Did she lie?"

"No, she didn't lie. I was fine."

But he wasn't now.

Heven's suitcase moved in front of me and I snagged it, dropping it in front of me. I wasn't sure I was ready to hear whatever he was going to say. This was Heven's mother we were talking about. Her family.

"Sam? I really missed you."

I turned my head to look at my little brother. He looked scared and confused. I wrapped my arm around him and pulled him in for a hug. "I missed you too, bud."

We stood there a minute and he made no move to pull away. "Whatever is going on, it's okay. Everything will be fine."

My giant duffle bag rolled around and I snagged it too.

"Come on," I said, hefting one bag in each hand. "Let's go. Heven's going to want to get right to the hospital. We'll talk then."

Logan nodded. He seemed a little calmer now. Maybe things weren't as bad as I thought. Maybe he was the one who found Heven's mom and was shaken up. Poor kid. Would he ever catch a break?

We hurried out of the airport toward Gran's car at the curb and I tossed the bags into the trunk and hurried to climb in. Heven was in the front seat, staring out the windshield, and I saw the sheen of tears in her eyes before she slid on her sunglasses and looked at me.

There wasn't anything I could say to make this better, so I gave her a reassuring smile and hoped that her mom would be okay. Logan was quiet on the ride to the hospital and I didn't dare try and talk to him in the car.

"You don't know anything about what happened?"

Gran shook her head. "Not much of anything. Poor Logan found her."

So I was right. He was upset because he found her.

Heven turned in her seat to look at Logan. "You found my mother?"

He nodded, fear creeping into his eyes.

"What happened?"

"I don't know," he said and looked at me. I nodded, wanting him to continue. "I came downstairs to get some water, it was late... she was lying on the floor in the kitchen. There was blood..." He looked down at his hands as his voice trailed away.

"Then what happened?" Heven asked, desperate for answers. I wanted to tell her to ease up, but she wasn't really being too harsh, she just wanted to know.

"I called 9-1-1 and the ambulance came. I went with her to the hospital and Gran came."

"Did she fall?" Heven pressed.

"I don't know," he said again. "I didn't see. There was water on the floor, like it was spilled. Maybe she slipped and hit her head."

Heven bit her lip and turned back around in her seat. Logan looked at me and I smiled, trying to tell him that everything was okay.

But the way he was talking... the way he looked. I'd seen that look in his eye before. Right after he trashed the second-hand store below my apartment.

* * *

The hospital was barren and quiet compared to the loud, busy airport we just came from. The walls were sterile white and the smell of antiseptic burned my nose. Beside me, Heven walked woodenly, solemnly. It made me angry because she had already been through so much and this was something that I couldn't protect her from. I knew that things between her and her mother

270

weren't very good, but lately, it had all been changing. Their relationship was growing strong again. I felt comfortable enough to leave Logan in her care and now I was wondering if that had been a mistake.

My fingers were wrapped around Heven's, ice cold and trembling. I released her hand to put my arm around her shoulders and pull her into my side as we made our way off the elevator and down yet another sterile hallway.

"Any change?" Gran asked, grabbing a nurse by the arm on her way down the hall.

"No, ma'am. Is this her daughter?" the woman asked, regarding Heven with kind eyes.

"Yes, this is Heven and her boyfriend Sam and you know Logan."

The nurse nodded. "Your mother is stable. There's some slight swelling in her brain and the doctor believes that when it goes down, she will wake up."

"Swelling in her brain?" Heven asked, alarmed. I took my arm from her shoulders and slid it around her waist for support.

"She had quite a fall, hit her head pretty hard," the nurse responded.

Heven made a small sound in the back of her throat.

"It's not so bad. She's going to be fine," the nurse assured her. "One visitor at a time. Immediate family only until she wakes up." The nurse looked at me and Logan as she spoke.

"Of course," Gran agreed.

Gran moved on down the hall and we followed, stopping in front of a closed wooden door. "Go on in. We'll wait out here," she said to Heven.

Heven pulled away from me and looked up. *I'll be right here.* I told her, wishing I had more to offer.

Without another word, she opened the door and disappeared inside.

Gran stood there a moment, then turned to Logan and me. "It's been a very long day and I'm going to go get a cup of coffee. Would either of you care for anything?"

We both declined as she moved off down the hall. When she turned the corner I looked at Logan. "Start talking."

His shoulders slumped and I thought he might cry. I grabbed his arm and led him to a room two doors down that was empty and I pulled him inside and pushed the door around.

"At first, everything was okay," Logan said. "Heven's mom, she's really nice. She cooked a lot and most of it was pretty good, except for the chicken. It was kind of like being back home."

"Then what happened?" I asked patiently.

"*He* started hanging around." His words tightened.

"Who? Henry?"

Logan nodded. "He was nice at first, too. But then one night he took me to the movies and for pizza. He said things…"

"What things?"

"That if you really cared about me you wouldn't have left me here and went to Italy. He said that you only cared about Heven." His voice broke.

"Logan, that isn't true," I said, reaching for him, but he backed away and continued to talk.

"He said that you didn't understand what was happening to me, but he did. He said he could fix me. I told him that he was lying and that you would help me and he got mad. He drove us to this empty lot, a field of grass and he made me get out of the car."

He started to cry and pure rage lit through my body.

"He hit me, Sam."

I was going to kill that SOB. As Logan talked, my limbs began to shake.

"He kept hitting me. He told me that I wasn't doing my job. That I wasn't submitting the way I was supposed to, that I was too strong." His voice broke again and in a small voice he said, "I'm not strong at all."

My vision was beginning to tunnel in and out. I was fighting for control. I was losing.

"He said he was going to break me. That I would do what he wanted from now on…"

I practically tore the door off the bathroom in the room and rushed in and yanked the faucet—the handle coming off in my hand. I looked in the mirror above the sink and glittering gold eyes looked back. *Get control of yourself!*

I splashed water on my face, ice-cold water, hoping to shock myself into calming down. I couldn't change here.

Sam? Heven's voice reached through my internal battle. *What's wrong? Why are you so upset?*

It was her concern, her downright weariness, that broke the tension in my body and I sagged against the sink. She needed me to hold it together. She was breaking right now in fear for her mother. I had to be the strong one.

Sorry, sweetheart. Logan was just telling me again about finding your mom. It made me upset.

She's so still.

But she's alive, baby.

Yeah, yeah she is.

Be with her. I'm okay now. Come out when you're ready.

I love you, Sam.

A long exhale released from my body and I pushed away from the sink. *I love you, too.* I tossed the broken handle into the sink bowl, and luckily, there was a water shut off valve beneath. I turned it to shut the water off and left the bathroom, closing the door behind me, grimacing at the way it hung loosely from its hinges. I hoped no one noticed it until we were gone.

Logan was there, tears staining his face. I sighed.

"I'm sorry. I got angry. I am angry. What he did to you, Logan. It's sick. He'll pay for what he did." He would pay with his life.

Logan threw himself at me and I caught him, hugging him hard, silently vowing to let no one hurt him again.

"Are you mad at me?" Logan asked, his voice muffled against my shirt.

"You didn't do anything wrong."

He pulled away then and looked at the floor. "I think I did."

Everything inside me stilled. "What do you mean, Logan?"

"As he was hitting me, I blacked out... When I woke up, I was standing over Heven's mom... with a glass water pitcher in my hands."

Horror sliced through me, but I kept calm. I would not freak out. I would not. "You said that you went downstairs for some water that night."

"There was blood on the pitcher, Sam. I beat her mother in the head with it and now she's here, in a coma!"

"Shhhh!" I whispered and looked at the door. I wasn't sure what I was going to do, but telling the entire hospital staff was not a good idea.

"I poured water on the floor to make it look like she slipped, rinsed off the pitcher and called 9-1-1."

"No, Logan." I shook my head. "You're just confused."

"No, Sam, I'm not. I can feel it. I did this. Me. There's something wrong with me..." His voice trailed away. "There's something inside me that's evil."

Denial, sharp and pungent, whipped through me. This was Logan. The little boy who loved to play football and pirates in the backyard. The little boy who trailed behind me every day after school and wanted to be just like me. This boy... this shell of a person that stood before me crying and confessing now was not my brother.

It dawned on me then.

He was right.

There was something inside him. And it wasn't a hellhound.

It was worse.

Heven

The curtain was drawn around the bed. It was white and made of thick, stiff fabric. The lights were dim and the shades were closed over the windows. I figured it was for when she woke up, in case her eyes were sensitive. She was alone in the room, with no roommate. There was a standard hospital bathroom to the left and a blue chair next to the bed, with the curtain separating the bed and the chair. I went forward, measuring the steps I took and counting the breaths that filled my lungs.

I never wanted this. I told myself.

Over the past months, my mother and I had our differences. We disagreed a lot and our once-close relationship drifted apart. I regretted it then, but it was easier to blame it all on her and be angry.

I should have tried harder.

And now it might be too late.

I could be an orphan before the age of seventeen.

Losing a father had been horrible, unbearable even. What would it be like to lose a mother too?

My sob was a loud echo in the room and it disturbed the stillness of the space around us. I wiped the tears from my cheeks and took a deep breath. I was stronger than this. It wasn't too late and my mother was not going to die. Even the nurse said so. I collected myself and pulled the curtain aside.

My mother looked small and pale against the white sheets. The scratchy blankets that the hospital used were draped over her still frame. Beside her, machines beeped and monitors recorded the beating of her heart. An IV was taped to the back of her hand and a large white bandage was wrapped around her head.

"Hi, Mom," I said, stepping closer to the bed. "I'm home from Italy. It was a good trip."

She gave no indication that she could hear me, but I kept talking. I told her about my trip and the plane ride. I told her about the places we went and the people we met. Soon, though, I fell silent, feeling awkward at the sound of my voice.

"What happened to you?" I whispered, taking her hand.

Of course she didn't answer. I leaned over her, studying her features. The machine next to us began to scream, beeping crazily. A nurse ran in and glared at me. "You're standing on the IV tube."

I jumped back like I'd been burned. "I'm sorry, I—I didn't know."

The nurse sighed. "It's fine." She came into the room and pressed some buttons. The beeping stopped. "Be careful," she warned before leaving the room again.

I sat down in the blue chair next to the bed, tucking my feet beneath me, making sure I was nowhere near the wires and tubes. I stared at Mom for a long time, wishing she would wake up.

She didn't.

But I did begin to feel my heart race and my hands shake. I was upset, but not like this. I realized that it must be Sam. Something must be happening.

Sam? What's wrong? Why are you so upset?

A few moments passed as I waited anxiously to hear his voice. I stood, ready to rush from the room if needed, but then his voice flooded my brain.

Sorry, sweetheart. Logan was just telling me again about finding your mom. It made me upset.

I was so relieved that I fell back into my chair, looking back at Mom. *She's so still.*

But she's alive, baby. She was and that counted for something. She would be okay. She would.

Yeah, yeah she is.

Be with her. I'm okay now. Come out when you're ready.

I love you, Sam. I needed to say the words, to hear them in return. To know that beyond this horrible thing there was something good.

I love you, too.

An hour later my legs were asleep and the bruises on my back were throbbing. I stood and, being extremely careful, leaned in to kiss her cheek. "I love you, Mom. I'm so sorry."

Guilt weighed me down.

This was my fault.

I took one last glance at her before exiting the room. Haunting words followed me out the door and I couldn't help but wonder if this wasn't the beginning of something terrible.

When everyone around you is dead...

Chapter Twenty-One

Heven

Night cloaked the farm as I stood out on the porch, leaning against the railing and staring out into the darkness. Usually, I could see the land and the trees, and it calmed me. But tonight, there was hardly a star in the sky and the moon was hidden behind dark clouds, so I could only see as far as the porch lights illuminated. I was hoping to see a shooting star, some kind of sign that everything was going to be okay. But no stars rained down, the sky was hidden and everything remained unchanged. Just like my mother. We spent hours at the hospital before Gran convinced me to come home and rest. I wasn't tired. I couldn't rest until everything was right again.

When would she wake up? What would she say? And where was Henry? His absence did not go unnoticed by me, although it seemed to by everyone else, except Sam, of course. When I asked Gran about him, she looked at me like I was crazy.

"Why would Henry be here, honey? He and your mother only had one or two dates."

But that wasn't true. I knew it wasn't. He was at Mom's house all the time and at all hours of the night—I talked to him. I didn't argue with Gran because her aura told me that she believed exactly what she was saying. Had someone influenced her memory?

Could a witch be capable of that?

I guess I couldn't quite hide my dismay over it all because Gran began making noises about how tired I must be and sent us home. She stayed at the hospital, keeping vigil over my mother.

I looked back up at the sky, searching for answers to all of my questions, but I knew the answers weren't in the sky. A noise from the kitchen brought my attention back to Earth and to another problem that was more troublesome than the rest.

Sam.

From the minute I left my mother's hospital room and found him pacing in the waiting room with Logan I knew—I *felt*—that something was wrong. When I asked him about it, he seemed all too relieved when my phone rang. It was Cole and I took the call to tell him about my mom. Then in the car, I could sense that he didn't want to talk and with Logan within earshot, I didn't press. The back door opened, but I didn't turn around, just continued to stare out into the nothingness of the yard.

His arms wrapped around me from behind and I leaned into him. I listened for Logan but I didn't hear him, he must still be inside.

"Thinking about your mom?" Sam asked, his voice right against my ear.

I nodded. "Do you think this happened because I lost the scroll? Do you think my mom's accident was my punishment?" The words kind of whooshed out of me and I hadn't really realized that I had been thinking that until I said the words out loud.

Sam's arms tightened around me. "I don't think you're being punished, Heven." His voice was hoarse with pain.

I turned in his arms to stare up at him. "What's wrong?"

He shook his head. "I hate to see you this way."

"That isn't all there is," I said gently. "Did something happen with Logan? Did he say something to make you upset with me?"

Sam made a sound in the back of his throat. "I'm not upset with you. You didn't do anything wrong, Heven. Unlike me... one mistake after another..." He said the last part almost as if he was talking to himself.

I grabbed his face between my hands. "What mistakes have you made?"

"For starters, I let the scroll get taken to Hell."

"You don't get to carry the blame for that. That scroll was my responsibility. Yours was protecting me. I'm still here, but the scroll isn't. This is my mistake to bear."

"Don't say that," he said, grabbing my shoulders. "I won't let you take the blame for this."

"So that's what this is about," I whispered. "You think Airis is going to take my life back because I failed."

"You didn't fail," he denied, looking over my shoulder into the darkness, almost as if he expected Airis to appear and strike me dead.

"There's one way to know for sure," I told him, wiggling out of his hold and going down the stairs into the dark yard.

"Heven, don't do this, please." His voice had grown quiet and desperate. "I can't lose you too."

I was already calling for Airis. But with his last words my voice died abruptly. "What do you mean lose me too?"

He was rushing down the stairs toward me, pulling me into his arms, but it was too late.

Everything went white.

* * *

The InBetween was as white and empty as always. I searched every space for my father, for the slightest hint of him, but as usual, there was nothing.

"Things didn't go as planned in Italy," Airis said.

Sam stepped around me, half blocking me from sight. "That's my fault. I didn't realize the greatness of the threat. I was unprepared for Hecate and for Kimber's betrayal."

"He's trying to protect me, to take the blame for something that I did."

Sam didn't even acknowledge that I spoke, but kept his gaze turned on Airis.

"You think that I'm going to take back the life I gave to Heven," Airis said to Sam.

"The thought did cross my mind," Sam said, once again trying to block me from her sight.

"She knows I'm here, Sam," I said, annoyed. Why did he insist on taking everything on himself?

There was a hint of a smile on Airis' face when she said, "If I was to take back the life I gave Heven, wouldn't it make sense that I would take yours back as well, Sam?"

His body stilled.

"I did give Heven back her life, but then I took yours in payment for hers. Then I gave it back as well, therefore I restored both of your lives."

"Leave Heven out of this," Sam said tersely, not bothering to deny that what she was saying was true.

"I gave your lives back to you because they are important. I do not give and take away life so frivolously. I will not be taking your lives away as payment for the loss of the scroll."

Sam practically stumbled from relief.

Airis actually looked like she was sorry for his fear. "Do not look at this as failure. Look at it as a bump in the road, a turn in the path you are walking."

"So it is possible to get it back," Sam said.

"I believe so."

"Do you know if they have gotten it open?" I asked.

Airis shook her head. "I do not think so. The key that you have. It isn't just any key. It's enchanted and has to be inserted into the lock of the Treasure Map by a Supernatural Treasure for it to open completely. It is why you were being lured into Hell by the Dream Walker."

"So he does need me to open it."

"Yes."

"We'll get it back," Sam vowed. "I know where a portal to Hell is."

This was news to me. "You do?"

He nodded. "It's a fountain in Portland. I've always been drawn to it."

"You showed it to me once," I said, remembering the day I walked in the rain to be with him. The day I tried my first bubble tea.

"That's the place," he said, nodding.

"It seems that you have somewhere to be," Airis said.

Sam took my hand and we waited for Airis to send us back home.

"Remember, sacrifices might have to be made in your quest. Not everyone can be saved."

For a moment my heart froze, I thought she was talking about my mother. But she was looking at Sam, whose face had gone unnaturally pale.

He opened his mouth to protest. I could feel the denial within him, but Airis cut off whatever he might have said by sending us back home.

* * *

Something wasn't right. The minute our feet touched the grass in the yard at home, I knew that something was wrong. I glanced around, realizing what it was. It was even darker here than when we left.

"Why is it so dark?" I wondered.

"The porch light is off," Sam said, looking in the direction of the house. I could make out the white stairs leading up to the porch and light was shining through the kitchen window and door. "Bulb must have burned out. I'll replace it in the morning."

"Oh." I laughed. I guess all that talk of death and sacrifice up in the InBetween creeped me out.

"That didn't go as bad as I thought it would," Sam said.

"Yeah, she even seems to think that there is a chance we could get the scroll back."

"We should leave as soon as possible to get it back."

"How did you figure out where the portal was?"

"It was something Gemma said while we were in Italy about remembering a place that I was drawn to—I remembered the fountain. The more I thought about it, the more it seemed to fit."

"I'll call Cole and tell him. We can leave tomorrow." I started toward the house, but Sam caught my hand and drew me back.

"Listen, Hev…"

I looked up at the hesitation I heard in his voice. "Yes?"

"There are some things going on with Logan… things that I haven't told you about."

"I know you feel caught between us, Sam. But you aren't. I understand that he's your family. Your brother. I won't ever ask you to choose between us. You don't have to."

"You don't know what he's done."

"I know that you love him. That's all I need to know right now. We'll figure the rest out."

"I love you too, you know."

"I know. It's because I am so hot and the total package," I joked. The turmoil within him was upsetting and I only wanted to take it away.

I saw his white teeth flash against the night and he laughed.

Just then Logan opened up the back door and stuck his head outside. "Sam?"

All the laughter died and Sam tensed. "I'm out here."

Logan looked toward us. "You coming inside?"

"Be right there." Sam moved by me and I caught his hand, threading my fingers through his. He gave my fingers a squeeze as we both walked to the house.

Whatever was going on with Sam had to do with Logan. Airis's warning came flooding back in my mind.

I truly hoped that the sacrifice that she was talking about was not Logan. I would never make Sam choose between me and his brother, but if I had to choose, it would be Sam every single time.

And if it came down to that, I was very afraid that Sam would never forgive me.

* * *

"You're sure this is the place?" Cole asked, staring at the fountain like he couldn't quite wrap his head around the fact that it would take us into Hell.

"Yeah, I'm sure. I can feel its pull stronger than ever before," Sam answered.

"Me too," Logan said, his voice and eyes thoughtful. "I was here before. This is where I met China. The air around the fountain seemed to shimmer. Now I know why."

I thought it was a little strange that Sam wanted to bring Logan. I was surprised when Sam told me this morning after I visited my mother that he filled Logan in on what happened in Rome and was bringing him along. As protective as Sam is over his little brother, taking him to the most dangerous place I could think of didn't seem right. But when I voiced that, Sam looked at me with those whiskey eyes and asked me to trust him. He said he couldn't explain now, but he would soon.

So, I let it go.

And here we stood at the portal. Me, Sam, my brother and his brother staring at a fountain, a pretty one at that, which supposedly led to a nasty, vile place. It was ironic really.

"So how do we, you know, use it?" I asked, looking dubiously at the fountain. There wasn't exactly a big handle and an arrow that stated 'Enter here to go to Hell.'

"Just jump at it. You'll get pulled in," said a familiar voice behind us.

Cole was the first to turn around, but the rest of us were close behind him. "Gemma."

Her gray eyes brushed over Cole almost like she was assuring herself that he was okay, even knowing that he was, before turning her gaze to the rest of us. "You guys going right now?"

"That's the plan," Sam said.

"I'm coming with you."

I smiled. For a girl who seemed to keep people at bay and not let anyone close, she sure was taking an interest in us. Or maybe it was just Cole.

"Are you sure you want to do that?" Cole said, going to her side.

She nodded. "I can help. I know things that you all don't."

"Like what?" Sam asked.

"Like how to get out of Hell once you're there."

"Isn't there another portal?" I asked, my nerves making my stomach shake. I thought there would be another portal like this one.

"No. This is a one-way portal. You cannot get out this way."

"Then how do we get out?" The thought of being trapped in Hell, that soulless, colorless place was a living nightmare.

"You can leave the underworld at any place at any time. All you need is a Lucent Marble."

"We don't have one of those," I said, frustrated. We didn't have time to find one of these Marbles; we needed that scroll back. Now.

"They are in Hell. You can get one when you get there."

"Where are they?" Sam asked.

"You can find Lucent Marbles at the bottom of any body of water," Gemma responded.

"But the water there is disgusting. It's thick and black — it looks like chunky oil," I said, recoiling at the thought of going into the water.

"How do you know?" Sam asked, alarmed.

"My dreams," I said simply. They were actually nightmares, but it turns out that they might be helpful.

"Of course they will be in a disgusting place," Gemma quipped. "Did you think that the way out of Hell would be easy?"

"How do you know all this?" Cole asked Gemma.

"I've been around a long time. Plus, I have the books."

"The books?" I asked, intrigued.

"Leather-bound books that pretty much tell you everything about Heaven and Hell." Gemma continued, "The Marbles are translucent, clear. It's why they're called Lucent. The water is so thick it coats them and makes it very difficult to see on the bottom. Sam is the only one that will be able to get them. He alone is strong enough to swim to the bottom; the fact that he's a hellhound and incapable of drowning gives him the time he needs to find them."

"I'll find one," Sam vowed.

I wondered why she didn't include Logan in her explanation. He was a hellhound too. Wouldn't that make him capable of going down there?

"To leave Hell, all we need to do is smash it onto the ground and a portal will open. Move quickly because they do not stay open for long."

"We could not have gotten this far without your help, Gemma. Thank you."

Gemma didn't know what to do with my sincere thanks. It seemed to embarrass her. So she said, "Let's get this done."

I turned away to join Sam at the fountain.

"Wait! There is one more thing you must know before we go," Gemma said quickly.

We turned toward her once again.

"This is very important. Our time in the Underworld is limited. You cannot stay there for long."

"What do you mean?" I asked.

"A human who has not died does not belong in Hell. It's the same reason you cannot go into Heaven, only the InBetween. Your soul is still in your body."

"If we can't get into Heaven, why can we get into Hell?" Cole asked.

Gemma smirked. "It's Hell. Of course it would allow you in, in hopes that you won't get out and you will lose your soul."

I hadn't realized I could get any more afraid than I already was. I pushed the feelings away before Sam picked up on them. He was already worried enough and rethinking his decision to allow me to come.

Gemma spoke again, drawing me out of my thoughts. "When you've been down there too long you will begin to feel your insides shake. A violent shaking. The outline of your body will begin to blur as your soul begins to separate from your body. You MUST leave when this happens. If you don't your soul will be stolen and you could be lost in Hell forever."

"Thanks for the pep talk," Cole quipped when we all stood there a little freaked out. "Way to give us some courage."

Gemma shrugged. "I never said this was easy, but knowing what you are walking into will give you greater odds of walking out."

I nodded.

"Let's go," Sam said, taking my hand. *Stay close to me.*

Lately his protective nature made me bristle, but not this time. This time I was grateful for it.

"Just jump at it?" Sam asked Gemma again, glancing at the fountain.

She nodded. "It will recognize you because you are a hellhound. It only opens for those it recognizes. As soon as you jump, it will open and we'll follow."

He glanced at me then back at the fountain.

Together we jumped.

* * *

Going through a portal to Hell didn't hurt, but it didn't feel good either. It was like being sucked through a giant vacuum and then being pushed out the other side. I would have fallen on the ground if Sam had not been there to catch me.

I rested my cheek against his chest briefly before he set me on my feet, trying to make the moment longer than I knew it could be. Cole followed me through the portal and hit the ground with an oomph. Gemma, of course, landed gracefully.

The portal snapped shut, instantly leaving us trapped in Hell.

We are not trapped, Sam reminded me before turning back to our first view of Hell. Well, *their* first view.

We were silent as we took stock of our surroundings. The place was as I remembered it: a completely colorless, barren landscape that appeared to have been destroyed by fire. The sky was sunless with nothing but gray, threatening low-hanging clouds. Beneath our feet was not grass, but dirt and sharp rock. The entire place spoke of despair and pain.

"I think we should find at least one Lucent Marble before we do anything else," Sam said.

"Good plan," Gemma agreed.

"Let's go," Cole said, clearly ready to do what we came to do.

We walked for what seemed like hours, but was really only minutes before we came to a wide river running through the ground without purpose or cause.

The thick black water was disgusting. The thought that Sam had to swim in that mess made me break out in a film of cold sweat. We all stared down at the slow-moving sludge as it went lazily down the river.

"Pretty gross," Cole observed.

"Smells too," Logan said.

Sam pulled off his shirt and handed it to me, then kicked off his shoes. "I'll be back in a minute."

"Wait!" I cried. How could he just dive in there? Just like that? But there was no other choice.

He bent so that we were at eye level and looked me straight in the eyes. "I will come back."

"There are those crocodile demons in there," I whispered, trying to sound confident.

He nodded.

Then his body shifted as he dove into the water.

Chapter Twenty-Two

Sam

The water was thick, sludge-like and coated my fur, pulling and yanking, almost like it was trying to claim me. For a mere second, I was tempted to give up the fight, to surrender. It would be easy. Simple.

I am better than that.

Even as I thought the words, the hound in me stretched out arrogantly and my limbs pushed through the sludge like it was butter.

This is what I was made for. I could do this.

All I had to do was reclaim the scroll, save the Map and then go to Airis. She would get that thing out of Logan once she saw all that I had been through. Then everything would be okay.

Except that you lied, a voice whispered in my head. I had lied. I lied to Heven. And it haunted me.

After Logan confessed what he did to her mother, after I figured out what was going on with him, I made him swear not to tell anyone. Including Heven. It wasn't that I wanted to lie to her, but I didn't know how to tell her. I was torn between my brother and my heart. Heven was rightfully upset about her mother—*I* was upset about her mother, but I couldn't undo what happened. I could protect my brother and protect Heven from more pain. And it was going to kill her when she found out who put her mother in the hospital.

I was going to tell her. But first, I wanted to get that thing out of my brother. I wanted to prove to her that he hadn't been himself. And truthfully, I wanted to prove to myself that I was right. I didn't want to believe the truth, but I had no choice. I'd buried my head in the sand for too long and I couldn't anymore. I loved my brother and so I had to do this.

A demon materialized beside me. It was completely adept at swimming in this thick, nasty "water" and it reached for me. I bit its hand off. It shrieked, but I couldn't hear a thing. Its mouth moved, but no sound reached my ears. In fact, it was utterly, eerily, silent here. There was no sound at all—the only things I could hear were my own thoughts.

With the loss of its hand, the demon shrank away, disappearing into the black void of sludge. I kept pushing downward, toward the bottom, wondering how deep this was, but not once stopping. I also took a moment to marvel at the fact I could see down here. It was pitch-black, almost suffocating in darkness. Combine the vast nothingness with the absence of sound and this place was like a void. Which, actually, was more frightening than anything I had seen on land in Hell so far.

My paw hit something solid and I kind of slid-dropped to the solid surface of the bottom. The "water" moved so lazily, so heavily, that I was able to stand on the bottom without difficulty. I began pawing the floor, looking for anything that felt round and hard.

The floor here was not sandy or rocky like other bodies of water. It was rock. Solid rock that didn't give way to my insistent paws. I moved off to another area and began searching again. Finally, I felt something roll beneath my front left paw. I hadn't given much thought to how I would pick it up and I stopped, pondering the thought briefly when my back paw rolled over what felt like two more balls. Taking advantage of my flexibility, I rolled the balls beneath my back paw up toward the front one. Then, with impatience, I bent down and took a huge mouthful of sludge. I swished (as good as you can swish sludge) around and confirmed that there were marbles in my mouth.

I pushed off the bottom and headed up. There was no light to guide me to the surface so I just kept going up, not once panicking that I wouldn't find the surface. I would. Eventually.

When my heart started racing and fear slammed through my chest, I knew it wasn't my own. *Heven.* I began rushing toward the surface, scrambling, fighting the urge to open my mouth and call out. Something was wrong.

I tried to calm myself with the realization that Cole was with Heven. So was Gemma. But I wasn't sure if even they would be a match for Logan if he decided that he wanted to harm Heven. So that left her, essentially, alone.

The girl I loved more than life itself was standing in Hell with my brother, my brother who, when he lost control, left chaos in his wake.

My paw broke the surface and then the other. I pushed myself out of the water with a great leap and landed on the unforgiving ground. Black goop coated my eyes and I stood there wondering what kind of view it was concealing.

Heven

Even as a hellhound I could see that Sam's strong limbs had to work for a moment before finding their way through the thick, black sludge. Soon he had disappeared beneath the surface and I was left to pace the riverbank. Cole knew he could offer no comfort so he took up position near the water and stared down as if willing Sam to hurry. Gemma didn't seem that worried, but I knew she was good at hiding her true feelings.

Logan was also staring down at the water, except it looked like he was waiting for something bad to happen. Like he hoped it might. I scolded myself for thinking such bad thoughts about Sam's brother. He was probably scared and worried for Sam right now.

I went to his side and rested a hand on my shoulder. "He'll be okay, Logan."

"Yeah." He shrugged my hand off him and walked a few steps away. I guess he didn't feel like talking.

Come to me…

The voice called to me and only me. One swift look at Cole, Gemma and Logan and I was sure. I knew what that meant. The Dream Walker knew I was here. I guess he somehow sensed me. From the minute I came through the portal, a familiar ache at the base of my skull asserted itself. Up until this point, I denied what it could possibly mean, but it was hard to ignore someone when they spoke to you.

I am waiting, little one…

My skin crawled. I hurried over to Cole's side, knowing that his presence wouldn't scare away the Dream Walker because I wasn't asleep, but still hoping his presence would make it easier on me.

"You okay, Hev?" Cole asked, his eyes narrowing on my face.

I nodded. "Worried for Sam."

Cole sighed and draped an arm over my shoulders. "He's tough, Hev. He'll be fine."

"Thanks for coming with us."

"Like I would let you come without me."

I rested my head against his shoulder and we both stared down at the water. It was really nice having a brother. "So…" I began.

"So…?" Cole responded.

"You and Gemma," I whispered.

"There is no me and Gemma." He glanced over to where she was standing and then gave me a look.

"You like her," I sang.

"She's a fallen angel, Hev." He said it like that explained everything and pulled away to cross his arms over his chest.

"You're a Supernal Being," I countered.

"I'm also human. I don't think Gemma is interested in a human. Now hush." He turned his face away to signify he was done talking about Gemma.

I wasn't so sure about that. I've seen the way she looks at him when she thinks no one else is looking and she did show up in Rome at just the right moment to save him. I was about to say as much when the world around us faded and a new place took shape. I jerked and looked over at Cole, but he was gone. His comfort was replaced instead with unpolished, black granite walls that held no windows or light. It was dark except for an ancient-looking lantern hanging against one wall with a flame that was fueled by oil. The floor beneath my sneakers was the same ground all over Hell, shale and rocks.

I shut my eyes and took a deep breath. This was not real. I was not trapped in a dungeon. Screams bounced around me, horrid, tortured screams. I suppressed a whimper. "Cole?"

All I needed was to hear his voice. To know this wasn't real.

"Heven?" Cole answered, but his voice was so far away. Above me, like I really was in a dungeon and Cole was up above, looking for me.

I resisted the urge to scream, because I knew that I was really right beside Cole on the bank of a nasty black river in Hell and I was waiting for Sam.

Sam! What if he needed my help and I was still stuck in this fake world? I ran to the wall in front of me and beat on it with my hands. The stone was unrelenting and didn't budge at all. I took a deep breath and stepped back, but stumbled over something. I landed on my butt in a tangle. I spread both hands out around me, to hoist myself up, but my hands didn't land on the ground. They formed around something icy cold and thin. I looked down.

Bones.

I landed on top a skeleton that had once been chained to the wall.

Screams echoed around me once more.

This time they were my own.

"Heven!" Strong hands grasped my shoulders and I was lifted off the pile of bones.

"Help me, Cole!" I begged.

"Everything's fine," he said, sounding confused and afraid at the same time.

"What's wrong with her?" I heard Gemma ask.

I felt his hands on me. I knew I was safe, but I couldn't stop staring at the broken pile of bones at my feet. Slowly, a few bones began to rattle. I took a step back, afraid of what I was about to see. A long bone—a leg bone—rolled away and a huge, lethal snake uncoiled from beneath. It rose and rose until it came to my shoulder and stared at me with beady dead eyes.

I whimpered.

It opened its mouth to reveal two very long, sharp fangs. At the same time, I heard an odd sort of sucking sound and the splash of water. The dungeon around me melted away and I fell back against Cole.

"Heven? What the hell is going on?" Cole demanded, gripping my arms.

As he spoke Sam leapt out of the black river to land at the water's edge.

All three of us ran forward with me closing the distance between us first. The thick black sludge was clinging to his black fur and coating his eyes, nose and ears. He blinked rapidly, trying to get the goop out of his eyes. I ripped off the sweater I was wearing over my tee, bringing it to his face and wiping the gunk from his eyes. It was sticky and clung to my sweater. As I cleaned him, I tried to catch my breath. It had been a trick. Just a nasty trick... When Sam could see he blinked up at me with flashing golden eyes.

What happened?

I couldn't help but look over at Logan. I denied it for as long as I could, but no more. I was positive that he was responsible for my momentary 'trips' into alternate places. In his eyes was the briefest flash of recognition and I knew without a doubt that I was right.

"You!" I screamed. "What did you do?!"

Logan looked at me like he was shocked I would yell at him. He portrayed the perfect mixture of hurt and disbelief on his fourteen-year-old face.

It really pissed me off.

"I don't understand. Why are you yelling at me?" he said, wobbling his lower lip.

"Oh, please. Cut the act, would you? Tell me what you did. How did you do that?"

Logan, of course, turned his eyes to Sam. "Sam? I don't understand why she's so upset."

I made a scoffing sound and Gemma frowned, looking over at Logan.

I turned my eyes back to Sam. He was watching me with a pained look in his eyes, but then he blinked and it was gone.

Hold out your hand, he said.

I obeyed and he opened up his jaws and unrolled his tongue. Three black gobs fell into my palm. They were icy cold and surprisingly heavy. When I closed my palm around them, Sam stalked over to where his clothes lay and morphed back into himself. He hurried to shrug into his clothes and we all stood there waiting to see what he would do after I yelled at his brother.

When he finally was dressed, he looked at me and then his brother. "Logan, trying to get between me and Heven isn't going to work. I won't choose. I love you both. Do me a favor and stop doing whatever it is you're doing to her."

Logan's mouth dropped open, but then he recovered to say, "I didn't do anything!"

Sam pinned him with a hard look. "You know that isn't true. I realize you didn't mean whatever you did, but it needs to stop. Now."

He turned to me. "Are you okay?"

I nodded.

"What the hell is going on?" Cole demanded again.

"We don't have time for explanations," Gemma said. "We have to keep moving."

"Can I see them?" Cole asked as we began walking. I noticed Logan kind of trudged behind us. I felt kind of bad for him because he had been so sure that Sam would choose him over me.

Sam scooped them out of my palm and used my already ruined sweater to wipe them clean and hold them out. We all leaned forward to see the Lucent Marbles. They were beautiful, which was a surprise because they came from such a desolate place. They looked like balls of glass, almost clear, without any imperfections.

"I'll hold onto them," Sam said, stuffing the trio into the front pocket of his jeans. I gave a silent sigh of relief that they were tucked away somewhere safe and away from Logan.

"How do we know where the Map is?" Cole asked.

I thought back to the voice that called to me moments ago. "I know where it is."

Four pairs of eyes turned to stare at me.

"This way," I said, ignoring them and walking away from the water.

"How do you know where to go, Hev?" Cole asked from behind me.

I peeked out of the corner of my eye at Sam, who was watching me with a tight frown on his face. "I've dreamed of this place," I answered.

"You mean when that guy was getting in your head?" Cole asked.

I nodded, feeling sick and not liking the thoughts swirling through my mind. "This is where I usually was. In Hell."

Everyone digested that. I felt Sam lace his fingers with mine. *Heven?*

He's calling to me, Sam. He knows I'm here.

I felt all the muscles in Sam's body tense and the familiar feeling of my insides fluctuating that I always got when Sam was about to shift. *No, Sam.* I squeezed his fingers. *He might know I'm here, but I'm not in danger. We can use this to find the scroll.*

How? Sam worried. *I thought I destroyed the thread he used to get into your head.*

I thought you did, too. Had it all been a ruse to lure me under a false sense of security?

We walked in silence for a while, stepping over broken, dead trees and stumbling through rocky, uneven terrain. Suddenly, I had a flash of recognition and I knew that just ahead was the valley from my dream. I skittered to a stop.

"The last time there were demons down there."

Without another word Sam and Cole stepped in front of me and were soon joined by Gemma and Logan. We all walked forward to stare down into the valley.

It was empty.

In fact, everything here was vacant and deserted. It wasn't anything like how I remembered it.

"He knows..." I murmured.

"Who?" Cole asked.

I looked up into my brother's concerned blue eyes. "The powerful one. He knows we're coming. He wants us to come; he doesn't want anyone to stop us."

"Who is this guy?" Cole wondered, turning to look at Gemma. Her face had gone pale.

That was not a good sign.

"Doesn't matter," Sam said. "I'm going to kill him."

Logan laughed under his breath.

Yet another clue that he was not who he seemed.

My eyes shot to Sam. He had to have heard his brother laugh. The area around Sam's mouth tightened and pain was the briefest emotion through the liquid honey of his eyes. But he smoothed out his features before turning to face his brother. "Something funny, little brother?" Was there an edge to his voice as he spoke?

Logan seemed to realize his mistake and looked regretful. "No. Sorry. I'm just nervous. I—I don't want you to get hurt trying to kill someone."

"It wouldn't be the first time I've had to kill someone," Sam responded patiently.

Logan nodded. "I know. But this man, he must be very powerful if he was able to get inside Heven's head."

"I was able to destroy the Dream Walker's thread," Sam reminded his brother. I kept my expression smooth, knowing he must not want Logan to know that we suspected the thread may not be broken.

I suppressed the urge to shudder. I knew the kind of power this man carried. It was unlike anything I ever felt before. I hated to admit it, but Logan might have a point. Would Sam be able to fight someone this powerful?

"Sam's not alone," Cole spoke up. "I may not be a hellhound, but I can fight."

Sam held out his fist and Cole pounded his against it.

Great, now I had to worry about the both of them.

Gemma rolled her eyes and started moving again.

I peeked over my shoulder at Logan, who seemed to be concentrating awfully hard. He caught my stare and gave me an odd sort of smile. I thought about telling Sam what happened back at the water, but now wasn't the time. We couldn't afford to lose focus on what we came here to do.

I shook my head and regretted the motion because the pain in the back of my skull was beginning to grow with a vengeance. "We're getting closer," I whispered.

We came upon a huge rock that jutted out from the ground. It obscured the view up ahead and was gray, covered in soot and had sharp jagged points sticking out at every angle.

I knew what was beyond this rock.

Him.

The back of my head was now splintering with pain and I felt like I was being tugged farther along. I dug my feet into the rocky terrain and stopped. *No!* I shouted as loud as I could in my mind.

Behind me Sam made a noise and was instantly at my side.

Welcome home, the powerful one called. The tug became stronger, but I fought, grabbing on to Sam's hand.

Sam let out a roar and tugged me against him, his arms forming iron bars around me. *You aren't alone!* the Dream Walker screeched. My ears rang with his madness.

"Is he always this way?" Sam choked.

I twisted my head back so I could see him. He winced with every shout and scream the powerful one made. "Can you hear him?"

Sam nodded. "As soon as I touched you. He's so close to the surface of your mind that I can hear him now too."

Relief made my knees go weak. Part of me was afraid that Sam would think I was going crazy.

"I must have only weakened the thread he left in your mind, not severed it," Sam whispered.

I nodded, already thinking the same thing. "It must just be easier for the Dream Walker to manipulate it here in Hell because we are closer."

Sam pressed a kiss to my temple. "I'm sorry I didn't get him the first time around. I won't make that mistake again."

"Oh, you severed the thread. But this is his hometown," Gemma said, coming to stand beside us. "He marked a claim on Heven, probably the first time he dragged her here. Whenever she's here, he will be able to get into her mind because he has been there before."

"Do you know who is doing this?" I asked.

"I have an idea," Gemma hedged.

Behind us Logan doubled over in pain and made a moaning sound. "Logan!" Sam yelled, rushing to his brother's side.

"It hurts! Oh God, it hurts!" he cried, falling onto his back and pulling his knees up to his chest.

How dare you bring them here! the powerful one screamed. A sharp pain radiated through my head and down my back. It felt as though he struck me inside my head.

"He thought you came alone," Sam said, looking up from Logan, who was groaning in pain. Sam looked back down. "Logan?"

"It hurts too bad. I have to give in. He says if I do, then it won't hurt anymore." To my horror, large red scratches bloomed down his arms.

"Heven, how about some answers? What's wrong with Logan?" Cole asked, coming to stand in front of me. His face was pale and drawn.

I shook my head and pointed. "The castle is just beyond that rock. He knows I'm here now. He thought I came alone."

"Is he that stupid?" Cole asked.

"You should have been alone."

We whipped around at the sound of Logan's voice. It was deeper and harder than I had ever heard before.

"Logan?" Sam asked, pain cracking his voice.

Logan laughed a sick kind of cackle as he climbed to his feet, shoving Sam away. "Logan's not home." As he spoke, a filmy white aura bloomed around his body.

I gasped.

"I'll give the kid credit, though, he fought. Harder than I thought the little brat would. Whenever his big brother Sam was around, he tried to get out."

"What the hell have you done to my brother?" Sam screamed and lunged, only to be slapped backward.

The thing that looked like Logan, but wasn't Logan, shrugged. "He's in here somewhere. No matter. When I leave him, he will die!"

"No!" Sam wailed and sprang forward. My muscles tensed, ready to join whatever fight Sam was about to have. He caught Logan by the throat and lifted him off his feet.

"Be careful, Sam. Don't want to hurt your baby brother," the voice inside Logan taunted.

Sam dropped him like he had been electrocuted. Indecision battled within him. He didn't know what to believe.

"What's going on?" I screamed, taking Logan's attention.

"The 'powerful one,'" he mocked "The one you call Dream Walker needed someone close to you, to keep an eye on you."

This was the Dream Walker's doing? "Who is he?" I asked.

"Someone you will never defeat."

"Why didn't you just kill me?" I asked. "And take the Treasure Map, since that's what you wanted."

"I wanted to. So many times. But *he* doesn't want you dead. You've become a trophy for him to acquire. His newest obsession. I tried to take the scroll a few times, but your boyfriend here was always watching. And then you hid it. Little Logan couldn't even get the whereabouts out of big brother. No matter how hard he tried to get between you. My only consolation prize was torturing you with the false worlds," Logan taunted. "That and watching Sam rip himself to pieces trying to 'fix' his baby brother."

"I knew it was you." But really, I had been wrong. It wasn't Logan... it was..."What are you?" I whispered.

Gemma stepped up beside me. "He's a demon, Heven. There's a demon living inside Logan's body. And now that demon wants out."

Sam

Gemma's words cut me like a knife. I stood there bleeding, aching and in pain. The words had been spoken. There was no going back.

The words were true.

For weeks a demon had been taking up residence in my brother's body. Fooling us. Fooling him. I should have seen it sooner. I should have realized that it wasn't possible for him to be a hellhound.

But now there was nothing I could do.

I couldn't destroy it because it would destroy him.

I couldn't destroy my baby brother.

"You sick bastard!" Cole roared and threw himself at Logan. They both went down in a tangle with Cole coming out on top, throwing punches, making Logan's head spring back again and again.

"No!" I yelled, lunging at Cole, sick inside, and pulled him off my brother.

Logan stayed on the ground and laughed. "You're pathetic," he spat through a bloody mouth. I was beyond torn. The thing living inside my brother was sick and twisted. It was hurting Logan, but fighting it meant destroying someone I loved.

Logan got up from the ground. "You don't want to fight me?" he screamed. "Then watch as I hurt her!" He lunged at Heven.

I roared and grabbed Logan by the front of his shirt, his body sagged like a ragdoll in my grip as he laughed. And laughed. And laughed. I paused.

"You won't do it," Logan taunted. "You will stand by while I kill you, and then Beelzebub will claim what he wants."

Who the hell was Beelzebub? Did he mean the powerful one?

Pushed to the limit, I reared my fist back and brought it down. "Sam?" Logan said, except the voice was no longer the demon; it was the voice of my brother.

"Logan?" I whispered, his fist stopping mid-air.

"What's going on?"

My voice caught. "Everything's going to be okay, Logan."

"I'm scared."

I couldn't do it. I couldn't hurt him. Instead, I pulled him against me. "I'm so sorry, Logan. You should never have been involved."

"I love you, Sam." Logan said.

I let out a low sob.

"Sam!" Heven screamed just as I heard the whisper of a dagger being brought toward my back. I didn't see what he was doing. I didn't think about being betrayed.

I threw the demon away, the dagger leaving a long cut down my bicep. Where the hell had he gotten a dagger? The demon threw the dagger at me, but I caught it and without thought, sent it spiraling back. The demon dodged it and laughed.

Cole charged with his own dagger drawn, but the demon leapt a few feet off the ground and landed behind Cole. He picked Cole up, Cole's feet dangling, and then tossed him up into the air like a father would a toddler, but instead of catching him, he grasped him around the neck and slammed him into a giant rock jutting from the earth. Cole went down and didn't move. Gemma rushed over to where Cole was lying in a crumpled heap.

"Cole!" Heven ran toward him, dropping to her knees beside him.

But she didn't stay there long. In the blink of an eye, Logan moved and grabbed her. Pinning her beneath him. "Get Cole away from him!" Heven told Gemma, more worried about her brother than herself.

"He said I couldn't kill you, but he never said I couldn't harm you." Logan cackled, reaching up and tearing a jagged piece of stone from the rock mountain and holding it above him, ready to strike Heven with it.

I realized then that this may look like my brother. He might sometimes talk like my brother.

But he wasn't my brother.

Gemma whistled and I looked up. She sent something spiraling through the air and I caught it. I knew exactly what I had to do.

In the end, I did have to choose between him and Heven.

"I'm so sorry, Logan," I said, the words actually hurting me.

I rushed him, caught him from behind, and dragged him away from Heven. Before he could react or turn, I plunged the dagger Gemma had thrown me into his chest.

Surprise flickered through Logan's eyes before they turned a flat black color.

I expected there to be blood.

There wasn't any.

But there was something worse.

Out of the hole the dagger created, something began to leak, to ooze… and as it filled the ground beneath my brother's lifeless body, it began to take shape. It began to fill out, it began to stand.

The demon.

A demon of huge proportions. He towered over me a good foot and was wide with muscle. His skin had a greenish tint and his teeth were yellow. He only had four fingers on each hand and his hair was buzzed off unnaturally short.

"Finally, I am released from my puny prison," he said, his voice deep. "Go to your master," he ordered Heven who was standing behind him in shock. "You cannot save these people."

Instantly, I shifted to full hellhound form. I watched the Lucent Marbles go rolling across the ground when my jeans tore from my body, but I didn't stop to pick them up. Heven rushed after them, scooping two up and shoving them in her pocket.

I launched myself at the demon, teeth exposed, ready to rip out his throat. I would tear him apart for what he did to my brother. He knocked me away with one swipe of his arm, but I wasn't done. The gash in my arm burned, but I ignored it. I focused completely on this vile creature before me.

Heven was pacing behind us, then stopped and squatted next to my brother. She touched his cheek with her hand and she frowned. Her tenderness distracted me and earned me another hard hit from the demon. Heven shot to her feet at the same moment I did and she began to look around wildly. She wanted a weapon so she could join the fight. I prayed she didn't find one. Moments later, she ran out of my line of sight and I was relieved. I didn't want her anywhere near this.

I took a chunk out of the demon's side, listening as it roared in pain and I lunged again, taking another out of its thigh. But on my third lunge, he kicked me and I went flying, landing hard against the large rock formation. I felt something crack and I wasn't able to spring right back up.

The demon moved fast, coming to stand over me, a manic expression on its face. It was holding the dagger that it tried to stab me with earlier. The very one that I had stabbed my brother with. It raised the blade above its head and I jumped to my feet as I saw the edge rushing down toward me.

"NO!" Heven screamed from close by and then she was in front of me shoving another dagger — Gemma's dagger — in the demon's chest. He stumbled backward, shock marring his nasty face.

Run, Heven, I urged.

Heven looked toward Gemma, who yelled, "You know what to do."

To my dismay Heven reached out and grasped the dagger and pressed the jewel on the hilt.

Then something remarkable happened.

The demon opened his mouth, but no sound came out. He dropped to his knees and fell forward as I pulled Heven out of the way. Bright light seemed to fill the inside of the demon. Pure, white light. We all watched as the demon writhed in pain as the light shined out from his eyes, ears and nose. He writhed for a long time. It was hard to watch because the more light that shined the more pain it obviously felt. He tried to scream, but it was as if his pain was so great, he couldn't manage the sound. He was trapped in a world of pain with no escape. Finally, I realized something and stepped forward.

Using my teeth I reached down and tugged the dagger free.

The light died instantly and so did the demon. He was left lying on the ground, blackened as if he had been charred in a fire, with smoke curling from its ears and mouth.

"It's like he was burned from the inside out," Cole said, now fully awake. There was a trail of blood down the back of his neck that curled around his ear and disappeared into his shirt.

"Cole! Did you break anything? How are you even awake?" Heven said.

Cole smiled. "Gemma has some serious mojo and fixed me up."

Gemma didn't seem to want to talk about her "mojo" and she motioned toward the dead demon at our feet.

"That's exactly what happened," Gemma said, taking the dagger from my mouth. "That vile creature was no match for the pure light of Heaven, which is exactly what just killed him."

We all looked at the dagger clutched in her hand with awe.

"I saw an image on the wall of the catacombs… it was of that dagger. That's how I knew what to do," Heven said, sounding shaken.

I morphed immediately while Cole stepped in front of me, yanking some pants out of the bag he was carrying. I hurried and shoved them on and ran to my brother, kneeling beside him.

"Logan," I choked out.

The dagger wound in his chest was gaping and blood soaked the front of his torn and dirty shirt. He was so pale and small. Smaller than he had looked since he first found me. I realized that the demon had made him look bigger, had somehow swelled his looks so he appeared stronger than he was. In truth, his shoulders were narrow and his body was thin. He seemed to have a hollow look about him and I wasn't sure if that was because his body was suddenly more empty than it had been or because he was so close to death. His dark blond hair fell limply over his forehead and beneath his closed eyes were purple smudges. He was so frail, so achingly fragile that I was afraid to touch him in even the smallest of gestures. His chest was rising and falling slightly, so I knew he was hanging on to what life he had left and I sat there, hunched over him, trying to think of a way to somehow give him some of my own life.

"Let me see him," Gemma said, pushing me aside and holding her hands out, palms down over his chest. The air between her hands and his wound began to glow. The wound magically began sealing itself up and the skin knitted back together.

"You can heal?" Heven asked from beside me.

"Like I said, she has serious mojo." Cole leaned close to Heven to whisper loudly.

Gemma nodded. "They might have taken my wings and banished me from Heaven, but I still have some powers. This is one of them."

"Will he live?" I asked, desperate.

"I don't know. But this will help him," Gemma said, standing up.

"Take him out of here. Take him back to my apartment, please," I asked.

Gemma nodded. Heven reached into her pocket and pulled out two Lucent Marbles. "I only found two; the third one is gone."

"It's all we need," I said, staring down at Logan, who was still unconscious. What would this do to him when he woke up? Would he remember what happened? Would he ever be the same?

"I'll get him home safely and watch over him," Gemma promised. She looked at Cole.

"I'm staying with them. They're going to need the help."

"Be careful. Beelzebub is very strong. If he is who you are up against, I would recommend just coming with me."

"I'm not giving up. This guy has taken too much from me. He's hurt too many people." Heven placed her hand in mine.

Gemma nodded. She knew that I would never run from a fight.

I crouched beside Logan and brushed his hair from his forehead. "I'm so sorry. You're going to be okay."

He didn't respond as I knew he wouldn't. But something did happen. The ground began vibrating beneath my feet and there was a shrieking in the sky.

What now?

Heven gasped and pulled my arm, pulling me up away from Logan.

"Get back!" Gemma yelled, pushing at Cole.

I stared in shock as a humungous dragon lowered itself from the dark, ominous sky and landed on the ground beside Logan.

Heven

"No," I whispered and started forward.

Sam pulled me back. "Are you crazy? Do you see the size of that thing?"

Yes, but if he understood what it wanted, he wouldn't be pulling me back. I twisted free and ran forward. Sam followed with a muffled curse. The dragon seemed to ignore us as it leaned over Logan's limp body and began opening its massive jaws. The whirring noise and a light sucking pulled at my clothes.

"No!" I yelled, coming to stand in front of the dragon.

Its golden eyes flicked to me. It opened its mouth wider.

"No!" I yelled, again, with all the force and strength I could.

Amazingly, the dragon closed its mouth and looked at me again.

"Good boy," I said, feeling silly.

"Heven, come away now," Sam begged, grabbing my hand. "I'll get Logan."

The dragon shrieked and roared, its putrid breath blowing us back. I pulled my hand away from Sam's. The dragon eyed us suspiciously.

I watched it to see what it would do.

It nosed Logan's body as if testing me.

"No!" I told it again.

It growled.

"Give me the bag," I said to Sam.

"Heven…"

"The bag, Sam."

He handed it over. Without taking my gaze from the dragon, I fished around inside and found what I wanted. I dropped the bag at my feet and loosened the wrapper around what I held.

"Are you serious, Hev?" Cole asked. Then to Gemma he said, "Is she serious?"

"I have no idea," Gemma answered.

The dragon stared at me as I held up the prize. With a quick flick of my hand, I sent the Snickers bar at him. The dragon caught it and, without chewing, swallowed it whole.

"Good dragon," I told it.

It opened its jaws and made a sound, almost like a response and showed me his teeth.

I stared at it as it turned and lumbered toward the dead demon's corpse. It nosed it and then crouched over it and opened its mouth. Amazingly, its golden eyes looked up.

I nodded and stepped back toward Sam who was already running to scoop up his brother from the ground. "Watch," I told everyone.

The dragon did his thing, opening his mouth and sucking what was left of the demons soul right out of him. When he was done, he looked up.

"What is that thing?" Cole asked, amazed.

"The Devourer," I whispered.

The dragon looked at me before it flew away.

"It was going to do that to Logan?" Sam asked, tightening his hold on his brother and looking to the pile of ash that used to be the demon that used Logan's body as a façade for its sinister identity.

"Yeah."

He turned to Gemma. "Get him out of here."

Gemma swiftly took Logan from Sam and asked me for a Lucent Marble, which I held out to her.

"Take care of him," Sam told Gemma.

"Don't worry about Logan. Take care of yourselves. At the first sign of real trouble, get out."

Sam nodded and, without another word, Gemma threw the Lucent Marble down and it shattered. A swirling portal of fog appeared. Gemma didn't hesitate to walk right through.

And then they were gone.

Sam, Cole and I looked at one another.

"I'm so sorry this happened," I told Sam, feeling just awful about his brother.

"I suspected a demon since we got home from Rome. I brought him down here, hoping for some answers. I hadn't expected all this though." He sounded weary and I couldn't blame him.

"Me either. I keep wondering who this Beelzebub guy is and why he's gone to such great lengths to torture us."

"That demon said he wants you, Heven. It isn't just about the scroll anymore, but you too," Cole said, his voice grim.

"Yeah, well, this guy is about to get a rude awakening," Sam said, grabbing my hand, and we started walking again.

Nerves knotted my stomach as I anticipated the one I knew was waiting for me just beyond the rock. When at last he came into view, my breath caught. He wasn't at all what I was expecting.

I knew him.

I watched as a fly circled his head and landed in his hair. I gasped in horror as I realized exactly what we had been missing this whole time.

Beelzebub was Henry. Henry was Beelzebub.

My mother was dating a demon.

* * *

Sam let out a roar and lunged at Beelzebub. He only laughed, flinging out his hand, and sent Sam flying backward onto the ground. Sam rebounded and stood, racing toward him again, but I caught his arm. *Stop, he's more powerful than we realized.*

Sam didn't lunge again, but I knew that he wanted to. I felt the restrained need in him to shift right there and fight.

"Are you the one who's been in my head?" I asked.

He laughed. "Thought you were clever by breaking that thread, did you? Guess you didn't really break it after all."

"That's only because I'm here, in Hell," I said, wanting him to realize that I knew more than he thought I did.

He cackled again and the hair on my arms rose. "Is that what you believe? Silly girl. I can still get into that head of yours anytime I please. That thread may have been broken, but it wasn't the only thread that I left in your mind. I've been leaving you alone because you were going to Rome. I wanted you to have a false sense of security, so that taking the Treasure Map would be easier."

"There's a demon in my head," I said, realizing that things were much worse than I had thought. I watched what that demon had done to Logan. Would the same thing happen to me?

"Demon is such a derogatory term." Beelzebub smirked. "I'm far above a lowly demon." He motioned with his hand and two demons, the kind he deemed lowly, came into sight carrying something.

A body.

Cole, Sam and I watched in horror and shock as a white twisting cloud rose out of Beelzebub, whose body—Henry's body—immediately dropped on the ground, lifeless and unmoving.

I realized it was his spirit. His soul.

It floated with purpose toward the body the demons were carrying and began traveling up his nose, and into his ears... then suddenly the body's eyes popped open and he stood.

This was the man from my dreams. Dark hair, pale skin and blood-red lips. This was the man who pulled me into Hell when I slept.

I have been being tortured by the same man who had the ability to change his form—his *body*. That explained the day I almost drowned, why I never saw a demon in the water with me. He wasn't using one.

"I am the Prince of Demons, The Lord of Flies! I am Second only to Satan!" he roared triumphantly.

The three of us stood there, not really reacting because we were all in shock. Besides, his title didn't scare me. His actions did. And really, the Lord of Flies? That's nasty. And pathetic.

It seemed to make him angry that the three of us didn't react or run away screaming. "Have I not done enough to make you fear me?" he said, his voice was deadly quiet, which was much more frightening than when he was screaming.

Of course I was afraid. We all were, but none of us were going to give him the satisfaction of admitting it.

He sighed dramatically. "I guess that's what I get for sending a worthless demon to get between you. The only thing he had been good for was giving me information about you, which I managed on my own by letting myself into your head. If he had done his job, you would have realized that you belong here and would have come running. It's a pity you already killed him. I would have enjoyed it."

I was feeling a little weird... shaky. The Lucent Marble in my pocket felt heavy, reminding me our time was running out.

"It's time I took matters into my own hands. I tried the nice way, the civil way, but no more!" he screamed and lifted his hands to the sky.

Purple lightning whipped through heavy clouds. It was so cloudy and hazy that the lightning looked florescent as it flashed. Sam pulled me behind him, placing his body directly in front of mine and Beelzebub laughed.

Then, like an orchestra conductor, he brought down his hands, a quick sweeping motion and with them came the lightning. It hit the ground with such force that the rocky floor exploded around us. Sharp pieces of shale flew everywhere and dust blew in my eyes. A loud booming sound filled my ears, the ground shook and I was falling...

Everything went black.

Chapter Twenty-Three

Heven

I heard my name being called. The voice was urgent and pleading. It was a raspy voice, a voice I liked, so I opened my eyes.

"Thank God," Sam groaned when I looked up at him.

"What happened?" I said, blinking and looked at Cole, who was leaning over Sam to stare down at me.

"We all blacked out and he locked us up in here," Cole answered, grimly.

I sat up, my head swimming. "Easy," Sam said.

"I don't feel right," I moaned.

There was a light tug in the center of my chest and I wondered if it was my soul starting to separate from my body. I glanced at Cole to see if maybe he was feeling the same way and he nodded once. His eye was swollen and beginning to blacken and the rest of his face was covered in soot and dust from the explosion. It was a stark contrast to the rust-colored trail of dried blood running down the back of his neck.

"We have to get out of here," I said, pushing to my feet.

Then I realized where we were.

In his castle. In his dungeon.

We were locked away behind iron bars. How long would he try to keep us here? My only comfort was that we had the Lucent Marble, so really, we weren't trapped.

"I know where the scroll is."

Even though the voice was raspy and low, it was familiar. Stunned silence froze us all for one long second. Then, Sam and Cole whipped around and I looked past them to peer into one of the dark cells across the hall. Kimber stood in the shadowed doorway, behind the bars. Her hair was matted and dirty, hanging around her gaunt, white face.

"Kimber?" I whispered.

"Turns out you were right. I chose the wrong side," she said, the words seeming to scrape from her throat. It was painful to watch.

"That day at the airport..." I said, thinking of the dark car she was climbing into—how I hadn't seen her since.

"I tried to get it back. I tried to make it right. I'm sorry."

They made her a prisoner here. They used her and then turned on her. Pity and sorrow filled me. Our friendship might be over, but I didn't want this for her and I still cared about her.

I rushed toward the bars. "How do we get out of here?"

She shrank back into her cell, darkness enveloping her and I wanted to scream out in frustration. But then I realized she wasn't trying to tease us.

She was hiding.

Beelzebub appeared, followed by a figure dressed in a blood-red robe. The hood was pulled forward, hiding the person's face, but I knew it was Hecate. She stopped in front of Kimber's cage and turned toward us. I couldn't see her stare, but I could feel it and I shivered.

Beelzebub looked completely unruffled and not the least bit dirty from the explosion as he stepped in front of our cage. I stumbled backward.

"Ah, you're awake." He was holding the bronze tube in his hands, the one containing the Map. "Tell me, little one. How is your soul fairing? Is it wanting out?"

"Please let us out," I said, no longer above begging for our lives.

"So it is," he said.

A low growl ripped from Sam's chest.

"Careful, kitty," Beelzebub taunted. "Make me angry and I will reconsider letting you out."

The iron door swung open and I lunged forward, but Sam pulled me back and once again put himself in front of me as he and Cole walked out of the door first. When it was my turn to go through, Sam put a hand on my arm as if to anchor me to his side—like he was afraid I would be snatched away at any moment.

Maybe I would be.

We were at the very end of the long hallway, the only light coming from flame-lit torches that lined the walls. Our cell was to the right and just in front of us where the hallway ended was a wide door, arched at the top and made of black steel. It was to this door that Beelzebub strode, throwing the lock and yanking the heavy door open wide.

Intense heat rushed at us through the opening. It was so hot that it took my breath. There seemed to be no floor and no walls inside the new room and the back of the door was blackened— scorched.

It was a fire pit. An endless hole of fire that I knew never went out.

As I watched the flames lick through the door, Beelzebub lashed out, grabbing Cole and dragging him toward the flames.

"Cole!" I cried, rushing forward only to be yanked backward by Sam.

"You have a choice," Beelzebub yelled as Cole fought and struggled to no avail. "You can open up this scroll case and give me the Map or watch as I send him to a fiery grave."

"Don't do it, Heven!" Cole yelled as sweat dripped from his forehead.

I wasn't about to let my brother die. I looked at Sam, his face set in a grim expression. He knew I wouldn't allow my brother to die, and after what just happened to his brother, he wouldn't ask me to.

"Okay," I said, my voice barely audible. But he heard me and smiled triumphantly. He took a few steps away from the flaming pit and I let out a breath. Cole was shaking his head, but I ignored him. I had to do this.

Acting nervous (not that it really was an act), I put my hands into my pockets and lowered my head, allowing my hair to fall and curtain my face, letting my shoulders shake—like I was trying to get it together.

"Now!" Beelzebub screamed.

My body was shaking now, and it wasn't from fear.

Hell was trying to claim my soul.

I yanked my hands out of my pockets, gripping the single remaining Lucent Marble and reached back toward Sam, pretending to want his comfort. He reached out and I dropped the Marble into his hand and turned back to Beelzebub.

When I get my hands on that scroll, bust that Marble and let's go.

Sounds like a plan, Sam answered and I didn't dare look at him for fear that Beelzebub would get suspicious.

"Let him go," I said, motioning to Cole.

Beelzebub narrowed his eyes.

I took the chain that held the key from around my neck, pulling it out from beneath my shirt. I swung it between my fingers, taunting my tormentor. "Let. Him. Go."

He shoved Cole away roughly and he smacked against the wall with a sick thud. I didn't look at him or Sam as I stepped toward Beelzebub and held out my hand. He ignored my outstretched arm and grabbed me roughly, yanking me against him. He wound his arm around my waist and I felt the hard metal of the scroll case through my T-shirt. With his free hand, he reached up and caressed my face.

I recoiled.

Behind us a menacing growl ripped through the air.

"You are a beauty," Beelzebub murmured as he ran a single finger down the left side of my face exactly where my scars used to be. "But I liked you better when you wore my mark."

I gasped.

We always thought maybe China hadn't been acting alone and now we knew for sure. My mother had been right all along. I had been marked.

Marked by evil.

Behind me I heard a scuffling sound and I knew Sam was about to shift—to attack. Beelzebub lifted his hand up as if to stop him. "You change right now, I will toss her into the fire. I prefer you in your weak human state."

Sam wasn't weak in any form. But he was more vulnerable to injury in his human form so I said, "I'm fine, Sam. Stay back."

Beelzebub looked at Hecate. "Keep him in line. Keep him back."

"My pleasure," she said from within her hood. My stomach knotted.

"Open it," Beelzebub snarled, grabbing me by the neck and holding me toward the fire. I looked down into the flames that seemed to go on forever. I might be holding the scroll in my hands, but Sam couldn't throw that Marble down because the minute he did, Beelzebub would toss me in the pit. I had to open it, make him

312

think I was doing what he wanted so I could get away, get closer to Sam.

I held up the key and brought it toward the lock, but my hands were shaking too badly to insert. "Please," I said. "Can we move back? I'm scared."

Beelzebub sighed dramatically, but he did move back and I sighed in relief. I took a chance and roughly pulled away from him, but he kept hold of my arm. I inserted the key into the lock and listened as the inner mechanism clicked and the lid popped off.

Beelzebub laughed.

It was now or never.

I swung the tube upward, hitting Beelzebub in the face and jerked free, yelling. "Now, Sam!"

Beelzebub roared and Hecate flung out her hand, sending Sam flying backward and crashing into the hard stone wall. The Lucent Marble rolled across the stone floor.

"Cole! Get the Marble!"

Cole was already moving, already diving at it, but he was too late and the Marble rolled into a darkened cell, behind iron bars. Out of reach.

"No!" Cole screamed, reaching out his hand. A hand that no longer had a true shape.

We had no way out of Hell.

We were trapped.

And we were out of time.

My vision was beginning to blur and my teeth were chattering as Sam lifted me to my feet. The bleakness of the situation pinched his face and eyes.

"You shouldn't have betrayed me!" Beelzebub screamed and ripped a length of chain hanging from the wall.

This wasn't the first time I had seen his anger. I knew how violent he could be so I anticipated his next move. He would go for Sam, the one thing that could hurt me most. Somewhere inside me, I found the strength and agility to move quickly and throw myself in front of Sam and take the hit intended for him.

"No!" Sam shouted and tried to shove me out of the way, which saved me from taking the full lash of the chain.

But the end of the chain still connected with my flesh and pain exploded through me.

313

I hit the ground. I was bleeding. I could feel the warm liquid ooze from my split face. I tucked the scroll beneath my body as Sam leapt into the air, shifting and landed on four sturdy midnight-colored paws. He planted himself in front of me, snarling.

Hecate held up both her hands and whispered a few words beneath her breath and flung Sam backward into a cell, the iron bars closing behind him.

I ran after him to let him out, but Beelzebub grabbed me, lifting me off my feet and carried me toward the angry flames. He was going to throw me. I was going to die.

Sam was throwing himself against the iron bars with all his weight and the metal was groaning under his intense weight and strength. A splitting sound went through the air as one of the bars cracked. In moments he would be free.

"Heven!" Cole ran forward, but he too was flung back with whatever magic Hecate was using.

It was up to me to save myself.

Using my teeth I pulled the loosened cap off the scroll and tossed it aside. Then I shook the case, flinging the Map out onto the floor. Beelzebub released me and went for the scroll, but I beat him to it, scooping up the delicate paper and holding it out. He froze and licked his lips. He wanted this so badly I could practically see the desperation dripping from him.

"Give it to me," he said, his eye fixated on my hand and what it held.

"You know, I'm pretty tired of this thing," I said, taking a step closer to the fire pit. "Who would have thought that a little piece of paper could cause me so much trouble?"

"What are you doing?" Beelzebub said and lifted his hand like he was going to do that little voodoo trick and fling me.

"Ah, ah ahhh," I sang. "I wouldn't do that if I were you. You take me down and I'm taking this precious piece of paper with me."

Anger flared in his eyes, but he dropped his hands to his sides. I held the scroll out away from me like I was going to release it and I looked back at him. "Sure does suck to be the one who isn't calling the shots, doesn't it?"

My taunting set him off just like I knew it would, and he let out a roar and charged me. I took a step back from the door opening, flung the Treasure Map away and kicked the empty bronze case that once held the scroll into Beelzebub's path. He tripped and reached out for me and being the good girl I was I helped him.

Right into the pit of flames.

Just before he plummeted, our eyes met and I made sure to smile. His own eyes widened in disbelief as he realized that he had been outsmarted. Even though I hated him, even though he was vile, his tortured screams were hard to hear. It was a long way down and we all heard every single one of his cries.

But I got over it. He deserved what he got.

Hecate grabbed the unprotected, fragile scroll off the floor and smirked at me. "I cannot wait to see how he makes you pay for that."

You mean that wasn't going to kill him? I shuddered. What exactly was this guy capable of?

I reached out to try to snatch the scroll from the witch, but was distracted by my arm. The outline of it (of my whole form really) was no longer there, and I knew that if we didn't leave now, my soul would be ripped away from my body and I would be trapped forever.

"Here, take this," a voice from a nearby darkened cell called. Something rolled across the floor as I turned.

The Marble.

"Kimber," Cole said, picking it up.

"Get out of here while you still can."

Hecate said something low and the door to Kimber's cell swung open. We all watched as Kimber's emancipated form floated out of the opening, suspended in mid-air. Even with Hecate's spell holding her up, her body still sagged in defeat. She looked like an empty shell. As we watched something else floated out behind her... what could only be her soul.

Kimber's soul had separated from her body.

But how was it still here? I just assumed that once a soul was released it would wander away and be corrupted by Hell.

"I did you a favor," Hecate said. "You should be dead. Your soul should be gone. If it wasn't for the magic I gave you and the spell that I cast on your cell you would be nothing but dust, your soul would have left, and turned into a lowly demon."

Kimber gave no reaction. In fact, her skin was beginning to crack. Thin, black cracks that started at the tips of her lifeless fingers and began working their way up her wrists and arms. I watched in horror, my own body shaking, as I wondered if her skin would begin to flake off her body until she was nothing but a pile of bones.

"Stop!" Cole screamed, standing below Kimber, his arms raised as if he would pluck her from the air.

Whatever spell that was keeping Kimber semi-alive within her cell was clearly not working now that she was outside its confines.

I looked around for something I could use as a weapon, something to stop Hecate from whatever she was doing.

But it didn't matter.

Hecate flung her fingers toward Kimber, who was tossed back into the dark cell, the door slamming with finality behind her. I couldn't see her anymore, but I heard a smack against the granite walls and a whimpering of pain. I took that as a positive sign that she wasn't dead. I was getting really tired of Hecate flicking her fingers and flinging people around.

Cole didn't waste any time and threw the Marble against the floor. It shattered and a swirling portal burst open.

"Let's go!" he yelled.

With a loud cry Sam charged the iron bars that confined him and sent them snapping outward as he broke free.

Hecate screamed in outrage at his strength. I took advantage of her distraction and ripped the scroll from her hands. She reacted quickly, jerking backward, and the fine paper of the Map ripped, leaving her holding the bottom section of the scroll. I threw what part I had to Cole and he tossed it through the portal and held out his hand for me to join him.

Sam charged the witch, slamming into her, and the torn piece of the Map fell from her hand. I grabbed it and looked down, not trying to read it, but feeling my mind click into place, retaining everything that on the page. Thank goodness for my new "ability" because a strong gust of wind pulled it right from my hands and into the burning flames.

"If I can't have it, no one will!"

The Map no longer mattered as Sam and I ran for the portal. We were mere inches from jumping to safety when I heard him yell. I turned, but he was no longer behind me. He was back in the cell that he had just broken out of.

I looked at Cole and the safety of the portal. I felt my soul literally ripping from my body. Safety called to me.

I turned my back.

"Sam!" I ran toward him, but when I reached the cell door, my body hit something and bounced off some kind of invisible shield.

Hecate laughed. "You can't get in and he can't get out. He's a prisoner now."

"I won't leave him!" I screamed, my voice coming out far weaker than I thought possible.

"Then, in seconds, your body will be ripped free of its soul and you will become a demon!"

You have to go, Heven.

Even through my blurry vision, I could make out every single beautiful line of Sam's face. His sun-kissed hair was sticking up and gray from soot. He was still the most gorgeous thing I'd ever seen and he was still everything to me. *I won't leave you here.*

You don't have a choice.

"Heven!" Cole said, grabbing my shoulder. "The portal is closing."

"No!" I screamed and flung myself at the invisible wall that separated me from my beloved.

Please go. I can't lose you, he begged and flattened his palm against the wall.

Yet if I left, wouldn't we lose each other?

Tears rained down my cheeks and blurred what was left of my vision.

I'll get out of here, Heven. I'll come home to you.

I pressed my shapeless hand up against his. We couldn't touch, but I swear I felt his warmth through the barrier. A sob ripped from my throat.

Sam nodded, but he wasn't looking at me anymore. He was looking at Cole. Suddenly, I was being lifted off my feet and carried away from everything that mattered.

Please forgive me, Sam said.

"No!" I screamed. "No!" I hit Cole. I scratched and kicked, but nothing I did would make him let go of me. Through my screams Hecate's laughter echoed around us.

I *hated* her.

I've never seen anyone look so miserable as he stood there and watched Cole tow me away. I hated myself in that moment for not being strong enough to get away.

"Sam," I sobbed my voice hoarse.

I watched as the full lips that kissed me so many times formed the precious words, *I love you, Heven.* I heard them as a whispered rasp through my mind.

And then Cole stepped through the portal.

Today, Hell was denied the souls it had been trying to claim, but in the end, it stole something much more valuable, something I wasn't sure I could exist without. My heart.

Chapter Twenty-Four

Heven

I wiped the tears from my face and blinked against the harsh light, realizing that it wasn't quite light outside yet, but it was still far brighter than where we came from. I didn't have the strength to pull away from Cole, but I didn't really want to. I wasn't mad at him for towing me away like that. He was only doing what he thought best. I glanced down at my hand and noted that the edges of my body were no longer blurred. My skin was pulled taut across flesh and bone and my soul was safely contained within my body. Sam traded his safety for mine.

I ducked my head into Cole's shoulder and tried to stop my insides from trembling, but it was no use. While my soul and body may have recovered from the horrible events that just occurred, my brain was still trying to catch up.

"Heven, look at me," Cole demanded, his voice sounding like he hadn't spoken in weeks. It made me wonder how long we were down in the pits of Hell.

Cole grabbed me by the shoulders and forced me away from his body, holding me out so he could study me. "How badly are you hurt?" he whispered.

Tears filled my eyes. Did he really even have to ask? We left Sam in Hell. The place that is most famously known for destroying a person's soul and turning them into evil zombies. While I knew that as a hellhound his soul would stay within his body, I was still beyond grief. The boy I loved most in this world was torn from me and I don't know when and if I would see him again.

"I'll get you to the hospital," Cole said, standing up and taking me with him. He swayed a little on his feet and I knew that he was trying to hold it together for me.

"I don't need to go to the hospital."

He looked at me strangely before slowly asking me if my face hurt.

I shook my head. The only thing that hurt was my chest, where my heart used to reside.

"Heven, focus," Cole said firmly and planted me on my feet. He kept his hands clasped around my biceps as if he thought I might crumble to the ground if he released me. "Your face."

I made a frustrated sound. What about my face? I flung my hands up and pressed them to my cheeks and stopped, my eyes flashing up to Cole's. Slowly, I lowered my hands noting that one set of fingers came away bloody. Visions of a swinging chain burst behind my eyes. Sam's anger and cry of protest rang through my ears and I remembered.

Beelzebub tried to lash Sam with a chain.

I got in the way.

"Doesn't it hurt?" Cole asked apprehensively.

"No."

The look on his face told me that he didn't believe me.

I tentatively touched the gash once more. "It doesn't," I whispered. The pain of leaving Sam in that horrible place was far worse than any physical pain could ever be.

"You must be in shock. I think you need stitches..."

He was waiting for me to freak out, to scream and melt down. I wasn't going to.

I didn't have time for that.

I had to be strong; I was Sam's only shot at getting out.

Sam. Sam, are you okay? Please God, let me still be able to reach him through our Mindbond. If we didn't have that I was sure I would crumble.

Heven! Did you make it out? Where are you?

I literally sagged with relief, swallowed past the lump in my throat and swiped at my tears with the back of my hand. I could still talk to him. We still had our link.

Yes, I'm fine. Cole and Logan are fine too. (At least I prayed Logan was okay.)

His rush of gratitude and relief strengthened the tether I had on sanity and made me all the more determined to get him out.

Thank God.

What about you? Did Beelzebub come back yet?

I'm fine. He isn't here. That was something at least. Still, how long until he came back, madder than ever? We had to work fast to get Sam out of there.

"Where are we?" I asked Cole looking around, trying to get a handle on my surroundings.

"The fountain," he said patiently, pointing a short distance away at the fountain that we had entered what seemed an eternity ago.

The Treasure Map was lying next to the fountain. Well, what was left of it. I retrieved it on wobbly legs. I didn't want the stupid thing. It had caused more pain and heartache than anything. I was beginning to wonder if any of it had been worth it.

Of course it had. I scolded myself as I tucked the scroll beneath my arm. *It brought you Sam.*

"I need to go check on Logan." I didn't know what kind of shape Logan was in, but I knew that I would do whatever it took to keep him alive. When Sam came home—and he *would* come home— his brother would be healthy and whole.

Just then a blur darted out from between a few parked cars and came at us. I braced myself, but the figure stopped just shy of barreling me over. "What took so long?" she demanded.

My muscles couldn't relax even though this person was not a threat. "Gemma, Sam is trapped in Hell. We were forced to leave him there. We have to go back and get him. We need a plan."

"What happened to you?" Her eyes widened as she came closer to stare at my face.

"It's nothing." I waved it away. "Can you help me get Sam back?"

"Of course I will help. But now isn't the time. You're injured."

I gritted my teeth. Didn't she see the urgency of the situation? I looked at Cole for some back up. He looked beaten up and exhausted. I sighed. "Could you check out Cole? He took a few hard hits down there."

Just like that she was gone and instantly at Cole's side. I turned to watch the pair together.

"Cole?" Gemma asked, her voice lowering in volume. "Let me see."

"I'm fine," he insisted, but didn't turn away from Gemma's seeking hands. She grasped his head lightly and pulled him closer to examine his injuries. She made a small noise in her throat as she studied the swollen, blackened eye.

"You'll live," Gemma declared. Her fingertips splayed lightly over his wounds, moving in an intimate caress. I wanted to look away. It was painful to see the connection between them and know I abandoned the one with whom I shared that kind of connection with.

But I couldn't look away. I couldn't tear my eyes from them. I felt a lump form in my throat and the threat of tears behind my eyes.

Just as I was about to lose all control, Gemma lowered her hand and stepped back. Cole's face was completely healed.

"The back of his head has a gash in it," I told her, so she would heal that too.

Cole glared at me for admitting to yet another injury and ruining his 'tough' guy image, but I didn't care. Sam was already in enough danger. I wanted my brother safe.

Gemma slid her hands through Cole's thick, dark hair and brought them together at the back of his head. When she pulled away, her fingers were red. She frowned at the smears on her fingers.

"Hey," Cole murmured, grabbing her elbow and breaking the spell his blood seemed to have over her. She looked up and blinked at him. "It's really not that bad."

Gemma nodded and threaded her fingers back into his hair, Cole's eyes fluttering closed. The next thing I knew, Gemma had released him and was coming toward me.

I backed up as far as I could go, but the fountain was at my back. "I don't want to be healed," I told her.

Gemma stopped and stared at me. "No?"

"No." Why should I be healed and pain free when Sam was down in Hell suffering? Panic welled up inside me. I couldn't leave him there. I couldn't.

"Heven, that's crazy," Cole said, striding forward. He stopped at Gemma's side. "She isn't thinking clearly. She…"

"Why don't any of you seem to get it?!" I yelled. "Sam is trapped in Hell! We have to go back, now!"

"And we will get him back, Hev," Cole said, using that patient voice again. I hated the way he talked to me like I was going bonkers. I turned my back on him.

"Please," I said desperately to Gemma. "I need you to do something for me,"

She nodded. "Anything."

"Take care of Logan. Keep him safe till I get back."

She didn't understand. "Get back?"

I nodded and began walking away from the fountain, then stopped and turned back, ready to launch myself at it the way Sam had.

"I'm going back to Hell to get Sam."

I started to run.

Gemma caught me around the waist before I could jump at the fountain and tackled me to the ground.

"Let me go!" I screamed, trying to shove her off. "I'm going!"

Gemma pinned me to the ground and I made a sound in frustration. I was done with being weak. If she wouldn't train me, I would find someone who would. "The portal will not open for you. It will only open for Sam."

I stopped struggling against her and a sob caught in my throat. I hadn't thought about that.

Her voice gentled when she said, "Even if you could, it's too soon. You're soul is still vulnerable and needs some time to root more firmly back in your body."

"My soul is fine," I growled.

"You will be of no help to Sam right now. You're injured, exhausted and your soul…"

"I have to get back there," I said flatly, cutting off the rest of her words. "Who knows what Beelzebub is going to do to him."

"Sam is very strong, Heven," Gemma tried to reassure me.

I heard her, but I wasn't listening. "I should go now while Beelzebub is preoccupied."

Gemma lifted a brow.

"Heven pushed him into this burning pit in his dungeon," Cole explained.

Gemma gasped. "You did that to Beelzebub?"

I shrugged. He deserved worse than that.

"Hecate seemed to think it was funny," Cole murmured.

"You saw Hecate!" Gemma exclaimed.

Which reminded me. "What about Kimber, Cole?"

Just the mere mention of her changed Cole. The lines around his mouth and eyes tightened, his shoulders tensed and his aura flashed muddy, cloudy colors.

"Who is this Kimber girl? Wasn't she in the catacombs?" Gemma asked, reading Cole's reaction.

"She's our friend—used to be our friend, anyway. Cole dated her," I answered, watching as Gemma slightly flinched.

"She betrayed us and sold herself to Hecate," Cole spat. He turned to Gemma. "I broke up with her a few weeks ago. Before we met."

"She's in Hell?" Gemma asked, turning toward me.

"In a cell right next to Sam. She helped us get out of there."

"You must wait to go back, form a plan," Gemma urged.

She knew as well as I did that no amount of planning would help me. I was on a suicide mission to Hell that I refused to back out of. At the very least, I was hoping to trade myself for Sam.

"Please," Gemma urged. "I'll help you get ready."

"You'll teach me to fight?" I asked.

"Yes," Gemma promised over Cole's dark cursing.

"Meet me later at the farm. We'll begin then," I said. "I have to check on Logan, but first I have something I need to do." Something I needed to be alone for.

Gemma nodded, but Cole frowned. "Where are you going?"

"Will you stay with Logan until I get there?"

"Hev." Worry and regret shone in his eyes.

I stepped forward and wrapped my arms around his waist. He returned the hug with force. "You don't have to worry about me. Meet me at the farm later."

"I'm sorry," he said.

"I understand why you made me leave," I told him. "Thank you." As much as I hated to admit it, Cole was right to pull me out. I would be of no use to Sam if my soul was gone. I have to make sure that he is out and safe before I sacrifice my soul to save him.

"We'll stay with Logan," Gemma promised.

As I walked away from them, I heard Cole's whispered words, "I feel like I should explain about Kimber…"

Gemma answered just as quietly as he had spoken. "Don't. Everyone has a past. Including me."

I didn't hang around to hear the rest. It didn't really matter.

Just as the city of Portland was awakening, I strolled away from the fountain and stared up at the newly lightened sky to yell, "Airis!"

* * *

The bright white of the InBetween was assaulting to my dark mood, but I ignored it, realizing that I asked to come here and it really wasn't fair of me to treat anyone (especially someone who would hopefully help me) to my unhappiness.

"Things haven't been easy lately," Airis said, appearing before me. Her blond hair shone brightly as it framed her face with loose curls.

"So you know what has happened?"

"To Logan and to Sam, yes."

"I have the Treasure Map," I said, holding out the bronze tube, hoping she would take it and I would be rid of its responsibility.

"It is incomplete."

I glanced down at its torn, jagged edge. "Yes. But I know what part is missing. I can replace it." Who would have thought that having a photographic memory would actually be helpful?

"Did anyone else read it?"

"No. It was burned."

As I held it out, a new bronze case formed around the scroll. The metal was smooth and perfect without any of the scratches and dents the previous case held.

"You're not going to take it back, are you?" I said, not being able to keep the disappointment from my voice.

"No."

"But why? It belongs in Heaven, where it is safe."

"It is incomplete."

"If I complete it, will you take it back?"

"When the time is right you will know what to do with the Treasure Map."

Not exactly the answer I was looking for, but I accepted it because the scroll wasn't why I was here. "Can you help me get Sam out of Hell?"

"I cannot." Airis bowed her head as if to apologize.

I wanted to weep and scream at the same time. I closed my eyes and took a deep breath as a perfect image of Sam formed behind my eyes. He was beautiful, all tan and gold with deep whiskey-colored eyes and a perfectly sculpted face. I couldn't let him down.

"Why?" I asked, calmly.

"I have no control over what goes on in Hell."

"Beelzebub has Sam."

"Did you know he's a fallen angel?"

I shook my head. That explained why he thought demons were beneath him.

"He became the Chief of Demon's on Christ's allowance. He is *very* powerful."

"You mean God appointed him Chief of Demons?" I asked, curious.

"Yes."

"But why?"

"There are many theories," Airis hedged, clearly not wanting to get into a religious debate.

I shrugged. I guess it didn't matter anyway. What mattered was what was happening now.

It was hard to believe that violent, cruel man once came from Heaven. "How can I defeat him?"

"I do not know. He is very dangerous. My advice would be not to go up against him. Avoid him at all costs."

At cost to Sam?

Hell. No.

"Can you give me some more supernatural powers that can help me get Sam back?"

"You have already been gifted supernatural powers."

Yeah, stupid ones. I didn't dare say it out loud because I didn't want to sound ungrateful, but I mean, really, seeing auras and having a photographic memory... I wouldn't even call them powers—just abilities to make me a freak. Yet, I couldn't say that they hadn't been completely worthless.

"So you aren't going to help me at all, help Sam? Not even after everything he has done to help you?" It just wasn't fair.

"You will have to do this on your own. Hell is not a place where I can help you."

"Send me home." I blinked back tears. "Please."

Airis studied me for a long moment and I had to struggle to hold onto my patience and my calm. I would not cry. I would be stronger than that for Sam.

"There is something I can give you," Airis said.

"What?"

"You only have minutes," she said and then disappeared.

"Airis!" I yelled. Why had she left like that? How was I going to get home?

A sob caught in my throat and I scrubbed my eyes with the palms of my hands. When I looked up someone was standing before me. I blinked back the tears to clear my vision... certain that I was seeing things.

"Heven," the familiar voice filled me with longing and warmth.

It took me a moment to realize he was really there. That he really spoke.

"Daddy?" I whispered.

He nodded and held out his arms.

I ran right into them.

He smelled exactly the same. All the years that he had been gone fell away and it was like he had never left at all.

"I've missed you," I whispered into his chest.

His arms tightened even harder around me and I felt the breath catch in his chest. "I've always been with you."

"I thought I wasn't allowed to see you."

"Things have been hard lately," he said, drawing me back and looking down at my face. Concern darkened his features, but I drank them in hungrily. He was tall, almost six feet with a strong build including wide shoulders. His hair was light—like mine, but his eyes were a deep brown that Mom always called puppy-dog eyes.

"Have you seen what's been happening?"

"Most everything," he confirmed.

"Not all?" I wondered which parts he hadn't seen and why he hadn't been watching.

His lips pulled into a quick smile and I was reminded of Cole. I wondered how I never put the resemblance together before. In fact, if I had been able to see my dad's aura, I was sure it would look a lot like my brother's.

"I wasn't able to see anything about your recent trip into the Underworld." His mouth pulled down in disapproval. "You're injured."

He held out his hands to my face, but I stepped away. The mention of Hell made my chest feel heavy and Sam's beautiful face flashed into my mind. As intensely glad as I was to have these few moments with my father, it just wasn't enough to shadow the pain I carried knowing that Sam was trapped in Hell. *Sam.*

I didn't realize — not at first — that the thought was spoken, an unconscious attempt at reaching out to my beloved.

I'm still here, Heven.

The whisper of his words and the intensity of relief that rushed through me almost brought me to my knees. I heard the sob that ripped from my throat and was powerless to stop it.

Every time I talked to him I was afraid it would be our last conversation.

I was afraid that the very fine thread that tethered me to sanity might snap and I would float away into complete grief.

Are you all right? I didn't know what else to ask. Everything else was too hard to broach. I'd left him there. What if he felt betrayed and hurt and didn't want to speak to me ever again?

I looked up at my father and swallowed. He was staring at me with a wary expression on his face. I cast my eyes back down, squeezing them shut, shutting out everything but Sam.

Don't worry about me. I can handle this.

I love you, Sam. I swear I'll get you out.

I'll find a way out, Heven. Don't come back here.

I wasn't sure what to say because I didn't want to argue and I *would* be going back to get him. He must have felt my resolve and desire to not fight because a faint laugh echoed through my mind. *I love you, Heven. Always.*

My eyes snapped back up to my father. I felt torn with guilt. Here, standing before me, was my father, the man whom I wished for every single day since he died and I had a chance that no one else ever got, and I was so wrecked from Sam's imprisonment that I couldn't fully enjoy this.

I rushed forward, throwing my arms around his waist and burying my face against his chest. I couldn't stop the hot tears that fell from my eyes or the burning in my chest from holding back my sobs.

"That's my girl," he crooned. "It's all right now."

"It's not!" I cried, lifting my face up. "Sam is trapped in Hell, in Beelzebub's dungeon. Kimber got caught up with Hecate and is trapped there too, and I'm pretty sure that her soul isn't inside her body anymore. Well, maybe it is…" My voice trailed away, unsure. If Kimber's soul was truly gone, she wouldn't have helped us escape. It was all so confusing.

He murmured some comforting words and rocked me back and forth. Soon my crying quieted and I was left listening to the soft humming of a song that he had sung to me when I was a little girl. I let the melody soothe the roughest parts inside of me before gently pulling away. "You didn't tell me about Cole." I didn't want to be angry, but I was.

My father nodded. "I wanted to. I loved Cole's mother very much and we dated for a while, but then your mother came into my life. Things got complicated. Two women, two babies… I wanted you both, but could only have one woman. Your mother seemed to need me."

"But what about Cole?" I said, cutting him off.

"I tried to see him, honey. Cole's mother was understandably hurt that I chose someone else and she didn't want me in his life. After all the pain I caused her, it was all I could do to honor her wishes. It was better that way."

"Not for Cole."

"Yes, for Cole. As I said, it was complicated."

I allowed his words to sink in, knowing that he only tried to do what was best. I didn't want to spend what little moments I had with him arguing over something that I couldn't change.

"I always thought that I would have the time when he was older to explain things…" His words trailed off and I hugged him again.

"It's all right, Daddy. I understand."

"How is he?"

I grinned. "He's great. So much like you."

Dad nodded. "A Supernal Being," he said, almost to himself.

"Did you always know what you are?"

He smoothed the hair away from my face and looked about to respond when his head tilted, like he heard something I didn't.

He frowned a bit, his brown eyes melting a little. "I have to go."

"No!" I hugged him fiercely as if to keep him at my side.

"I'll be watching over you, always."

"Please stay," I begged.

"Be strong and be careful." He pressed his lips to my forehead before gently pulling away.

"Wait!" I cried. He looked back at me with love. "I love you, Daddy."

"I love you too, angel."

Fresh tears slid down my cheeks as I watched him walk away. As he began fading away he smiled. "Tell your brother that I'm sorry and that I love him."

I nodded. "I will."

Just before he vanished completely, I saw him smile. "And Heven?"

"Yes?"

"I'm proud of you."

* * *

The night sky looked like rich navy velvet, pulling me toward the window and promising to cocoon me in peace. I ignored the pull of the silver studded stars and pushed the window closed, my fingers grazing over something that wasn't necessary until now.

The lock.

My fingers stung and my eyes burned as I shoved the lock home. *It's temporary.* I promised myself as I pulled shut the shades and curtains. I walked stiffly away from the window, my muscles protesting with every movement I made. Training today with Gemma had been exhausting. I hurt in places that I didn't even know I had, and I felt beaten down with the knowledge of how weak I really was.

But it didn't matter because tomorrow I would be stronger.

Every day I would get stronger and the pain and weakness in my body would give way to a warrior capable of going into the pits of Hell and achieving the only thing in this world that I wanted.

Sam.

But not just Sam.

Sam *and* retribution for what was done to everyone I loved.

It didn't matter that Airis couldn't help me. It didn't matter that even with supernatural powers I was still achingly human. I didn't care that Beelzebub was somehow going to return from the fiery pit that I punished him with and make me pay.

And I had no doubt he would make me pay.

I thought about my best friend, who may or may not be soulless and punished for working with the most heinous witch ever. I pictured my mother, lying unconscious in a hospital bed, a casualty of a war she had no knowledge of. I thought about Logan, who lay just down the hall, sleeping and barely alive from the damage that the demon had done to his frail body.

And the lies I told Gran about Logan and Sam? Just a means to an end.

With single-minded determination I would take the steps that would free everyone I loved from what had been done to them. I would get revenge and I would do whatever I had to do in order to do it.

Beelzebub would pay for what he has done.

I looked down at my bruised arms and legs and took pride in their pain. Pain was merely weakness leaving my body—a weakness that simply wouldn't do. I needed strength, strength of mind *and* body.

I went to the mirror above my dresser and looked straight at my reflection. What I saw would have sent me into a full-blown panic attack. *Before.* But this was *After.* What I saw wasn't what defined me anymore. But it was definitely a scar. Or what was going to be a scar. Right now it was still raw, red and open. I didn't see it as something awful though or something that represented a blank spot in my memory. I knew how I got this scar. I knew why.

I was strong.

Stronger than I ever believed and I would wear this scar with pride.

It was why I couldn't let Gemma or even my dad heal me. I was meant to carry this mark, and whenever I looked at my reflection, I would be reminded of my strength and everything that I am capable of.

I glanced over at my bed, knowing that sleep would make me stronger, but I turned away from it abruptly; I couldn't face sleep right now. The minute that I went to sleep, I knew he would come for me. After what I did, I wasn't sure anything would keep him away. I shuddered and reached into my desk for some paper.

Sleep wasn't an option, but that was okay because there were other ways that I could build my strength. I sat down at the desk and arranged the paper in front of me. Reaching for a pen, I paused to look up at my bulletin board that was filled with snapshots of me and Sam. The way the sun kissed his hair and his smile was so genuine. My favorite snapshot was taken by Kimber, in happier times, of Sam and me kissing. I remembered it perfectly, the way his lips melted against mine just right and the delicious heat of the sun's rays against my skin. I reached my fingers to the photograph expecting to feel the heat I remembered from the sun. Instead, the paper was smooth and cold, lifeless against my fingers. The pen I was still holding snapped in my hand. I turned away from the photos. They were distracting me.

Distractions weren't welcome right now.

I had plans to make.

Cambria Hebert grew up in a small town in rural Maryland. She is married to a United States Marine and has lived in South Carolina, Pennsylvania, North Carolina and back to Pennsylvania again. She is the mother of two young children with big personalities, is in love with Starbucks (give the girl a latte!) and she is obsessed with werewolves. Cambria also has an irrational fear of chickens (Ewww! Gross) and she loves to watch Vampire Diaries and Teen Wolf. Her favorite book genre is YA paranormal, and she can be found stalking that section at her local Barnes and Nobles (which happens to be her favorite place ever!). You can find her never doing math. It makes her head hurt.

Cambria is the author of the Heven and Hell series, a young adult paranormal book series. The series begins with *Before*, a short story prequel and is followed by the first novel in the series *Masquerade*. Look for all her titles where all books are sold.

Cambria also co-hosts a live, internet blog radio talk show, *JournalJabber*, (www.blogtalkradio.com/journaljabber) where she dishes about books, publishing and everything in between: hair in a can, toilet snakes, chicken phobias, etc..

You can find Cambria on Facebook, Good Reads, Twitter and her website http://www.cambriahebert.com for her latest crazy antics and the scoop on all things Heven and Hell.

Lightning Source UK Ltd.
Milton Keynes UK
UKOW042017290513

211457UK00003B/529/P